THE

COLOR

OF

SILENCE

THE COLOR OF SILENCE

A Dreamers' Dragon Novel

Book One

By

— C.J. Gryffin —

DEDICATION

For my family, who waited eighteen patient years for this story to move from words in my head to words on the page.

For my husband, who listened, encouraged, and reminded me that this first book had to be Darius's story. He was right.

For my children, Christian, Mason, and Mikky, who inspired me to keep going, and for my beautiful granddaughters, who inspired some of the characters still to come.

And for every person with autism, every parent and family member who has given so much in love and sacrifice, and for my students and their families.

This story was shaped by your courage, your endurance, and your lives.

SOUNDTRACK

When *The Color of Silence* first found its way into Window Light Studio, none of us expected what would happen next. But once I stepped into its pages, I couldn't stop writing. Beginning with *Somewhere Past the Window Light*, the story sparked something deeply personal in me. As the creator of the soundtrack — and the father of a son with autism — I found in these pages emotions I had carried for years, finally given a voice through music.

The result became an original 22-song soundtrack, with each song intentionally written to accompany a specific chapter of the book. Like the score of a powerful film, the music expands the emotional depth of the story, creating a richer, more immersive experience for readers and listeners alike.

For me, this project is more than a soundtrack — it is a personal testimony told through story and song. The soundtrack is available separately or as part of a bundle at cjgryffin.com

Scan for the Soundtrack

AUTHOR'S NOTE

The Color of Silence is a work of fiction, but it is rooted in realities that many families know well.

Darius is not a real child. Though his name was inspired by a real little boy, his character is a fictional creation shaped by many students I have taught over the years, as well as the families who have loved and fought for them. His autism is not meant to represent every autistic child. It cannot. As the saying goes, "If you know one person with autism, you know one person with autism." This is one imagined child, one family, and one possible experience.

This story is also a speculative look at what autism might have looked like before it had a name, before therapies and support systems were widely available, and at a time when families were often given little hope and few humane choices. In that era, many children like Darius were misunderstood, hidden away, or sent to institutions. This novel imagines what it might have meant for one family to love such a child fiercely in a world that did not know how to see him clearly.

I know this story may be a difficult read for some, especially for parents and caregivers of autistic children. Some scenes may feel painfully familiar. But one of the deepest truths I hoped to hold onto in writing this book is that there is hope. Communication matters. Therapy matters. Support matters. And love matters.

Children like Darius are not broken. They are deeply loved, even in homes stretched thin by exhaustion, fear, isolation, and misunderstanding. Parents and caregivers are often carrying more than the world can see. A child having a meltdown in public is not a sign of bad parenting. It is often a sign of a family doing its best under strain that others may never fully understand.

Too many families raising autistic children live with isolation. They may pull back from gatherings, avoid public places, or lose connections with friends, relatives, and community because their child's needs make others uncomfortable or because the effort of going out is simply too great. These families do not need judgment. They need support, professional services, patience, and grace.

If this book leaves you with anything beyond Darius's story, I hope it leaves you with a wider heart for the children and families who live this reality every day.

CHAPTER ONE

ASLEEP

Summerset Nursing Home, Atlanta, Georgia, 2025

Most said he was a miracle. Some believed he was cursed. But the old ones, the ones who remembered rumors of strange stories — they called it madness.

Darius Turner was none of these. He was a dreamer.

He was born in 1925 and had outlasted wars, presidents, and the people who once called his name. When his hundredth birthday arrived, it passed with no celebration. No cake. No balloons. Just a tarnished plaque nailed to the wall and a nurse, flat and distracted, humming as she tucked the blanket tighter around his chest. He hadn't opened his eyes in years. Hadn't spoken for even longer. Yet his fingers moved as if tracing something only he could see.

The silence started the year of his birth. Six years without words: no mama, no dada. His mother, Sadie, counted each wordless day while neighbors whispered of her unusual child with wild eyes. The Turner boy, they said. Something is wrong with him. Then came the night everything changed. The night Azure came to him in his dreams.

And after that, he spoke of Azure and of places no child should know, and of creatures no one had seen before.

Some called it imagination. Others suspected something darker.

And Darius learned to stop sharing his peculiar story. He simply dreamed.

Somewhere far from that peaceful room, far from this world, in Somnoria, realm of the Dreamers' Dragons — a dragon opened an eye.

PART I

CHAPTER TWO

STORMS

Chapters 2-4: September 23, 1930 - The Autumn Equinox, Atlanta, Georgia

As dawn crept through the gray mist, it cast soft shadows on the small wooden house at the edge of the Atlanta neighborhood. Today marked the equinox, when the day split evenly between light and dark, summer and fall, and at this hour their home sat eerily quiet. While Sadie Turner moved through her kitchen, her tired, aching limbs and thin frame bore the marks not of time, but of the weight of the past few years.

Outside, dirt roads were still damp from the night's shower, and the morning air carried a faint chill, the kind that reminded you the season was changing and settling its cloak over the city. When the sun finally broke the horizon, the rhythms of the morning began: water splashing in basins, beds creaking as children stirred, and the familiar soft rocking sound from the front room, where Darius sat watching the world wake around him.

"Mama, Darius won't come eat!" Theo said, his voice loud enough to pull Sadie from her thoughts.

Sadie looked up from the stove, her wooden spoon suspended above the pot, and peered around the corner at her youngest son. "Leave him be," she said, her voice level. "He'll come when he's ready."

Lula, small, motherly, and already dressed for the day, appeared beside her brother in the doorway. "He's been in that chair all morning," she said, frowning with the kind of worry that belied her eight years. "He's rocking and rocking."

As the smell of an overripe peach tree drifted through the kitchen window, it blended with the warmth of breakfast on the stove. Each child converged into the kitchen, their sounds announcing the arrival of morning, while the creak of the chair in the front room, occupied by Darius, undercut all others.

Darius was five years old and still silent. No "Mama." No first word waiting in reserve. Nothing more than guttural sounds and a thin swell of a hum. A few weeks ago, his birthday passed without notice — no birthday wishes, no cake, and no candle lit. The family learned that even a celebration could provoke him, and some moments were safer left untouched.

He was a beautiful child, and his eyes made strangers step back, with that uncanny blue, bright and wrong against his skin. Those eyes that didn't match his deep brown skin; that didn't match anything anyone could explain. But behind those eyes, behind that brightness lived something reticent and shut away.

The rocking stopped.

When Sadie peered around the corner, discomfort settled in her chest at the sight of Darius sitting frozen in his chair, one hand raised, fingers splayed toward the window where a cardinal perched, its bright feathers a stark contrast to the dull morning. Darius closed one eye while the other eye tracked the bird's every twitch between his stretched fingers. When the cardinal flitted away, his hand fluttered after it, then lowered as he fell back into the steady cadence of his rocking, his way of keeping pace with the world that did not meet him halfway.

"Mama! Ezra took my hairbrush again!" Lula's cry pierced the weathered calm, followed by the thunder of stomping feet across the worn wooden floor.

"Did not! Wasn't even in your room!" Ezra shouted back, exasperation flaring in his voice, the very accusation absurd, as if he'd ever touched a brush.

As Sadie braced her hands against the counter, she summoned her patience. "Theo, help your sister find her brush. Ezra, help me with breakfast. You all got ten minutes before you need to leave for school."

Theo, the eldest at twelve, let out a wary sigh and steered his younger sister back toward her bedroom. "Come on, Lu. It's probably fallen under your bed again."

"Wasn't under my bed yesterday!" Lula's voice trailed behind them as they disappeared down the narrow hallway.

The noise pulled little Gunny from sleep. She toddled into the kitchen, hair flattened on one side, her nightgown hanging loose and oversized, arms raised as if the effort of standing had exhausted her. "Mama, up."

"Morning, sunshine. Let's get some food in you," Sadie said, lifting her youngest onto a chair near the table. She turned back to the stove, pouring the steaming grits into five waiting bowls.

Five plates. Biscuits. Grits. Her hands moved on instinct, imbued with the weight of long days, nights of interrupted sleep, and dreams sacrificed to necessity.

Behind her, Darius rocked with growing insistence; each rise in volume from the other children intensified his movement. She kept part of her attention fixed on that shift, alert to the signs she had long since learned to read.

Augustus departed before sunrise for his shift at the rail yard. The colored men worked the dirtiest line, coupling cars, shoveling coal, hauling freight until their backs gave out, but he never complained. Work was work, and in 1930s Atlanta that meant survival. While neighbors lingered on porches waiting for word from the WPA office, Augustus kept his head down and his hands moving. By day's end, soot had settled so deep into his skin no lye soap could touch it. Before he left, he pressed a quick kiss to her forehead. "Good luck today," he said, already pulling on his cap. As he walked into the gray dawn toward the rail yard beyond the trolley stop, the air always tasted of iron and smoke. She didn't correct him anymore. They both knew luck had nothing to do with it.

"Mama, you need to sign my school paper. Teacher says it's important." Theo placed a crumpled sheet on the table beside her.

"Put it there. I'll look at it before you go," Sadie replied, sliding plates of grits and biscuits toward hungry hands.

When Lula reappeared in the doorway, she brandished the missing hairbrush. "Found it in Gunny's toy box."

"Wasn't me!" Gunny chirped through a mouthful of food, her eyes wide with innocence — a small solace against the morning's chaos.

The voices and noises in the house rose and fell in uneven waves, and through it all Sadie's eyes remained fixed on Darius. The rocking intensified. Quick, rhythmic movements erupted at his sides, as if he were trying to shake off something invisible. One hand rose to shoulder level, fingers flicking and wrists snapping in tight arcs. As the noise around him surged, so did the height of his movements — arms lifting above his head, then dropping again, faster each time. Faint moans, like the hum of an animal in distress, came from the front room.

She knew these movements. The lift of his shoulders, the frantic twitch of his fingers. None of it was random. It was the start of something swelling inside him, gathering strength.

His eyes darted between the kitchen table and the window, searching for a place to land, caught between the clatter of the house and his need to find solace in his world by the window.

"Quiet down some." She didn't raise her voice, but her words carried caution born of experience. "Y'all know better than to get too loud this early."

The warning came too late. Not more than a moment later, Ezra knocked his glass over, sending milk crashing across the wooden table. The sudden splash and Gunny's shocked squeal tipped the delicate balance.

It was as if a switch flipped.

Darius leapt from his chair with a high-pitched wail that cut through every other sound, a raw manifestation of his overwhelming distress. Hands clamped over his ears. His body stiffened, eyes wild and wheeling, searching for refuge.

"Here we go." Ezra shrank back, fear creeping into his voice.

As Sadie moved toward Darius, her actions remained deliberate and measured. "It's all right, baby. It's spilled milk. Nothing to worry about."

But the scream intensified. He dropped to the floor, both fists clenched tight, striking the wooden floorboards with violent force. His body curled in on itself, then unfurled as his hands struck the floorboards again.

"Mama, we gotta go now or we'll be late." Theo clutched his books, his eyes darting toward the doorway, desperate to escape the scene unfolding before him. Gunny pressed close to his back, her small frame trembling.

"Theo, take Gunny to the back room before you go," Sadie urged, her voice restrained despite the storm that raged in the front room. He turned without a word, ushering his sister down the hall, the sound of Darius's cries trailing them like a haunting echo.

"Go on to school. All of you. I got him," Sadie said.

"Sorry, Mama." As Lula stepped back toward the door, her eyes brimming with tears, the children filed out, leaving Sadie alone with the tempest that was her middle child.

The slam of the door carried more than footsteps; it carried their unspoken relief at stepping away from a scene that left its mark every time.

Darius thrashed on the floor, his small body tormented with emotions he couldn't express. When Sadie knelt beside him, she remained present, not reaching out yet, allowing him to find his way back to her. She hummed a low, measured melody. Darius continued to cry out, but Sadie noticed the pauses between his screams lengthen.

"That's it, baby. Mama's here," she said, risking a touch to his back.

Outside, the neighbors might watch and judge. They talked of institutions and "proper help." None saw Darius as she did — not broken, different.

His screams faded. His breathing, still ragged, evened out. Sadie continued humming. "Don't you know how tired I am? You're gonna wear me down to nothing, child."

But her voice bore no anger, only bone-deep exhaustion wrapped in an unwavering love that terrified her. This hadn't been one of his worst episodes, maybe twenty minutes; time was difficult to gauge during these moments. Sometimes they stretched for hours, leaving both of them hollow-eyed and spent. When Darius finally uncurled himself, tears streaking his face, his eyes were red but calm. Something in the distance caught his attention, a woman in a vibrant yellow dress crossing the street, and the storm passed. He crawled back to his chair by the window, resuming his rocking as if nothing had happened.

His quiet had returned, but not his peace. His body still contained the storm. This morning was a warning shot.

As Sadie rose, her knees protested after too long on the hard floor. Her left knee clicked when she stood, the one she'd twisted last month trying to keep Darius from running into the street. She sighed as she surveyed the aftermath of the morning's chaos. It wasn't too bad this time. An overturned glass, a toppled Bible, picture frames and books scattered across the floor, and the remnants of a family struggling to hold itself together. With movements of habit, she cleaned and stole glances at her son, who now looked to be perfectly at peace, rocking in his silent world.

And so, the morning ended as it had begun, rebuilding from ruin, sweeping away the evidence of a war no one else could see. When Sadie caught sight of herself in the hall mirror, she wondered when those lines had carved themselves beside her mouth. Thirty-four years old, and she looked like her mother had at forty-five. At times, she appeared as venerable as the Bible now scattered on her floor, its leaves discolored and delicate, mirroring her patience.

The morning light strengthened, warming the small home to an uncomfortable heat even for this time of year. In one of these patches, Darius's shadow rocked back and forth, a small, steadfast silhouette against the day's unfurling brightness. While weariness tugged at his mother's shoulders, she watched him, committing this calm to memory, something to hold on to when the storms returned.

A sharp rap at the door startled Sadie out of a moment of peace. She straightened the toppled photograph on the side table and brushed her hands against her apron before turning the tarnished knob. Mrs. Jenkins stood on the porch, her generous frame blocking the morning light, eyes already sweeping past Sadie to catalog the disarray within. The woman's lips pressed together in that familiar expression of pity mixed with judgment, wrapped in the guise of neighborly concern.

"Morning, Mrs. Jenkins." Sadie stepped back, opening the door wider.

As Mrs. Jenkins entered with a sigh, she pulled half the heat in with her. "Lord have mercy, Sadie. Looks like a hurricane blew through here." She bent to retrieve a book from the floor, placing it pointedly on the shelf.

"We had a bit of a rough start." When Sadie's eyes moved to Darius, she saw him rocking by the window, his body taut and trembling. His hands still hovered near his ears, as if he were trying to shut the world out, yet his shoulders jumped as if reliving each remembered sound.

"My Arthur said the screaming near woke him from across the street. Said it was like somebody was being murdered in here." She pulled back the curtain as she said it, her eyes sweeping the street where the church steeple peeked over the rooftops, two blocks away.

Sadie's fingers tightened on her apron. "Darius gets overwhelmed sometimes. It passes."

"Mm-hmm." The older woman's gaze lingered on Darius, her perspective shifting to concern. "Where's my little Gunny-girl? Lila's been asking for her since breakfast."

"In the back room. The noise upsets her."

Relief washed over Sadie. This was why Mrs. Jenkins came most mornings to take Gunny to play with her granddaughter Lila while Sadie managed the household and took care of Darius. This arrangement had started months ago after an especially hard day when Mrs. Jenkins had found Sadie collapsed in tears on the front steps, Darius screaming inside, and Gunny wailing in her arms.

"I'll fetch her." As Sadie moved toward the back of the house, she remained conscious of Mrs. Jenkins's eyes following her. In the small bedroom, Gunny sat on the floor surrounded by paper scraps she'd been tearing into smaller pieces, a habit she'd developed during Darius's episodes.

"Look who's here for you, sunshine. Mrs. Jenkins is taking you to play with Lila."

"Lila! Lila has dollies!" Gunny jumped up into her mother's arms. She gave her mother a big kiss and a hug. Gunny always knew that Mama needed a little extra lovin' after mornings when Darius lost control. As they walked together into the front room, Gunny scrunched her face, her cheeks puffed, lips puckered, eyes crossing enough to look ridiculous, then spun in place with an exaggerated hip-sway, her cotton dress flaring. "Gottago, Mama! I got dollie' to ten' to!"

Mrs. Jenkins chuckled. "That child don't do nothin' without a show."

Sadie shook her head, grateful for the spark Gunny brought, even on mornings like this.

Mrs. Jenkins swooped the three-year-old into her arms with practiced ease. "There's my sweet girl! You ready to come help me make some biscuits with Lila?"

Gunny nodded with royal gravity, then thrust one finger dramatically into the air. "Portant. Biscuit. Cookin'. Mama!"

"You're a lifesaver, truly," Sadie said, brushing a loose curl from Gunny's forehead as the girl waved goodbye with her usual flair. "She needs space to shine. And I... I need quiet to keep him calm."

The gratitude was genuine. Those precious hours when Gunny played next door gave Sadie time to clean up after Darius's outbursts, catch her breath, and sometimes even close her eyes for fifteen blessed minutes.

She never said it aloud, but some days that bit of relief felt like the one thing standing between her and complete collapse.

"Happy to help, child." Mrs. Jenkins bounced Gunny on her hip. "The Lord says, 'Bear one another's burdens.'"

But the moment of appreciation soured as Mrs. Jenkins's attention returned to Darius. She clicked her tongue; her head tilted toward the window. "That boy needs a firm hand, Sadie. All this coddling…"

"We've tried that. It makes things worse," Sadie said.

"Then he needs more prayer." Mrs. Jenkins's voice was loud, as if Darius couldn't hear or understand what she was saying. "Pastor John was saying last Sunday about how some folks got spirits troubling them. Demons of the mind, he called it."

While Darius paused his rocking, he traced patterns on the glass, his eye skittering between the yard and the two women; Sadie sensed his attention and wondered if he knew they were speaking of him.

"He ain't got demons, Mrs. Jenkins." The words came out sharper than Sadie intended. She softened her tone. "He's different. His mind works in ways we don't understand." She'd heard what happened to children deemed "possessed" in some communities. The institutions where children disappeared, never to return. She'd die before letting anyone harm Darius in the name of salvation.

"Different, huh?" Mrs. Jenkins shifted Gunny to her other hip. "That's what the doctors call it?"

"The doctor said he's…" Sadie paused, remembering the cold, clinical assessment six months ago. "He said Darius's brain didn't develop right. Called him… well… an ugly word… feebleminded. Said there were places for children like him. State places."

"And you don't think that's the devil's work? He's got a beautiful soul; I know it. But that boy's got spirits pressing on him. You ever seen a child so quiet and so wild, both at once?"

Though Sadie's smile didn't fade, her jaw tightened. She'd learned to let these comments pass, to live with the little prices to pay for kindness. "That isn't going to help," she said, her eyes drifting toward the window where Darius sat rocking, his short legs swinging beneath his little frame. "He doesn't understand. He can't tell me what he needs."

She crossed herself, then softened. "I don't mean harm, Sadie. Lord knows I don't. I want to see you rest easy."

When Sadie squeezed her eyes shut for a breath, she gathered her worn resolve before meeting the woman's gaze. "Thank you for your concern."

Mrs. Jenkins sighed. "You think love can fix everything, Sadie. It can't."

"Maybe not," Sadie said. "But it's all I got."

Mrs. Jenkins huffed, adjusting Gunny's weight. "Well. If you change your mind, the prayer circle meets Wednesday evenings."

"I appreciate that." Sadie opened the door.

"Come on, sweet pea," Mrs. Jenkins cooed to Gunny. "Let's go make those biscuits."

"Bye-bye, Mama!" Gunny's small hand waved over Mrs. Jenkins's shoulder as they descended the porch steps. Mrs. Jenkins set the little three-year-old down on the porch, and Gunny's shoes clomped down the wooden stairs, louder than needed and how she liked it. On the sidewalk, dust puffed up beneath her feet as they passed the peach tree on the corner lot, its crooked branches almost bare.

"I'll bring her back after lunch," Mrs. Jenkins called without turning.

"Thank you!" Sadie called after them, the words catching in her throat.

When the door closed, she leaned against it, exhaling. Gratitude and resentment tangled in her chest, the weight of both equal.

CHAPTER THREE

CLOSET

After the morning's upheaval, stillness settled over the Turner home, a rest that felt earned. Sadie lingered in the doorway, dishtowel twisted between her fingers, looking at Darius's profile at the window. The early light cascaded around him, catching the curve of his round cheek and full pouty lips — lips that had never formed her name.

It was the unique color of his eyes that transformed him into something ethereal. Sadie often contemplated if those eyes held the key to his silence, if they connected him to a deeper understanding of life. Sometimes she wondered if he saw patterns or truths the rest of them missed entirely. In these private interludes, she experienced connection and yet painful distance, an observer standing at the edge of his uncharted territory, a world she could not enter. She would watch him intently in these quiet moments, when her son was at peace, when the world aligned right to grant him stillness from whatever war raged inside him.

Outside, a rooster crowed somewhere near the Jenkins' side yard, and the faint noise of a screen door slapping shut traveled from two houses down. Men headed for the trolley stop for shifts at the rail, boots scuffing the packed dirt. A milk wagon rattled through the alley. The church bell marked the hour as it always did. Through all this, Darius lifted one hand, fingers splayed, rotating it in the beam of sunlight as it poured through the window. His eyes followed the shadows his fingers cast on the opposite wall. He repeated the motion, endlessly fascinated. Then he followed the light as it spread across the floor and touched the faded wallpaper and the pile of mending in the corner of the room. It was a simple motion, repeated with patience, a game that held him completely.

When Sadie returned to the kitchen, she left the door open enough to keep him in sight. She plunged her hands into the basin of soapy water, tackling the breakfast dishes with methodical efficiency. The rhythm steadied her, a familiar mantra: wash, rinse, dry, put away.

With the real world shuttered away, she pictured the home she once envisioned, a home much like the one she grew up in, with rooms filled with laughter and music, children's voices rising in sweet harmony while she stirred pots and baked bread. She turned her head back toward Darius. "You know what I think?" she said, her voice barely above a whisper, as if they shared a secret between them. "I think you see things the rest of us can't. Things too beautiful for words."

She often spoke to him this way when it was the two of them — casual, open, as if they were any mother and son sharing the intimacy of morning thoughts. But the doctors' dismissive words echoed in her mind, their clinical assessments ringing like distant church bells. "He doesn't understand; might as well talk to the walls." Yet, deep within that silence, Sadie refused to believe that her son was unreachable. Somewhere in the depths of his being, she knew he was listening, absorbing the world with an understanding that transcended language.

The memory of the first time she noticed something was different flashed through her mind, a painful clarity. Darius had been over a year old, sitting in a patch of sunshine, spellbound by the dust motes swirling through the light.

Other babies she'd raised would laugh and babble, smile with round, toothy grins and reach for objects or her face. Ezra and Lula had been early to everything — walking, talking, and stealing attention with their vibrant personalities. Theo had toddled down the block to the corner store by two, bursting with energy. But Darius... Darius had always looked inward first, transfixed by the world within him, never seeking to connect with anything or anyone outside of his world.

When she had called to him, touched his cheek to break his concentration, he would cry out, flailing his arms and legs with such fury that it left her reeling, stumbling back in shock. The fear had settled in her gut, a dark seed of worry sprouting roots that intertwined with her heart.

At four years old, when he still hadn't spoken a word or answered to his name, Augustus had insisted they see a doctor. "Something ain't right," he said, fear overriding hope.

Dr. Simmons, a broad-shouldered, tired-eyed man and one of the few Negro physicians serving their community, examined Darius in the cramped back room of his office. The boy never looked at him. He flinched at the doctor's touch, covered his ears when the metal tray clattered, and rocked hard enough to rattle the chair legs.

Simmons watched all of it, his mouth tightening the longer it went on.

As he set his stethoscope aside and straightened, his shoulders sagged under the weight of what he didn't quite understand. "Mrs. Turner... Mr. Turner... I'll be honest with you. Children with... actions like these don't grow out of them."

Sadie's hands froze in her lap. Her fingers curled inward, nails biting into her palm hard enough to sting, as if pain might keep the words from settling. She didn't look at Augustus. She couldn't risk seeing his face change.

"He doesn't look when called, he startles at everyday noises, he moves the same way over and over." Simmons hesitated, lowering his voice. "Some doctors call it a feebleminded state."

Heat crawled up Sadie's neck, her skin prickling as though the room had shrunk around her. She swallowed once, hard, the back of her throat aching, and pressed her feet flat to the floor to keep from swaying.

Dr. Simmons continued, "Others think it's a… damage at birth. A weakness of the nerves." He shook his head once, uncomfortably. "No one agrees on the cause."

He didn't hide the pity in his eyes. Or the fear.

"I don't see signs of illness," he went on. "It isn't deafness. And it isn't something medicine can cure. This… condition tends to stay the same, sometimes worsen as the child gets older." He wiped his palms on his coat as if trying to rid himself of the words. "Once he grows… once he's too big to handle… most families turn to Milledgeville. It's harsh, but it's the only place set up for long-term care."

Sadie's body shuddered at the word. Milledgeville.

Her breath caught, sharp and shallow, as if the air had turned thin. She folded one arm tight across her middle, pressing her hand there as if she could hold something in place before it broke loose.

Simmons rushed to soften the blow, though his gentleness only made it worse. "You are wonderful parents. Anyone can see that. But be prepared. You'll need to keep him safe as long as you can. Keep breakables put away. Doors secured. Maintain the established ways of doing things." His gaze drifted to Darius, still rocking, still lost somewhere the doctor couldn't reach. "Children like him don't manage the world on their own."

When Sadie nodded, she barely heard him. The room pulsed faintly at the edges of her vision. She stared at the worn seam of the floorboard beneath her shoe, afraid that if she lifted her head, something raw and animal would come out of her instead of words.

The silence after that settled thick and unmoving, like a verdict already sealed. Sadie felt it press inward, heavy and relentless, each breath a little harder to take than the last.

For months, that sentence lived inside her. It followed her through the house, into the night, into the quiet moments when she watched her son sleep and rested her hand on his back to feel him breathing. Some days it sat on her chest so heavy she had to stop and brace herself against the counter, afraid that if she let go, she might fold in on herself and never quite stand right again.

16

She drew a slow breath and turned back to the moment in front of her.

"Pass me that towel, won't you, baby?" she called, gesturing toward a dish towel near his chair without looking up, her voice laced with hope.

Darius remained still, unresponsive, his fingers twitching as he traced the sunlight dancing across the floor. Sadie hadn't expected him to move; even so, she offered these small invitations to join her world, unwilling to let go of the possibility that someday he might accept.

She wiped her hands and moved to the laundry basket, sorting clothes for washing. Through the doorway, she watched Darius slide from his chair onto the floor. He crawled toward the wall where sunlight cast prismatic patterns through a jar of preserves she'd left on the table. His fingers danced along the wallpaper, tracing the delicate shapes with an intensity that stirred something deep within her. Painful gratitude mingled with grief.

"That's red," she said, her heart aching with love. "And that one's yellow. Pretty, ain't they?"

Sometimes, she imagined he understood colors more profoundly than others. He could spend hours watching light refract through water or glass, suggesting a perception that lay far beyond ordinary sight.

As she hung the laundry, swept the floor, and darned a tear in Augustus's shirt, she kept Darius in her sight. The heat clung to her skin, September refusing to surrender to fall. The air, thick and electric, pressed against her, a constant reminder of the challenges that loomed outside their door. At the window, Darius leaned close, his face flat against the glass, utterly absorbed, studying something in the yard.

Curious, she edged closer, peering through the window at what held him so captivated. A stray cat sat on a fence post, its orange coat brilliant in the sunlight. Darius's hand lay on the glass, fingers spread wide, as though he were attempting to touch the animal from afar.

"You like that kitty?" She knelt beside him.

For one fleeting second, Darius turned, and their eyes met for a rare moment. Then, as swiftly as it came, his gaze slid back to the cat, and the instant evaporated, leaving her with a lingering ache of longing.

"Hopefully, we'll see him again tomorrow," she said, her voice thick with emotion.

Sadie observed what lay beyond her small home, the window bearing witness to daily routines that moved on in their ordinary, unbroken rhythm. Outside, neighbors hung laundry, while children too young for school played in the dirt, and men moved to and from shifts at various jobs. The low hum of a distant radio drifted from someone's window. Inside their little bubble of sunlight and silence, Sadie and Darius existed in a world apart, governed by different rules and expectations.

When she touched his shoulder, she held the warmth of his skin beneath her fingertips. He stiffened but didn't pull away, a flicker of trust that ignited hope within her.

"We'll be all right, you and me," she whispered, letting her fingers linger a moment longer. "No matter what they say."

The simple peace of this moment eased the bruised places in her heart, battered by doctors' verdicts, neighbors' judgments, and the unrelenting fear of an uncertain future. She didn't know how to fix her son; she didn't know if he even needed fixing, but rather understanding. Yet she knew, with a certainty that would not yield, that she would never stop trying to reach him, never stop fighting for him.

As the morning light began its slow transition into the heavy, humid air of an Atlanta afternoon, Sadie wiped sweat from her brow while kneading bread dough. She stole glances at Darius, who had moved to the center of the room, arranging small objects in meticulous lines across the floor. His focus was absolute, a sanctuary of order in a tumultuous world.

Through the open window, men's voices drifted in from next door. Augustus's deep tone mixed with Mr. Carter's raspy drawl. He had come home early from his shift at the railyard. The men lingered in the narrow alley between their homes. She could hear the slap of dominoes on a wooden crate, the clink of a soda bottle against brick.

They thought she couldn't hear them, but their words floated through the air, sharp and clear as the train whistle drifted from the tracks: "place for boys like him," "can't keep living this way," and "Milledgeville Home takes them as young as six."

Sadie's hands stilled in the dough, her heart plunging at the mention of Milledgeville, the institution where families sent children they could not manage. That word alone sent an icy shiver through her veins.

"They've got doctors there," Mr. Carter was saying, his tone matter-of-fact. "Specializes in the feebleminded. My cousin's boy has been there three years now. Family can visit on Sundays."

With a surge of anger, Sadie pushed the window shut more forcefully than intended, cutting off Augustus's response and trapping the words of judgment within the confines of her home. He had never suggested sending Darius away, but she had caught him reading pamphlets from the doctor, serene and contemplative, and had noticed the way his gaze lingered on their other children — Theo, Ezra, Lula, and the vibrant Gunny — who laughed and played like children should.

As she returned to the dough, she pounded it with renewed vigor, pouring her feelings into the kneading. Behind her, Darius's arrangement of buttons, spools, and pebbles stretched across the floor in perfect rows, each piece a testament to his meticulous nature that often eluded her.

The afternoon ticked on, thick with expectation. Mrs. Jenkins hadn't returned with Gunny yet; she sometimes kept her through dinner, especially on days when Sadie looked spent from caring for Darius. Normally, those tranquil hours with Darius were a cherished respite, but today the silence appeared charged, as if something dangerous lingered beyond reach.

The first warning sign came when Darius froze, a spool of thread suspended in his small hand. His head tilted, listening to something Sadie couldn't hear, a flicker of unease creeping through her before the moment unraveled. Outside, a truck backfired once, twice; a sharp crack that rattled the windows and sent a tremor through the air.

The spool dropped. Hands flew to his ears, body tensing as the world crashed in around him. "It's a truck, baby." Sadie wiped her hands on her apron, crossing the room toward him, heart racing. "Darius, it's all right. The truck is gone."

But the rocking came, a low hum building in his throat, tension mounting with each passing moment. Fingers curled into tight fists. She moved closer, careful not to disturb his meticulous arrangement on the floor.

"Let's sing your song, hmm?" She knelt beside him, not touching, present, her voice wrapping around them like a lifeline. "Hush, little baby, don't say a word..."

Her melody didn't penetrate the storm brewing inside him; the aching vocalizations, long and strained, rose in volume as the rocking turned frantic. When the neighbor's dog began barking at the passing truck, hands slammed against his ears with a wail that ripped through the house.

"Shh, shh, it's all right." She risked touching his shoulder, her hand trembling. The response was immediate and explosive. Lashing out, his small fist connected with her cheek with surprising force, pain blooming like a harsh reminder of their reality.

"Darius, please…!"

Another scream. He launched himself forward, sending buttons and spools skittering across the floor.

His body jerked and surged with an impossible strength, arms and legs pounding against the overwhelming sensations that assailed him.

As Sadie backed away, her heart pounded, each beat a reminder of the rising tide of these episodes. They had come more frequently now, lasting longer, erupting from calm to chaos in mere moments.

He threw himself against the wall, then the floor, forehead repeatedly striking the wood with sickening thuds.

Blood beaded above his eye, evidence of the injury she could not stop, shattering her heart.

"No!" She lunged forward, grabbing him around the waist, desperate to keep him safe. He bucked in her arms, screaming with a raw desperation that brought tears to her eyes. Fingers clawed at her arms, drawing blood.

"I'm sorry, baby. I'm so sorry."

With strength born of desperation, she propelled his thrashing body toward the narrow linen closet in the hallway.

His head snapped back, striking her chin. Pain exploded across her jaw, but she pressed on, knowing this was the safest course to take.

"I can't... I can't do this..."

Her fingers fumbled for the latch, vision blurring with tears. The closet was empty except for a folded quilt on the bottom. She used the small space when all else failed, as a last resort to protect them.

As carefully as she could manage, she set him inside, closing the door and sliding the bolt across. Immediate silence enveloped her, broken only by his fists pounding against the wood, muffled yet still piercing — a sound that echoed her own feelings of failure.

The moment the lock clicked, shame dropped into her like ballast, dragging her under. She sank to the floor outside the door, wrapping her arms around herself and rocking in unconscious mimicry of her son.

"I'm sorry," she sobbed, pressing her forehead against the cool wood. "I'm sorry, I'm so sorry."

Inside, Darius continued to wail, the cry tapering only to surge back with renewed force. She should open the door. She should hold him, comfort him, be the mother he deserved. But her body refused to move, paralyzed by exhaustion and despair.

How long she sat there, she couldn't say. The afternoon light shifted, casting shadows across the hallway. Darius's cries softened to hiccupping sobs, then silence, broken by the occasional thump as he rocked against the door.

"Sadie?"

Augustus's voice startled her. She hadn't heard him enter, his presence filling the narrow hallway.

"What happened? Why are you on the floor?" He stepped closer, noticing her tear-stained face and the scratch marks on her arms. Understanding dawned in his eyes. "Darius?"

She nodded, a silent acknowledgment of the turmoil that lay between them.

Augustus set down his lunch pail and lowered himself to the floor beside her, his workman's frame seeming too large for the narrow hallway. He took her hand, his calloused fingers gentle against her skin, a grounding reminder of the strength they had built together.

"Bad one?"

"I don't know what to do. I have no idea how to help him." The words escaped in a broken whisper, laden with the years of fear and love that had accumulated in her heart. "I put him in there like he's an animal. What kind of mother does that?"

"The kind who's doing her best." Augustus squeezed her hand; the warmth of his grip anchored her in that moment. "The kind who hasn't slept through the night in five years."

A tempered thump came from inside the closet. Darius still rocking, but calmer now.

"I heard you talking to Mr. Carter." She forced herself to meet Augustus's gaze, dread pooling in her stomach. "About Milledgeville."

Augustus sighed, heavy with guilt and exhaustion. He shook his head and looked up at the ceiling, desperately wishing she hadn't overheard that conversation. "He brought it up. His wife's cousin has a child there."

"You thinking about it?" The question hung in the air, thick with unspoken fears.

"Aren't you?" The inquiry held no accusations, only shared pain. "Sometimes, Sadie. Sometimes when I see what this does to you, to the other children..."

"He's our son."

"And we're killing ourselves trying to help him." Augustus rubbed the weariness from his face, the day's rail yard grit still etched in the lines of his skin. "Doc said his mind won't ever work right. Said boys like him need special care."

"Doctors told Mrs. Washington her baby would die before his first birthday. That 'baby' started working at the drugstore." Sadie's voice was low, but with purpose. "Doctors don't know everything and they can be mistaken."

"Special care." The words twisted in her mouth, leaving a bitter taste lingering. "You've seen those places. They warehouse them. Forget them."

There was another thump from the closet, softer this time, but enough to send a shiver down her spine.

"I can't send him away." Her voice cracked on the last word, a plea wrapped in desperation. "I won't."

Augustus didn't argue. He wrapped an arm around her shoulders, drawing her against his solid warmth. They sat together in the dim hallway, two weary soldiers in a battle they hadn't chosen but couldn't abandon.

"We'll figure something out," he murmured, his voice low and filled with love. "One day at a time."

With Augustus steadying her, Sadie unlatched the closet door. The hush that followed was thick and solemn — a hush that held regret and resolve, and the last tremors of a storm. Darius sat collapsed on the folded quilt, knees pulled tight to his chest, head bowed. The shadow of the bruise above his eye was deepening to purple, a stark, silent indictment of the battle waged within him.

As Sadie knelt, her movements slow and deliberate, she remained careful not to startle him. The air in the narrow hallway was heavy, smelling of sweat and dust, and the faintest trace of blood. She reached toward her son, her touch as gentle as breath. "Come here, baby," she murmured, the words trembling between apology and love.

He didn't resist. He never did, not when the storm was spent. His limbs were limp, his face streaked with drying tears. One small hand found the fold of her dress, clutching it with more need than strength. Sadie gathered him up, feeling the weight of his exhaustion, the surrender in the slack of his muscles, and carried him through the dim hallway toward the front room.

Augustus cleared away the scattered objects from the floor. A trail of buttons, spools, and pebbles marked the chaos left behind. He furrowed his brow, pressed his lips tight, and handled each object carefully, reverently, as though they were pieces of Darius's inner peace that needed restoration.

In the front room, the last light of afternoon slanted across the floor, burnishing the worn boards to the color of old honey. As Sadie settled into the rocking chair, she pulled Darius into her lap, his body fitting against hers as naturally as roots to earth. She began to rock, the motion slow and measured, humming a lullaby that her mother had sung to her in the harmonious hours of her own childhood, the same melody she'd once hoped would fill the house alongside laughter and song.

Darius's head rested against her chest, each breath growing softer, each shudder further apart. She stroked his hair, the warmth of his scalp beneath her palm, a small comfort for both of them. "Shh, you're safe. Mama's here. We're both still here."

Augustus lingered in the doorway, watching them with eyes that housed too much worry, fatigue, the remnants of pride and hope battered but not yet extinguished. The house settled into a somber stillness, the storm contained, but the bruises — both visible and invisible — remained. When Sadie met his gaze across the room, they exchanged no words. The silence allowed them to rebuild something: a bridge of understanding, forgiving each other for the unwanted choices.

The scent of cooling bread drifted in from the kitchen, underscored by the heat of the late summer afternoon, while Sadie rocked her son, the rhythm even, her heart aching but resolute. "One day at a time," Augustus had promised, and for now, it was enough.

CHAPTER FOUR

AFTERSHOCKS

As dusk settled over the Turner house, the children drifted home, tracking dirt and noise behind them. Ezra and Theo burst in first, books and mitts under their arms, arguing about a missed catch. Lula followed, clutching a handful of wilted wildflowers. Mrs. Jenkins delivered Gunny last, her cheeks sticky with evidence of afternoon cookies and a limp biscuit in one hand and a pink button in the other, prizes from the makeshift tea party Lila hosted under the laundry line.

The house was awake, its bones creaking under the weight of converging lives. Yet Darius remained in his corner, back pressed against the cool plaster, watching the ebb and flow of his family with wary, luminous eyes that appeared to miss nothing and revealed even less.

"Mama, teacher says I got the best spelling in class," Lula announced, her bouquet presented with a flourish. "Miss Thompson let me pass the chalkboard and said my letters looked as nice as Mrs. Avery at the county office."

Sadie accepted the flowers, arranging them in a chipped cup at the table's center, their delicate blooms a small defiance against the day's wear.

"I helped Ezra with his arithmetic," Theo declared, his voice edged with pride.

"Did not," Ezra shot back, arms crossed. "I solved it myself."

"After I showed you how!"

"Boys," Augustus's voice carried from the kitchen. "Less talking, more helping your mama."

Obedience, if reluctant, followed. Theo gathered plates, Ezra filled glasses, and the current of rivalry yielded to the muscle memory of routine. Gunny trailed Sadie, small hands clutching her skirt, narrating her day in half-formed sentences as she swayed between the comfort of her mother and the allure of the biscuit still clutched in her fist.

Noise swelled, a familiar tide: clattering cutlery, grease popping in the cast iron, laughter chasing scoldings, and the small, sharp cries of children negotiating space. Each noise stacked atop the next, building a crescendo that pressed against the boundaries of what Darius could bear.

When Sadie's eyes found him, she saw his fingers twitching in a rhythm of warning — a cue she had learned to read. The purple bruise on his forehead lingered as a reminder, an echo of earlier battles and storms that no one else could predict. She caught Augustus's gaze over Gunny's head, a silent message passing between them. *Watch him.*

"Dinner in five minutes," Sadie called. "Lula, bring the bread, please."

As Augustus moved through the kitchen, he offered affection where he could: a quick kiss to Lula's crown, a tousle of Theo's hair, a squeeze to Ezra's shoulder, and lifting Gunny for a quick hug.

"Daddy, can we go fishing Saturday?" Ezra asked, pressing close to Augustus. "I heard the catfish at the pond are biting."

"If your chores are done and your mama can spare us." Augustus's arm settled across Ezra's shoulders, his affection understated, the rare intimacy of father and son.

Across the room, Darius rocked, eyes fixed on the exchange. Something changed in his expression, a yearning almost visible, a child on the outside of glass, watching warmth from the cold. He took a tentative step toward the family circle, elbows bent, hands fluttering near his face.

Sadie held her breath, everything in her aching to scoop the other children aside and clear a path, but she knew better. Too much sudden movement, too many eyes, could shatter his courage.

"Look who's joining us," she said, her voice an invitation.

Hope flickered across the children's faces. Lula edged behind Augustus's legs. Theo straightened, watchful but not cruel. Gunny, guileless and full of grace, beamed at her brother and patted the chair next to her.

"Dari!" she crowed, using her special name for him. "Come eat!"

Darius moved closer, each step an act of will — halting, brave, dissolving in the glare of the kitchen lights, the press of voices, and the layered scent of dinner. His fingers and wrists flickered faster, minute bursts near his cheeks.

"Set his place at the end," Augustus murmured to Theo. "Where it's quieter."

They'd learned these adaptations through painful trial and error. Darius needed space, needed less noise, and he needed escape routes. The family learned to bend around his needs, never forcing, only making room.

When Darius reached the table and hesitated at its edge, his eyes darted from face to face, never quite meeting anyone's gaze, yet he appeared to absorb every gesture, every tone, every shadow of expectation. Sadie wondered, as she always did, what he saw: the shape of love, or nothing more than the movements that mimicked it?

"Sit down, son. Food's almost ready," Augustus said.

For a single heartbeat, possibility lingered, almost within grasp. The dream of a normal family dinner hovered, fleeting as dew. But peace in the Turner household was always on borrowed time.

A spoon clattered to the floor.

Darius screamed, high and raw, his body pitching forward as the room rushed in on him.

The family moved at once. Theo and Lula cleared the plates. Augustus swept Gunny back and she closed her eyes and covered her ears. Their retreat was silent, practiced.

Sadie stayed.

When the storm burned itself out, Darius crumpled to the floor, sobbing, and Sadie knelt beside him, humming as the house settled again.

She hadn't envisioned this life, yet they endured the chaos and calm. They were still here. Still trying. Tomorrow would come soon enough.

CHAPTER FOUR

CHAPTER FIVE

DROWNING

Chapters 5 and 6: September 23, 1930 –

Later that night and the next morning

The amber light from the streetlamp cast across the floor, catching the edge of Darius's chair where he rocked in an unbroken rhythm. Sadie remained on the threshold, dishcloth still clutched in one hand, watching her son's profile against the window. The house had settled into its nighttime stillness — Theo and Ezra breathing deep in their shared bed, Lula curled around Gunny in the girls' room, Augustus's familiar snore drifting from their bedroom. It was here, in this in-between space of the front room, that wakefulness persisted.

She should go to bed. Tomorrow would bring its own battles, its own exhaustion. But something held her there, studying the way the light softened her son's face. The bruise on his forehead had darkened to deep purple, but in this gentle illumination, even that mark of today's struggle appeared softer. He pressed his small hands to the cold window, exhaling a hazy cloud across the glass. Even as the fog spread beneath his lips, he continued his slow back-and-forth rocking, the sole motion that kept him tethered to the room.

The creak of wood against wood repeated itself. One she knew by heart. One-two-three forward, pause, one-two-three back. The same rhythm that had governed so many of her nights when he was an infant. Her arms remembered the weight of him, how she'd walked circles through this very room, bouncing him with each step while exhaustion blurred her vision. Other mothers spoke of colicky babies who cried for hours. But Darius's crying had been different, not the angry demand of hunger or discomfort, but something deeper, more desperate, more primal, as if the very air he breathed and his own skin burned him.

Memory pulled her backward, five years dissipating like sugar in water. She saw herself again, younger, less worn, standing in the same doorway with a screaming bundle pressed against her chest. Three months old and he'd never once slept longer than twenty minutes at a time. She'd tried everything — swaddling tight, swaddling loose, warm baths, cool cloths, every remedy the older women suggested. Nothing worked. While Theo slumbered through thunderstorms and Lula dozed in her basket while Sadie cooked, Darius resisted sleep as though it were death itself.

Those first months had nearly broken her. She'd walked him through the house until her feet went numb, hummed until her throat went raw, rocked in the chair until her back seized with pain. When Augustus could, he would take turns, but his work at the railyard demanded strength and alertness. A man couldn't handle hot metal and heavy machinery on no sleep. So, it fell to her, this endless motion, this constant soothing of a child who couldn't be soothed.

The other babies she'd carried had prepared her for none of this. Even Ezra, stubborn from birth, had settled when she sang to him. They'd look at her face, recognition dawning in their dark eyes, tiny fingers reaching for her cheeks. But Darius had never reached. His gaze, shocking against his brown skin even then, would fix on points beyond her shoulder, tracking obscure patterns he alone could see. When she tried to turn his face toward hers, he'd arch away with surprising strength, his cries escalating to shrieks.

She'd discovered the window by accident. One night, delirious with exhaustion, she'd stumbled during her endless pacing. To collect herself, she paused by the front window, shifting Darius's weight in her aching arms. The crying stopped so suddenly that she thought something was wrong. But no, his eyes had locked onto the streetlamp outside, his small body going still for the first time in hours. She'd stood there, afraid to move, afraid to breathe, watching her son watch the light.

After that, the window became their refuge. She'd pace him there during the worst nights, letting him stare at the warm glow while she counted trolley bells in the distance. The counting kept her grounded when exhaustion threatened to pull her under. Sometimes she'd drift into half-sleep standing up, Darius's weight the one thing keeping her upright.

The memories encased the present — that desperate young mother and this weary one, both watching the same child seek the same light. The front room had become his domain gradually, a natural evolution born of necessity. First, they'd moved his crib here when his night screaming kept his brothers awake. Theo had school, so he needed his rest. Then the crib became a mattress on the floor when he'd learned to climb the rails. Finally, the chair by the window, where he could rock himself through the long hours while the family slept.

The arrangement brought relief. She couldn't deny that. No more midnight disruptions, no more exhausted boys at breakfast. But it also meant Darius lived apart even within their home. While his siblings whispered secrets in their shared rooms, while they giggled over private jokes and squabbled over space,

Darius remained here, separated by more than walls. The special place near the window that gave him peace also kept him apart.

Sadie's fingers clenched on the dishcloth. Love could feel like drowning sometimes, like being pulled in directions that threatened to tear her apart. She loved him with a fierceness that frightened her, loved him more desperately perhaps, because he seemed so unreachable. But that love came braided with guilt — guilt that she experienced when he was calm, guilt that she'd chosen the other children's sleep over keeping him close, and the shame that some mornings she stood in this doorway and wondered what their lives might have been if he'd been born different.

The chair creaked on. Darius's eyes remained fixed on the window, on that small circle of light that gave him something she never could. Peace. Predictability. A constant that never demanded he be anything other than exactly what he was.

When Sadie pushed the bedroom door open, Augustus stirred anyway. Fifteen years of marriage had tuned him to her movements, the particular way she tried not to wake him that always did. The oil lamp on the dresser cast slanting shadows across the narrow room, over his work clothes draped on the chair, her Sunday dress hanging from a nail, and the wedding photograph in its tarnished frame.

"Come lay next to me." His voice was rough with near-sleep, one arm extended across the space beside him.

Sadie hesitated at the foot of the bed, exhaustion weighing her bones. "Augustus, I'm too tired tonight. I can't…"

"That's not what I want." The hurt in his voice made her look up. His eyes were open now, locked on her with unusual intensity. "Come here. Please."

She studied his face in the coppery light, seeing not desire but something rawer. Need. Not for her body but for her presence, for the comfort of not being alone with whatever thoughts the darkness brought. She understood that need. She'd clung to it every night for five years.

Removing her housedress, she slipped on her nightgown and slid beneath the thin sheet. The mattress was still warm from his body heat, the pillow sweet with the pomade he used on Sundays. Augustus pulled her against him, her back to his chest, his arm heavy across her waist. She noticed the tremor in his hands, the way his breathing stayed shallow.

"You stood there watching him a long time." His breath stirred her hair.

"He was peaceful. Didn't want to disturb him." As Sadie paused, she reflected on the vision of Darius sitting in the window. "He's always peaceful at night. Like the darkness makes more sense to him than day-light."

They lay still for a moment, listening to the house settle around them. Through the thin walls came the distant creak of Darius's chair, rhythmic and relentless. Augustus's arm tightened around her.

"Remember when he was born?" When Augustus nodded against her neck, Sadie continued. "The midwife said he was the prettiest baby she'd ever delivered. Those eyes — she'd never seen anything like them."

"Neither had I. Still haven't," Augustus said.

"I thought they meant he was special. Blessed." Sadie's voice dropped to a whisper. "But it wasn't that kind of special, was it?"

"He don't look at me." The words came out rushed, as if Augustus had been holding them back. "Not once, Sadie. Not one time has that boy looked me in the eye. I'm his father, and he looks through me like I'm made of glass."

"He never makes eye contact with any of us. Not exactly."

"He looks at you sometimes. I've seen it."

"At my shoulder, maybe. Or past my ear. But not at me, not so much." She shifted in his arms, turning to face him. In the lamplight, she could see the lines strain had carved around his eyes. "He looks at light more than people. Always has."

"What else does he do that ain't right?" Augustus's jaw tightened. "I mean, I see things, but I don't know what they mean."

Sadie weighed her words. "He lines things up. Spends hours arranging buttons or stones in perfect rows. Gets upset if anyone moves them."

"The spinning and the rocking."

"When he's happy, yes. Spins until he falls down dizzy, then gets up and spins again. And you know the rocking is the one thing that keeps him calm."

"The hitting." Augustus's voice stiffened. "His own head, Sadie. What child does that?"

"One that's hurting in ways we don't understand." She touched his face, feeling the day's stubble beneath her palm. "The world's too loud for him, too bright, too much. When it overwhelms him, the pain's got to go somewhere."

"I watch Ezra and Theo, how easy they are with each other. Wrestling, joking, being boys." Augustus's voice broke. "And then I look at Darius… I don't know how to help him. I'm unsure how to be his father when he won't let me close enough to try."

"You think I know? You think any of this comes naturally?" Sadie's voice was low but edged, the kind that comes after too many quiet battles. "Every day I wake up and try something new. Every day I fall short. He's slipping through my hands, Gus, and all I can do is keep trying different ways to reach him. Some days are harder than others. Like today."

When Augustus turned toward her, shadows cut sharp across his face. "I feel like we're being punished. Like God's tellin' me I ain't worthy."

Sadie's head snapped toward him. "Don't!" she said, the word flat and final. "Don't you dare make this about God's judgment. Darius didn't choose this. Neither did we."

"Then why?" His voice cracked on the question.

"There isn't a why," she said, softer now, as though the force had gone out of her. "There's what is. I don't have answers, but I know this much … God doesn't hand out children as punishment. He doesn't pick favorites or sinners. He gives us what He gives us, and we do the best we can with it. That's the whole of it."

He was silent for a long moment, his breath shallow. "You truly believe that?"

"I have to," she said. "If I start thinkin' otherwise, I won't have anything left to stand on."

The room grew somber again. A streetcar rattled somewhere in the distance. When Augustus reached out and found her hand, rough against rough, he asked, "You think God's still watchin'?"

"I think He never stopped," Sadie said. "And maybe that's enough."

He drew her close, their foreheads touching, two people clinging not to certainty but to each other. The heat pressed down, the night settled,

and through the stillness came the faint, steady rhythm of Darius's rocking — mild, but constant.

Sadie's hand drifted to her stomach, flat beneath her nightgown. "I
can't have another child." The words came out in a rush. "When I found
out about Gunny, with Darius not even walking… I'd lie awake counting
the hours in the day, dividing them between four children, and coming
up short every time. Thank God she slept through his worst spells.
Thank God for Lula's little arms, always ready to hold her while I…"
Her voice caught, remembering those endless days of division, of never
being enough places at once.

"Sadie…"

"Mrs. Jenkins helps. The older kids help. But I'm emptied out, Augustus. Got nothing left to give a new baby. Can barely give enough to the
ones we have."

"I wasn't asking for more children," Augustus said, squeezing Sadie a
little tighter.

"But you want them. I see how you look at the Baker family with their
seven. Like we're unfinished."

"We got five beautiful children. That's enough. More than enough."
He paused, choosing his words. "It's that every man wants to protect his
family. Keep them safe. But how do I protect him from his own self?
How do I keep the world from crushing a boy who can't handle hearing
spoons clinking?"

The question hung between them, unanswerable. Sadie pressed closer,
feeling his heartbeat against her palm, a warmth and love that had carried
her through fifteen years of marriage.

She placed his hand over her heart, running her fingers over the calluses that told the story of his days at the railyard. "You protect us by
providing. Even when the foreman cut hours. Even when Mr. Daven-
port wouldn't extend credit at the store." Her voice softened. "You
found a way."

"Any man would do the same."

"No, not any man." She traced the scar across his palm where he'd
caught himself on a coupling pin last winter, working through the

infection rather than lose a day's pay. Her thumb lingered on his wrist. "Some men drink away their troubles. Some men's fists get loose when life gets hard. But you... you keep showing up for me, for the kids... for Darius." She looked up at him, her eyes wet in the dimming light. "That's what Darius needs. That's what I need and the kids do too. Steadiness and that heart of yours."

Augustus pulled her tight against him, his face buried in her hair, breathing in the scent that had been home to him since he was a teenager. "Then I'll keep loving you all the best way I know how."

"We both will."

As they held each other, the lamp burned lower, its light fading. Augustus's breathing deepened, evening out into sleep. But Sadie remained awake a while longer, listening to the subdued sounds of her house. Theo's snore, so like his father's already. Gunny's sleeping mumble. And beneath it all, constant as a heartbeat, was the creak of Darius's chair — forward, pause, back again.

The rhythm followed her down into sleep, where she dreamed of oceans rocking, boats that never reached shore, a beautiful boy with sapphire eyes standing always beyond her reach, watching lights she couldn't see.

36

CHAPTER SIX

REFLECTION

From his place in the front room looking out into the world he couldn't reach, Darius sensed the house ease around him as the last footsteps faded and the evening rustle of voices receded into silence. The silence brought relief. No clanging, no chaos. Only breath, glass, and darkness. Darius rocked, comforted by the predictable motion. He pressed his forehead to the pane, letting the smooth, cool glass ease the pounding behind his eyes while moths circled the porch light outside in frantic loops, their wings forming designs he followed even as tears rolled down his cheeks. Outside, yellow squares of light marked neighboring windows, some flickering from gas lamps, others flickering behind handmade curtains. Each was a different world where people spoke and laughed and touched without the armor of fear he wore like a second skin.

His tears came in silence. They always did. They arrived the way everything inside him arrived — sudden, encroaching, and too tangled for him to explain. He had not meant to scream, or to swipe the table clear, or to send his family scattering, yet each noise earlier had struck him like a pebble thrown into still water. One crash rippled into another. Ezra's laughter. Gunny's shout. The plate hitting the counter. Each sound built upon the last until the pressure filled every part of him, and the only way out had been forward.

Now the memory replayed in bursts that made his stomach tighten. Gunny with tear-streaked cheeks. Ezra stepping back with wide, startled eyes. Mama gathering the pieces of a supper no one had eaten. The heaviness in the room afterward had settled into his chest, and even though he couldn't put words to it, he knew the sadness belonged, in part, to him.

Another tear slid down, warm against the cool window. He didn't wipe it. He curled closer to himself, drawing his knees in and rocking with slow, constant motion meant to remind his body where it ended and where the world began. The window helped with that. Light and shadow obeyed rules here. The shapes of fence posts, telephone wires, and neighbors' windows stayed where they belonged. The world outside didn't shift shape the way people did.

From the back of the house came the faint creak of his parents' bed, followed by his father's inaudible murmur and his mother's softer reply. He couldn't make out their words, but he heard his name woven into their voices that pulled at something deep inside him. Earlier he had wanted to reach them. He remembered that clearly. He remembered the feeling of what he wanted, a simple touch, the gentle weight of a hand on his shoulder like Papa had placed on Ezra's. But the wanting had been sharp enough to hurt, and the path toward it vanished before he took a step.

Then the spoon fell. And the storm overtook him.

A dog barked across the trolley line, two sharp bursts of sound that made him flinch. He waited for the next bark, bracing for the noise that cut straight through him, but the night held. His reflection swam in the glass — wet cheeks, tight jaw, eyes still bright with leftover fear. The colors around the edges of the night deepened, as they often did for him. The yellow lamplight grew warmer, and the dark outside shifted into layered shades of blue and violet that eased some part of him he could never express.

When Darius pulled the sheer curtain across his face, he created a thin veil between himself and everything, dimming the room and muting the colors. When he pushed it aside, the world sharpened again. That change soothed him, the simple cause-and-effect people never quite provided.

If he could tell Mama about the colors — tiny worlds painted on the wall when sunlight hit a jam jar right. The faint trails the butterfly had left in the air that morning. But the words that might explain it stayed trapped inside him, fluttering without form.

A soft, muffled sound drifted from his parents' bedroom; his mother crying. The noise froze him. Her sadness found him in ways nothing else did. He wanted to go to her, to stop her pain, to erase whatever part he had played in making it. His body didn't move. His hands fluttered instead, absorbing the emotion because there was nowhere else for it to go.

He pressed his palm over his reflection's face on the glass. A new tear slid down. Then another. The distant clang of the factory bell carried across the street, marking the end of one shift and the beginning of another. He wanted to reach them. He wished to be understood. He desired to cross the invisible barrier.

He rocked again, slower this time, and let the tears fall until the rhythm thinned and the glass cooled beneath his forehead.

***

Morning arrived in stages. First the rooster from two streets over, then the milk wagon rattling past, sunlight creeping across the kitchen floor where Sadie stood grinding coffee. Her hands moved through the familiar ritual while her mind wandered to the boy still rocking by the window.

"You're up early." Mrs. Jenkins appeared at the back door, basket in hand. "Brought some biscuits. Thought you could use them after yesterday."

Sadie accepted the basket, inhaling the warm scent. "Thank you. That's right kind of you. Coffee's almost ready."

As they settled at the kitchen table, the house remained still around them. Mrs. Jenkins studied Sadie's face, taking in the shadows beneath her eyes.

"Bad night?"

"No worse than usual." Sadie wrapped her hands around her cup. "Three meltdowns yesterday. Two the day before. Four on Tuesday."

Mrs. Jenkins's eyebrows rose. "You're counting?"

"Augustus started marking them on the calendar. Hoping he might get better, but he ain't. To prove to ourselves we're surviving." Sadie traced the rim of her cup. "You said 'after yesterday.' But yesterday was like the day before. And tomorrow will be the same."

"Lord have mercy, Sadie. Every day?"

"Every single day. The screaming fits come like clockwork. Getting him from bed to breakfast. Unexpected sounds. Too much touching, too little space." She glanced at the calendar on the wall, its squares marked with Augustus's careful tallies. "Seven days this week. Fifteen meltdowns. I keep washing blood from his forehead where he bangs it."

Sadie's eyes filled with tears. "I don't mean to complain, Evelyn. I love him with everything I got. It's that I'm so wore out I don't know if I'm coming or going some days. Can barely remember my own name." She wiped her eyes. "I'm grateful, truly. For you taking Gunny during the day especially. Lord knows what I'd do without that help." A small smile crossed her face. "I hang on to the little things. Theo's grin when he masters something new. Lula humming while she braids her hair. And Gunny, when she hugs me, I hold her a little tighter, a little longer than she probably wants. But bless her heart, she seems to know I need it. She melts into me and pats my back with those tiny hands like she's the mama."

Mrs. Jenkins leaned forward. "You ought to write it down. Keep a journal."

Sadie laughed, bitter and short. "When? Between the screaming and the cleaning? Besides, what would I write? Today, yesterday... tomorrow they are all the same."

"Honey, you can't live like this."

"We are living like this." Sadie's voice stayed level. "This is what our life looks like. Every sunrise brings the same battles, same victories measured in seconds of eye contact, same exhaustion that settles into my bones like the stain of sweat."

Mrs. Jenkins pursed her lips. "You've done rearranged this whole house for that boy. Cleared the shelves, took down the doors ..."

"We make do. Same as any family would."

"Most families don't have children like ..." She caught herself. "Well, they say..."

Before Mrs. Jenkins could mention the state hospital, Sadie cut her off. "Darius ain't going anywhere." Sadie set her cup down harder than intended.

"But what about the others?" Mrs. Jenkins pressed. "Theo... Ezra..."

When Sadie stood, she moved to the window where she could see Darius still in his chair. "You know what I see? I see Theo learning to move with care when his brother needs calm. I see Ezra figuring out which sounds hurt and avoiding them. Yesterday, during the worst of it, when everything was chaos and noise and splintering — Darius reached for me. Not past me or through me. For me."

From the front room came the sound of Darius's chair slowing, then stopping. Both women listened as his bare feet padded toward the kitchen. He appeared in the doorway, not entering, standing there in his nightclothes, looking past them toward the window.

"Morning, baby," Sadie said as her eyes followed him.

He didn't respond, but he stepped into the kitchen, moving to his usual seat near the window where morning light rested on his skin.

As Mrs. Jenkins watched him settle, his fingers found the table's edge and traced its familiar grain. "Does he ever... does he know you?"

Sadie poured milk into a cup, set it where Darius could reach it without looking at her directly. "He knows which footsteps are mine. Which laugh is Lula's. He knows when Augustus is tired before any of us notice."

"But does he love you back?"

The question hovered in the air. Sadie watched her son's fingers trace the marks on the table.

"I don't know if he loves the way we love. But that reach yesterday, in all that chaos..." Her voice dropped. "That's enough. That has to be enough."

The morning sounds of the house began with beds creaking, voices mumbling, water splashing in basins. Soon the kitchen would fill with children wanting breakfast, Augustus needing coffee before the rail yard shift. Another day, like the one before.

As Mrs. Jenkins gathered her basket, she paused at the door. "You're stronger than you know, Sadie Turner."

"No," Sadie said, watching Darius lift the milk cup with both hands, careful not to spill. "I'm as strong as I have to be."

CHAPTER SIX

Chapter Seven

Azure

Chapters 7 & 8: October 1930

Darius understood family, even if he could not join it the way he wanted. He saw it in the way his siblings leaned into one another, how their laughter rose and folded together like a melody. His love for his family was rooted deep within him, but the feeling had no outlet. The words stayed locked inside, and his hands refused to reach out. He sat separate, watching his family through the invisible wall, wondering if they knew he was trapped on the other side.

The same invisible wall that kept him from their touch kept him from the world outside the door.

Last week, he'd tried to follow Lula outside. The sunshine had called to him, yellow rays stretched across the porch steps. He'd been so close, three steps from the door, two steps, one step to the threshold, then the screen door slammed behind his sister. The sharp crack detonated in his mind like a firecracker, and something inside him broke loose.

He remembered the screaming, his own voice, raw and wordless. He remembered his fists pounding against the door, his head banging against the wood. And then Mama's arms had locked around him from behind, pinning his arms to his sides.

"Stop it, Darius! Stop it now!" Her voice had trembled in his ear. "You're gonna hurt yourself!"

As her grip tightened, his arms flailed and legs kicked, his body twisting and going limp all at once, making it impossible for his mother to hold him. He jerked and bucked, swinging wildly and clawing at her hands as her warm tears dropped onto his neck, and he heard her prayers whispered into his ear. "Lord, please help my boy. Please show me what to do."

Darius hadn't understood why she held him so tightly. He knew that the door, and the world behind it, remained closed to him while everyone else walked through it freely. In Mama's arms, he'd felt both her love and her fear, but he also felt trapped.

Now he watched through the front window as a group of children chased each other down the dirt road, skirts flying, bare feet slapping red clay. Their laughter drifted through the glass, mingling with the scent of iron and dust that always rose when the road dried after rain. He set his fingers against the pane, feeling the vibration of their footsteps on the ground outside.

One Sunday, Daddy rested a cautious hand on his chair near his shoulder. "One day you'll be ready to go outside. We gotta wait till you're bigger."

But Darius didn't want to wait. The outside pulled to him, the deep blue of the sky, the rustle of leaves, the mysterious shapes of clouds. He counted the children as they played: seven, then nine, then six as some ran home for supper. He noted their colors, brown skin in different shades, bright clothes, and white teeth flashing in their smiles.

Tonight, Darius curled up on the couch where he could still look out the front window at the moonlight, the rough fabric beneath him, his head resting on the feathery pillow Mama had placed there long ago. Wrapped in his blue blanket, the one that had a slight smell of sunshine from drying on the line, he closed his eyes to the familiar hush of the house. The echoes of the day faded. His breathing slowed. Sleep crept upon him. His limbs grew weightless, as if the floor had forgotten he was there. Heat from the day's fire slipped from his skin.

Then came air, fresh and cool on his face. When Darius blinked and sat upright, he found himself on the front porch. The door behind him was closed. No arms held him back. No voice told him to stop. He was outside, alone. Air and space and freedom. The air startled him as the cool, wide, uncontained world touched every part of him at once; it was overwhelming and thrilling in the same breath. His heart jumped with fear, but beneath it ran a thread of something sharper — joy.

A slender smile crept across his face, shy and bright.

The road stretched out before him like a silver ribbon from Lula's hair, with nothing but the distant sounds of dogs barking. Houses lined the block, but their angles seemed steeper, blurred at the edges like chalk drawings bleeding in the drizzle of a gentle rain. Trees swayed without wind, their branches twisting into peculiar shapes. The stars above were endless, more than he knew could exist, bright enough to light the shadows but not enough to explain them.

Darius leaned into the night. No fear. Only the thrill of being free from the walls of his home.

The air seemed different against his skin. When the breeze brushed his face, he closed his eyes to focus on the sensation. Unlike the daytime touches that pressed and scratched, this one skimmed across his cheeks, cool and weightless.

The first raindrop landed on his cheek. Darius froze, eyes flying open. Another drop struck his forearm, then his shoulder. Within seconds, a gentle shower surrounded him, each drop tapping against the ground, the roof, his skin. He waited for the panic to rise, for the sensory assault to crash over him, as it always had.

Instead, a curious calm settled over him. Each drop, soft, cool, and wet felt distinct yet part of something greater. Darius lifted his face to the sky, letting the water trace paths down his cheeks and his neck, soaking into the collar of his nightshirt. The sensation didn't hurt. It didn't crowd his thoughts or scramble his senses. It was cool, rhythmic, and orderly in its randomness.

When he stepped off the porch and into the center of the street, the rain intensified, plastering his clothes to his small body, but Darius didn't mind. The water created a barrier between himself and the world, softening every sensation to something he could bear. He could see the colors in each raindrop, prisms of light, reflecting in every direction.

His feet carried him down the street, past houses where he'd primarily been an observer. He trailed his fingers along fence posts, touching the rough wood, the peeling paint, and the slick wetness of rain. He crouched to examine a puddle forming in a pothole, watching his reflection fracture and reform with each falling drop.

The stray dog with the white eye patch appeared from between two houses, regarding Darius with curious caution. Neither retreated. When the dog shook itself, sending water flying, Darius laughed, a silent laugh that bubbled up from somewhere deep inside him, a place that had never found expression.

Lightning flashed in the distance, and Darius counted until the thunder followed — one, two, three, four, boom. The thunder rolled across the sky, but in the open air, even this didn't overwhelm him. He spread his arms wide, letting the storm wash over him, through him.

The rain slowed, leaving the street glistening and transformed. Darius knew he should return before the house woke, before Mama discovered his absence. But something urged him onward, toward the empty lot at the end of the street where tall grass grew wild between broken fence posts, once part of a garden plot now overrun.

Something waited for him there, large and impossible, outlined by clearing rain.

The shape was too large to be a dog, though that was Darius's first thought. It stood motionless in the grass, rain sliding off its back as the moon traced a luster of electric blue, not dull like his faded blanket, but alive, like lightning trapped in glass.

When Darius froze at the edge, his bare feet sank into mud. The thought of Mama finding him there tugged him back. Something deeper pulled him forward. The creature turned its head, eyes like a winter sky meeting his without threat, recognition. It moved with deliberate movements as if it knew how much he could bear.

When it sat, wings tucked close, Darius saw it wasn't a dog at all. Jewels glimmered between the scales on its face; feathers edged its ears; wings flexed in the rain.

Dog? It was the one word his mind offered.

The creature twitched in response, lowering its head in what felt like an invitation. When Darius reached out, his fingers trembling, he touched warm, thrumming scales. It didn't sting or startle. It felt… right.

A deep rumble vibrated through the creature's chest. Darius, who shrank from even his mother's gentle hand, laid his palm to its cheek, tears rising, stemming not from fear, but from something unnamable breaking open inside him. A luminous wing arched over him, sheltering him from the drizzle. Darius wondered if this was a dream. A thought deep in his mind, not his, answered inside his head.

Both, the thought answered. *And we are here together.*

Darius understood the creature's thoughts. He regarded the giant blue dog with a look of surprise, confusion and relief all at once.

Hello, Darius. I've been waiting for you.

And no, I'm not a dog.

My name is Azure.

The words formed perfect shapes in his mind, pressing gently like warmth held inside his chest, shaping thoughts he had never heard aloud. His hand dropped. Stepping back, Darius watched as the creature moved toward him. How he knew this creature came for him, he didn't know how he knew. He just did.

Don't be afraid.

The creature bowed, lowering its massive head until it warmed Darius's face.

My kind are called Dreamers' Dragons. I am your guide and teacher in the realm of dreams.

Darius tilted his head to the side. *Teacher?*

To help you find words, Azure said. *And to shape this place.*

Find words? Darius asked.

Not all at once. When Azure dropped his eyes, their eyes were level. *Not tonight.*

The idea overwhelmed him. Darius had tried before — tried to tell Mama what he needed, tried to pull the words out of his head and into the world. They never came the way he wanted. They slipped away somewhere between thinking and saying.

He tried anyway.

His lips parted. He shaped the word in his mind, pushed it forward, willing it to take form.

Nothing.

His throat seized. The word lodged there, heavy and sharp. His fingers curled. Rocking once, then again, faster, his hand struck his leg hard.

It's all right.

Azure's presence settled around him, not pushing, not pulling.

You've done nothing wrong.

Breath came in short bursts. His eyes burned.

You've spent a long time being asked for things before you were ready, Azure said. *Here, that doesn't happen. You decide when we begin. I'll be waiting.*

The rocking slowed. Darius's hands loosened.

When Darius reached out, he brushed his fingers across Azure's scales. Warm. Familiar. Safe.

Blue, he thought.

Yes, Azure replied at once. *Blue.*

Darius traced the jewels along Azure's cheek, counting silently.

Seven.

Nine.

Az…ure.

A rush spread through him — not loud, not sharp, but lifting.

That's my name, Azure said. *You found it.*

Darius didn't speak aloud, but Azure had heard him. Exactly.

Something new stirred in his chest.

You'll come back? Darius thought suddenly. The thought came fast, tangled with urgency.

Azure's gaze fixed.

Yes. But through dreams.

He shifted barely, angling his body so Darius could see the closed door of the house beyond the rain.

When you are asleep. When your body is safe inside. That's when you'll find me.

Darius's fingers stilled.

Not outside, Azure continued. *Not in the daylight. The world beyond that door isn't built for you yet.*

Darius remembered the slam of the screen door. The sharp crack. Mama's arms holding him too tight.

You don't come looking for me there, Azure said. *You wait. And I will come to you.*

When Darius pressed both hands to Azure's face, he thought the word clearly.

Promise?

Promise.

The word settled, firm and sure.

And Darius knew, without being told, that this would not be once, or twice, but an untold number of nights, stretched long into the years ahead.

Darius's thoughts tumbled faster than his hands could move. He wanted to touch everything — scales, wings, tail, claws, the cool jewels set along Azure's face. He needed to know how each part felt.

Azure's tail curled.

Go on.

Darius began at the shoulder. The scales were warmer than he expected, firm but not hard. He pressed, then traced where one ridge overlapped the next, finding the narrow seam between them.

Jewels, scales, wings, claws, Azure said, a note of quiet humor in his thoughts. *New dreamers always investigate. Once, a boy tried to count my teeth. He made it to nineteen before he sneezed in my face.*

Darius paused, then lifted his hand again.

He reached higher, fingertips brushing along the edge of the wing.

That one tickles, Azure said, a low rumble rolled through him.

Darius's eyes narrowed. He pressed the same spot again.

The rumble returned. *Definitely tickles.*

He tried once more, careful and exact.

The sound came again, deeper this time.

A small, sly smile crept across Darius's face.

He moved on — claw, tail, wing — then back again, mapping Azure by touch and response. The wing felt smooth and taut, its edges fluttering faintly with each breath Azure took.

All dragons are different, Azure said. *Some sharp. Some soft. But we are never small.*

Azure straightened, wings lifting as rain slid from them in shining sheets. Then the air shifted.

That's enough for tonight, Azure said, gentle but firm.

Darius stilled at once.

Azure inclined his head until its warmth brushed Darius's cheek. The touch didn't overwhelm him. It didn't scatter his thoughts.

We have time, Azure said. *More nights than you can count yet.*

Mist curled around them, and Azure's shape blurred, thinning into rain and shadow until nothing more than the slight hush of water remained.

Darius woke with a start, his cheek resting against the cool glass of the front window. His small wooden chair creaked beneath him as he shifted, blinking in confusion at the morning light. The familiar street stretched before him, puddles from the night's rain already drying in the Georgia sun. Across the way, Miss Ruth was already hanging laundry from the clothesline, and the distant clang of a streetcar echoed down the road.

No enormous blue creature.

No glimmering scales.

No voice in his mind.

Only the window.

The rocking chair.

The world he had always known.

His hands opened and closed, searching for the sensation of warm scales beneath his fingers. How had he gotten back to his chair? The last thing he remembered was standing in the deserted lot as Azure faded into the mist. Had he walked home? Had someone found him? The space between that moment and this one remained blank, a page torn from a book.

Nose pressed against the glass, Darius scanned the street for any sign of Azure. The lot sat vacant, a patch of weeds and mud where no dragon waited. The rain had stopped, but the sky stretched gray and unwelcoming. His small chest tightened. Eyes remained fixed on the vacant lot, willing Azure to appear.

Emptiness spread through him. Had it all been a dream? The rain on his skin, the midnight wandering, the creature with eyes like blue ice — had his mind created it all? Darius's hands began their familiar flapping, uncertainty triggering the need for motion.

"You up already?" Mama's voice came from behind him, warm with sleep. "You're up before me today."

Darius didn't turn. He didn't move.

When Mama's hand came to rest briefly on his shoulder, she said, "Lord, child, your clothes are damp. Did you leave that window open in the rain?" Her eyes traveled downward, widening at the sight of his feet. "Darius Turner! There's mud between your toes! How in heaven's name…" She knelt, examining his feet, then his nightshirt, her brow furrowed in confusion. She touched the windowsill, finding it dry, then checked the locks. "This doesn't make a lick of sense," she muttered, more to herself than to him.

Before she could think further, Lula shrieked from the back room, Ezra hollered his innocence, Gunny cried, and the kettle rattled toward a boil.

Sadie sighed, the kind of sigh that came from surviving too many mornings. "Stay put, baby. I'll wash you off in a minute."

She hurried away, already pulled by everything else that demanded her first.

When Darius looked down, he saw his nightshirt clinging to his skin, damp and cool. The mud squished between his toes as he shifted his weight.

Was it a dream?

But the mud was real. The wet cloth was real.

It had to be.

Somewhere between dream and waking, between night and day, he had met Azure. He had heard.

A few minutes later Mama returned, dish towel in hand, crouching again at his feet. She blinked. The mud had thinned to faint smudges. The pale grass blades were gone. Nothing but dull, ordinary dust remained, the kind that drifted in from the yard or trailed in on the children's shoes. When Sadie frowned, she touched the dry boards around his chair. "Huh," she murmured. "I must've been more tired than I thought. Looked worse a minute ago." Her voice carried relief and dismissal in equal measure, the mental triage she had grown accustomed to living life with five children and a husband: if it wasn't dangerous this second, she'd usually move on and forget about it.

She wiped the last specks away and stood. "There now. All clean."

But Darius knew what had been there before it faded. His toes still tingled from the cool mud. His skin remembered the rain.

His thoughts felt different too, clearer along the edges, as if someone had opened a window, and the ache of Azure's absence followed him. Would he come back? The street outside looked so ordinary now. The neighbors emerged from their homes to begin their daily routines, men pulling lunch pails toward the trolley stop, women hauling wash tubs to the backyard. Children skipped toward school with books tied in belts or tucked under arms, their shoes scuffed and their braids bouncing.

But something had changed. He sensed it in the new awareness of his tongue behind his teeth, in the memory of words forming in his mind and being understood. He felt it in his hands, which had touched something beyond explanation and found acceptance there. He carried it inside his head, where Azure's words had untangled his thoughts.

Twenty times throughout the day, he returned to the window to check the vacant lot. Each time disappointment settled over him when he found it empty. Perhaps it had been a dream.

Yet something warm remained lodged in his chest, a small ember of hope that refused to die. Azure had promised to find him in dreams. Tonight, when darkness fell and the last of the day faded, Darius would close his eyes and see if that promise proved true.

From her place at the kitchen table, Mama watched him with new intensity, as if sensing the change in him but unable to place it. "You all right today?" she asked once, her voice careful. No answer came. The words weren't there yet. But they hovered closer than before at the edge of silence, no longer distant — waiting.

As the sun lowered, Darius climbed into his chair once more. His eyes followed the path he had taken: the porch steps, the wet road, and the lot where magic had waited.

Tonight, he would sleep.

And he would look for Azure.

CHAPTER EIGHT

COUNTING

Under his blue blanket, Darius counted the ceiling's water stains: one, two, three. The house creaked softly, settling around him. Tonight, he was going to find the dragon, and sleep welcomed him. One moment, he sensed the scratchy fabric of the sofa; the next, cool grass brushed his feet.

An open field stretched beneath a sky pierced with stars, tall grass swayed at his knees. The air was heavy with the scent of rain, reminding him of the night before when he first met the dragon. Everything felt calm and anxious all at once.

When he climbed a small rise, he scanned the horizon. His heart sank. No Azure. Nothing but open sky and a meadow of purple and yellow wildflowers.

Darius tugged at the hem of his nightshirt. He cupped his hands and tried to call out, but no words came. His hands dropped, fists tight with frustration. Rocking began. First slow, then faster. Where was Azure?

Then he remembered: Dreams are where *I'll find you*. Azure had promised.

He drew in a breath, folded his legs beneath him, and settled into the grass.

Time shifted in this place. The moon hung motionless. The crickets chirped in perfect timing, mesmerizing his senses. His fingers twisted blades of grass into thin ropes, one after another. In the waking world, stillness often warned of a storm building inside him. Here, the stillness soothed him and he savored the connectedness to the silence.

A shadow cut across the moon. Darius tipped his head back. Something vast drifted overhead with a slow, deliberate grace.

The night went silent around him, but the quiet held layers he could sense. The cool hush pressed close, breathing faint colors into the darkness, and his gaze slipped past the ordinary world toward something wider, something that trembled beyond consciousness.

Azure glided above the mountain with wings spread in a sweeping arc. The blue along his hide shifted as he moved, deep along the center, bright at the edges, flashes of pure azure where moonlight scraped across his scales.

Inhaling sharply, Darius stood stunned. Fingers tapped against his shoulders, quick staccato movements full of restless anticipation.

The dragon circled lower. Jewels along his face and spine caught the light, and the curved ridges of his horns framed his head with quiet symmetry, but it was his gaze that kept Darius still. The blue inside those eyes deepened until it seemed to draw the world inward.

As Azure descended, a rush of wind pressed against Darius's skin. His shirt pulled tight against his chest. The earth quivered beneath him when the dragon landed, claws carving into the ground with a weight that felt both real and impossible at once.

Darius's rocking stopped. Every sense caught. Scales gleamed, rows of shifting blue that shimmered under the moon.

Then Azure looked at him.

Eyes, glacial and endless, locked onto his. Darius didn't look away.

The fear that usually knotted his stomach didn't come. No buzzing in his ears. No urge to hide. Stillness and wonder.

He stepped forward without realizing it.

I knew you would find your way back.

When Azure lowered his head, Darius's palm rested against warm scales.

"Welcome back, little one," Azure said out loud.

The sound didn't simply reach his ears. It rolled through his chest, down his arms, and settled in his stomach like a far-off rumble. Not loud. Not frightening. Steady. Solid.

He didn't have words for it, not even in his head, but something inside pushed back. A small tug.

He turned toward Azure and touched his chest. Then his own.

Then tapped the air.

"Ah." Azure's eyes narrowed with understanding. "You like when I speak out loud, not in your thoughts?"

He nodded toward Darius's chest. "You feel it."

Darius gave the smallest of nods.

"Then I will use it more often," Azure said. "Words should be felt. You deserve to feel them."

Darius looked up at him, genuinely looked, and nodded again.

When Darius touched his throat, he formed the wish silently.

"You wish to speak aloud," the dragon said.

He nodded. Tried. Nothing.

His hand dropped. Frustration surged through him and he pointed at his temple, then at Azure. Can you still hear me?

"Yes. Not out loud, but inside. Your mind speaks clearly."

Relief softened his posture. Circling back to the face, he counted the embedded jewels: one, two, three… pausing to notice how some were cool and glassy while others held tiny imperfections inside, like bubbles caught in ice.

"You count often," Azure said. "It steadies you."

Darius nodded.

"That is a strength. Not everyone can see the world that way."

They stood in silence, head to snout. When Darius pressed his forehead to Azure's scales, the heat calmed him.

"You are not lacking, Darius. You are listening in ways others have forgotten."

They walked into the dream.

When they reached the crest of a hill, Darius hesitated, hand again on his throat.

I want to try.

"Then try," Azure said. "This place is meant for you."

Taking a breath, Darius opened his mouth.

Nothing.

His knees hit the ground. His forehead slammed into the earth.

Instinct.

Hard.

Again.

At home, the wood floors were cool and unyielding, giving him pressure, sensation, and most importantly, control.

But here the ground pushed back like supple clay. His head bounced off something spongy, unreal.

Jerking forward harder, he tried to break through it, desperate to feel something. His forehead struck again. But the dream wouldn't let him. A mild resistance caught him, firm but unbreakable. It gave no pain, no feedback — it erased the one thing that had always helped.

A frustrated cry escaped, silent but shaking. His arms flailed. He clawed at his head. His whole body trembled with the mismatch between need and reality.

No! His mind screamed. No, no, no.

"Darius. I know what you're trying to do," Azure said.

Darius didn't stop, still tangled inside his surge of emotion. His fists pounded the sides of his head now, desperate to find some relief. The blows came fast, then slow, then fast again, wild, uneven. His world was shrinking, collapsing inward.

The air shimmered around Darius. As he swung again, something subtle and lambent appeared, an invisible barrier that caught his hand mid-strike, holding it still without force.

When Azure stepped forward, he lowered his enormous head. "This place is different. I won't let you hurt yourself here."

Darius froze. His breath caught again, this time from confusion, not pain.

"In the waking world," Azure said, voice soft, "pain becomes your signal. It's how you find control when nothing else works."

The jewels across Azure's face lit from within, restrained at first, then brighter. The colors turned, from sapphire to emerald to amethyst and back again. A sequence emerged, unwavering, calm. One. Two. Three.

Blinking, Darius drew a slow breath.

Follow the colors.

Blue.

Green.

Purple.

Stay with me.

His fists lowered.

"You don't need pain to be understood," Azure said. "I will teach you other ways."

The lights continued to pulse, gentle, calming, in a predictable order.

His body stopped fighting, the gentle rocking continuing as the panic ebbed.

And when he finally looked up, the tears were still there, but so was trust.

"This is how we learn," Azure said. "Not by force. But by choosing something new."

No words came in response. But he sat down. The rocking slowed. His hands stilled.

Then, when he eventually looked at Azure, his eyes were clear.

Will you leave me?

"No. Never. They will not take you from me," Azure said quietly. "Not while I can reach you."

In the waking world, the whispers had a name — Milledgeville State Hospital. He didn't need to ask who they meant.

Azure lowered his body beside the boy, a comforting presence in the grass.

"You are not broken. You are building. That is why I'm here. To help you build, to grow, to learn."

The words didn't undo the pain. But they made room for it. They let Darius breathe.

"You see what others don't. Patterns. Light. Truth in small things."

The boy wiped his face with the sleeve of his shirt. Gradually, he sat upright again.

When Darius reached out to Azure once more, his fingers moved to the embedded jewels along the dragon's cheek, one, two, three, counting the familiar pattern. Each number brought calm, and a little more peace.

When he reached the last jewel, Azure nodded.

"No one has ever counted them all."

Pride stirred in Darius's chest, warm and unfamiliar. He had done something real. Something whole.

"What seems small to others," Azure said. "Is often sacred to us."

They continued, then the dream shifted.

When Azure lifted one wing, a gust of wind spiraled outward. The field folded away into mist, and from the mist rose a forest, trees stretching into shadow, their leaves silver in the moonlight.

In the clearing ahead was a pond, still as glass. Moonlight pooled across its surface. It didn't reflect the trees, only the stars.

"This place is for you," Azure said. "To try. To grow. To make mistakes safely."

When he stepped forward, his reflection greeted him — calm, centered, unmarred. He reached out. The water rippled. His image fractured, then returned.

"Out there, every stumble leaves a mark," Azure said. "Here, you try again."

No words were needed to understand. He stayed.

When Darius knelt beside the water, he watched his face look back: rounded edges, bright eyes, a quiet mouth. But no shame. Him.

"Do you see yourself differently now?" Azure said.

Darius opened his mouth.

No pressure. No push. Presence.

And from within, the word came.

"Blue."

A faint whisper. Not forced. Not broken.

Azure did not cheer. He nodded.

Yes. Blue.

When Darius pressed his hand to Azure's scales one last time, he lingered.

"This bond, this dream doesn't fade. You'll carry it with you," Azure said. "Not only here in the dream realm, but during the day, when storms rise and the world feels too loud, you'll remember. What we practiced will stay with you. You'll feel it, even if no one else understands why."

The stars dimmed. Mist rolled in.

Dawn comes. I'll return each night.

The dragon's form faded, but warmth remained.

Darius woke under his blue blanket, fingers at his throat.

"Buh…oo…" Darius tried to say, with a wisp of breath.

Mama froze mid-step. "Darius? Baby, did you — ?"

He looked past her, toward the window. Not for her. Not yet.

She lingered, studying him, then sighed and moved on. But her steps were slower.

He knew she'd heard. And he knew she knew it mattered.

Darius didn't want to wake up.

Long before his eyes opened, his body curled tighter under the blanket, seeking the lingering warmth of dream. He clung to the last moments of sleep with desperation, hoping Azure might return if he held still enough, quiet enough. Real life felt too loud and too bright.

He pressed his face into the blanket, fingers fluttering against the worn edge. Go back. Please. I need to go back.

Footsteps. Mama's.

"Darius?" she called from the doorway. "Time to get up, baby."

And Darius stayed.

Motionless, his body remained a statue, breath shallow, eyes open but vacant. Not absent. Somewhere else entirely.

When she crossed the room, she crouched beside him. "You all right?" Her fingers brushed his forehead. No fever. No tears. Unreachable.

She watched him for a long moment, then exhaled. "I'll fix you some grits. Come on when you're ready."

Darius didn't stir. His thoughts clung to the riverbank of dreams, willing the water to rise and carry him back.

Azure stood beside the dream-river, waiting.

"You came back fast. Have you even left your bed yet?" he asked.

Darius nodded once, head low.

"You're upset," Azure added, circling him, trailing wisps of dream-matter in his wake."

I want to talk, Darius thought, fists clenched. *But it won't come out. I can't make it work.*

"Words are difficult for you in the waking world. Your mind knows them, but your lips and tongue struggle to form them."

Why? The thought crept in with frustration.

Azure stopped walking and lowered his head to Darius's level.

"Because your mind works differently than most. The path between your thoughts and your mouth is tangled," Azure said. "Like roots growing through stone."

He conjured an image in the air, an opalescent outline of Darius's head. Pathways lit up across the image, flickering with effort as Darius watched.

"See?" Azure said. "Your messages take the long road. That takes time."

When Darius reached out, he pointed to the flickers. *They're real?*

"Yes." Azure nodded. "And they will get brighter. But you must be patient with yourself. Your silence isn't emptiness; it's a waiting place."

Darius's jaw tightened. *It still hurts. Not talking.*

Azure's voice softened. "I know. But your thoughts are strong. Clear. Don't mistake quiet for weak."

When Darius's gaze dropped, he thought clearly.

Touch... hard too.

"Yes. For you, touch doesn't feel kind or safe. It's sharp. Loud. Like too many people talking at once inside your skin."

Darius nodded once. His fingers twitched.

Even Mama. I don't want to hurt her. But when she touches me... I want to run. Scream. Like my body gets too full too fast.

Azure's luster dimmed, softening like twilight through fog.

"What feels small to others can feel like fire to you."

The dragon's form shifted; his outline grew misty, less solid.

"May I try something? I'd like to help you with touch. Here, in the dream world, we can practice without it hurting."

Darius hesitated. His fingers curled against his palm.

"You're in control," Azure said. "If it's too much, think stop. I will."

After a moment, Darius gave a small nod.

Unhurried, Azure approached, mist trailing like smoke. It reached out, not to grab, not to press, but to be near. The fog wrapped gently around Darius's hand. No pressure, presence.

"This is fog," Azure whispered. "Let it move between your fingers. Focus on your breath. In... one… two... three... out... one… two... three."

Darius closed his eyes. Counted silently.

Then Azure added weight. Barely enough to notice. The sensation shifted, first the warmth of a blanket, then the whisper of a feather, then something like grass on bare skin. Each time, Azure waited. Gave him space. Darius flinched once, but didn't pull away.

Breathing.

Waiting.

"Touch doesn't have to chase you," Azure said. "It can wait. And when it's too much — breathe. Count. Move. Say when."

Darius's hand hovered, then reached forward. He touched one of Azure's luminescent jewels.

Cold, he thought.

They practiced beneath the fading sky, color draining from the clouds until everything turned velvety violet. After, Darius stopped tensing. His hand didn't jerk away. He noticed. He measured the touch.

"When you wake," Azure said, "try this. Once. Let someone near. There is no need for you to return the touch or speak. Don't run. Not this time."

Darius looked down, uncertain.

"I'll be watching," Azure said, his voice wrapped in warmth. "Not always close, but never far."

***

Evening settled over the Turner home, and Darius remained at his post by the window, his silhouette etched against the fading light. His bright eyes caught the first stars appearing in the twilight sky. Behind him, the family moved in their evening routines, Augustus reading the newspaper, Theo helping Ezra with sums, and Lula braiding Gunny's hair while the little one squirmed and giggled. The sounds washed over Darius like distant waves, separate from the shore where he sat watching and waiting.

"Hold still, Gunny. Can't make you pretty if you keep wiggling."

"Don't want pretty. Want to play."

"After your hair's done. Mama said."

Theo looked up from Ezra's notebook. "That ain't right. Seven and eight is fifteen, not fourteen."

Ezra frowned and gripped his pencil tighter. "Is too fourteen."

"Count it out then."

Darius's fingers traced scratches on the windowpane, invisible maps of thoughts he couldn't express. Inside him, words and feelings swirled, beautiful in their movement but impossible to catch or order. He wanted to turn from the window to join the circle of warmth behind him. The wanting stayed with him, but the path from desire to action vanished in fog.

When Sadie entered from the kitchen, she wiped her hands. "Gunny, time for a bath before bed."

"No bath!" The three-year-old scrambled away from Lula's hands, launching herself toward Darius's corner. "Hide with Dari!"

Before anyone could intercept her, Gunny crashed into Darius's space, her small body colliding with his legs. The sudden contact jolted through him like electricity. His body tensed, hands flying up, breath catching.

"Gunny, no!" Sadie moved fast, voice sharpened by fear. "You know better."

The room froze.

Everyone waited for the storm — screams, flailing, broken glass, or worse. Darius's fingers curled tight against his palms, breath shallow, rocking suspended in tension. He counted as Azure taught him. One. Two. Three. Breathe.

The scream didn't come.

His hands floated down. He didn't touch her, couldn't, but he didn't push her away either. The rocking resumed, faster, processing the contact without shattering.

Across the room, Augustus lowered his paper, his voice low. "Well, look at that."

Gunny, oblivious to the tension around her, patted Darius's knee. "Dari, hide me."

Sadie approached cautiously. "Gunny, come to Mama. Let's give Darius his space."

Lula leaned in, studying her brother's face. "It's all right. He ain't upset. Look."

Fingers flicked near his face. Deliberate. Not distressed.

Darius's gaze stayed pinned to the window, but his body had made room for Gunny.

Augustus didn't move. He looked at his children sharing the same space for the first time and stared in silent awe.

Sadie knelt a few feet away, unwilling to disrupt this delicate moment. "Darius? Is it all right that Gunny's sitting with you?"

No response came, at least none they could interpret. But the absence of distress spoke volumes. The family watched, hardly daring to breathe, as Gunny leaned against Darius's leg, content in the moment's peace.

Darius continued to count. One. Two. Three. Breathe. One. Two. Three. Breathe.

Ezra returned to his sums, Theo to his corrections, but their eyes flicked frequently to the unlikely pair by the window. Lula edged closer, emboldened by Gunny's success.

"I finished my book today," she said, carefully choosing each word. "The one about the rabbit. He found his way home at the end."

Darius continued rocking, but something in his posture suggested awareness, not of Lula's words perhaps, but of her presence, her voice.

When Sadie moved to the window, she kept a respectful distance. "Stars are bright tonight," she said, following his gaze upward. "Like little holes poked in the dark, letting light shine through."

No response came.

Still, she stood beside him, sharing the view, if not the experience, of it. After a moment, she reached toward him, her hand hovering near his cheek without touching.

"I don't know where you are, baby, but I'm waiting right here for when you find you're ready."

Later, after bathing and tucking the other children into bed, and after Theo and Ezra went to their room to say goodnight as part of their ritual, Sadie returned to find that Darius was still at his window. The night settled in the Turner home, Augustus's gentle snoring from their bedroom, the occasional creak of the old structure, and the distant whistle of a train crossing town. Mama looked at her youngest son, her heart bursting with hope.

When she placed his blanket and pillow on the sofa where he slept these days, she smoothed the fabric with care. "Whenever you're ready," she said, the same words she spoke each night.

CHAPTER NINE

BREAKTHROUGH

Six months later - April 1931

Spring arrived in Atlanta with a gentleness that made winter feel like a distant dream. Theo and Ezra bickered over a pencil. Lula braided her hair with a ribbon she'd sworn she lost two days ago. The Turner household still woke to the usual scramble of shoes, breakfast crumbs, clinking spoons, and raised voices tumbling through the walls.

But beneath the chaos, something had shifted.

Augustus no longer marked his careful tally marks on the kitchen calendar. The grid of marks that had tracked Darius's storms for months now hung unmarked since February. Where once the calendar bore witness to daily battles, some days marked with two or three desperate tallies, now whole weeks passed clean and white.

Darius still rocked. Still flinched at sharp noises. But there was a calm in him now, a softness the others felt.

Sadie noticed it first. Then Augustus. Then everyone.

And they were grateful.

Through it all, Darius sat by the window.

Still rocking. Still moving his hands in quiet, circling bursts near his head.

Not in distress, but in peace.

Watching.

A knock came at the door.

Mrs. Jenkins approached the porch with a sense of mission, cookies bundled in wax paper, chin lifted like a woman on holy assignment. The morning air carried the sweet perfume of wisteria and honeysuckle. She wore her good blue housedress, and her hair, tucked under a scarf, caught the ten o'clock light that filtered through the blooming dogwood branches.

Beside her, Lila peeked out, a pale-yellow dress catching the dappled shadows.

"Well, look at you, Sadie Turner," Mrs. Jenkins said, her voice broad and warm as sunrise and her grin full of mischief. "You ain't even dressed for the Lord's day? Shame on you."

Sadie half-smiled, conscious of her everyday apron. "It's not Sunday yet, Evelyn. It's a plain old Tuesday."

"And I'm headin' to choir practice. You're comin' with me. I could use your alto, Sadie. Easter service is comin', and the choir's thin. God don't mind what day you come to Him, honey," Mrs. Jenkins replied. She stepped inside, ushering Lila forward, her eyes already moving through the room, lingering where chaos used to live.

Sadie smiled, but her reflex was to decline. "You know I can't."

When Evelyn tilted her head toward Darius, she studied him with the practiced eye of a woman who'd witnessed his transformation. "He seems calm today. Real calm. Not like before." She paused, remembering that morning months ago when she'd found Sadie sobbing on the kitchen floor, talking about putting things in high cupboards and doors being removed. "Remember what you told me? About how improvement looks different for Darius?"

Sadie's throat tightened at the memory. "I remember."

"Well, seems to me you were right. Boy hasn't had one of his fits in weeks, has he? Augustus hadn't touched that calendar in weeks." Mrs. Jenkins gestured toward the kitchen. "And look at him now. Peaceful as a Sunday morning. A little walk and sunshine might do him some good."

Sadie looked over. Darius was still by the window, eyes following the lazy drift of pollen through the morning light. He wasn't distressed. Not today. The April warmth had softened something in him, as it had coaxed the azaleas into bloom.

"I don't know..."

"I'll help with the girls," Evelyn offered. "Lila will keep Gunny busy, and they will be fine. Besides," she added, "when's the last time you sang with the choir? How long has it been since you did something for the joy of it?"

The question hung between them. Sadie remembered their kitchen conversation, how she'd insisted they were still a family, still finding their way. Now here was proof — the possibility of leaving the house with Darius.

"Choir?" Sadie asked.

"Choir," Mrs. Jenkins said. "And coffee. And gossip." She smiled, softening the edge. "You need it. And that boy of yours might surprise you. Seems to me he's been doing a lot of that lately."

"Let me put on my shoes."

"Take your time," uttered Mrs. Jenkins, moving to the sofa and lowering herself with a grunt. Lila followed, keeping a watchful but curious eye on Darius.

When Sadie slipped to the back room, her mind turned over Evelyn's words. She found Gunny curled up with a storybook and lifted her into her arms. "Want to go see the church ladies, sweet girl?"

Gunny nodded, burying her face in Sadie's neck. "Will there be cookies?"

"Yes. Mrs. Jenkins never comes without cookies."

"Can I bring Dari?"

Sadie nearly laughed at the request — months ago, it would have been impossible. "Of course, he's coming too."

The group set out together into the mild April morning. The air hung warm but not yet heavy, carrying the green smell of new growth. Bees droned lazily in the blooming azaleas, and the sidewalk was dusted yellow with pine pollen that would need sweeping by afternoon.

Skirts swayed in the slight breeze, and feet crunched over gravel still damp with morning dew. Gunny and Lila walked ahead, their chatter a musical backdrop, stopping to examine a line of ants or point at a cardinal. Evelyn carried her plate of cookies in one arm and hummed a hymn under her breath.

Sadie walked beside Darius. Six months ago, she would have been gripping his wrist, ready to restrain him if he bolted. Now he walked freely beside her, his bare feet careful on the warming pavement.

He didn't take her hand, but he stayed close. His head turned at every bird call, every flicker of wind through the new leaves. The world always seemed too loud to Darius, but today, he seemed to walk with it instead of against it. When a butterfly crossed their path, Darius's eyes followed it as if it were leaving invisible trails of color only he could see, and his lips curved ever so slightly.

"Boy's grown so much over the past months," Mrs. Jenkins said, glancing back at Darius. "Remember when you couldn't even get him to the corner without him dropping to the ground? Look at him now, walking proud as you please. You oughta be celebrating, Sadie."

"I am," Sadie replied, her voice thick with gratitude. Every peaceful morning was a small miracle.

When they reached the church, a modest white building with weathered steps and flowerbeds full of early petunias and struggling zinnias, the April sun had climbed higher. The warming painted boards released the smell of old wood and linseed oil. The doors stood open, warm voices already drifting out as the choir gathered.

70

Mrs. Jenkins marched ahead, her gait proud and purposeful, fanning herself with her hand against the building's warmth. She called out, "We're here!" as she entered.

Sadie lingered on the threshold, a memory surfacing from last autumn. Darius had waved his arms during the sermon, small hands rising and falling in quick, uneven bursts. High, broken notes had spilled from his mouth — not words, but bright, melodic notes all his own. The congregation shifting in their pews. The whisper that floated loud enough to bruise: "Poor thing."

She'd carried him out before the final hymn and let him finish his song on the church steps.

But that was before. Before the calendar marks had dwindled. Before the storms had gentled to occasional squalls. Before whatever wonder seemed to intervene with her son.

He was calmer now. Stillness and quiet weren't guaranteed, but they no longer felt impossible.

She squeezed Gunny's hand and stepped inside.

The sanctuary offered blessed coolness after their walk, though the air was already growing close with the promise of afternoon heat. Nearly empty pews stretched before them, dust motes dancing in the colored light from stained glass. A row of women filled the choir section, sheet music rustling like leaves, fans working against the warmth. When they turned as the group entered, their faces broke into surprised but genuine smiles.

Mrs. Alma adjusted her glasses, gave a polite wave, and returned to her sheet music. "Welcome, Sadie," she called out, dabbing her forehead with a handkerchief. "So nice to see you. And Darius too — my goodness, how he's grown!"

"It's nice to be seen," Sadie replied, feeling the truth of it. Being seen without pity, without the careful distance.

She settled Gunny next to Lila and guided Darius to an empty pew. She let him choose his spot. When he slid to the far end, he positioned himself where the morning light through the window could warm his face, and arranged his blanket carefully on the seat. He reached into his pocket and withdrew a smooth river stone he'd picked up on the walk, rolling it between his palms.

Eyes fixed on the piano, he sat quietly, giving his full attention.

When the choir director lifted her hands, her fingers arched in the air. "All right, everyone, let's take it from the top. Page 1."

A hush fell so complete you could hear hearts ticking and the lazy drone of a wasp against the window. Then the music began.

From the front, the choir launched into "His Eye Is on the Sparrow."

As Sadie watched Darius, his body shifted uneasily at the first note, his hands gripping the stone. She leaned forward as if to reach him, but the moment the first notes touched the air, Darius slipped somewhere she could not follow. The world around him receded, leaving the music and the place it carried him.

Soft. Measured. A slow, swaying rhythm enveloped him.

Why should I feel discouraged...

At first, it was the melody, notes he'd heard many times, floating between the rafters where dust sparkled gold in the morning light.

Why should the shadows come...

But now the air itself seemed to quiver, as if the music had grown a body, breathing beside him.

Why should my heart feel lonely...

His muscles softened. His head lifted, eyes drifting past anything fixed or real. The music reached him. It felt like the rain that night, the first night he'd found peace in his dreams. He remembered the way each drop had shielded him, how the water had turned the world down to a hush. This melody did the same. Each note pressed inward, sinking deeper.

When Jesus is my portion...

My constant friend is He...

Tears came suddenly, hot and unexpected. When Darius closed his eyes and gripped his smooth stone so tightly his knuckles turned white, it was not for comfort, but to stay tethered to the world. His head swayed back and forth, drawn by the melody, as the music stirred something deep within him, a place no one had ever reached.

The voices rose and folded over one another, the organ swelling until the air itself seemed to press against him — a susurrus that left no space to breathe. His breath caught as the choir gathered force, deep and resonant. He wanted to cry out, to step into the beauty of it, but nothing came — tears and joy. They spilled down his cheeks faster than he could wipe them away.

He wasn't sad. He wasn't afraid.

His eye is on the sparrow...

Sadie saw it before anyone else — his closed eyes, head swaying, and the wetness streaming from the corners of his eyes. She rose from her seat, mother's instinct surging. Six months ago, tears meant disaster was coming.

When Mrs. Jenkins reached out and gripped Sadie's arm, she said, "Wait. Look closer. He's not upset."

Sadie pressed a hand to her chest, fighting the urge to go to him.

"This is his way," Mrs. Jenkins said. "It's joy."

And it was. Darius wasn't crying — he was weeping. Something in the music had found him, touched him, filled him. And in that moment, all anyone could do was bear witness.

One by one, the other voices faded.

Except one.

Sister Alma stepped forward, her voice rising like a prayer torn from the soul. It was not merely music, but a calling, reaching for Darius in the quiet place where no words had ever gone. The morning light through the windows seemed to brighten, casting rainbow edges on everything it touched.

I sing because I'm happy... I sing because I'm free...

A shiver raced down his spine despite the warming air. Goosebumps prickled his arms and the melody carved a tunnel into his heart.

His eye is on the sparrow...

And then, across that sea of faces, his gaze found hers.

His mother.

In that moment, everything he had ever needed was there.

And I know He watches me.

Across the sanctuary, Sadie saw the change before she understood it. The music softened, the room steadied, and her gaze narrowed to her child on the pew. Whatever had been happening inside him had reached its crest, and she moved toward him as if pulled by something older than memory. She crossed the sanctuary, every step unsteady. She no longer heard the choir. She heard only the silence between them, stretching back almost six years.

She collapsed to her knees beside him, trembling.

When Darius turned toward her fully, his tears still flowed, unashamed, lips parted in awe. Then, with agonizing care, he lifted one hand.

He placed it, light as breath, on hers.

His fingers barely curled around her wrist.

But it was not random or tolerated. It was not accidental.

It was intentional.

And Sadie broke.

A sob tore from her chest, followed by another. She pressed her other hand atop his, anchoring herself to the moment like it might vanish. This was the boy she'd found locked in chaos months ago. The boy she'd cried over in her kitchen, wondering if improvement would ever come.

And here he was, reaching for her.

Behind her, the choir women stood in silent reverence. No one moved or spoke. Alma stepped backward, her voice fading into tears of her own. Even Mrs. Jenkins, who'd seen plenty in her years, dabbed at her eyes with her handkerchief.

Darius looked at his mother. He gazed directly at her.

And he smiled.

It wasn't wide. It didn't last long.

But it was.

And it was for her.

Sadie could barely see through the flood in her eyes. She bowed her head, holding his hand to her chest, her whole body trembling from the weight of it.

A woman in the back pew whispered, "Mercy... The Lord is in this room."

74

Another crossed herself without thinking.

The stillness in the church wasn't empty — it was full. Full of awe. Of love and of something sacred.

And in that sanctuary, where April light filtered through old glass and the air hung sweet with promise, the boy who never reached, never looked, never let anyone close, had done all three.

The walk home came at noon, when the April sun stood high and warm overhead. The morning's gentle warmth had ripened into something heavier, and Sadie could feel perspiration gathering at her temples. The children ahead of them had slowed their pace, Gunny's earlier energy wilting in the heat. Even the birds had quieted, seeking shade in the thick canopy of oaks that lined the street.

Darius walked differently. His steps were still careful, still measured, but something had loosened in him. The stone stayed in his pocket. His hands hung quiet at his sides. Once, when they passed under a magnolia heavy with blooms, he stopped entirely, face turned up to catch the sweet, lemony scent that drifted down.

Mrs. Jenkins walked beside Sadie, both women silent for the first block. Finally, Evelyn spoke.

"In all my years," she said, "I've never seen anything like that."

"Neither have I," Sadie admitted.

"You were right, you know. What you said that morning in your kitchen. About improvement looking different," Mrs. Jenkins said. "When you were crying about those broken dishes and removed doors, saying how you'd keep trying, keep adjusting — I thought you were fooling yourself."

A lump formed in Sadie's throat as she remembered.

"But look at him now," Evelyn continued. "Reaching out to you in church." She shook her head.

"The Lord works in mysterious ways," Mrs. Jenkins said, then paused. "Though I suspect He had some help. You never gave up on that boy, Sadie Turner. When everyone else would have sent him away, you kept believing he'd find his way."

When they arrived at the Turner house, the church bells chimed at noon. The door creaked open, letting in the scent of rain-damp grass from last night's shower mixing with the dusty heat of midday. Sadie stepped through first, her good shoes in hand, stockings damp with perspiration. Gunny darted past her, humming the hymn under her breath, already forgetting the weight of the morning's miracle.

Darius paused on the threshold. His eyes scanned the room as if it might have changed while they were away. The curtains billowed in the warm breeze, the front window still streaked from yesterday's rain. Nothing had changed. And yet everything had.

When Sadie set her shoes by the wall, she moved straight to the couch, easing herself down with a sigh. She didn't call Darius. She didn't beckon or reach out. She hummed.

It was the same song Sister Alma and the choir had sung, now stripped of words, bare and soft. The melody drifted through the room, light enough not to disturb a thing. Darius's head tilted.

Sadie settled deeper into the couch with Gunny curled beside her despite the heat. She opened a picture book, turning the pages slowly so the little girl could study each one.

Darius hovered near the doorway. For a long time, he stood there, watching. Then, with a slow and unsure motion, he crossed the room and climbed onto the sofa. He sat next to them, not at the far end.

He didn't lean in. He didn't ask to be included. He sat, holding his rock and blanket, eyes fixed on the book.

Sadie noticed, but she didn't say a word.

She read aloud, her voice composed, Gunny's head heavy in her lap. She felt the warmth of Darius beside her, closer than he'd ever dared before.

She read another page. And then another.

They sat like that through the afternoon heat with the memory of music and the comfort of closeness. Sadie never looked directly at him, but her voice never wavered.

For a moment, the memory unexpectedly surfaced — the linen closet, the pounding fists, her sobs muffled behind the door.

When her fingers brushed the edge of his blanket clutched in his hand, she whispered, "Thank you," not sure if she meant it for him or someone else entirely.

Darius blinked once.

He turned his face toward her. Lips parted.

He mouthed a word, "Mama."

No sound. No breath behind it. The shape of the word, offered like a question.

Sadie didn't see. Her eyes were on the book as she continued to read to her children.

Somewhere between music and silence, between reaching and being reached, a bridge was being built.

One unmarked calendar day at a time.

CHAPTER TEN

MUSIC

Night wrapped around the Turner house, stars punching tiny holes in the darkness outside Darius's window. He curled beneath his blue blanket, eyes fixed on the ceiling, waiting for sleep to claim him. His mind buzzed not with the usual chaos of sensations but with the memory of music, of his mother's warmth beside him on the couch, and of the word he'd shaped but couldn't voice. Sleep arrived swiftly, engulfing him like a wave.

When Darius opened his eyes, he stood in the same moonlit field where he'd met Azure the second time. Tall grass swayed against his legs. He turned in a slow circle, searching.

A flicker of blue light caught his attention. Azure descended from the night sky, wings stretched wide, scales catching starlight in rippling waves. He landed with a gentle rush of air, folding his magnificent wings against his sides.

"You're steadier," Azure said, his voice flowing directly into Darius's mind. "I can sense it."

When Darius reached out, he placed his hand against Azure's warm scales. The connection steadied him, grounding him in this place where touch brought comfort instead of pain.

"Come with me tonight," Azure continued. "I want you to see where I go when I'm not with you."

Azure lowered his body, an invitation clear in the gesture. Darius hesitated for a moment before climbing onto the dragon's back, settling between the ridges of his spine. His hands found purchase on the smooth scales, cool and warm at once beneath his fingers.

"Hold on," Azure instructed. "The shift can twist your stomach."

Azure's wings unfurled, sharp and smooth at once, like silk tearing. He rose into the air, powerful muscles bunching beneath Darius. The ground fell away. The stars rushed closer. Darius gripped tighter, heart hammering, not from fear but from a wild, unexpected joy.

The world around them blurred. Colors stretched like taffy, stars smearing into long lines of light. Darius closed his eyes against the vertigo. Wind rushed past his ears, carrying whispers he couldn't quite understand. The air grew thin, then thick, and changed entirely.

"Open your eyes."

When Darius lifted his eyelids, he gasped.

Below them stretched a landscape of impossible beauty. Mountains of crystal rose like frozen waves, catching and fracturing light from twin moons overhead. Valleys glowed with luminescent plants. Lakes of liquid silver reflected auroras that floated across the sky, curtains of color Darius had never seen, hues that might not have words in the world outside his dreams.

Azure circled lower, slow enough for Darius to absorb the wonder. The air sang with strange harmonies, not quite music, not quite wind, but something between. Each breath filled Darius with energy that tingled through his limbs.

"This is Somnoria," Azure said. "Home."

They glided over crystal spires that reached skyward like grasping fingers. Within those transparent peaks, movement caught Darius's eye, flashes of color, winged forms in flight.

"My kin," Azure added. "Dreamers' Dragons."

He banked toward the largest mountain, where an opening like a massive doorway yawned in the crystalline face. Inside, the space opened into a cathedral-like cavern. Light filtered across the faceted walls, creating contours that shifted like beings made of thought and shadow.

Dragons filled the chamber, dozens, perhaps hundreds, in every color imaginable. Ruby-red dragons adorned their scales with garnets. There were also dragons with emerald eyes and jade scales. The golden dragons trailed sparks as they moved. All adorned with jewels matching their hues, all radiating strength and wisdom.

When Azure landed on a wide ledge overlooking the chamber, Darius slid from his back, legs wobbling underneath him as they adjusted to the ground.

Several dragons turned. Their eyes, of so many shapes and colors, fixed on Darius. He fought the urge to hide behind Azure's leg.

"Don't be afraid," Azure said. "They're curious. This place isn't meant for most dreamers."

A dragon with scales flickering like burning flames approached. Rubies glinted along her hide. Her eyes, warm bronze flecked with gold, studied Darius.

"This is Seraphina," Azure said.

"Another child with sapphire eyes," Seraphina said.

Darius stiffened. *Another?* His eyes darted to Azure. He wanted to ask, but the question tangled in his chest. Another meant there were more like him. Or had been.

Azure held his gaze. "Not yet."

"Do not keep him blind," Seraphina said, heat beneath her words. "The threads are already pulling. He deserves to know he is not alone."

"Alone?" Darius echoed, his voice barely audible in the vast hall.

When Azure lowered his head, jewels caught the shifting light of the archives. "You are part of a weave larger than any single dreamer. In time, you will see the others. For now, hold to this: the Luminaries do not waste their sight."

Darius's thoughts raced. Others with sapphire eyes. How many? Where? The questions crowded, but Azure was already moving.

"Come." Azure stepped away before Darius could press further. "There's more to see."

They walked deeper into the mountain, passing dragons of every description. Some nodded to Azure. Others studied Darius with gazes that seemed to peer into him. None came too close, as if honoring a silent boundary.

Azure guided Darius from the vast chamber through a winding tunnel of crystal. It opened into a small grotto tucked inside the mountain's heart. Water trickled down the walls in silver beads. The chamber, smaller and curved, carried sound with unusual clarity. When Azure settled on a wide stone, his tail curled neatly around his feet.

"Sit with me," Azure said, showing a smooth outcropping across from him.

When Darius settled next to Azure, the surface vibrated faintly beneath his palms. His eyes lifted, more intent than before. "Another child," he said. "With sapphire eyes. Like me."

Azure inclined his head, neither confirming nor denying.

"Who?" Darius asked.

"There will be a time," Azure said. "Not tonight."

"But there are others?"

Azure's jewels lit faintly. "Yes."

Darius frowned, unsatisfied. His gaze dropped to the cave floor where water dripped in a continuous metronomic precision, one, then another, then another. He counted silently. One... two... three. The sound calmed him.

Azure nodded toward the dripping water. "Listen."

One drop. Then the next.

"That's how this comes," Azure said. "One piece at a time."

Darius's frown eased. He didn't like waiting, but the rhythm made sense.

"Trust the order of the weave," Azure said. "If every secret unraveled at once, the whole cloth would tear."

Darius perched on the edge. The ground trembled mildly under his hands.

"I was with you today," Azure said. "In the church."

Darius looked up, eyes wide.

"Not like that," Azure said. "But I felt it when the music started."

The memory surged, voices rising, the hymn unraveling something tangled inside him. He shed tears not out of sadness, but from a more profound depth. When Darius touched his chest, he chased that moment again.

"You see now why I brought you here," Azure said, gesturing around the grotto. "This place holds sound. Dragons come here to practice their songs."

Darius tilted his head. Dragons sing?

Azure's mouth curved. "Where do you think dream music comes from?"

Azure released one clear note. The crystal walls caught it and sent it back in layers. The note vibrated through his body, from the floor, through his fingertips, into his soul.

"That's why it reached you," Azure said. "It gets in where words can't."

When Darius closed his eyes, he remembered the choir's voices rising toward the rafters. His hands moved unconsciously, tracing music in the air.

Darius opened his eyes. Can it help me talk?

"Yes," Azure answered. "It already has. Remember the church, how music opened something. You reached for your mother. You nearly spoke."

Darius nodded.

"Listen," Azure said. He hummed a simple melody that rose and fell like waves. "Each note has shape, movement, and weight. Words are the same."

His humming shifted into a phrase: "Blue sky, blue eyes, blue light."

"Try. Out loud," Azure said.

Darius's throat tightened.

"Not hard," Azure said. "Follow the rhythm."

Darius took a breath. "B… bl…"

The word faltered, collapsing inward. His arms twitched, hands fluttering near his chest.

"Don't force it," Azure said. "Ride it."

He hummed again. When Darius closed his eyes, he let it carry him. His body swayed.

"Blue," Azure sang, drawing out the note.

"Bl... blue," Darius said.

Azure's eyes lit up. "Yes! Again."

"Blue," Darius repeated, louder. "Blue!"

Joy surged through him. He slapped his hands on his thighs, not in frustration, but in triumph.

"Sky," Azure prompted.

"S... sk... sky," Darius managed, clumsy but persistent.

"Blue sky," Azure sang.

"Blue sky," Darius repeated, arranging the words like a string of beads.

His voice was strange, higher, raspier, than he'd expected. Tears welled up. He wiped them with his sleeve, beaming and shy.

"Again," Azure urged. "The whole phrase."

Darius breathed deeply. "Blue sky. Blue eyes. Blue…" He faltered.

"Light," Azure supplied.

"Light," Darius said. Then, steady: "Blue sky. Blue eyes. Blue light."

The phrase hovered in the air, reminiscent of a wisp of color. Azure's gaze shone with pride and fierce, quiet love.

"In the waking realm," Azure said, "start with song."

How?

"Simple," Azure said. "Find the tune first. Then hang the word on it."

Mama sings?

"Yes. Listen to her."

The idea thrilled and frightened him. To speak aloud in the world he woke to each day? To push through the barrier that had always kept him silent.

But here, in this quiet chamber with echoes of music still hanging in the air, he had done it.

"It'll be harder when you're awake," Azure said. "But it's real."

When Darius stood, he placed his hand on his throat, feeling the muscles move.

"Say my name," Azure said.

Darius paused. Two syllables. This was the most complex word he had yet attempted.

"A..." he began. "A... zur..."

The dragon bowed his head. "There."

"Azure."

"Yes," Azure said, quiet and proud. "Now we begin."

Begin what?

"Dream weaving," Azure said. "I'll teach you next time."

When Darius pressed his palm to Azure's cheek, the connection vibrated through him with triumph and promise.

"Tomorrow," Azure said, "when you wake, remember this. Music bridges worlds. You have a voice, Darius. It's been waiting for you."

Darius nodded, fingers tracing the jewels on Azure's face. One, two, three, a song all their own.

A silent promise: *I will try.*

The crystal light pulled inward, softening the chamber. When Azure lifted his head, he said, "Dawn approaches. We should return."

As he rose, wings arching wide, something in his stance appeared heavier. Darius nodded, his fingers brushing his throat, as if trying to hold the voice he'd found.

They turned toward the tunnel. A sudden chill crept in. The crystal light flickered. For a heartbeat, the air seemed to tighten, as though something vast had taken notice.

Azure moved closer, wings flared.

"Something heard us," Azure said. "A fallen one."

Darius stilled.

"Obsidian," Azure added.

He paused. "Not tonight."

When Darius pressed his hand against Azure's scales, he didn't understand everything, but he understood this: music could help him find his voice, and he intended to use it.

CHAPTER ELEVEN

WEAVING

Darius sat on the Turner back porch with one knee up, a stick clenched in his fist. He scratched endless loops into the dirt at his feet, never quite circles, never quite lines. Each pass erased the last. Sunlight pressed down, warming him and the wood beneath him.

A few steps away, Gunny hopped from shadow to shadow, counting each one with wild bursts of joy.

"Six! Seven! Eight! Nine!" She stomped the porch's edge, then bounded into a patch of dandelions. "Ten!"

Darius's eyes followed her, counting alongside Gunny in his mind, six, seven, eight, nine, ten. The rhythm fit neatly inside his head, built from numbers he'd heard from his brothers, from Lula helping with homework, from Mama reading recipe cards. He hadn't been to school yet, but he already knew the count to ten and most of his letters. He gathered things by watching and listening, storing them away like marbles in a jar. Getting them back out, into words or actions, was the hard part.

When Gunny twirled in the dandelions, he rocked with her, small, constant motions against the porch rim.

A sharp squeal from her game made him flinch. His arms jerked up, hands working the air in quick, uneven bursts, but he didn't drop the stick. The motion picked up for a moment, then stilled as he pressed harder into the dust.

From the kitchen door, Sadie watched through the torn screen, arms crossed, mouth tightening with cautious relief. A year ago, she wouldn't have dared let him out of sight. If he ran, no one but Ezra or Theo could catch him. Now he stayed in the yard, moving between porch and dandelions, counting shadows with Gunny. He didn't stray, didn't bolt, played, silent but near.

When Gunny chased a bee through the yard, she tumbled through a patch of clover, then leapt to her feet, grass-stained and triumphant. "Come! Dari, come see!" she cried, trailing a fistful of clover and a ladybug crawling along her wrist.

Darius didn't answer but flicked his eyes up, then away, then back again. When Gunny dropped beside him, her nose nearly touched the porch's edge.

"Draw me, Dari!" she begged, jabbing an elbow into his ribs, tender but insistent. "Draw my name!"

The stick hovered. He pressed it down: a spiral, a line, two ovals, nothing like letters, but enough for Gunny. She squealed, clapped, and collapsed backward, legs in the air.

Sadie stifled a laugh, but her eyes never left her son. She eased down the steps beside his shoulder.

"You hungry, Darius?" she asked.

He didn't look at her. The stick carved a slower line, then paused. She waited. He tapped it three times. Sadie counted each like a heartbeat.

"I'll make you a sandwich," she said. When she stood, her skirt brushed his cheek, and she stepped inside. Gunny followed.

Darius remained on the porch. He watched the shadow of the rail stretch and shrink across the boards. A butterfly, blue and gold, too vivid for the yard, drifted down and landed on the back of his hand.

He sat still and watched. The wings opened and closed, the colors shifting with each beat, sometimes blue, sometimes nearly silver. His eyes traced the formation.

He wanted to speak to it. To tell it something. His lips parted. Nothing.

The butterfly crept up his arm, wings brushing his skin. He flinched but didn't shake it off. At the bend of his elbow, it paused, wings flat.

The butterfly lifted, circled his head, and vanished in the light.

When Gunny returned with bread in her mouth and crumbs on her chin, she plopped beside him. "Did you see the butterfly? It was blue, blue like your eyes, Dari!"

He didn't answer, but his hand drifted toward hers. When Gunny caught the motion, she pressed her palm to his, matching fingers as if reading them.

Sadie stood, hands trembling, tears daring to escape her eyes, her mouth a tiny curve edging into a smile.

Evening passed without trouble: dinner, homework, bath-time all folding into a quiet rhythm. The Turner home sank into calm.

One moment in bed, the next standing barefoot on smooth, silver-gray stone. The air shimmered faintly, carrying the quiet of a place between breaths.

Azure waited ahead, tall and still, wings folded like jeweled sails.

"Come," the dragon said. "Your hands are ready to learn."

They walked into a wide, open space where the floor seemed to fall away into starlit depths. Overhead, countless strands of light arched down from unseen heights, some pale and thin, others rich with shifting color. They bobbed back and forth, like kelp in a deep ocean.

"These," Azure said, "are threads of memory and possibility. They carry pieces of dreams, some from you, some from others, some not yet born. They are the foundational pieces of dream creation."

When Azure bowed his majestic head, he looked directly at Darius. "Close your eyes."

He did.

The dragon's voice came steadily. "Feel the pattern. Where it bends, bend with it. Where it resists, ease away."

Something satiny brushed Darius's fingers. When he opened his eyes, he saw a silver-blue thread coiling toward him. When he touched it, warmth spread into his palm, a ripple of Gunny's laugh, the smell of clover, sunlight on the porch.

Darius pinched one between thumb and forefinger. It flexed but didn't break. When he tried to lift it, it darted sideways like a fish, slipping from his grasp.

Azure chuckled low in his chest. "Patience."

When Azure lowered his head, his eyes were level with Darius's. The boy's threads trembled in the air, half-woven, ready to collapse.

Darius watched as Azure moved the strands little by little.

Then he guided Darius's hands with his own.

Afterwards, he stepped back. "Now you try."

Darius's jaw tightened, but his hands steadied. The pattern held.

This time, Darius moved slower. The thread arced toward him, wrapping around his finger like silk. Another followed, and another, until three strands floated before him, swaying in unison.

"Begin," Azure said.

When Darius twisted the first two together, they tightened, then loosened, then unraveled completely. He scowled, gripping the air. The third thread darted away, flashing like quicksilver.

Azure stepped closer, one talon resting lightly on the stone. "Weaving is not force. It is rhythm. Feel it before you shape it."

When Darius closed his eyes, the hum returned, faint but present. He caught one strand, then another, then the third, loop here, pull there, until a small circle hovered between his hands, whole and unbroken.

It trembled. For a heartbeat, he thought it would dissolve. Instead, light bloomed along its edges, scattering particles into the air like fireflies.

"Now shape it," Azure said.

When Darius caught the strand between his fingers, he coaxed it into a slow arc. It followed, curving until it joined with a thin green thread that had been swaying nearby. The two pulsed faintly, then settled into a new design, a loop that shimmered once before floating higher into the air.

"That is the beginning of weaving," Azure said. "Small changes, joined in the right place, can shape the dream. But for now, what you create here will fade. In time, you'll learn to make shapes that endure."

They moved deeper among the strands. Some bent toward Darius; others swayed away. He practiced guiding them, sometimes with ease, sometimes fumbling so badly the thread dissolved into sparks. Azure corrected him with a claw's nudge or a tilt of his wing.

At last, Azure stopped beside a lustrous braid, three threads wound together, colors shifting like a sunset reflected in water.

"Some sequences are too important to pull apart," Azure said. "Even when they are tangled, they must remain whole."

When Darius studied the braid, he stepped back without touching it. Azure rumbled low in his chest, a signal Darius had learned meant approval.

When they turned toward the archway that would take him home, Azure spoke again, quieter now.

"You won't always see me," he said. "Not in every dream, and not when you are awake. But I will be there, near enough to catch you if you fall, steady enough to guide you when you falter. You will never walk this path by yourself."

Darius looked up at him, eyes reflecting the threads above, his hands tracing their motion in the air.

Chapter Twelve

Birthday

September 1, 1931

The days slid into weeks, then months, each marked by changes the family couldn't ignore. Sometimes, at dusk, Sadie stood in the kitchen doorway and marveled at the hush that had settled over the house — a hush that no longer felt heavy with dread, but softly miraculous.

When September came again, they baked a small cake for Darius and set it on the table by his window. Lula pressed a crooked, half-burned candle into the icing and grinned. As Sadie watched the flame flicker, gratitude welled in her chest so fierce it nearly ached.

There had been a time, not so long ago, when she couldn't picture this moment — couldn't even dare to hope for it. Back then, the idea of the whole family gathered around Darius, celebrating him, had seemed like something out of another life. She remembered past birthdays, when she'd baked a cake but ended up eating it with the other children, her heart breaking as Darius retreated to his corner, untouched by all their efforts. She'd learned not to expect too much.

But now, here they were. All of them together, the room bright with the golden spill of afternoon light and the simple miracle of presence.

"Six years old," Augustus said, as if naming the number would make it sink in. He settled a gentle hand on Darius's shoulder — an act so ordinary and so new that Sadie had to blink away tears.

Theo leaned against the wall with his easy confidence, a hint of pride in his voice. "He's almost as tall as Lula now. Won't be long before he's catching up to me."

Ezra folded his arms, a quiet smile playing on his lips. "He minds himself better than he used to. Don't see him upset near as often."

When Sadie reached over to smooth the shirt she'd mended for Augustus, her hands needed something to do. "He's settled, somehow. Quieter, yes, but it's a peaceful sort. He comes and sits with us more. Why, last night he let Gunny lean against him during the story."

Lula beamed. "He likes being with us. I can tell."

Gunny, perched on her knees, peered closely at Darius. "But his eyes are still blue," she said. "I thought maybe they'd turn brown like mine once he stopped going wild all the time."

When Sadie smiled, she brushed a stray curl from Gunny's forehead. "No, baby. His eyes are his own, special as the sky. They don't have a thing to do with how he acts."

Gunny nodded, satisfied, and Darius's gaze flickered to her. For a heartbeat, the edges of his mouth curved into the smallest of smiles.

Darius's eyes fixed on the flame. He didn't touch the cake, but his stillness drew them closer, each of them wishing for something more and grateful for what they had. Sadie watched him closely, feeling the distance between them shrink, little by little. She believed he heard every word they spoke now, or at least she hoped he did.

She remembered the nights she'd lain awake, praying for a sign — a word, a glance, a moment like this. Now, the words still stayed locked inside Darius, heavy in his throat. Here, though, he leaned nearer to the flame, and Sadie let herself believe that maybe, he was listening.

A year had passed in the everyday world, and she could see the change in him. At night, when the house settled into shadows, he climbed into bed without protest, his eyes drifting closed with something that looked almost like anticipation. No one knew what world waited for him behind those eyes, but Sadie saw the difference: he woke lighter, steadier. Changed.

Darius sat in his familiar spot by the window, rocking, but with a new calm that puzzled the family. Sadie often watched him from the kitchen doorway, a dish towel twisted in her hands and a quiet wonder blooming in her chest.

"There is a stillness in him he's never had before," she said one evening, as Darius lined up marbles by color instead of flinging them across the floor. "He's starting to belong. His fits are less frequent and shorter. He'll sit near the other children now, close enough to be part of their world. He lets me touch him, even if only for a moment. And lately, he sits on the couch with Gunny and me during reading time. It's been slow, quiet... but he's finding his place with us."

Augustus nodded, his eyes cautious and unsure whether to trust this peace. "I think he's maturing."

But Sadie knew it was more than growing up. It was a transformation — something mysterious and sacred. She didn't know where it came from, only that it felt like a blessing.

The moment his eyes closed, the pull began, smooth at first, like a tide rolling in. His body lightened.

Mist unfurled in slow ribbons, and beyond it, the sky opened in a deep indigo sweep, streaked with moving colors that shifted and bled into one another like wet paint on glass. Floating islands drifted on invisible currents, some lit from within, others trailing waterfalls that fell into the void.

Azure was waiting, coiled on a broad slab of rock suspended in the sky. The dragon's scales caught every shifting hue, each facet flashing a different blue, from pale glacier to deep ocean.

Welcome back, my young dreamer.

Over the year of nightly visits, Azure often used his true dragon voice. The words didn't echo; they resonated — a low vibration through bone and chest. When Azure lowered his head, one golden horn hovered above the mist curling at Darius's feet.

"You remember what we practiced?"

Darius's lips moved, slow but certain. "Dreams … real, and … true."

Azure's chest rumbled with approval. "Good."

When the dragon turned, he tilted his claw slightly, and the space around them shifted. A thin stream of fire unfurled from his mouth, not fierce, but warm, and it curled into a shape. The flame folded in on itself, becoming the trunk of a tree. Leaves sprouted, then shimmered away into starlight. The starlight condensed into a figure: a mother, a father, children holding hands.

"Name them," Azure said.

Darius pointed. "Tree."

He pointed again. "Star."

His gaze lingered on the figures. "Family."

The word wavered at the edges, but it landed.

"Again," Azure said.

And so it went, flame becoming water, water becoming birds, birds scattering into flowers. Each shape was a challenge, each word a step. Darius's tongue stumbled sometimes, but they kept coming.

"You've done very well speaking out loud in the dream realm. Now it's time you start to speak beyond your dreams," Azure said at last. "Each word you speak here will make the next words easier when you wake."

Darius's gaze fell to the mist. "Mama… cry when I can't."

Azure's great head tilted, eyes narrowing in thought. He stepped closer until his breath stirred Darius's hair.

"I know," Azure said. "Speaking in the waking world will come as soon as you trust yourself to try. That is why we practice here in the dream realm."

The dragon's wing curved forward, vast and sheltering, the blue stretching high overhead without touching. Darius stood within its arc, embracing the stillness.

"Now," Azure said, drawing the wing back, "once more, before you wake."

They practiced again, slower this time, as if savoring each victory. Tree. Star. River. Sky. The words felt like they stayed in his mouth a little longer before slipping away.

When Darius finally faded, returning to waking consciousness, Azure touched his forehead one last time.

"Remember, young dreamer. The words are in you. The courage is in you. We will meet again tomorrow night."

Chapter Thirteen

Words

Yesterday's birthday candle, the crooked stub of wax Sadie hadn't had the heart to throw away, still sat in the dish by the stove. Sadie stood at the sink, her hands moving through the familiar ritual of washing breakfast dishes while the house maintained its blessed quiet. School had claimed the older children. Gunny was already at Mrs. Jenkins' home playing with Lila. Darius remained, sitting at the table in his usual spot, fingers tracing invisible shapes on the wood.

Six years old. Her baby was six years old yesterday, and he'd let them sing to him. Let Augustus touch his shoulder. Let them exist in his space without fleeing.

The plate in her hands was already clean, but she kept washing it, needing something to do with the restless energy that had lived in her chest since yesterday's birthday gathering. Since that almost-smile he'd given

Gunny. Since he'd leaned toward the candle flame like he understood what it meant.

Behind her, she heard the mild scrape of his finger on wood. The same scratching that had become the soundtrack of her mornings. She'd learned to find comfort in it — the consistency of his presence, even if that presence felt like standing on opposite sides of glass.

She hummed without thinking, the melody rising from somewhere deep. "His Eye Is on the Sparrow" — the hymn that had broken through to him in church five months ago. She'd hummed it every morning since, hoping maybe the memory would bridge something between them.

The scraping stopped.

Sadie didn't turn around. She'd learned not to react to his every shift and pause. Too much attention sent him retreating. So, she kept humming, kept washing the same clean plate, kept her back to him while every nerve strained to know what had changed.

It was a mother's instinct, that awareness of being watched by your child. She'd experienced it with all her children, but with Darius it was rare as snow in Atlanta. Precious.

Unable to resist, she glanced over her shoulder.

He was looking right at her. Not through her. Not past her. At her.

Their eyes met — his sapphire blue to her brown — and held.

When Sadie's hands stilled in the water, she turned around, afraid any sudden movement might shatter whatever was happening. Water dripped from her fingers onto the floor. She didn't notice.

"What you looking at, baby?" The words came out soft. She'd asked him this question a hundred times before, never expecting an answer. It had become another way of filling the silence between them.

His mouth opened.

Closed.

Fingers fluttered at his sides — not the frantic flapping of distress, but something else. Something lighter.

Sadie waited, barely breathing. She'd learned to read his silences, the different qualities of quiet that surrounded her son. This was different. Expectant. Like the air before lightning.

She returned to the sink, not wanting to pressure him with her attention.

"Mama."

The word hit her like a physical force.

Sadie's whole body went rigid. The plate slipped from her nerveless fingers, splashing back into the sink. She didn't even feel the water splash up soaking her apron.

Had she imagined it?

Had her desperate, yearning heart conjured the name she'd been praying to hear for six years?

She turned back to him, her movements underwater-slow. "What did you say?"

Darius rocked once in his chair. His jaw trembled with effort, the muscles working as if the word was fighting its way out.

"Mama."

Stronger this time. Clearer. Real.

The sob tore from Sadie before she could stop it. Six years. Six years of silence. Of wondering if he even knew who she was, if he understood she was his mother, that she loved him with a force that terrified her.

Her legs moved without her permission, carrying her across the kitchen in uneven steps. She dropped to her knees beside his chair, tears streaming unchecked down her face. Her hands reached toward him, then stopped, hovering in the space between them.

"Oh, my sweet boy..." The words broke apart on her tongue. "You... you said Mama."

He watched her cry with those startling eyes, his fingers returning to their tracing on the tabletop. But he didn't pull away. Didn't flee. He stayed there with her falling apart beside him.

Six years of locked doors. Of him trapped inside himself while she stood helpless on the outside. And now — this word. This bridge. This miracle.

"Can I hug you, Darius?" The question shook out of her. "Would that be all right?"

She expected him to rock away, to retreat to his window. Instead, he leaned forward. An inch. But toward her.

Permission.

When Sadie gathered him into her arms, she embraced him with the careful reverence of holding spun glass. His small body stiffened at the contact — she felt every muscle lock — but he didn't pull away. She held him loose enough that he could escape, close enough to feel his heart beating against hers.

He smelled like soap and sleep and something uniquely him. Her baby. Her boy who had called her Mama.

"If it's too much, tap my arm," she whispered against his hair.

For three heartbeats, four, five, he stayed. Then came the small tap against her forearm.

She released him immediately, scooting back to give him space, wiping her face with her apron. But the smile breaking across her face was unstoppable.

"Thank you," she said, her voice thick. "Thank you for calling me Mama."

He returned to his tracing, but the space between mother and son changed. It was lighter. Thinner. Like maybe that glass wall had developed a crack.

When Sadie stood on shaking legs and returned to the sink, she gripped its edge for support. Her reflection in the window above it was a mess — red eyes, tear-stained cheeks, the raw joy that bordered on pain.

She heard his chair scrape. Delicate footsteps. Then he was beside her, not touching, but near. He reached for the dishrag and handed it to her. A gesture so normal, so simple, that fresh tears spilled over.

"Thank you, baby."

He stayed there while she finished the dishes, a warm presence at her elbow. When she began humming again, Darius tried his own humming and joined her music. Not quite the same tune, not quite in melody, but trying.

Together.

By the time Augustus came home for lunch, Sadie had been hugged by Darius three times. Three separate times he'd allowed her arms around him. The last time, he'd lifted one hand and patted her back — awkward, uncertain, but intentional.

She met Augustus at the door, practically vibrating with the need to tell someone.

"He talked," she said, gripping Augustus's hands. "He said Mama."

Augustus's face went through a series of changes — disbelief, hope, something that might have been fear.

"He talked?" His voice came out rough. "He truly...?"

"Mama. He said Mama. Twice. Clear as day." She was crying again, couldn't seem to stop. "And he let me hold him. Real holding, Augustus. Not a second before running away."

When Augustus looked past her to where Darius sat on the floor, he saw their son lining up his blocks in perfect color order. Darius looked the same as always — focused, separate, absorbed in his thoughts. But Sadie knew better. She'd seen behind the veil today. Her son was in there, finding his way out.

"What changed?" Augustus asked, his voice barely above a whisper.

Sadie thought of the church service, the music that had reached him. The months of storms diminishing one at a time. The birthday candle he'd leaned toward. The calendar that no longer bore witness to daily battles.

That afternoon, when the older children tumbled through the door, Sadie gathered them in the kitchen.

"Your brother said his first word today."

The eruption of questions and excitement filled the house. Theo wanted to know what word. Ezra asked if he'd say it again. Lula started crying joyful tears like her mother. Gunny ran straight to Darius and plopped down beside him, chattering about how she knew he could talk, she knew it.

And through it all, Darius continued arranging his blocks and spools. But Sadie noticed he'd moved closer to where his siblings sat. Not joining them, not yet. But closer.

That night, after the children were asleep, Sadie stood in the hall watching him. He lay on the couch in the front room, still refusing the bedroom with his brothers. His breathing was deep and even. In sleep, his face relaxed into something peaceful.

She thought of all the nights she'd stood here, wondering if she'd ever reach him. All the prayers that had felt like shooting arrows into the dark. All the times well-meaning people had told her to "be realistic" about what Darius would never do.

Speak. Connect. Show affection.

Today he'd done all three.

"Mama," she whispered to the darkness, tasting the miracle. Her son had called her Mama.

She didn't know what tomorrow would bring. Maybe he'd retreat into silence. Maybe this was one moment of grace in a lifetime of struggle.

But today — today her son had found his voice. He had made his way to her.

And that was enough.

That was everything.

That night, as sleep claimed him once more, Darius found Azure waiting, the dragon's scales gleaming with approval.

"You did well today," Azure said.

A beam of pride shone from Darius; it warmed him like sunshine. "I said Mama," he told Azure. In the dream world, his words came with less difficulty, and this practice gradually turned into progress in his waking life.

"In the months to come, there will be more," Azure promised. "One step at a time, young dreamer. One word, one touch, one breath."

Darius nodded, understanding what the dragon meant. The walls separating him from the world were still high, still thick. Until this moment, he had never found a way to peek over them — and the view from the other side was worth the climb.

104

CHAPTER FOURTEEN

THREADS

Christmas 1931

The Turners' living room was lit in the soft yellow wash of the kerosene lamp, its small flame steady against the quiet of the evening. The walls were bare of greenery, but Sadie had looped a short chain of paper scraps across the mantle, cut and pasted by Lula from old newspaper, the uneven circles and links swaying slightly whenever the breeze slipped through the open window. On the table, a single candle burned low, its wax pooled and hardened from being used and saved again. The faint glow caught the worn arms of the old couch where Augustus and Sadie sat close together, their shadows stretching long across the floorboards. Nearby, the children gathered around the small table, their faces warmed by the candlelight as the room filled with the soft hush of voices and the quiet promise of Christmas.

As Sadie sat close beside Augustus on the old couch, their hands intertwined — a habit they'd fallen out of for years while worry kept them drifting in their own orbits. Now, his thumb brushed the tender skin at the base of her hand, warmth sparking in her chest. She leaned her head against his shoulder for a fleeting moment, feeling not like a mother, but a woman, a wife. Sometimes, when the house was quiet and the children's voices faded, she found herself dreaming again of a fuller table, another small hand to hold, a new laugh to braid into the family's song.

"Let's sing one for Christmas," Sadie said. Gunny clambered into her lap, as she clutched the doll Sadie had stitched from leftover cloth, its button eyes wobbly but dear.

Lula stood tall, smoothing her dress, and began in a clear, sweet voice. Silent night, holy night…

Ezra joined in a beat later, low while Theo tapped the side of his chair, palms keeping time like a drum. When Sadie's alto slipped in next, it was rich and certain, and the small room filled with harmony.

While she sang, Sadie watched the room — the drowsy candle, the neat chain of paper scraps, the faces of her children. Rocking melodically, Darius sat near the window, as the music wrapped around him. His hands stilled in his lap. He mouthed the words silently, shaping each word with careful lips. He didn't make a sound, but she could see the rhythm of the song move through him.

Gunny sang too loud and half a step ahead, grinning at her own mischief. When Lula giggled, faltering on a line, Ezra gave her a mock glare before raising his voice louder, turning the verse into a playful contest.

Sadie smiled, rocking with Gunny's weight against her chest, listening as her children's voices braided together. Once, she had wished for a house filled with song, lessons and laughter carried on the air. In this moment, it was real: the house, the song, all of it. Hunger and worry slipped to the edges, replaced by harmony she had dreamed of.

As the hymn wound to a close and the last soothing notes faded, Sadie reached and squeezed Augustus's hand, a quiet promise blooming between them and the silence that lingered felt like the hush after prayer, tender and whole.

"All right," Sadie said, brushing Gunny's hair back. "Bedtime."

Darius rose, the song still moving in his limbs. He washed and changed, the last strands of the song still curling through his mind.

***

When he lay down, eyes half-shut, instead of the usual slow drift into dreams, there was a moment, sharp and bright, where the room tilted. And in the breath between one blink and the next, the weight of his quilt became the cool mist of another place entirely. Mist curled up from the ground and cooled his cheeks, clinging to his legs as he stood on a wide ledge of smooth black rock. Far below, water cascaded in dozens of what looked like iridescent strings, each glistening faintly in colors that didn't belong to daylight — pale greens, blues, and golds that shifted like woven silk in the wind.

Halfway up the cliff, Azure waited. The dragon's cobalt-and-azure scales caught the spray, wings folded tight, gaze fixed, as if he had been watching long before Darius arrived.

"This is Threadwater Falls." Azure's voice rolled over the falls.

Darius tilted his head. Beneath the crash of water, another tone surfaced, softer, like a hymn slowed to half its tempo.

"Do you hear it?" Azure's eyes narrowed. "That rhythm belongs to you. Every dreamer carries one. It is called a vein, the life-thread of your being. It cannot be altered."

Darius's chest tightened. For an instant, he thought he sensed the pulse in his fingertips, deep, constant, unyielding. It thrummed like the beat of his own heart. He pulled his hands back.

When Azure lowered his head, he guided Darius forward again. "There is another kind. Threads."

The water split around Darius's arms. Light streamed between his fingers in long, bright strands. Unlike the heavy pulse of the vein, these vibrated with variety, quick, slow, sharp, smooth. Some flickered; some shone intense; some even tangled together and pulled apart.

"These are dream-matter," Azure said, steering Darius's hands with his claws. "They can be caught, joined, shaped, or unraveled. That is weaving. Veins are fixed. Threads are possibility."

Darius pressed closer. The vein lay like stone beneath his skin, immovable, absolute. But these threads bent, darted, even reached toward him, alive with movement. He caught one, then another, their movements aligning under his grip.

"Now," Azure murmured, "we weave."

Accompanied by the dragon's guiding claw, Darius crossed the strands. A burst of blue light spiraled outward, curling into the shape of a feather. It hovered between them, then rose on the mist, carried upward into the endless fall.

Darius's mouth lifted at the corners, the smallest of smiles. "Made it."

Azure's rumble echoed deep and warm. "You did. Your first true weave. Remember this difference: a vein holds who you are. Threads hold what you can become. One you must never break. The other you are meant to shape."

When the dragon's gaze shifted toward the falls, he said, "There is more to see."

A section of water parted, revealing a narrow path cut into the rock. When Azure led him through, the thunder of the cascade softened until it became a distant whisper.

They stepped into a chamber lit by a pale, endless effulgence. Shelves curved away in every direction, rising higher than sight, each stacked with rolls of woven light, restless and slow, as if responding to the air.

"This is an annex of the Cerulean Archives," Azure said. "Every lasting weave is kept here. What you made tonight is already among them."

When Darius turned, searching, Azure pointed with his snout, and there it was, his feather. The feather looked small among the towering shelves, but pride rose in him when he saw it resting beside the others.

Darius's breath caught. It stayed.

"The Luminaries set dragons as guardians so no weave would be left unheld."

His eyes met Darius's. "You shine, young one. Brighter than you know."

When Darius's hand twitched toward the feather, it stopped short. "Who keeps them?"

"We do," Azure said. "They are preserved here in the Archives. Threads are not solely for creating. They can be pulled apart, unbound, destroyed. What you weave with care, another might unweave with cruelty."

The words settled heavy, and Darius's gaze returned to the small flickering feather. Pride and unease warred inside him.

"Come," Azure said, guiding him back toward the falls. When his wing lowered like a ramp, Darius climbed onto it. Together they rose until they were level with the highest threads. From here, the strands seemed endless, stretching into a sky where stars burned even through the mist of daylight.

"Touch them as we pass," Azure said. "Each has its own texture, smooth, rough, warm, cold. Learn them. Remember them."

They glided along the curtain of falling dreams. Darius brushed his fingers across thread after thread: a blue one that slipped like running water, a pink one plush as wool. Another brushed his wrist — cold, brittle, wrong. He pulled his hand back without knowing why.

"Someday," Azure said, "you will weave threads that carry your own light into another's dream. You will mend broken strands, create bridges, shape dreamscapes."

Darius's thoughts leapt to Lula's ribbon, Ezra's off-key singing, Theo's steady drumbeat, Gunny's clapping hands. If he could weave a dream that moved and felt like that song, maybe someone else could know what he knew, what words never carried.

When they circled back to the ledge, Azure lowered him to the rock.

"That is enough for tonight," the dragon said. "The threads will wait. Your hands must be ready before they can hold more."

Darius nodded, his eyes lingering on the luminescent falls. He didn't want to leave, not now that the colors and sounds had begun to make sense, but the mist was already thinning, the ledge fading, and the dream was letting go.

PART II

CHAPTER FIFTEEN

"BLUE"

March 1932

It was the March after Darius's sixth birthday. The windows stood open, a cool breeze slipping through the house and stirring the curtains. He sat in the front room with his siblings, the last light of evening spilling across the floor.

Darius held the ball in both hands, his fingers tracing the seam as if it concealed a secret. Then, without warning, he said, "Blue."

The room froze.

When Ezra blinked, his mouth fell open. "Did he just ...?"

"He did," Theo breathed, a slow grin spreading across his face.

Lula clapped her hands, eyes wide. "He said blue! Mama, he said blue!"

Their mother stepped into the room, drawn by the unusual hush followed by a burst of laughter and joy. She paused in the doorway, taking in the sight, Darius positioned centrally in the room, cradled by his siblings' amazement.

Her fingers rose to her parted lips. "Oh, baby…"

Lula, eager and gleaming with pride, picked up a green block from the floor. "What color is this one, Darius?"

Darius looked at it. In his mind, he saw the color — green. But when he tried to say it, his mouth betrayed him.

"Blue," he said again, this time more strained.

He frowned. His fingers twitched.

Ezra leaned forward, suddenly cautious. "It's all right, D. You're fine."

The wrong word had come out, and he knew it was wrong. His body tensed, hands rising near his face.

Before anyone else could speak, Mama crossed the room and knelt beside him. "Sweet boy," she said, reaching for his favorite blanket. "You said blue. That's a beautiful word."

She unfolded the blue cloth and held it up. "Look here. Your blue blanket. Like your word. Can we breathe now? In… and out…"

Darius hesitated, eyes darting from the blanket to her face. Cautiously, he touched the corner of the blanket, bringing it to his cheek. His breathing steadied.

"That's it," Mama said, wrapping an arm around him. "You said blue. That's enough for today."

She kissed the top of his head, her voice thick. "Do you know how big that is? You know the color blue. The ball is blue, your blanket is blue, your eyes are blue."

Darius clutched the edge of his blanket, his chest still rising and falling as the last waves of frustration faded.

"That little word?" she said. "It's not little at all. I don't need all the words at once."

Behind her, the other children remained still, their excitement now softened into something sacred.

"Blue," she said again, brushing his head with her fingers. "That word was perfect."

They didn't see him step through the back door.

He stood there a long moment, silent, unmoving, half-cast in the fading light, watching a miracle unfold. A word had cracked open something in his son. Not a flood, but a trickle. And in that small word carried hope.

Their father had never heard Darius speak. Not once. But today, something had changed.

And it began with a single word. Blue.

Countless nights he'd sat on the edge of the bed, shoulders hunched, listening as his wife wept beside him, her tears spilling over worries she could never say aloud in front of the children. He had tried to be strong, to be reliable, to be the man who fixed things. But Darius had been beyond his reach. Beyond words. And he'd hated himself for not knowing how to help.

Now, watching his son hold a blue ball and say its name aloud, something in his chest loosened. A knot, tight for too many years, uncoiled.

Darius was still Darius. He was still different. He continued living in a world apart from the one his siblings so easily inhabited. But today, this word, this moment, it was a bridge where once there had been only distance. They didn't understand everything. But something had passed between them.

And that something was everything.

Later that evening, once the excitement had faded and the children were settling into their nighttime routines, Darius's father took him outside to the small patch of yard behind the house. They sat side by side on the back steps, no words, no touch, watching the clouds drift across the deepening sky.

After a long while, his father spoke, voice low and rough with emotion he'd never learned how to share. "I heard you say 'blue.' I'm proud of you, son. That was a big step. Like when you said 'Mama.'"

Darius didn't look at him, but his head dipped in a small, almost imperceptible nod.

"Can you say 'Daddy'?"

Silence.

Darius's fingers tapped against his thigh, his jaw tensing as he struggled to pull the word from his mind into his mouth. Nothing came.

His father exhaled, not with disappointment, but with acceptance. "That's all right. No rush."

He pointed toward a lone flower blooming in the garden bed, its color catching the last of the daylight. "What color's that one?"

Darius followed his gaze. He knew it, yellow. He knew the word in his head, clear as a bell. But if he tried to speak, he knew what would come out.

Blue.

So, he said nothing, letting the question hang in the air.

His father nodded, as if Darius had answered anyway. A smile tugged at his lips' edges, softening the usual stern lines. "That's yellow. It's called a marigold. Your mama planted those last spring." His voice softened. "It's still standing."

They sat together a while longer, the silence between them no longer empty, but full.

Interlude: Practice

In the weeks after the word "blue," the house moved differently around Darius. Nobody asked him to perform. Nobody tried to pull more than he could give.

Some days, he said nothing at all.

Other days, in the quietest parts of morning, Sadie would hear a small mutter from the table. Not a word, exactly. More like a test of one. A breath shaped with intention, then released.

Once, when she offered him water, he looked at the cup and managed, "Yes," so muted she almost missed it. She nodded like it was ordinary and returned to the stove.

Months had passed, and Darius gradually added a word here and there, simple ones like more, yes, and no. With each small success, a routine took shape in their home. In the still moments of the day, especially when

114

the house was hushed, and he sat by the front window, Darius practiced. He shaped words with his mouth, whispering them into the silence. Sometimes, he succeeded. Red. Yellow. Green. Words he knew in his mind, words he dared not yet speak aloud in front of others. But he was trying, testing the precarious bridge between thought and voice, and gaining confidence with each whispered triumph. Words did not arrive in a straight line, but they came.

Interlude: Story-time

By June, the evenings came later. The kerosene lamp turned the front room gold, and Sadie's voice filled the space the way it always had, calm, patient, unhurried.

Most nights, Darius stayed close to the window, rocking, separate but near the rest of them.

This night, he sat on the floor with the others.

When Sadie opened a book of fairy tales, she began, "Once upon a time in a land far away, there lived a brave knight who discovered a dragon living in a cave near his village."

Darius's head snapped up and he gave his full attention to his mother's words.

Sadie read on, the knight approaching not with a sword, but with an offering of friendship. The dragon, lonely after years of silence, let the boy into a cave filled with treasures and knowledge.

When the story ended, Lula shifted beside Darius, eyes wide. "Mama…"

When Sadie lowered the book, she asked, "What is it?"

Lula leaned closer to her. "He said something. Now."

Darius stared at the floor, fingers tracing the edge of the rug.

"What did he say?" Sadie asked, careful with her voice.

Lula swallowed. "It sounded like… Azure."

Sadie remained still. She looked at Darius, searching his face.

"Azure?" she repeated. "What's that mean, baby?"

Darius did not answer. He did not retreat, either. He sat there, breathing, holding something private in the open.

When Sadie closed the book, she kept her voice gentle. "All right. Bedtime."

Later, when she turned out the lamp, the word stayed with her like a hymn that would not leave.

INTERLUDE-STORYTIME

CHAPTER SIXTEEN

LEARNING

The house exhaled. Floorboards settled, the kettle's last hiss faded, and Darius sensed his body ease and the dream stirred. He knew this feeling now, the lightness in his limbs, the peace that came before Azure arrived. The dream realm stretched ahead, no longer strange, but something he was understanding, like a story he could finally follow. When he settled into his dream, Azure was waiting. He was floating on a slab of silvery stone, its edges trailed by a warm rain of sparks into a twilight that had no horizon. The dragon stood with calm grandeur, coils gathered, wings tucked, one brilliant eye warm as lamplight.

"You come with more assurance now," he said.

Darius nodded once. He didn't rush. He drank in the scene the way he drank in music, with his whole body. The colors steadied him. The deep blues and violets settling into place, and a thin ribbon of pink and green running through Somnoria, bright and familiar, like the ribbons Lula tied in her hair.

"Tonight," Azure said, uncoiling, "we walk further. You will see where memory is kept and where some dreamers learn to work."

He lowered a wing. When Darius climbed without being told, he settled between the ridges, fingers combing the warm geometry of scales he knew by number and texture. The wing rose; the stone slid away; the sky, if sky it was, opened like a book.

They flew.

Below, mountain spines of crystal rose and fell like sleeping dragons, catching twin moons in a thousand facets. Valleys blazed with phosphorescent grasses. Far to their left, a waterfall dropped in shimmering strands, Threadwater Falls, a curtain of threads too distant to touch yet close enough for Darius to hear the faintest murmur of patterns braided within them. He itched to reach, and his fingers flexed.

"Later," Azure murmured, and Darius eased.

A shape surfaced from the dusk ahead: a many-spired structure that seemed carved from one endless sapphire. As they drew near, its walls turned translucent, then clear, revealing light nested inside incandescent scrolls, tablets, and lenses of frozen light drifting in ordered arrays.

"The Cerulean Archives," Azure said, pride threaded through the words. "Where our bonds are remembered and our wisdom tends itself."

Mist peeled away, and the chamber opened before him.

Shelves soared into shadow, curving outward until they disappeared beyond sight. Every surface brimmed with rolls of woven light, hundreds, thousands, maybe more, each shifting as if breathing.

His mind jumped to the smaller chamber behind Threadwater Falls; the shelves there had housed a few rolls, one of them his own feather-shaped weave. This was the same, but vast enough to swallow the sky. The same low hum lived in the air.

When Azure stepped beside him, he said, "The Cerulean Archives. You've walked its threshold before. That was an annex, a whisper of the whole."

Darius's fingers itched to find his feather again, to see if it had followed him here.

They surfaced upon a hewn balcony, stone cut and shaped by hand, the marks of the chisel still ridging its surface. The air rang here, barely audible, braided with a thousand whispers. When Darius slid down, his palms met smooth stone. It buzzed faintly beneath his skin, the way pews did when the choir held a final note.

Inside, the first hall widened into a vault whose ceiling was a living mural, light painted with light.

"The Luminaries," Azure said.

High above, the white dragons turned, wings crossing, stars spilling from their paths.

"They shaped us to guard what humans could not yet hold safe on their own," he continued. "Dreams are powerful. Unguided, they fracture. We keep the veil between our worlds from tearing."

They walked beneath the moving sky. Along the walls, scenes unfolded in simple sequence:

A small child in rough linen slept; a dragon, deep indigo like one of Mama's blueberry pies, bent over the bed, touching brow to brow.

A different child, older, standing on a cliff with a dragon, with iridescent green wings like that of a dragonfly Darius had once seen on the porch with Gunny.

"Our purpose," Azure continued, "is simple and unending: guide, mend, guard. We do not command minds. We keep them from breaking."

Darius's hands hovered toward a display where ribbons of script floated in columns. The characters were not letters he knew; they shifted like ripples, aligning to his gaze, becoming patterns he could count. Rows of sevens. A cadence of three-then-five.

"Those are records of bond," Azure said. "Not people, but their shapes. Each bond has a pattern, and no two are the same."

They reached a circular well, flooded not with water, but with suspended memory.

Threads?

No, Darius thought. These were not threads. The light here branched and branched again, infinitely detailed, like frost taking a window in winter. The sight of it melted the tension resting in his shoulders.

"Veins of light," Azure said, hearing the unasked question. "We spoke before of threads and veins, but here you see them side by side. Threads fall free. Veins root and branch. Both matter, but their purpose is not the same. Veins represent people and memory currents. You may look. You never weave them."

Darius's eyes met the great dragon's gaze and he carefully placed his hands behind his back to remind his body to only see.

Azure guided him down a side passage that narrowed, then opened suddenly onto a high mezzanine. The gallery overlooked Threadwater Falls from within the Archives, an impossible vantage where falling strands were both far and near, each thread bright enough to follow with a fingertip, each carrying its own pulse.

"This is the Spiral Loom Room," Azure said, lowering his head until snout and boy were level. "Here, young weavers learn to steady threads beyond their own. Tonight, you will make your first stitch for another."

When Darius drew closer to the balustrade, he ran his fingers along the cool stone rail between the evenly spaced columns. From here, the difference was obvious; the threads were cords of light, taut and tangible. The veins in the Archives had branched like trees; these ran like rivers you could clasp.

When Azure swept a claw and caught one as if catching the end of a ribbon on a clothesline, a tremor passed through Darius's fingers at the same moment, soft, familiar. Laughter, quick and high. He smelled clover. Gunny.

He froze.

Azure released the thread and it slid back into the falling curtain with a satisfied hum. "You see we listen before we touch," the dragon said. "Strands pass near one another at times, the ones you love will always be close. But we work purely with the freely falling, and never twist a sleeping mind to our will."

Darius breathed out, slow. Some part of him had understood since his first night by Threadwater Falls.

When Azure drew a different thread, thin, pale, shivering as if cold, the beat within it was uneven. Darius's stomach quivered. First a stutter, a too-fast flutter, then a drop.

"Someone's storm," Azure said. "Not your family. A child you'll never meet." His voice was gentle. "You will not alter who they are. You will lay a line of steadiness across their growing storm, then release."

"How?" Darius asked aloud.

Azure's jewels brightened, one after another: blue-green-violet. "With pattern. Choose a rhythm your body trusts."

Without thinking, Darius's hand found the railing and began its quiet tap, the same gentle cadence that steadied him at the kitchen table and in pews when the hymn would not end. He let the taps gather in his shoulders until his breathing slowed.

"One," Azure murmured. "Two. Three."

The thin thread vibrated. Darius reached, hesitated, reached again. It met his fingers with a cool give, like wet silk that felt like rope. He didn't pull. He laid his rhythm alongside it, the way you lay twine along a line before you braid. His fingertips found the smallest over-under-over. Not a knot. A tack.

The pulse smoothed a fraction. The tight places in the strand loosened. The thread's light warmed from pallor to dawn.

Darius's chest stung; not pain, exactly, effort. Sweat pearled at his temple.

"Enough," Azure said. "Release."

He let go. The strand slipped back into the falling body with a whisper, like a blanket being gently set down. Darius's shoulders dipped; he'd poured a little of himself into the stitch, and his body knew it.

When Azure lowered his head, a warm exhale washed Darius's face. "Small weave, small cost. You did not change the child. You offered a safe beat, then left them to their own dream."

Darius sighed, relieved, a shy spark of pride flickering in his eyes. He made a mental tally, over, under, rest, and set it next to the familiar sequences he kept in pockets of his mind.

Azure led him from the Loom Room through a ribbed corridor of crystal that opened onto a long, high terrace, their third vantage, all of Somnoria spread like a map. Below, he could see everything: the Archives' perpetual purple night sky edged with green, pink and orange spirals of light; the distant glitter of Threadwater Falls, and islands that flowed rather than drifted. Nearer to the terrace, stood a vertical face of glass-smooth stone veined with light.

The veins here were breathtaking: branching, re-branching, filling the surface with a living filigree. One cluster, fine, bright, close-knit, pulled his eye. He lifted his hand by reflex.

Azure's tail tapped the back of his wrist. "Look," he said, voice low. "Do not touch."

Darius tucked his hands under his arms and squinted his eyes to study and memorize the angles of light. Out from far across the half-seen sky, not above or below but at the place where distance itself seemed to crease, a wind rose, no sound, only the temperature dropping. The terrace's light dimmed a hair, and a line appeared, hair-thin, and ink-black, no wider than a split in old paint.

Azure's jewels flared, quick and bright; the air warmed at once. His wing curved instinctively, sheltering Darius without touching him.

Darius pointed. "What is it?"

"An old wound," Azure said.

When Azure's wing eased away, he said, "You have seen enough for a first stitch and a first truth." He gestured with a claw toward the tumbling distances. "Truth one: threads can be shaped, never owned. Truth two: veins of light are to be honored, never woven. Truth three: the work costs part of you. You pay in concentration, in patience, in rest you must later take."

Darius pressed two fingers to his sternum, then set them on the railing. He understood both the cost and the worth in the same breath.

"In time," Azure said, and there was something like a smile in the slant of his eye. "Your body must rest. A weaver who ignores rest ties knots he cannot undo."

They walked back through the Archives at an easy pace. When Darius looked up once more at the living mural, the overhead, snowy white upon milky white, and the sparkle of the jewels mesmerized him as their wings crossed. He stared at them in reverence, watching, not wanting to interrupt the moment, yet wanting to get closer and reach to them and touch them. He did not know who they were. But the feeling was familiar. It was the same feeling he had in church, after the singing ended, when the room went still after the lingering notes of the choir faded.

Back on the balcony, Azure lowered his head. When Darius placed his palm to Azure's scales at the jawline, he counted the facet-stones there without looking: one, two, three, four, five, six, seven.

The balcony's edge dissolved to mist; the calming colors of trust from his dragon dimmed to the ebony of a familiar room. The grandeur of Somnoria eased into the simplicity of his view of the window; the terrace's cool shifted to the knit warmth of a blanket.

He woke with the shape of an over-under stitch still in his fingers and a quiet cadence ticking in his chest: one, two, three and the echo of a wider world still in him. A world where learning did not bruise and silence was not absent. The house returned around him, close and ordinary, its limits pressing back into place. He did not resist it. He remembered that elsewhere, in his dreams, something patient and luminous waited.

CHAPTER SEVENTEEN

DRAWINGS

On a humid July evening, Darius sat in the yard with his siblings. Summer was in full sweltering heat, and the air heavier now, the red clay holding the heat of the day. The peach tree near the fence had bloomed small fruit, scattering pale pink petals across the ground like scraps of paper. They had invented a game called "Darius Says," a twist on Simon Says where he pointed and named objects, and the others scrambled to touch them.

"Tree!" he called, finger aimed at the oak towering over the yard.

They bolted toward it, tagging the bark as if it were treasure.

"Blue!" They scattered, hunting for jay feathers, bits of painted wood, and scraps of fabric.

When Lula adjusted the ribbon in her hair, she gave him a smile so wide it wrinkled her nose. She ruffled his curls.

"You're getting so good at this."

He grinned back. "Again!"

When they tired of running, they settled on the back steps, and his brother taught him a clapping game. Darius's coordination still lagged behind his age, his hands sometimes refusing to follow his brain's instructions, but he persisted until he could complete the simple sequence.

"You did it!" Ezra held out his hand toward Darius for a celebration clap. Darius stared at the outstretched hand, then carefully pressed his own against it.

"I did it," he echoed, the three-word sentence emerging whole and clear.

Inside, their mother paused in her cooking, listening to her children playing together. Not that long ago she would have been hovering anxiously, ready to intervene when Darius inevitably broke down. Now, she allowed herself the luxury of trust, trust that he could manage, trust that his siblings knew how to include him, and trust that the peace they'd found wasn't a temporary reprieve but a new way of living. As she looked at her boy — with those eyes that were so stark against his skin — she thought of the words the midwife had gasped the day he was born, crossing herself in awe. Special child, she'd said. The blue-eyed ones see things others don't.

Sadie had dismissed it as superstition at the time, but now… watching how his gaze stayed locked on, she wondered. What did he find in the light and shadow that the rest of them missed?

That evening, after dinner, Darius approached his father, who sat whittling a small piece of wood.

"Daddy."

His father looked up, accidentally dropping the little wooden piece in his hands. "Yes, son," he said, voice rough with emotion. "What can I do for you?"

When Darius reached for his father's free hand, he tugged. "Come."

Curious, his father set aside his knife and wood high on a shelf and allowed himself to be led to the kitchen table. Darius pointed to the cup holding his siblings' pencil stubs and the stack of scrap paper their mother saved for schoolwork.

"Draw," Darius said, the word new to his spoken vocabulary, though Azure had taught him its meaning months ago.

His father raised his eyebrows. "You want to draw something?"

Darius nodded, hands fluttering with a mixture of excitement and frustration at the limits of his speech. "Draw something," he said, echoing his father's words.

The rest of the family gathered, drawn by the novelty of this request.

"Lula, bring me some crayons from your room," Mama said as she smoothed out the paper, while his siblings watched with curiosity.

When Darius grasped a blue crayon awkwardly, his fine motor skills, like his speech, developed at a much slower pace than those of other children his age. But Azure had shown him in dreams how to hold a stick, how to wield it with intention rather than chance.

The first lines were shaky, uncertain. His face was scrunched with concentration, tongue caught between his teeth. His father reached out, wanting to help, but his mother touched his arm, shaking her head. This was Darius's battle to win or lose.

Bit by bit, the random marks began to hold. A curve settled into place, then a line answered it. His siblings leaned closer, heads nearly touching. After several minutes of fierce concentration, Darius set down the blue pencil and chose a black one, anchoring the shape with careful, deliberate strokes.

When he finally sat back, the family stared at his creation in silence. It wasn't the crude scribble they'd expected from a child who had never shown interest in drawing. On the page was a dragon, its body formed of sweeping blue curves layered with intention, its eyes two deep-blue ovals, and unmistakably aware.

"Dragon," Darius said, tapping the paper with one finger. "Azure."

Sadie remembered this word. Azure. He had said it the night she had read a story to the children. He had whispered the word to himself and only Lula had heard. His mother picked up the drawing, studying it with wonder. "Azure is a dragon? From your dreams?"

Darius nodded, a smile spreading across his face. "My dragon."

His siblings exchanged glances of confusion and amazement. His father cleared his throat. "You dream about dragons, son?"

"Yes." Darius reached for another piece of paper. "More."

For a moment, the joy in the room ran too bright, as if something beyond it had noticed.

For the next hour, the family watched as Darius captured a world only he could reach, mountains with caves, skies streaked with light, and islands suspended in space. Between each drawing, he spoke a word or two: "Somnoria" and "Dream."

His sisters made up stories about the images, weaving tales about the blue dragon and his adventures. Darius listened, nodding sometimes, shaking his head at other times when they got details wrong.

"You been keeping all this inside you?" his mother asked, touching one of the drawings. "All this time?"

Darius looked at her, then pointed to his head. "Inside. Words... hard." He pointed to the paper. "Draw... no hard."

His father squeezed his shoulder gently. "You got a whole world in there, don't you, son?"

Darius nodded solemnly. Then, with careful deliberation, he spoke the longest sentence they had yet heard from him: "I go... sleep. I... dream."

The family fell silent, absorbing the magnitude of this communication. It wasn't the words themselves, but the complex thought behind them, the awareness of his dream life, the ability to convey its importance, the desire to share something so personal.

His mother wiped a tear from her cheek. "Is it a good place? This dream world?"

"Yes." Darius's crystal eyes shone with conviction. "Azure... teach me."

"Teaches you what?" she asked.

Darius considered the question, his face working through the effort of translating his thoughts into words they could understand. "Words. Touch." He paused, then added: "Learn."

His eldest sister picked up one of the drawings. "Is that why you're different now? Why you can talk to us and play with us?"

Darius's eyes lit up and he bobbed his head, "Yes."

Gunny, his youngest sister, who had been unusually quiet during this revelation, suddenly piped up. "Can I have a dragon too?"

He had never laughed like this before, not a giggle, but full-bodied joy that shook his small frame. When he caught his breath, he shook his head. "Me... dream."

"And you're a special dreamer?" his father asked, pride creeping into his voice.

When Darius stood, he reached for a fresh sheet of paper. With new confidence, he drew a simple figure, a boy with a round head and stick limbs. He colored in the eyes last, two careful circles of blue, clear and bright, then added the dragon beside him in the same shade, larger, curved, watchful. When he finished, he set the pencil down and pointed to the page.

"Me... dreamer," he declared, the words clear and strong. "Dragon... Azure."

His family stared at him, seeing him anew, not as the burden they'd carried, the problem they'd faced, the child marked by difference and difficulty. They saw instead a boy with secrets and strengths they were beginning to understand, a boy whose differences might be gifts in disguise.

When his mother reached for him, he stepped into her embrace without hesitation. "My boy," she said into his hair.

Sadie watched as her family gathered the drawings, their voices tender with wonder. She pressed one picture close, the blue dragon's eyes meeting hers with an unsettling familiarity. Azure. Darius had said. A word she had never spoken, and a creature she couldn't imagine.

She thought of that morning years ago, the wet nightshirt, the mud on his feet — not a footprint in sight. The puzzle of it had haunted her ever since. She had stood in the dark, watching her son stare out his window and wondering if she'd imagined it all. That was when things had changed: Darius allowing touch, reaching out, speaking and now — drawing. Was it real? A child's wild imagination? Angels? God Himself, moving unseen? She pressed a hand to her mouth, overwhelmed by gratitude and confusion, praying for answers she might never receive.

And yet, tonight, watching her son so present, showing them a world none of them had known, she let herself believe, for a moment, that some mysteries were meant to remain, and that joy might be found in the not-knowing.

As night settled over the house, the drawings were carefully set aside, and the family drifted toward their rooms. The sense of something holy, delicate as new leaves, lingered in the quiet.

***

Darius sat by the window, his eyes looking sapphire in the reflection of the faint moonlight, and something he'd never known before swelled in him. He had shown them. His drawings, his words, they had seen and heard. For so long, the dream world and the waking world had been divided by a wall only he could feel. Tonight, he created a bridge with his drawings. The longing to be known, not as "different," but as a dreamer, pulsed through him. He lay down quietly, heart fluttering, and let sleep take him.

The realm of dreams opened with silver light spilling over crystalline spires. Azure waited, vast and blue, approval shining in his ancient eyes.

"You shared our secret today."

"Drew you. Family saw," Darius said.

"And how did that feel?"

Darius considered the question, searching for the right word. In dreams, his vocabulary expanded beyond his waking limitations. "Free," he said. "Unlocking a door."

Azure's scales rippled with pleasure. "You're growing stronger. In both worlds."

Darius straightened, pride filling his chest. "I am dreamer."

"Yes," Azure said. "You are a dreamer. And one day, you will be much more."

When Azure leaned close, he examined the picture that Darius drew of him. His eyes, twin pools of blue and shadow, gleamed with something beyond approval.

"This," he murmured, "is more than marks on paper."

Darius tilted his head.

"When a dreamer cannot speak, they find other paths. Yours is the path of lines, shapes, and patterns, a way of finding truth. But your hands, still tethered to waking limits, cannot yet show what your mind sees."

When Azure raised one claw and brushed the air above Darius's head, filaments of silver light shimmered into view, trailing from the dream realm into the boy's fingertips.

"Now," Azure said, "what your soul sees, your hand will begin to echo. Not all at once. But soon, others will feel what you see."

As they soared together over the dreamscape, the truth of those words settled into his heart. The path ahead would not be easy, Azure had shown him glimpses of the challenges to come, the darkness that threatened both his worlds. It had never happened before, but that night, Darius Turner believed in his own strength, his own voice, and his own worth.

Darius was no longer the boy trapped in silence, but a child beginning to speak with growing confidence who drew with purpose, and who understood that his differences were not flaws but gifts. The dragon had awakened the dreamer, and the dreamer had stepped forward.

In the small house on the outskirts of Atlanta, the family kept his drawings safe, evidence of a journey they couldn't fully comprehend but they were starting to accept. And in the realm of Somnoria, the Dreamers' Dragons watched with growing interest as the boy with sapphire eyes — not dark like the gem but crystalline, fierce, and unmistakable — took his first steps toward a destiny that few suspected.

But elsewhere, where dreams pressed too hard against the fabric of day, seams split.

And something watched back.

Chapter Eighteen

Bouncing

August 1932

The world once called Darius broken. But in his dreams, he was becoming whole. Almost two years of dreams had carried Darius from single words to sentences. At home, the changes were steady enough for his family to trust they were real. He could sit through supper without bolting from the table, dress himself most mornings without a fight, and follow instructions without becoming overwhelmed. He even tolerated the scratchy Sunday shirts his mother insisted on for church, though only if she let him unbutton the collar halfway through service.

His father had noticed too. Some evenings, Augustus would linger in the doorway after work, watching Darius sort marbles or sketch with his head bent low. He didn't always speak, neither of them did, but there was a quiet exchange in the glance they shared. Something that hadn't existed before Azure entered Darius's nights.

Weeks before his seventh birthday, his speech was no longer a rare event but a part of daily life. Words weren't perfect, but they were his. And with each success came something even rarer: ease.

That night, when the familiar pull took hold, Darius found himself in an open expanse of blue sky — the kind with no ground and no ceiling. Azure waited in the distance, wings casting long, slow shadows across the clouds.

"Tonight," Azure said, his tone lighter than usual, "we bring the waking world with us."

Nothing seemed strange at first.

Then Lula's blue ribbon changed color with every note she hummed, flickering from red to green to gold. Ezra's chair legs stretched longer with each rock until he was nearly touching the ceiling.

Gunny burst through the door without knocking, her braids swinging, Theo right behind her. Theo wore two different boots — one his, one much too small — and no one seemed to notice.

Darius blinked.

The air had shifted. It was brighter, warmer, carrying that sweetness that only ever showed up here.

A low rumble came from outside. When Azure's head appeared through the kitchen window, his eyes crinkled with amusement.

"No lessons tonight," the dragon said. "Sometimes dreams should be dreams."

The floorboards rippled beneath them. Chairs lifted and drifted into the next room. The walls stretched, corners bending into angles that made no sense.

Darius took a step.

The kitchen door opened onto a hallway made of marshmallow — cushioned and squeaky underfoot. His weight sank enough, then steadied.

Lula darted past him, now wearing a hat shaped like a rooster's comb. Ezra dropped from the ceiling clutching a fistful of peacock plumage.

134

Gunny skidded in from the other side with both hands full of sugar drops that bounced like rubber balls.

Theo followed, sweeping a broom that neighed like a horse with every stroke.

The room shifted again.

Now it was a giant parlor lined with mirrors. In one reflection, Lula had dragon wings. In another, Ezra sported a mule's tail. Gunny's reflection was covered head to toe in icing. Theo's hair had gone wild — twice its usual size, a whole cloud trailing him.

Laughter broke loose.

They tore through doorways that led nowhere and back again. Feathers flew. Lemon drops ricocheted. Chairs bounced away from grasping hands.

Someone yelled, "Push it!"

In the center of the room sat a large red button marked DO NOT PUSH.

They crowded in — Darius, Lula, Ezra, Gunny, Theo — and Azure's claw pressed in beside them.

The button clicked.

The room exploded into motion.

Rubber balls burst from every direction, bouncing off walls, ceiling, even each other. Each made its own noise when it struck — piglet squeals, goose honks, a cow's low moo, the sharp yip of a puppy.

One stuck to Darius's shoulder with a goat-like boing, clinging there like a stubborn barn cat.

When Ezra lunged for it, he missed, and stumbled backward into three others that mooed, quacked, and barked in quick succession. He spread his arms like a fence, trying to corral them, but a ball the size of a watermelon honked like a goose and bowled him flat.

His laughter came in hiccupping bursts.

Lula streaked through the chaos, quick as a sparrow. She scooped up a red ball and hurled it at Ezra. It crowed so loud and sudden that half the others leapt higher in response.

Gunny dove headfirst into the rolling noise, vanishing beneath honks and squeals. She popped back up with an armful and flung them at Theo.

Armed with the neighing broom, Theo batted the balls away.

"Not today, varmints!" he shouted.

Lula nearly folded over laughing.

A small yellow ball rolled to a stop against Darius's foot and bleated like a lamb.

He bent, feeling the supple give beneath his fingers, and tossed it toward Gunny. When she caught it, she squealed back in perfect imitation.

The balls ricocheted everywhere — off walls, off each other, even off Azure's claws. The dragon rumbled and flicked one with the tip of his tail. When Theo leapt and smacked it like a baseball, he sent it spinning into the rafters.

The air carried the faint scent of fresh hay and warm earth.

Darius knew none of it was real.

His chest had loosened. His jaw ached from grinning.

This was his house. His people. His joy.

Something broke free in him — not a simple smile, but a deep, shaking laugh that left him bent over, gasping. His siblings laughed until they couldn't breathe. Even Azure's rumble joined in, thunder threaded with delight.

For a while, Darius forgot the waking world entirely.

Here, nothing fought him. His body moved without effort. Sounds came when he wanted them. His brothers and sisters didn't slow or wait; they met him exactly where he was, as if they always had.

He wanted it to last.

He wanted to keep laughing until his chest burned, to keep watching Gunny's icing-smeared grin and Theo's broom-neighing heroics, to hear Lula's ribbon change color with every breath and Ezra's ridiculous mule tail swish behind him.

If he stayed here, maybe nothing would ever be too loud or too fast again.

The edges softened.

Color bled like paint in water.

Darius reached for it, willing it to stay —

BANG.

A bedroom door slammed. His eyes flew open to pale morning light and the faint rattle of the windowpane.

He stayed still, staring at the ceiling, holding the dream in place before it slipped away. He could still feel the sugar drops bouncing past his legs, hear Ezra's snorting laughter, see Gunny's hands flinging candy into the air. The warmth of it lingered in his chest, the kind that made waking feel like losing something.

It was the smell of breakfast that reached him as he sat up, the smile from the dream still caught on his lips.

When Darius took his usual seat at the table, his spoon balanced between his fingers. His scrambled eggs cooled on the plate before him, yellow mounds already separated into three equal portions. He barely noticed. His attention drifted somewhere else, the smile still there, small but wider than normal.

Lula came in dressed for the day, hair pulled back with the blue ribbon she'd found last week. She grabbed a bowl, ladled herself grits, and dropped in a pat of butter that melted into a glossy pool.

When she sat across from Darius, her spoon hovered.

"You're smiling."

The words landed softly, not quite a question. Grits dripped back into her bowl.

Darius looked at her. The smile stayed. Not one of the quick flickers that vanished when noticed. This one held, as if he'd forgotten to tuck it away.

When Ezra crashed into the kitchen with his shirt half tucked and sleep still clinging to one eye, he poured a glass of milk, drank half of it, and came up with a white mustache he ignored.

"What's wrong with him?" He jerked his chin toward Darius, curious rather than worried.

"He's smiling," Lula said, like she was announcing something rare.

Ezra leaned back on two chair legs, grinning wide.

"Bet it's 'cause school's starting next week," he said. "Finally gets to show off all them words Azure been teaching him."

Darius's fingers tapped the table, light and uneven. He took a bite of eggs and chewed slowly, the smile never quite leaving.

Their mother turned from the stove with a plate in her hands. She studied him, the looseness in his shoulders, the calm in his hands.

"Good dreams, baby?"

Darius nodded. Then, after a beat, he said, "Funny dreams."

"Funny how?" Lula leaned forward.

His eyes flicked between them. The images were still close. His siblings hadn't been there. He knew that. But they had been exactly themselves.

"Bouncing," he said. "Lots of bouncing."

Ezra snorted milk through his nose.

Lula shrieked and lobbed a napkin at him. Their mother swatted at Ezra with a dish towel, trying to restore order. The kitchen filled with noise and motion, familiar and loud.

Darius watched it all, the smile widening a fraction.

They hadn't been in the house with the bouncing balls. Still, something was different. Seeing them there, even in his own making, had changed how the memory sat in him.

"You gonna eat them eggs or grin at them?" Ezra asked, recovered.

When Darius looked down at his carefully divided portions, he dragged his spoon through them, mixing them together.

"School," he said. "Teacher."

"Miss Thompson," their mother said. "She's supposed to be real patient. Good with special learners."

The words slid past him. He was special. Azure had said so. Different, not less.

"I hope she likes dragons," Lula said, then hesitated. "I mean, if you want to tell her."

Darius thought of the dream house, the button marked DO NOT PUSH, the way they had all pressed it, anyway. Sharing felt less heavy than it once had.

"Maybe," he said.

When Ezra thumped his chair back down, he grabbed toast. "You should show her that picture you made last week. The one with the flying islands."

"Somnoria," Darius said.

"Yeah, that," Ezra said. "Bet she never seen anything like it."

Breakfast carried on around him. Plates clinked. Water ran. His siblings talked over one another. Darius stayed slightly apart, not pulled away, holding something of his own.

His mother's hand hovered near his shoulder.

"You ready for school next week?"

He looked at her, then at Lula finishing her grits, at Ezra stacking toast crusts into a wobbling tower.

"Ready," he said.

The smile stayed with him through breakfast, small and private and entirely his.

Chapter Nineteen

School

The morning was cold as Theo added more wood to the fire and stoked the stove. Grease popped in the skillet, and the smell of salt pork and hot cornmeal filled the house.

Darius sat on the edge of his bed, fingers working the buttons of his shirt while Lula darted around her room. She sang a church song under her breath, gathering papers and tucking them into her frayed satchel.

"Mama says we need to hurry," Lula said as she tightened the ribbon in her hair. "Miss Thompson don't like it when we come in after the bell."

Darius nodded. His movements stayed precise. When he reached for the notebook on his nightstand, its corners thinned from use, pages thick with drawings, his fingers rested on the cover a moment before he slid it into his bag.

Sadie appeared in the doorway.

"You two ready? Got your lunch pails?"

She lingered, watching Lula straighten Darius's strap, the easy way her children stood side by side. Not long ago, even the word school had tightened her chest. When Darius's screaming fits were at their worst, neighbors and kin whispered the name Milledgeville State Hospital, always low, as if saying it aloud could make it happen. Sadie had lain awake many nights, clutching her son and praying she would never be forced to let him go.

Now he stood dressed, lunch ready, eyes bright with something distant and sure. Going to school.

"Yes, Mama," Lula said. She lifted the tins and handed one to Darius. "I packed extra cornbread for him today."

When Darius took the pail, his gaze drifted past Sadie's shoulder. He did not speak, but his hand hovered near Gunny's foot dangling off the bed.

"You have a good day at school, baby," Sadie said. "Listen to Miss Thompson. Listen to your sister."

Darius blinked once in reply.

Sadie murmured a quiet prayer of thanks for the morning, ordinary and rare all at once.

Theo and Ezra headed out first. Lula and Darius followed a few steps behind, into the crisp air. Doors opened down the street. A delivery truck rumbled past. A dog barked and then went quiet.

When Lula took Darius's hand, he let her.

They walked the dirt road, stepping around puddles left by last night's rain.

Since September, Darius had made this walk each morning with Lula and Ezra to the one-room schoolhouse. Ezra, thirteen and long-legged, set a quick pace in pants handed down so many times they stopped well above his ankles. Lula, ten, filled the space between them with questions and half-sung hymns.

"Mama says I might get new shoes for Sunday if Daddy's work stays steady," Lula said, hopping over a cracked patch of sidewalk. "They won't be new-new, but new to me from the church box. I hope they're brown. Black shows every speck."

Darius watched a crow land on a fence post. The bird tilted its head and preened one wing, then the other.

"Ezra says there's a spelling test," Lula went on. "But I don't think so. Miss Thompson would've told us." She squeezed his hand. "Did you practice the animal words?"

Darius nodded.

"You remember how to spell dog?"

He traced the letters in the air. D O G.

"That's right," Lula said. "And the numbers worksheet? The patterns one."

Another nod, firmer this time.

A girl with braids and a patchwork dress fell into step beside them.

"Morning, Lula. You finish that history reading?"

"Sure did," Lula said. "All about the colonies."

When the girl glanced at Darius, she said, "Morning, Darius."

His eyes flicked toward her, then away. His grip tightened in Lula's hand.

"He says good morning back," Lula answered, her voice easy and familiar. "In his quiet way."

The schoolhouse rose ahead of them, weathered wood and peeling white paint. The yard was packed dirt, worn smooth by generations of feet, with a few stubborn tufts of grass.

An oak shaded one corner where children clustered, tossing a ball and trading secrets. A bell hung from its post, waiting.

Lula guided Darius around the louder groups. She leaned close.

"Letters this morning. Math after lunch. You can draw during free time."

Darius's steps picked up.

Inside, the schoolhouse opened into a single room. Older students filled the back benches. Younger ones sat up front where Miss Thompson kept her voice slow and even, chalk tapping out a cadence Darius could follow.

Sunlight streamed through the tall windows, catching dust motes and the scarred surfaces of mismatched desks. The chalkboard stretched across the front wall, yesterday's lessons still faint beneath the fresh slate.

It had taken time for the room's noise to stop feeling like a storm.

Desks creaked. The slap of chalk on slate. Voices overlapped.

Over time, patterns emerged. Recitations. Copy-work. The scrape and pause of chalk. The hours lined themselves up until they made sense.

Two months ago, Darius had drawn Azure for his family. His mother slipped the picture between the pages of the Bible to keep it safe. That night, in dream, Azure traced the air with a wingtip and told him he'd drawn the light true.

The faint smell of dust and chalk, musty old books, and a rich, sweet, woody smoke from the small hearth fire filled the room. Charts of the alphabet, multiplication tables, and curling maps lined the walls.

When Miss Thompson stood at her desk, she sorted papers and greeted students as they entered.

Lula led Darius to their usual spot, two desks near the side wall. She arranged his things: pencil on the right, notebook tucked in the cubby, lunch pail beneath.

As other students filed in, their voices lowering, Darius kept his eyes down, fingers tracing initials carved long ago.

"That's the Turner boy," someone said. "The one who don't talk."

"He draws real good," another added. "Saw his dragon picture last week. Looked almost real."

"My ma says he's touched in the head," said a third. "Not in a bad way. Different."

When Lula lifted her chin, she said, "He can hear you fine. And he's smarter than all of y'all put together."

The whisperers fell silent.

Darius's hand brushed Lula's elbow, a small thank you.

When Miss Thompson rang her bell, she called, "Good morning, children," her voice warm but firm. "Let's begin with the pledge, then our morning scripture."

The class rose. Darius stood a beat later, hand over heart, lips still.

They sat again. When Lula opened their Bible to the marked page, she angled it for Darius to see.

The school day had begun. Darius was present, anchored by his sister's steadiness, his eyes taking in everything.

Miss Thompson stood tall at the chalkboard, chalk dust on her fingers and hem.

"Today we continue penmanship," she said, writing with practiced grace. "This sentence has every letter in the alphabet," she explained. "Neat, even letters with proper spacing."

She passed out lined paper. When she reached Darius and Lula, she lingered.

"How are we today, Darius?" Her voice softened.

Darius traced the lines silently.

"He's good today," Lula said. "Did all his practice."

"Guide, but don't do it for him," Miss Thompson said.

"Yes, ma'am."

Older kids passed pencils. A boy with scuffed knees dropped one on Darius's desk.

Ezra sat at the front, pencil already moving. Younger kids further back wrestled with their letters.

When Lula leaned in, she said, "Start with 'T' like we practiced." She placed his fingers on the pencil.

Darius gripped too tightly. His first letter came out jagged, but legible.

"Good," Lula said. "Now h. With the little loop."

He pressed harder. Each letter took effort. Lula supported him, but let Darius do the work by himself.

"Q next," she said, voice soft. "Remember the tail."

A girl two rows up turned, nudging her neighbor.

Darius paused.

Lula moved her slate, blocking their view. "Us and the letters," she said.

He resumed. "Brown" came slow, "fox" slower. Sweat dotted his brow.

Miss Thompson passed by, saying nothing, but noting the scene. Her eyes met Lula's briefly, in what looked like approval.

After twenty minutes, Darius had a complete sentence. Lula blew the flecks of lead to avoid smudging and turned it in.

"Very good effort," Miss Thompson said, noting the labor in every line.

She moved to the board. "Now arithmetic. Look for patterns."

She drew: Circle, Square, Triangle, Circle...

"What comes next?"

"Square!" a boy called.

"Correct."

Another followed. Two, four, eight, sixteen.

Ezra raised his hand. "Thirty-two. It doubles."

Miss Thompson nodded.

Then she drew again. Three squares. Four circles. Five triangles.

Pencils tapped. Lula frowned at her slate.

Darius sat still.

Then, suddenly, his chalk flew across his slate. He extended the pattern. Seven circles. Eight triangles. Nine squares.

When Miss Thompson noticed, she asked, "Do you have an answer, Darius?"

He held up his slate.

She examined it. "Exactly right. You continued the sequence perfectly."

She turned the slate so the class could see. "He followed the pattern forward. Numbers and shapes, increasing together."

"How did you know so quickly?" she asked.

Darius pointed — slate, eyes, circle.

"You saw it as a whole, not part?"

He nodded.

Throughout the lesson, his slate stayed active. Each time, his answers were right. No triumph, quiet understanding.

After ringing the bell, Miss Thompson made a note in her book:

146

Darius Turner, exceptional pattern recognition. Consider advanced number work. Build on this strength. -Miss T.

She watched Lula gather his things. The contrast between his strained writing and natural math stunned her.

Eight years of teaching had taught her many kinds of minds. Darius's was one of the rare ones, quiet, vivid, deep.

Chapter Twenty

Dragons

"Lula," she called. "Make sure your brother has time to draw during his free period. I'd like to see what he creates today."

Lula nodded. "Yes, ma'am. He draws dragons. He always draws dragons."

"Dragons?" Miss Thompson's interest sharpened. "How fascinating."

Darius didn't look up, but his hand drifted to the notebook in his satchel, his fingers resting on its worn cover.

Mid-morning light passed through the windows and free time had arrived, that precious half-hour before lunch when lessons paused and children chose quieter pursuits. Some huddled over checkerboards made from cardboard scraps. Others bent over shared books. Feet shuffled and voices murmured, a gentle backdrop rising and falling like waves.

Darius reached for his satchel with unusual eagerness. His fingers found the worn notebook, extracting it with care reserved for treasures. The cover bore smudges from constant handling, its binding reinforced with cloth strips Sadie had sewn to keep the pages from falling out.

When Lula glanced over, she asked, "You're drawing Azure again?"

Darius nodded, already opening to a fresh page. The paper wasn't clean; faint pencil marks lingered. Paper was too precious to waste.

He selected a pencil and tested its point. Too dull.

From his bag, he took the small paring knife Sadie allowed him to carry for this purpose and shaved the wood back with short, practiced strokes. Fresh lead emerged. He set the knife aside.

The pencil touched paper.

His shoulders relaxed. His breath slowed. His eyes locked on the page.

The first lines came with confidence. Sweeping curves appeared, suggesting motion.

A head took shape, long and elegant, crowned by a slight crest. The neck followed, sinuous and strong. The body emerged next, with scales suggested by careful arrangements of light and shadow.

Wings stretched across the page, their membranes thin enough to imagine light passing through. Each stroke built on the last with a certainty at odds with the hands that fumbled over letters.

When Thomas peered over his shoulder, he said, "Dang, D, when did you get so good?" Darius smiled without answering.

Ever since Azure brushed the air above his head, Darius no longer just drew with his hands. Each line came from somewhere deeper, as if his soul had found a way to speak without words, as though the paper understood.

Still drawing, Darius added detail to the eye, an oval with a vertical pupil and flecks of light inside.

"It's a dragon," Lula said when Thomas didn't move away. "Azure."

"Dragon?" Thomas repeated, curious. "Like from a storybook?"

A girl with braids crept closer, standing on her toes to see. "That don't look like no storybook picture," she said. "That looks real."

The word real drew more eyes.

A third student joined, then a fourth. They formed a loose semicircle, intrigued but respectful. Ears pink at the edges, Darius continued working.

His pencil moved steadily, claws curled like scythes, jewels embedded in the brow catching imaginary light, scales layered with mathematical precision. It wasn't just good; it was uncanny. Azure appeared on the page not as fantasy, but as something remembered.

"He's been drawing the same dragon for months," Lula said, pride in her voice. "Gets better every time."

"Does it breathe fire?" asked a younger boy.

Lula shook her head. "Azure doesn't need to. He has other magic."

"How's he know what a dragon looks like?" someone asked. "They ain't real."

"This one is," Lula replied. "To Darius."

The whispers followed.

"Look at those wings."

"It looks like it's moving."

"I wish I could draw like that."

Darius set his eyes on his drawing, though a faint flush colored his cheeks. His hand moved slower now, adding deliberate details, three jewels along Azure's jaw, evenly spaced, each catching imagined light. One, two, three. Every time.

"Can he draw other things?" Thomas asked.

"Sometimes. But mostly Azure," Lula said.

"Why's it called Azure?" Thomas asked.

"Because he's blue," Lula said. "Like the sky. Blue like…" She stopped, glancing at her brother's eyes.

A girl reached toward the notebook. "Can I touch it?"

When Darius's hand shot out, it covered the drawing. His pencil clattered to the desk. The students stepped back, startled.

"Don't touch his drawings, please," Lula said, calm but firm. "It upsets him when people touch his drawings."

The girl withdrew her hand. "Sorry. It's so pretty."

Darius gradually relaxed. He uncovered the drawing but kept his hand beside it, his boundary. After a moment, he picked up his pencil and resumed sketching clouds near Azure's feet, as if the dragon floated above them.

The students lingered, but seeing Darius wouldn't engage, they drifted back to their activities. Still, eyes flicked back toward his desk, drawn to the image taking shape.

Thomas lingered.

"Could you draw me one sometime?" he asked softer now. "A dragon of my own?"

Darius kept his eyes on his drawing, but his pencil paused.

He gave a slight nod.

Thomas beamed. "Thank you." He retreated, glancing back as if confirming the promise was real.

When Darius sat back, he studied his work. No smile, but something close. He traced the edge of Azure's wing with a finger, a gesture of recognition.

Lula leaned in. "He looks right. Best one yet."

Darius smiled.

In the drawing, Azure's eye contained a knowing gleam, as if the dragon looked back at his creator with approval.

When Miss Thompson rang the small bell on her desk, games and books vanished. Darius closed his notebook carefully, sliding it into his satchel. The dragon disappeared, but the impression remained, on the students who glimpsed a world they couldn't explain, and on Darius, who carried it within.

CHAPTER TWENTY-ONE

CASSIUS

Late morning, the arithmetic lesson halted mid-equation when three sharp knocks arrived at the classroom door. Miss Thompson set down her chalk, leaving a half-completed division problem suspended on the board. The students straightened in their seats, curiosity rippling through the room in whispers and shifting postures. Visitors during school hours were rare enough to warrant attention.

When Miss Thompson opened the door to a woman in a pressed cotton dress, a boy bounced lightly at her side.

"Mrs. Williams, good morning," Miss Thompson said. "And this must be Cassius."

The boy stood next to his mother, his round face framed by closely cropped hair. He wasn't thin like many children in the neighborhood; his cheeks were full, his frame solid. A small scar curved beneath his right eye, pale against his brown skin. His eyes darted around the room, taking in everything at once with interest.

"Yes, ma'am," Mrs. Williams said, her hand resting on her son's shoulder. "We moved from Macon last week. The principal said he could start today."

"Of course. We're delighted to have him." Miss Thompson gestured for them to enter.

Cassius entered without hesitation, his shoes squeaking against the floor. A grin spread across his face as he surveyed his new classmates, displaying confidence unusual for a child entering a room of strangers.

"Class, we have a new student joining us today," Miss Thompson announced. "This is Cassius Williams. He's come to us from Macon, and I expect you all to make him feel welcome."

Twenty-three pairs of eyes fixed on Cassius. He didn't shrink from the attention; if anything, he seemed to expand under it, rocking forward onto the balls of his feet.

"Hello!" he called out, not waiting for Miss Thompson to finish. "I'm Cassius, but you can call me Cass. I'm ten years old, my daddy drives trucks, I have a dog named Rex, and we live on Cedar Street now."

The rapid-fire introduction hung in the air. A few students giggled. When Miss Thompson smiled, she rested her hand on his shoulder.

"Thank you for that enthusiasm, Cassius. Now, let's find you a seat." She scanned the room, her gaze settling on the empty desk near Darius and Lula. "There's space right there, next to Lula Turner."

Cassius's mother bent to kiss his forehead. "You be good now. Mind Miss Thompson."

"I will, Mama." He was already moving toward his desk, unconcerned about her departure.

When Cassius dropped into the seat with a thud, the desk legs scraped. He turned immediately to Lula. "Hi! I'm Cass. What's your name? Do you like dogs? Mine's brown with a white spot, and he can fetch sticks. Once he caught a squirrel, but Mama made him let it go because she said it was dirty."

Lula blinked. "I'm Lula," she managed. "And this is my brother, Darius."

Cassius swiveled toward Darius, taking in his silent presence. "Hello! You don't look like your sister. Your eyes are blue. That's different. My cousin has light eyes too but they're more yellow. Mama says it's because his daddy was mixed. Are you mixed? I like your shirt. It's blue like your eyes."

Darius stared at him, expression unreadable. On his desk, hands curled into loose fists, then relaxed. The motion was subtle, controlled, not the self-soothing movements Lula had learned to recognize.

"Darius doesn't talk much," Lula said.

"Don't matter," Cassius replied without missing a beat. "My uncle Don doesn't talk much either. Mama says the war took his words. Did something take yours? Or do you not want to use them? I talk a lot. Mama says I talk enough for three people, so maybe I can talk for you too."

The offer was made with such guileless sincerity that Lula's defensiveness melted into surprised amusement.

"Children." Miss Thompson cleared her throat. "Arithmetic, please. Cassius, we're working on long division. Do you know how to do that yet?"

"Yes, ma'am!" Cassius called back. "My teacher in Macon taught us. I'm good at it except sometimes I forget to bring down the next number. One time I got every problem wrong and had to stay after school and do them all again."

He continued in a lower voice, now addressing Lula and Darius as Miss Thompson returned to the board. "I don't like staying after school. It's boring. What do you do after school? I like to play baseball but I'm not very good at catching. I'm better at batting. I hit a ball over Mrs. Peterson's fence once and broke her window."

Darius's eyes tracked Cassius's animated face. Something subtle shifted in his posture, a loosening, a settling. The stream of words washed over him, requiring nothing in return.

"We help our mama after school," Lula said, conscious of Miss Thompson's resumed lesson. "Sometimes we play jacks or marbles."

"I LOVE marbles," Cassius exclaimed, too loudly. Several heads turned. "I have a cat's eye and a steely that's all blue and…"

"Cassius," Miss Thompson interrupted. "I'm sure you can tell Lula and Darius all about your marbles at lunch. For now, please study what is on the board."

"Yes, ma'am. Sorry, ma'am." Cassius ducked his head, but briefly. Within seconds, he was whispering again. "Do you bring lunch? I brought mine. Mama made cornbread and beans, and there's a peach too. Do you like peaches? I like the soft yellow ones best. The green ones, when they ain't ripe yet, make your stomach hurt, but I still sneak 'em sometimes."

For the rest of the lesson, Cassius maintained a whispered monologue, pausing when Miss Thompson looked directly at him. He covered topics from his favorite foods to descriptions of every room in his new house. Each subject tumbled into the next, a stream-of-consciousness flow requiring no response.

Lula glanced at Darius, expecting tension.

Instead, she was surprised to see him watching Cassius with quiet fascination. His eyes followed the new boy's expressive hands as they punctuated each declaration. When Cassius paused to breathe, Darius's gaze remained unbroken, almost expectant, waiting for the flow of words to resume.

Once, when Cassius described a blue jay he'd seen that morning, Darius nodded, a small but definite acknowledgment that made Cassius beam with disproportionate pleasure.

"You like birds? I knew you would. You look like someone who notices things. I notice things. Mama says I notice more than I should, and that's why I can't stop talking about everything I see."

Lula caught Darius's eye and raised her eyebrows with a silent question: Should I?

Darius answered with the slightest upturn of his lips, not a smile, but the closest thing to it he'd shown all day. In Cassius's unstoppable chatter, he'd found unexpected comfort. Here was someone who filled the silence completely, who didn't wait expectantly for answers Darius couldn't give.

For once, silence wasn't waiting on him.

Afternoon sunlight streamed through the classroom windows. Miss Thompson had announced fifteen minutes of drawing time while she prepared materials for the history lesson. Paper was distributed, one precious sheet per student, and worn-down colored pencils were shared among tables. Children bent over their desks, tongues caught between teeth in concentration, creating bright houses, stick-figure families, and impossible animals with more enthusiasm than skill.

Darius pulled out his notebook rather than using the provided paper. His fingers traced the cover briefly before opening to a fresh page. Beside him, Cassius attacked his paper with a stubby red pencil, creating bold, erratic, and chaotic strokes.

When Cassius paused mid-scribble, noticing Darius's notebook, his eyes widened at the glimpse of previous drawings visible as Darius flipped through pages.

"What's that?" Cassius pointed, his voice carrying across several desks. "Those aren't school drawings. They're too good."

Darius froze, his hand hovering over the page he'd settled on. His eyes darted to Lula.

"That's his special notebook," Lula explained. "For his dragon drawings."

"Dragon?" Cassius scooted his chair closer, the legs scraping loudly. "Like in stories? Can I see? Please? I love dragons. My granddaddy told me stories about dragons that lived in the mountains back in Africa before people captured them all."

When Darius hesitated, he turned the notebook toward Cassius. The page showed Azure in flight, wings extended, scales catching imaginary light. Unlike his earlier sketch, this one included color, blue pencil layered to create depth and shadow.

Cassius went still. His mouth formed a perfect O. For five full seconds, he said nothing, a silence so uncharacteristic that Lula glanced at him with concern.

Then he exploded.

"That's the most amazing thing I ever saw in my whole life!" He grabbed the edge of his desk, bouncing in his seat. "It looks REAL! Like it could fly off the page! How'd you make it look like that? The wings are perfect! And those jewels, are they magic? I bet they are. Is it a nice dragon or a mean one? What's its name?"

The barrage of questions came without pauses for answers. Students at nearby desks turned to look, drawn by Cassius's volume and excitement.

Darius didn't recoil. Instead, he carefully turned to another page, revealing Azure from a different angle, this time perched on a crystal spire, tail wrapped around the column, head tilted as if listening.

Cassius gasped. "There's more! It's the same dragon but in a different place! That's so smart. I can draw the same thing looking exactly the same every time."

When he stood up suddenly, the chair tipped backward with a clatter. "EVERYONE! You have to see what Darius drew! It's the best dragon in the whole world!"

Miss Thompson looked up sharply. "Cassius, please sit down and lower your voice."

"But Miss Thompson, it's important! Darius can draw dragons better than anybody! Better than books even!"

Several students giggled at Cassius's unbridled enthusiasm. Thomas, who had asked Darius for a dragon drawing earlier, nodded.

"He can, Miss Thompson," Thomas said. "They're special."

Miss Thompson's expression softened. "I understand, but we still need to maintain a reasonable volume. You may show interested classmates quietly."

Cassius righted his chair and sat again, but his excitement didn't dim. He turned to the students nearest them.

"Come see," he stage-whispered, gesturing emphatically. "It's not like regular drawings. It's like he's seen real dragons."

A small cluster of children gathered around their desks. Darius didn't pull away or cover his work. Instead, he carefully turned pages, revealing different aspects of Azure, in flight, resting, perched on crystalline formations that defied gravity. Each drawing held the same uncanny precision, the same sense of something observed rather than imagined.

"What do you call your dragon?" Cassius asked again, finger hovering near but not touching the page.

Darius's lips parted a little. His gaze remained on the drawing.

"Azure," he said, the word barely audible but clear.

Lula's pencil clattered to the floor. Her head whipped around, eyes wide with shock. In all the months at school, Darius had never spoken aloud to anyone but her, and even that was rare.

Cassius, unaware of the significance, continued naturally. "Azure. That's perfect because he's so blue. Does he live in the sky? Is that why he's called Azure?"

Darius's fingers traced the dragon's wing. "Somnoria," he whispered, the familiar word rolling off his tongue with ease.

"Somnoria?" Cassius tested the word. "Is that a country? Is it far away? I've never heard of it."

"It's... home," Darius said, each word careful and measured. "Dragons live."

The surrounding students exchanged glances of surprise. Those who had been in class with Darius since the beginning of the year had never heard him speak.

"He talks," said a girl with braids.

Lula recovered from her shock and shot the girl a warning look. "Course he talks. When he wants to."

Cassius, blissfully unaware of the stir he'd caused, leaned closer. "Can Azure breathe fire? Or ice? My granddaddy said dragons breathe ice instead of fire."

Darius shook his head. "Talk. In dreams."

"That's even better!" Cassius declared. "A talking dream dragon! Can you teach me to draw him? I want to draw him too but mine would look terrible. My horses look like dogs, and my dogs look like potatoes."

Something slipped out of Darius, a faint burst caught between a cough and a laugh. He ducked his head, but Lula caught the spark before it faded.

"Darius is the only one who can draw Azure right," she said, voice thick with pride. "He sees him special."

"Well, I think it's the best drawing in the whole school," Cassius announced, loud enough for Miss Thompson to hear. "And Darius is the best artist, and I'm sitting next to him, which makes me the luckiest new kid ever."

The simple compliment brought a flush to Darius's cheeks. No response, but his posture opened, shoulders lowering, hands relaxing.

When Miss Thompson approached, drawn by the commotion, she bent to examine the open notebook, her expression shifting from curiosity to surprise.

"These are remarkable, Darius," she said quietly. "Truly remarkable."

The interruption came with a metallic clang, jerking them out of the moment. Students shuffled back to their seats, glancing over shoulders. Darius closed the notebook, slid it into his satchel, and let Cassius steal one last look.

"I draw… dragon…you," he said, so softly that only Cassius and Lula could hear.

Cassius's face lit up brighter than the sunbeams crossing the classroom floor. "You mean it? My own dragon? Can it be red? Red's my favorite. Or blue, like Azure. Or any color. I don't care as long as you draw it."

Darius nodded once, definitively.

Lula watched with wonder. She'd spent years interpreting Darius's silences, translating his smallest gestures. Now this whirlwind of a boy had drawn out words long locked away.

She caught Darius's eye, raising her eyebrows in silent question. The barest smile answered her, not the blank stare he often wore, but a knowing one.

160

Returning to her desk, Miss Thompson noted in her book: *Darius spoke today. To the new boy, Cassius. About his drawings. Significant. -Miss T.*

Chapter Twenty-Two

Time

The house creaked in the quiet. No footsteps, no voices, the delicate hush of night pressing against the Turner home. Sadie stood in the doorway, arms folded, watching her son.

Darius sat on the floor of the front room. His body in an unusual stillness. No rocking, hands still. Buttons spilled in a loose ring around him: some old, some shiny, some dull and dented from wear. But he didn't sort them by color or size. He touched each one, held it to his cheek, then pressed it to his ear, listening.

Click. Pause. Press. Tilt. Set aside.

Click. Stroke. Hold still. Set aside.

He wasn't simply playing. He was tuning in, like each button possessed a secret vibration that he could hear.

When Sadie leaned on the doorframe, her breath caught. The tone he made was low and melodic. It wasn't words, but it had sound. A low hum, round and rising, like the beginning of a song without melody. Her heart caught on the moment.

"Darius?"

He didn't startle. He turned his face toward her and mouthed a word. "Gun... ny."

He didn't repeat it. But his lips curled a bit.

She sat beside him on the floor, knees pulled to her chest. He picked up a smooth pink button, touched it to his own ear, then to hers.

Nothing but silence.

But to him, it said something. Maybe a vibration. Maybe a memory of Gunny's laugh stitched into wood.

That night, after the button game ended, and the quiet settled in, Sadie stayed on the floor beside him longer than usual. Darius leaned against the arm of the couch, fingers still tracing the button's rim. He didn't speak. He didn't need to. Something about the way he had touched it to her ear, so tenderly, so deliberately, stayed with her. When she finally stood to gather the pillows and fold the blankets, her hand slipped between the cushions.

She found a drawing.

Folded once, tucked beneath the corner of the sofa cushions. Two children, both older than Darius, stood in a meadow with tall grass of purple and yellow wildflowers. In the sky behind the children was a clear drawing of a dragon, not Azure, flying in the air. The boy had shaggy light hair and unusual shoes. The girl had wild brown curls, fists on her hips, and sparks around her feet.

She ran her finger over the boy's eyes.

Bright blue. He drew them the same color as his own.

But the skin, light.

Both of them white.

Her mouth tightened for a second. Not in anger. Not even judgment. Wondering.

Where would he have seen children like this?

Not in their neighborhood. Not at school. Not on the trolley.

Not in this life.

She looked up.

"Darius, where'd you see these children?"

He pointed to the window and then to his head.

Darius remembered sketching without thinking, his fingers tracing curves and angles before his mind caught up. The girl's hair was curly, like coils of wire. The boy's eyes were rounder than his. Their clothes were different, and he didn't understand. They were colorful. His pencil paused midline. He didn't remember ever seeing these children. He didn't know them.

But… had he?

That night, the drawing glistened faintly on the floor beside his bed. Not bright. Enough to nudge his thoughts awake. Darius rolled onto his side. Then the room rippled.

The window near the sofa, wooden frame, cracked glass, the one he stared through, moved.

It didn't vanish. It followed him.

As sleep took hold, the frame of that window twisted into the dream with him, bending light around itself like the rim of a mirror catching fire.

He woke up in his dream standing, and buttery moss covered the ground, damp under his feet. He sank with each step — not too much that he lost his footing. At the center of a floating platform, Azure waited.

"You brought your world with you," Azure said without turning.

"Sorry," Darius said as he gazed back. The frame of the window hovered like a door without a wall, light bending inside it. The stars of his world glittered on the other side. Then, without fanfare, it faded.

Gone.

He stared at the picture of the children, then at Azure. The drawing suspended in midair, folded from a single sheet of paper that seemed to breathe.

"I didn't mean to draw them," Darius murmured. "They were ... in my head."

When Azure approached, he rested a claw on the table's edge. "Dreams don't always wait for their dreamer."

Azure folded a paper in half where the edges met. "But dream-time curves. One layer might brush another. The future might lean close enough for your hand to catch it, even if your mind hasn't."

Darius blinked. A laugh echoed faintly, childlike, clear. It wasn't his.

He pressed a hand to the drawing. "I saw them before I met them?"

Azure nodded. "You glimpsed them before you knew you had. The folds bring what hasn't happened close enough to touch. Sometimes the dream arrives second. Sometimes the dream leaves fingerprints before it enters the room."

When he pressed his claw through the layered fold, the surface shimmered. Darius recognized it in his fingertips first, a faint vibration, like the pluck of a string. "Is that … a doorway?"

Azure's eyes glimmered. "That is dream-time. And through it… you may glimpse what was. Or what may be. Let me show you."

Azure unfolded the paper. He drew a dot at each end, then a line connecting them.

"This is how time works in the waking world. You move forward from one point to the next in a straight line."

Azure then folded the paper again and the two dots lined up. "In the dream world, you can move in time with a step in either direction."

A child's laugh broke through the stillness. High. Familiar. He somehow knew her.

The paper rippled, and an image swam into place.

It was her. The girl from the drawing.

"Her name is Sara," Darius said.

They stood in the open meadow, the grass tall and still. Their clothes matched nothing Darius knew, bright, strange, and colorful. Their hair, their posture, even the way they moved seemed different from anyone he'd ever known or seen before. But it wasn't the children that captivated him.

It was their dragon.

It wasn't bigger than Azure, but it looked different, its scales a mix of green-blue and deep purple. The dragon had one wing of solid gold that flickered in the sunlight. When the dragon lowered its head, the children walked toward it without pause.

Darius watched, unblinking.

"They don't see me," Darius murmured.

"They aren't meant to," Azure said. "Not yet."

They didn't seem to notice the world shifting around them.

But it noticed them.

They were Dreamers.

They were inside a dream.

When Darius pressed a hand to the image, it rippled.

The meadow dissolved into a steep mountain pass under a burnished sky. A girl stood there, taller, older, red hair tumbling over a fur-lined cloak. In her hand, a sword caught the firelight.

A dragon towered at her side, every scale bright with flame.

"Seraphina," Darius whispered. He remembered the fiery red dragon he met in Somnoria.

The girl beside her, barefoot, with a sword strapped across her back, shouted something into the wind. He couldn't understand the language, but her voice struck with the cadence of certainty and determination.

She looked different from the others. It wasn't just in clothing or hair, but like she carried the past on her shoulders. Where the laughing children had seemed to bend the dream to their joy, this girl stood inside it like a blade.

He stepped closer.

The mountain cracked.

And the image vanished.

"Who are they?" Darius hesitated. "They had eyes like mine. All of them. The boy, the girl with sparks. Even the one with the sword."

He turned to Azure. "Do all dreamers have eyes like mine?"

Azure's expression grew solemn. "No. They do not. Sapphire eyes are rare, even here in the dream realm. They are a sign, not of strength alone, but of belonging. Those you saw are dreamers, yes. But they are not ordinary. They are like you."

Darius's brow furrowed. A memory. Another child with sapphire eyes, Seraphina had once said. He looked back toward the fading images. "Is this what she meant? Was she talking about them?"

Azure's gaze deepened, a note of recognition threading the air. "Yes. She saw a fragment of what you now glimpse. Not one child, but many. They walk their own paths, but the threads draw them toward you."

"Like me how?"

"They will matter," Azure said. "To this realm. And to you. Perhaps not yet. But the threads have begun to pull taut."

Darius squinted at the empty air where the images had been. "So they're real? Will I meet them in my dreams?"

Azure tapped the folded seam again. "You will, but not now. That time has not come. There is still much for you to learn. Understand that sometimes dreamers walk the same ground from very different directions. The lass with the sword, she does not walk beside the one with the sparks. Their footsteps echo across very different hills."

Darius tilted his head. "They're not from the same... now?"

"No," Azure said. "Nor are they from your now. But their paths curve toward the same center. The dream knows what the waking mind cannot."

"They are real," Azure said. "Even if your steps never meet on the same patch of earth. Even if your suns rise in different skies. Dreamtime holds them together, not like marbles in a jar, but like notes in a song. Each plays its part. Each echos through the others."

The image folded in on itself and vanished.

"You know them?" Darius asked.

"I know their dreams," Azure replied.

CHAPTER TWENTY-THREE

FRIEND

Light filtered through curtains as Darius's eyes opened. He lay motionless, listening to the house settle, the creak of boards and snores of his brothers. His blanket lay smooth across his chest, untouched by restlessness.

A dream lingered, Azure, speaking without effort. They had practiced dream weaving again, the threads more responsive this time. Remembering that progress steadied him.

When he sat up, he reached for his notebook. A blank page. His fingers traced the edge.

Cassius wanted a red dragon.

He pulled a pencil from his bag and began sketching, not the fine details, a beginning. This dragon would be somewhat smaller than Azure, with different scale markings and a spiral tail. Not sleek and feathered, Cassius's dragon would be lean, young, and powerful.

He worked in silence, unaware of the waking house. When Sadie entered to stoke the fire, she paused at the sight of her son, dressed, drawing intently at the corner table.

"You're up early," she said. "Sleep well?"

He nodded, pencil moving continuously.

"What are you drawing today?"

He didn't answer, tilted the notebook. The dragon taking shape was broader, flames curling from its nose.

"That's not Azure," Sadie noted.

"Cass," Darius whispered.

Sadie froze, then nodded as if this happened every morning, grateful for her son's peace and his newly discovering a gift for drawing.

"That's kind of you," she said. "I know he'll love it."

The morning commotion filled the kitchen. Sadie's wooden spoon scraping the oatmeal pot, Gunny's sleepy protests, Ezra and Theo arguing over water duty, all without the tension of Darius having an outburst. By the time Lula came in, braiding her hair, the drawing was half-finished.

Breakfast followed its routine, Darius's food separated, his cup three-quarters full, spoon on the right. He ate in order: oatmeal, peach slices, cornbread. But today, he looked up during the conversation.

As breakfast ended, Darius carried his plate to the basin without prompting. Sadie stilled. He returned to his satchel, checked the notebook, and closed it with care.

"Almost time for school," Lula said. "You ready, Darius?"

He nodded and headed to the door, brushing the bag with one hand.

"Don't forget your lunch," Sadie said, handing them their pails. "And mind the clouds. If it rains too hard, stay put till it lets up. Have a good day."

Darius didn't answer, but as he stepped onto the porch, Lula saw him looking straight ahead, not at his feet, not at tracings in the dirt. His steps had purpose.

They walked through the neighborhood, Lula beside him, chatting about her dream where she fell in a river.

Halfway there, she noticed Darius ahead of her. Usually, he lagged or matched her exactly. This time, he led.

"You in a hurry?" she asked.

He shook his head, hand brushing his satchel again.

Understanding bloomed across her face. "You want to show Cassius your drawing."

It wasn't a question, but he nodded.

"Is it a special one?"

"His own," Darius replied. "Red dragon."

Lula looked curiously at Darius. Two spontaneous responses. She adjusted her pace and smiled.

"He's gonna love it," she said. "Probably talk your ear off all day."

The corner of Darius's mouth twitched. They turned onto the main road where other kids had started walking.

Darius slowed as they joined the crowd, his shoulders tensing with the rising noise. But he didn't retreat. His eyes scanned ahead for one person, Cassius.

Darius hesitated, then stepped forward, once, then again. His hand found the strap of his tote, fingers curling around it. He was excited and nervous all at the same time. Wondering if Cassius would like the drawing of the dragon he had made for him.

Lula watched him walk toward Cassius and toward a first in his life, friendship. She smiled — it held both happiness for her younger brother and a little sadness for herself as she knew it was the beginning of her letting go, and the start of something new.

A sharp clang rang out across the schoolyard as Miss Thompson rang the hand bell from the front steps. When Cass spotted Darius crossing the yard, he bounded down the steps, kicking up little clouds of dust with each stride. His grin stretched wide, crinkling the corners of his eyes and the scar beneath one.

"Darius! You came!" he called, as if Darius might not come to school. He jogged over, skidding to a stop short of collision. "I was telling everyone about how Rex chased three chickens into Mrs. Wilson's yard and…" He stopped, noticing Darius's grip tightening on his bag. "Did you bring it?"

Darius nodded, eyes shifting between Cass and the ground. He worked at the clasp with practiced care.

"The dragon? Is it done?" Cass bounced, hands flexing. "Can I see now, or do I have to wait? I barely slept. Mama said I went on about dragons all through dinner till Daddy told me to hush and eat my beans."

When Darius pulled out his notebook, its edges weathered from handling, he flipped through pages, then carefully tore one free.

Lula, watching from a few steps back, gasped. He never tore pages.

"For you," Darius said in a low voice.

Cass accepted the paper like prized possession. The dragon that emerged wasn't Azure. This one had a thin frame, overlapping scales like armor. Its tail coiled in a spiral, ending in a diamond tip. Rubies crowned its brow, trailing down the spine. Smoke curled from its nostrils, rendered so precisely it seemed to shift on the page.

"Crimson," Darius said, touching one wing.

Cass stared, silent for once. He traced the dragon's outline in the air, not daring to touch.

"He's perfect," Cass said. "Looks like he could burn down a whole city, but wouldn't. Is he nice?"

Darius tilted his head. "Brave. Protector."

"A brave protector," Cass echoed. "Like a knight. Or a firefighter. My cousin wanted to be one, but Auntie said it's too dangerous. But that's what brave means, right? Doing the hard stuff?"

At the doorway, Miss Thompson observed quietly. Cass's animation was expected, but it was Darius's fixed attention that captivated her. He leaned forward, watching Cass's face, attuned.

When Cass folded the drawing with care and tucked it into his shirt pocket, he patted it twice. "I'm keeping him right here," he said, "next to my heart."

Darius's mouth twitched in the faintest smile.

Inside, the day unfolded at its usual pace. During arithmetic, Cass counted under his breath, foot tapping the floor. Twice Miss Thompson looked his way, ready to intervene, then noticed Darius beside him, calm, focused. The stable tempo grounded them both: one found comfort in sound, the other in its predictability.

At lunch, students scattered into the yard. Cass followed Darius to a quiet spot near the fence, away from tag and marble games.

"Mama packed cornbread again," Cass said, opening his pail. "And a boiled egg. Do you like eggs? I like the whites. The yellows stick to my tongue weird. Want to trade? What'd your mama pack?"

Lula hovered nearby, uncertain. When Darius caught her eye, he gave a slight nod.

She smiled, mouthed "thank you," and turned toward a group of girls under the oak.

Cass didn't wait for answers. He tore his cornbread in half, handing the bigger piece to Darius without breaking his story about how Rex once stole a ham off a neighbor's windowsill.

"… and then he had the hiccups for two days! Mama said he deserved it, but he looked so miserable, like this." Cass performed a hiccup so dramatic it jolted his whole body.

A few kids nearby laughed. On another day, Darius might have retreated. Now, he watched, eating calmly, letting Cass's whirlwind orbit him.

Across the yard, three boys took notice.

"Turner's sitting with the new kid?" said the first boy.

"Never seen him with anyone but his sister," added the second boy.

"That Williams kid talks enough for two. I guess," said the other.

After lunch, Miss Thompson announced a free period. When Cass eagerly pulled out Darius's drawing, he unfolded it with careful hands.

"Could you teach me?" Cass asked, his voice dropping to what passed for a whisper in his world, still loud enough for three desks to hear. "I wanna draw Crimson too, but mine would probably look like a lumpy rock with legs."

Darius considered, fingers tapping on his desk. Then he nodded, scooting his chair closer. From his satchel, he pulled a spare pencil and placed it in Cass's hand, then with care, covered it with his own, as Lula often guided him when he learned to write.

"We'll start with the eye," Darius said.

Together, they traced a circle. Darius's hand hovered lightly, letting Cass feel the motion rather than forcing it. When the eye took shape, Darius tapped the center once.

"Look."

"At what?" Cass glanced around.

"Inside." Darius touched his chest. "See it first."

"Oh! Like imagine it before you draw it?"

Darius nodded, pleased.

Their heads bent together over the paper. With great effort, Cass's dragon took shape: clumsy, uneven, but clearly Crimson. When they finished, Cass held it up, beaming.

"Look! I made Crimson! Well, we did. It's not as good as yours, but way better than anything I've ever drawn!"

A few students turned to look, some smiled, others curious. Thomas wandered over.

"That's pretty good," he said. "Better than I could do."

"Darius showed me," Cass explained. "You gotta see it in your head first. Start with the eye, then build the rest, like a recipe, but with pencils instead of flour."

Thomas nodded. "Could you show me too?"

"Sure! Darius and me could teach a dragon class. We'll charge a penny a lesson and get rich!"

Darius didn't laugh out loud, but the idea made him proud that Cass thought he drew well enough to get rich.

When the final bell rang, students gathered their things. When Cass tucked both drawings, Darius's masterpiece and his own humble version, into his rucksack with great care, he announced, "Tomorrow I'm bringing my marbles. I've got seven cat's eyes and one steely big as a robin's egg. Do you play marbles? I could teach you. You taught me drawing, so I gotta teach you something. That's how friendship works, right? Equal exchange and all that?"

174

The word friendship hung between them, new and weighty.

Darius didn't answer aloud, but as they stepped into the sunlight, his shoulder brushed Cass's, deliberate, fleeting.

Cass lit up like he'd been handed a prize. "See you tomorrow, Darius! I'll tell Rex all about Crimson!"

At the road's fork, they split. Miss Thompson watched from the steps, noting how Darius tucked his notebook carefully into his satchel, then turned to watch Cass disappear down the path.

She made a quiet note in her book:

Friendship is blooming. Darius speaking more. Cass listening. Both are better for it. Miss T.

***

That evening, the family room was dim with the cast of a faint lamplight. Lula braided Gunny's hair while she sat cross-legged on the floor, flipping through one of Darius's dragon books. "He talks more than Gunny," Lula declared, glancing up. "He talks while he breathin'. I don't even know how that's possible."

Ezra snorted. "Cass, I like him, he's funny. He has a brother, Sam, who's not at all like him, Sam's quiet. His brother don't act all high and mighty either. Not like most older brothers I seen," he said loud enough that Theo could hear him from the next room.

Darius curled on the couch between his parents, sketchbook on his knees. He drew Thomas a green dragon and Cass's red dragon again, with ruby-lined wings. When Gunny leaned over his shoulder, munching an apple, she said through a crunch, "I wanna meet this kid. Someone who talks all the time? Maybe he can be my new best friend."

Sadie smiled, her hand resting gently on Darius's back. "It's good, baby. Real good, having someone to talk to about dragons and dreams."

Augustus leaned in, voice low. "He's not bein' nice to you 'cause of your drawings, is he?"

Darius shook his head once, a faint smile lifting the corners of his mouth. "He's different," he said quietly. "Like me. But loud."

Gunny giggled. "Loud like me."

Theo peeked in from the kitchen doorway, holding a mug of hot sweet tea. "Well, he ain't as annoying as you, Gunny," he muttered. "But maybe close."

CHAPTER TWENTY-FOUR

CRIMSON

The next day at school, rain drummed the schoolhouse windows, turning them to rivers of smeared light. Students pressed their faces to the panes, watching familiar play areas drown in puddles. Indoors, the air hung heavy, the kind that made bodies shift and pencils stall mid-word. Even the studious ones fidgeted, sighing over their papers, stretching legs beneath desks, forcing attention through the lull of energy stored up from being trapped inside all day.

Miss Thompson had assigned quiet work, facts about the American Revolution copied into lined notebooks. The classroom settled with the familiar rustle of pages, the scratch of graphite, and the occasional creak of a chair, while outside, thunder steadied its way closer to the school-house.

Darius bent over his notebook, copying dates and names. His handwriting remained labored, each letter requiring effort, but he pressed on with determination. Lula worked steadily beside him, occasionally glancing over with approving nods.

On Darius's other side, Cassius squirmed in his chair. His pencil tapped an irregular beat on the desk. His feet swung, knocking against the legs. His page remained mostly blank, with one title scrawled across the top in uneven letters.

"George Washington crossed the Delaware in December," Cassius said, pointing at a picture. "That's why there's ice. Can you imagine being in a boat in winter? I fell in a creek once in November, and my teeth wouldn't stop chattering. Mama gave me tea with so much honey I got a stomachache."

Darius didn't respond, but his pencil paused before continuing.

"Cassius," Miss Thompson called. "Fasten your attention to your own work. This is silent work time."

"Yes, ma'am," he replied, voice too loud. "I was explaining the ice to Darius."

"Darius seems to be managing fine. Your paper is still empty."

Cassius looked down with a frown. "I don't like writing facts. It's boring. I like the stories better."

"Nevertheless, please complete the assignment," Miss Thompson said, calm but firm. "Five facts, copied neatly."

Cassius slumped, sighing loud enough for others to look up. He copied a few words of one fact, pressing hard enough to tear the page.

Darius watched from the corner of his eye, his own work slowing. He recognized the signs, the difficulty sitting still, the frustration. Familiar, though different from his own.

Five minutes passed. Cassius finished his one fact, then stopped. His foot tapped faster, and fingers drummed the desk edge. The noise grew louder until Miss Thompson looked up from her grading.

"Cassius, that's disturbing others. Please stop tapping."

"I can't help it," Cassius said. "My mind runs too quick, and my hands gotta do something."

"Try holding your pencil," Miss Thompson suggested. "Channel that energy into work."

When Cassius grasped the pencil again, he tapped it against his paper — just as loud, just as disruptive.

Miss Thompson rose and crossed to his desk. "That's still too loud. Please respect your classmates."

"But I can't think when it's too quiet!" Cassius protested. "My brain gets jumbled!"

"Perhaps you could…" Miss Thompson started to say.

"No!" he snapped, his voice sharp with anger. "I ain't doin' it! This is stupid! Why we gotta write about dead folks anyway?"

The room went still.

Every pencil froze.

Twenty-three pairs of eyes turned.

Miss Thompson's voice stayed even. "Cassius, we don't speak that way here."

"Well, I do!" He slapped both hands on the desk.

"I hate writin'!" Slam.

"I hate sittin' still!" Slam.

"I hate keepin' quiet!"

The last slam sent his pencil flying across the floor. He didn't move to pick it up.

"That's enough," Miss Thompson said. "If you need a moment, put your head down."

When Cassius glared, he crossed his arms on the desk with exaggerated drama and buried his face, shoulders hunched in sulking silence.

Miss Thompson nodded once, satisfied with the compromise, and returned to her desk. Order crept back into the room, even as eyes kept drifting toward Cassius's slumped form.

Through the entire exchange, Darius had remained still, pencil frozen above his paper. His eyes never left Cassius, tracking each movement with unusual intensity. Not fear, but concentration, as if studying a revelation.

Lula touched Darius's arm. "Keep working," she said. "Don't worry about him."

Darius resumed writing, but his gaze drifted back to Cassius, who sighed into the crook of his arm.

Minutes later, Cassius peeked out. His eyes were dry, only frustration now. He noticed Darius watching and puffed out his cheeks dramatically.

To Lula's surprise, Darius responded, setting his pencil down, placing both palms on his desk, mirroring Cassius's earlier motion.

Cassius blinked. Then he straightened, glanced at Darius's hands, then his own. Something clicked, not fully, but enough.

"I still don't want to write," he muttered, softer now.

Darius nudged his notebook forward, revealing a neat list of facts, three, but each letter carefully shaped.

"You're good at it," Cassius said, surprised. "I thought you didn't like writing either."

Darius tapped his pencil once, then pointed to the clock: It takes time.

Cassius hesitated. Then his fingers curled around the pencil again. Under his breath, inaudible to anyone but himself, Cassius breathed, "He gave me that dragon drawing. He made it special for me." His cheeks began to flush with embarrassment. "What if he thinks I talk too much or bad?"

His eyes flicked toward Darius's paper again. "I want him to think I'm smart too. Or at least trying." He bent his head and began writing. Hurried. Sloppy. But with purpose.

From her desk, Miss Thompson observed without interrupting. The shift didn't escape her. She'd expected to manage Cassius's outburst, perhaps pull him aside later. Instead, she watched one student's presence calm another in a way no redirection ever could.

When Cassius finally picked up his pencil, still sighing, still reluctant, but writing, Miss Thompson said nothing. She made a mental note of it.

As the lesson continued, Darius glanced at Cassius's paper, nodding when a new sentence appeared. Cassius moderated his fidgeting. His foot still tapped, but softer now.

When Miss Thompson announced that time was over for their assignment, Cassius had written three facts, sloppy, but done. He held up his paper to Darius with a mix of pride and defiance.

"Did enough," he said with a shrug. "That's what my old teacher always told me. 'Cassius Williams does enough to get by.'"

Darius made a slight noise, like a half breath, half laugh. His hand drifted toward the paper, not touching, but acknowledging.

The rain had thinned to a mist, and the windowpanes blurred more with light than water. Sensing the restlessness of her students, Miss Thompson allowed a quiet break, books, drawing, or rest at their desks.

She caught Darius's eye across the room. No words passed between them, but her nod said enough, recognition, approval, and maybe even thanks. In his still, unspoken way, he'd reached Cassius where her instruction could not.

She retrieved her notebook from her desk and made a note:

Cassius Williams had a spell of frustration during quiet writing today. Not oppositional, has difficulty staying still and retaining attention during independent work. He struggles to concentrate when things are too quiet. Like Darius, his mind works differently. Needs patience, not punishment. I will try more active tasks next time. - Miss T.

Darius sat, pencil racing across the page. His eyes narrowed, chasing something beyond the lines. Each mark fell in time with the raindrops outside, steady and constant. Around him, classmates read, whispered, napped, but Darius's mind was elsewhere.

When Cass slid into the seat beside him, his fingers were sticky from the half-eaten peach.

"Whatcha drawing? Crimson again? Or Azure? I like both, but Azure's got those feathers, makes him look like one of those fancy hats rich ladies wear."

He leaned in to peek, his shoulder brushing Darius's. This time, Darius didn't flinch.

It was Azure. But this version had a focus and detail even greater than before. Scales shimmered with light, feathers defined with crisp lines.

The dragon's eyes, two ice orbs, stared out from the page, intense and unblinking.

"He looks mad," Cass said, taking a bite. "Or… not mad. Worried? Like my mama when I climb too high in the pecan tree."

Darius nodded and added detail to Azure's crest. His pencil moved faster now, urgency showing in the tension of his shoulders and the furrow between his brows.

"Is he worried?" Cass asked. "Is something bad happening in Somnoria? That's where he lives, right? You told me that once."

The pencil paused.

Darius looked up, surprise flickering across his face. He hadn't realized Cass remembered that.

"Dragons gotta worry sometimes," Cass went on. "My granddaddy says that's what makes a good guardian, he says they see trouble before anyone else does."

When Darius returned to his drawing, he worked on Azure's jewels, three sapphire stones along his jaw. As he shaded the last one, something strange happened. The blue darkened, richer than any school pencil should allow. For a second, the gems flickered with a tempered pulse matching the staccato of the falling rain.

Cass dropped his peach. "Did you see that?" His voice dropped, for once a true whisper. "They lit up. The jewels, they moved like lights!"

Darius stared at the drawing. The light was gone, but he'd seen it too, a flash of real color, of life bleeding through. But his fingers still tingled, as if warmth had brushed them.

When Thomas looked up at Cass's raised voice, he asked, "What lights? Let me see."

Cass waved him over. "They were glowing! Blue. Like jewels in the sun."

Thomas studied the page, shrugged. "All I see is a pencil. Still good, though."

"They were glowing," Cass insisted, but Thomas had already turned away. Cass looked back at Darius, half-excited, half-doubtful. "You saw it, right?"

Darius tipped his head once.

"How'd you do it? Is it the pencil? Or..." Cass leaned in. "Is it magic? Magic from Somnoria?"

Darius had no answer. He traced the sapphires again. No warmth, no shine. Just different.

When the bell rang, Miss Thompson called them to geography. Maps were passed out, one between each pair. Darius and Cass shared, and Cass immediately launched into a tale about his uncle boating down the Mississippi.

"... and he says there's fish as big as dogs, but I think that's made up. Fish like that live in oceans, right?"

Darius half-listened. Something strange was happening in his right hand. He turned his palm upward. Beneath the skin, a faint pulse moved, blue scales flickering across his knuckles in ripples, then vanished.

He froze. Carefully, he opened and closed his hand.

Normal.

Cass noticed his distraction. "You all right? Cut yourself?"

Darius shook his head, eyes still fixed on his hand.

"Let me see." Cass looked at his hand and examined it. "Huh. For a second I thought I saw something sparkly. Like sunlight on water. But it's gone now." He tapped the skin. "Maybe it was light."

When Miss Thompson walked by, her shadow fell across the desk. "Finding those tributaries, boys?"

"Yes, ma'am," Cass said. "We were tracing the Missouri. My uncle says it's muddier than the Mississippi even though it's smaller. But shouldn't bigger rivers be messier? Like how my bedroom gets messier the more toys I have?"

Miss Thompson smiled. "Rivers aren't quite like bedrooms, Cass. Trace the Missouri with your fingers, please."

As she moved to the next pair, something blue caught her eye, a small feather near Darius's chair.

She picked it up.

The color was unlike any local bird, too vivid, almost metallic. She glanced at Darius, but he was examining the map.

She slipped it into her pocket.

Rain tapped steadily through the afternoon. During spelling, Cass leaned in, his voice low.

"I've been thinking about Azure and Crimson," he said. "Crimson's a drawing, right? But Azure... he's different."

Darius looked up.

"Azure visits you. In dreams or something. That's how you draw him so perfect. You've seen him, haven't you?"

Darius didn't answer, but his stillness said enough.

"I wish I had a dragon like that," Cassius said quietly. "A real one. Big and strong. Crimson would be right. We'd fight off the bad guys, help folks, maybe even be heroes."

He stopped, self-conscious. "Don't you think that's something a baby would believe?"

"No," Darius said.

"You think someone like me could have a dragon? I talk too much. Mama says I'd wear one out in a day."

Darius thought for a moment. Then shook his head. "Dragons are patient."

"Even with me?" Cass's question carried a rare vulnerability beneath his usual chatter.

Darius nodded, then returned to his spelling. But as he wrote, a strange sensation crept up his spine, not from the rain, but from something un-seen. He glanced at the window, half-expecting Azure's face beyond the glass.

Instead, he caught a flicker — it was dark, swift, larger than any bird. Gone before he could set his eyes on it. The rain shifted, striking the pane in three distinct beats. One, two, pause, three.

By day's end, the rain faded to a gentle patter. Students packed up, eager to stomp through puddles. When Cass closed his knapsack with unusual care, he made sure Crimson's drawing stayed dry.

"Tomorrow's Saturday," he said, disappointment creeping in. "No school. But... maybe I could come over? We could draw dragons. I'll bring my marbles."

Before Darius could answer, Miss Thompson approached, holding another blue plume, larger than the first, its edge tinged silver.

"I found this near your desk," she said. "It's unusual. Any idea where it came from?"

Darius stared.

It matched Azure's crest exactly.

His skin prickled. His heart skipped a beat. He'd never expected to hold one in the waking world.

Dreams were not supposed to follow him here.

But something had.

CHAPTER TWENTY-FIVE

BALANCE

Darkness enveloped the Turner house like a warm quilt. Darius lay still, listening to the last drops of rain against the roof. The day played again in fragments, the glowing sketch, the scales on his hand, and… the feathers.

His breathing slowed. One finger traced designs on his blanket. Then, without a jolt or blur, the shift came. A change in air. In light.

He opened his eyes.

He stood inside a crystal chamber buried deep in Somnoria's mountains. The walls shone softly, the light rippling across the floor like water.

Azure waited at the center, wings partly furled, tail wrapped tightly around his front claws. The jewels along his jaw pulsed in sync with the walls.

"You've made a friend," Azure said, warmth layered beneath something sharper.

Darius nodded, stepping closer. When he touched Azure's foreleg, he grounded himself in the dragon's cool scales.

"Cass," he said. "He talks a lot."

"And you don't mind?"

Darius traced the spot on his palm where scales had briefly appeared.

"He doesn't need answers."

Azure's mouth curved slightly. "No, and that's what makes it a rare kind of friendship. One speaks without needing a reply. The other listens without needing to speak. There's balance in that."

"He wants someone to listen."

"I'm glad," Azure said, sincere now. "True friendship is beautiful, especially when both friends understand each other without needing to explain."

Darius nodded, remembering the peace of drawing side by side, sharing cornbread, watching Cass laugh at his own stories.

"But I sense something else," Azure said, lowering his head. "Something about the boundaries."

When Darius lifted up his palm, he turned it over. "Light. Here. Then gone."

Azure's eyes narrowed. "And the glow in my drawing. The feathers. Miss Thompson saw them?"

Darius nodded. "She kept one."

Azure rose, wings spreading slightly. He circled Darius once, his tail leaving faint trails across the crystal floor.

"Boundaries are softening," he said. "Your friendship strengthens you. But it also creates openings, paths that didn't exist before."

"Is that bad?" Darius asked.

"Not always. But when something crosses from dream to waking without intent, it means emotion is bleeding through unchecked."

Azure paused.

"Items can slip through the veil when they're saturated with feeling, grief that won't release… or love freely given. Those emotions anchor things. Sometimes they leave behind fragments."

Darius's fingers closed.

"But it shouldn't be happening so easily," Azure continued. "Not feathers or in the drawings."

He halted in front of Darius.

"You've made huge strides. You speak. You touch. You give. But Cass's energy may overwhelm yours."

Darius kept still.

"His noise and motion are part of him," Azure said. "But don't let his pattern erase your own."

Darius thought of the afternoon. He had laughed. He had felt safe. Tired too, and stretched thin in a way he couldn't make understand.

"Balance," Darius said.

"Exactly," Azure's tone softened. "And awareness. Use your tools, breath, stillness, space. Step back if you need to."

"I will," Darius promised.

"There's more," Azure said, tone darkening. "The edges between worlds aren't meant to bleed."

The chamber dimmed, as if listening.

"My essence leaking into your world means something is changing," Azure said. "Something fundamental."

The crystals flared briefly. One. Two. Pause. Then a third. Then calm again.

"Did you notice anything unusual today," Azure asked, "besides what manifested from me?"

Darius remembered the window. The rain. The shape that crossed too fast to understand.

"Something watched," he said. "Through the rain."

Azure went still. "Describe it."

"A shadow," Darius said. "Big. Fast."

"And the rain?" Azure asked. "Did it change when the shadow passed?"

Darius's eyes widened slightly at Azure's precision. "Two beats, pause, then one beat. Then normal again."

A low rustle rumbled in Azure's chest, not quite a growl.

"There is a dragon in Somnoria who hunts openings," Azure said. "A shadow with a mind behind it."

Darius swallowed. "A bad dragon?"

Darius waited.

"The Obsidian Dragon," Azure said.

The words landed heavy.

Darius stared, confusion at first. He had never heard that name.

"What is that?" he asked.

"A force that watches for weakness," Azure said. "He watches connections. He watches for change. He watches you."

"Why?" Darius asked, a chill creeping up his backbone despite the warmth.

"Connections create strength," Azure said. "They also create vulnerability. He seeks paths he can twist to his advantage."

Azure paused. Then, quieter and reflective, as if speaking to himself:

"He was not always this. Once, he stood among the stars." Azure shook the memory away. "But that story is not for tonight."

"Shall we continue your lessons?" Azure asked, his tone lightening. "Come. Tonight, you'll shape more than you ever have."

The crystal chamber rippled and dissolved, revealing a plain of pure white sand stretching in every direction. Above, the sky was colorless, endless, with threads that were thin, gleaming as if conscious, and drifting down like slow-moving strands of starlight.

"Begin," Azure said.

Darius reached for the nearest thread. It jerked away, slippery and defiant. Another coiled toward him but dissolved before his fingers closed. Frustration burned hotter with each failure until two threads tangled themselves midair, collapsing into a knotted mess around his wrists.

"They hate me," he muttered as he struck his thigh with his fist in frustration.

When Azure bent low, his talon sliced the knot apart without harming the strands. "They don't hate. They mirror. Show them calm, and they will hold still."

Darius took a single deep breath and closed his eyes. When he opened them, the threads swayed lazily, waiting. He lifted his hands. This time, they settled into his palms like weightless ribbons.

He twisted once, and a button formed, smooth and perfect. He shaped another into a spool. It hovered.

Azure's eyes glinted. "Good. Again."

His fingers worked quicker now, pictures rising in his head before the threads brushed his skin as confidence grew. He shaped a button, then another. A spool followed, then a feather so light it almost floated from his palm. Last came a cube that turned with control, and was solid under his touch.

Then, blindly, he reached higher, gathering a cluster of threads at once. They wove under his hands, braiding and spiraling until they took shape: a tiny model of Azure himself, silver-flecked wings outstretched, and perfect in miniature. It floated between them, glowing softly.

Darius stared, breath caught. "I made that."

Azure's tail swept the sand in a single arc. "Not just made. You held it stable. That is balance."

The miniature dragon dissolved into light, scattering into the air like sparks. Darius's grin broke wide and unguarded.

"Tomorrow," Azure said, "we build more."

Darius lay still in sleep, one hand tight on his blue blanket, the other open on his chest. For a heartbeat, three sapphire sparks pulsed under his skin, then faded. The room looked unchanged, but the boundary between dream and waking pressed closer with each breath.

And far beyond the white sands of Somnoria, in the waking world, a shadow moved past Cass's window, pausing, as if it too had felt the breakthrough.

Chapter Twenty-Six

Pyrrhos

In the Williams home that evening, Cass burrowed into bed, the quilt pulled to his chin as rain tapped his window.

His mind raced: Darius's drawing, the blue feathers, the promise of Saturday adventures. Sleep crept over him like a tide, not in Darius's orderly way, but in fits and starts. Thoughts tumbled until they became something else. The boundary between waking and dreaming blurred, then vanished.

Cass was running.

A field spread beneath his feet, grass flashing green, then purple, then blue in three strides. The ground felt springy, like it wanted him to keep moving.

Trees burst upward, full grown in seconds. Their branches sagging with candy. Cass laughed and plucked a chocolate peach, its sweetness sticky on his fingers.

"Best dream ever!" he shouted.

The field stretched, then compressed, the landscape shifting faster than the view from the trolley. His bedroom flashed past and dissolved into a playground with cloud-high swings. Cass jumped on one, pumping until he soared.

"Bet you can't swing higher than me!" a voice called.

Cass looked around, confused to hear a voice in his dream, but he answered it anyway. "No, you can't."

"Course I can," Rex said, his mouth moving. "Dogs are better at everything."

Rex bounded across the grass, no longer a medium brown dog but massive as a pony, white chest spot now a perfect star. He leaped onto the other swing, hind legs somehow gripping the seat.

Cass nearly fell off the swing seeing his dog larger than himself and talking. "You can talk!"

"In dreams." Rex's tail wagged as he swung. "We talk in the real world too, but humans don't listen."

"What do dogs talk about?"

"Smells. Food. Running. Chasing chickens." Rex grinned. "Belly rubs. Not boring stuff like school."

The swings dissolved beneath them.

They floated to the ground. The playground became Cass's backyard, then a field of chiming flowers.

Rex bounded through them, his steps ringing musical notes. "Dogs don't worry about tomorrow or yesterday. Just now."

"But dogs can't draw dragons," Cass said. "Or go to school."

"Who needs school when one fence post holds a thousand stories?" Rex asked. "Every dog knows the secret paths."

"What secret paths?"

The question hung unanswered.

Rex vanished like mist. His final bark echoed.

The flowers wilted and became stepping stones over a river of molten gold. Cass hesitated, then stepped onto the first.

"Don't be afraid," a voice called from the far bank. "The river can't hurt you here."

Cass squinted.

A shape emerged. Large. Winged. Brilliant. Each step brought it into focus. A dragon, red as apples in morning light.

Not red, but every red. Deep crimson, bright cherry, rubies along brow and spine. Its wings cast half the riverbank in shadow, membranes luminescent like stained glass.

"Crimson?" Cass said. It was Darius's drawing, but a real breathing dragon.

The dragon chuckled like distant thunder. "Close. I am Pyrrhos."

Cass approached without fear. "You look like the dragon Darius drew! Even the curly tail. Are you real? Or a dream?"

"Both." Pyrrhos lowered his head. Eyes copper with black flecks. "I am your Dreamers' Dragon."

"Like Azure?" Cass bounced. "I've got my own dragon! Wait till I tell Darius!"

Pyrrhos nodded, scales shifting like fire. "Every true dreamer has a dragon. Some take longer to find their dreamers."

"But why me?" Cass touched his snout. It was warm and solid. "Darius is special. I'm just regular."

"There's no such thing," Pyrrhos said. "You see the world in motion. In color. In constant possibilities. Your mind never rests. That is your gift."

The riverbank melted into a mountain path spiraling upward. Crystal spires rose, laced with red and gold.

"Somnoria?" Cass asked.

"A part of it," Pyrrhos said. "Each dreamer sees it differently. Darius sees patterns and colors. You see change."

They ascended together. Cass peppered Pyrrhos with nonstop questions.

"Do you breathe fire? Fight bad dragons? Know Azure? Can I ride on your back? Do all dragons have jewels?"

Pyrrhos answered each with brief amusement. Yes, to fire. Yes, I know of Azure. Jewels marked all Dreamers' Dragons.

"So, rubies are yours," Cass said, pointing to the gems.

"Yes."

Pyrrhos stopped at a plateau.

Below them lay Cass's house, school, and dreamlike oddities, floating islands, rivers flowing up, forests with walking trees.

"This is amazing!" Cass spun, trying to see it all. "Can we come here every night?"

"When you're ready. Dream-walking takes practice."

Cass frowned. "But I'm here now."

"Yes, I brought you here." Pyrrhos touched his forehead. "Next time, you must find the way."

The dream thinned.

Colors faded.

Morning light pressed at the veil.

"I think I'm waking up," Cass said, disappointment clear in his voice.

"Remember what you've seen," Pyrrhos said, his form beginning to blur. "And Cass, dragons choose their dreamers carefully. Never doubt that you were chosen for a reason."

The dream dissolved completely, red scales and crystal spires giving way to the familiar ceiling of Cass's bedroom. Outside, birds announced the arrival of Saturday morning, but unlike most weekends Cass didn't immediately jump from bed.

He lay still, holding the dream close, afraid it might slip away if he moved too quickly.

"Pyrrhos," Cass said, testing the name in the waking air.

It sat right on his tongue, solid and real as the morning itself.

Monday arrived with clear skies and the promise of warmth. Students gathered in the schoolyard, trading weekend stories and comparing scraped knees from Saturday adventures. When Cass arrived earlier than usual, he scanned the yard until he spotted Darius entering with Lula.

He bolted across the dirt, narrowly avoiding a jump rope game and abandoning a conversation with Thomas. His face gleamed with the unmistakable light of someone carrying a secret too big to keep.

"Darius! Darius!" Cass skidded to a stop, dust blooming around his shoes. "I have to tell you something amazing! You won't believe it but it's true, I swear on Rex's tail!"

Lula stepped closer to her brother, brushing his elbow in the protective gesture she'd perfected over years. "Good morning to you too, Cass."

Cass barely registered her. "I need to talk to Darius. It's important. More important than arithmetic or spelling or even lunch."

Darius watched him steadily, not retreating from his energy but not moving toward it either. His satchel hung at his side, notebook safely tucked inside.

"Can we go sit by the tree?" Cass could barely contain his energy, lowering his voice to what he considered a whisper. "It's private. It's about dragons."

Darius glanced at Lula.

"Go on," she said. Her smile lingered. "I'll see you inside."

Cass didn't wait. He grabbed Darius's sleeve and pulled him toward the old tree in the schoolyard corner.

"I had a dream," Cass began the moment they sat. "Not a regular dream with flying or showing up to school without pants, a real dream. Like yours."

Darius tilted his head.

"I met my dragon," Cass said, voice thrumming with excitement. "His name is Pyrrhos. He's red, not one red, but all the reds you can think of, like melted crayons that never mix."

Darius's eyes squinted in a questioning look.

"He has rubies on his back like Azure's sapphires! His eyes are deep amber. He breathes fire. He took me to Somnoria, but not like you said. Pyrrhos said dreamers see it differently. Mine had candy trees and rivers that went upside down and…"

"Slow," Darius murmured.

Cass stopped. Drew in a breath. "Sorry. I'm so excited I could burst."

He tried again. "Pyrrhos said I'm a true dreamer. Like you. That's why we're friends, because we both have dragons."

Darius looked down, then back at Cass. Confusion crossed his face. "How?"

Cass blinked. "How did I meet him? I went to sleep and…"

"No." Darius shook his head. "How you? Dreamers are… rare."

"That's what I asked him!" Cass said. "Pyrrhos said there's no such thing as being regular. He said my mind never stops, and that's my gift. Not like yours. Different."

Darius tapped his knee, one, two, three. After a moment, he spoke again. "Don't tell."

"Don't tell what? About Pyrrhos?"

Darius nodded. "Our secret. Dragons… private."

"But why? Wouldn't everyone want to know dragons are real? We could tell Miss Thompson…"

"No." Darius's voice was firm. "Only us. Promise."

Across the yard, Lula watched the two boys huddled beneath the tree. Cass's hands moved in animated gestures while Darius listened with rare attention.

Something twisted in her chest, not quite jealousy, not quite worry, but something tangled.

For years, she'd been Darius's bridge to the world.

Now Cass, with all his chatter and energy, had carved out his own space beside him.

"What are they always whispering about?" asked a girl with braids.

"Dragons," Lula said honestly. "Cass thinks they're real."

The girl giggled and moved on, satisfied. But Lula knew better. She'd seen the drawings. The blue feathers. The change in her brother.

The bell rang.

Cass jumped up, offering Darius a hand, which her brother accepted. Another small step.

Inside, students settled into their seats. Lula slid in beside Darius. Cass dropped into the seat on Darius's other side.

"I forgot to tell you the best part," Cass said. "Rex was in my dream too, and he could talk! He said dogs are smarter than people because they don't worry about silly things like school."

"Cass," Miss Thompson called without turning. "Is there something you'd like to share with the class?"

"No, ma'am." Cass straightened. "Telling Darius about my dog."

"Perhaps save pet stories for recess?"

"Yes, ma'am."

A minute passed before Cass leaned toward Darius again. "Do you think Azure and Pyrrhos know each other? Pyrrhos said he knew of Azure? They both live in Somnoria, right?"

Lula cleared her throat.

Cass glanced at her. "Sorry."

It lasted seconds.

"But for true," he whispered. "Do they?"

Darius shrugged, then gave the faintest nod.

"Can you ask Azure about Pyrrhos tonight?" Cass said. "I'll ask Pyrrhos about Azure. Then we can compare!"

Darius nodded again, the corners of his mouth lifting ever so slightly.

Lula pressed harder with her pencil until the lead snapped.

Both boys looked over, but her eyes stayed on the broken tip.

"Are you all right?" Cass asked.

"Fine," she said sharply. "Trying to pay attention to the teacher. Like we're supposed to."

Cass quieted, but by the time Miss Thompson called them to the front for reading groups, he was whispering again.

"What if someday we dream at the same time and meet up in Somnoria? Wouldn't that be amazing? We could see each other's dragons and…"

"Cass Williams," Miss Thompson cut in. "Please join your reading group."

"Yes, ma'am. Sorry, ma'am." Cass stood, but not before whispering, "Let's talk more at lunch."

As he bounded to the front, Lula noticed her brother watching him, not with sibling interest, but with understanding.

She'd seen that look before.

It had always been hers.

Now it belonged to someone else.

"You like him a lot," she said.

Darius nodded, eyes still on Cass.

"Do you think his dragon is real?" she asked. "Like Azure?"

When Darius turned to her, surprised, he studied her face, then answered, "Ask Azure."

Those two words said more than a full explanation.

Lula's expression softened. "I don't want you to get hurt."

Darius touched her hand. "Won't."

His certainty calmed her.

That evening, Miss Thompson sat at her desk long after the sun set behind the trees. She opened a blank sheet of paper and stared at it.

Your boy sees the world differently, she wrote. I think we need that.

She didn't sign it. Didn't seal it. Folded it in half and slid it into the back of her drawer, next to the attendance sheet and a broken pencil sharpener.

Maybe someday she'd send it.

But not yet.

Sleep claimed Darius quickly that night.

Cass's excited stories drifted through his thoughts as his mind slipped beneath the surface of waking. But the transition was different. Sharper. More deliberate.

When he opened his eyes, he stood in a chamber he'd never seen before.

Walls of shifting blue stone curved overhead like frozen waves. Veins of crystal threaded through the rock, carrying light that pulsed and flowed, illuminating a circular space that felt both newly formed and impossibly old.

At the center hung thousands of delicate threads.

200

They stretched from ceiling to floor, drifting as if stirred by unseen currents. Some blazed like stars. Others flickered faintly. Many were nearly invisible unless the light caught them right.

Darius moved toward them, then paused.

"You may touch them," Azure said.

The dragon appeared at the far edge of the chamber, moving through the threads without disturbing a single strand. When he reached Darius, his eyes asked a question he already knew the answer to.

"Something troubles you."

Darius nodded, reaching for Azure's foreleg. "Cass has a dragon."

"Tell me."

"His name is Pyrrhos. Red with rubies. Like my drawing, but real."

"When did this happen?"

"Saturday night. First dream. Pyrrhos said Cass is a true dreamer."

Azure's tail swept across the floor once. He turned toward the threads. "Come."

They stopped in front of a thread blazing sapphire blue.

"Yours," Azure said.

It vibrated softly, singing in a frequency that hummed beneath his ribs.

Then Azure moved to a second thread, dull amber.

"Cass Williams."

Darius frowned. "It's not red."

"No." Azure's voice stayed gentle. "If Pyrrhos truly bonded with him, it would burn crimson. This is scarcely brighter than before you met. Still the thread of a child without a dragon."

"But he saw Pyrrhos," Darius said. "In a dream."

"He saw something," Azure said. "Whether Cass is truly a dreamer or Pyrrhos is his Dreamers' Dragon remains to be seen."

Darius rocked on his heels. "He wasn't lying."

"I believe him," Azure said. "But not everything in dreams is what it seems."

They moved deeper into the forest of threads.

Bright ones, dim ones, some entirely dark.

"At any moment," Azure said, his gaze distant, "no more than a thousand children across all lands carry the bond. Most sleep through their chance. Some touch it once and forget. Fewer remember. Fewer still keep the connection as they grow."

"Like me?"

"Your thread shines differently." Azure looked at him. "There are dreamers. And there are dreamers of consequence."

The weight of that distinction settled in the air.

"Cass may be a dreamer," Azure continued. "His mind is quick. Tuned differently than yours. But the timing... the dragon naming himself after your drawing…"

"Coincidence?" Darius asked.

Azure's wings shifted. Nearby threads swayed.

"There are no coincidences in dreams," he said. "Merely patterns we haven't yet recognized."

"Is Pyrrhos real?"

Azure did not answer at once.

Darius walked among the threads, stopping occasionally to examine ones that caught his eye. A brilliant green one that twisted in spirals. A silver one that split into three halfway down. A cluster of seven that seemed to pulse in unison.

Then he stopped.

Before him hung a thread darker than the others. It did not radiate light. It absorbed it, creating a small void in the luminous forest.

"Don't touch that one," Azure said sharply, moving fast.

Darius withdrew his hand.

"The Obsidian Dragon?" Darius asked.

"His influence grows," Azure said. "Which brings me back to your friend. If Cass truly met Pyrrhos, then his gift has awakened at a precarious time. If what he met was not Pyrrhos —"

"Then what was it?"

"A deception," Azure said. "A test. Or a trap."

Darius's hands lifted toward his chest, fingers fluttering as his mind worked through the implications.

"Those without a full bond are vulnerable," Azure continued. "He seeks entry points."

"Should I tell Cass?" Darius asked.

"Not yet," Azure said. "First, we must be certain."

"And if Pyrrhos isn't real?"

"Then we protect him."

There was no hesitation in Azure's voice.

Darius's shoulders loosened.

Light thinned above them. Morning pressed at the edges of the chamber.

"Before the dream lifts," Azure said, "watch."

He reached into the space between them, talons barely grazing two drifting threads. With a slow, deliberate motion, he wove them together, each twist forming a tiny arch. The arches linked into a tight bridge no wider than Darius's hand.

"Shape guides purpose. A bridge connects. A net captures. A vessel carries. Choose what you wish to make."

Darius hesitated, then extended both hands.

Two threads floated near, gliding like ribbons on a breeze.

He steadied his breath, remembering the tangled knots from before.

This time, he didn't grab, he waited.

The first thread curved toward his palm. He coaxed it to hover.

The second wavered, flickering at the edges, but he adjusted the tilt of his hand as if tuning an invisible string until it stilled.

He began to weave them, looping each strand over and under until a small pouch took shape in the air. Its edges were uneven, but it rested, warm and weightless in his hands.

Darius glanced around, then spotted a tiny dream-moth drifting past, its wings painted in shifting colors. He lowered the pouch beneath it, and the moth settled inside as if the light itself were a perch.

For a few breaths, the creature rested there, safe within his weaving.

Azure watched. "Good. You made something that contains."

Darius grinned, watching as the moth lifted free and the pouch unraveled into pale light.

"Tomorrow," Azure said, "you'll try again. Stronger patterns. Tighter concentration."

"Our time grows short," Azure added, his gaze drifting toward the horizon. "Remember, Darius, friendship is a powerful thing, but it also creates connections that others may use. Be watchful."

Darius nodded, the shape of the braid still echoing in his fingers. His thoughts flickered to Cass — loud, impatient, loyal.

Different, but not so different.

Before the dream released them, Azure turned, his gaze narrowing.

Cassius's thread, normally amber and dim — surged.

Not wildly. Not brilliantly.

But in clarity.

For one brief instant, it burned with the red of conviction, pure and precise, before dimming again to its usual flickering hue.

A coincidence, perhaps.

Or the beginning of a deceptive design.

When Darius opened his eyes, the ceiling above him yielded no mystery, but his hands still remembered the rhythm.

Not the sea of tangled dream threads.

But the memory of that single braid. It was simple, and was brilliantly his.

And for the first time, he believed he might learn to shape this world, one strand at a time.

CHAPTER TWENTY-SEVEN
DISTRACTION

Sunrise painted the schoolyard in shades of honey-gold as students filtered through the yard before the school. Darius stood at the entrance, his eyes scanning the crowd with unusual intent. His fingers tapped against his satchel, one, two, three, while Lula watched with interest. He had never hurried to school before, had never looked forward to the noise of all the children's chatting and the chaos that came with it. But today, his gaze fixed on every approaching figure, searching for the familiar round face and boundless energy of Cassius Williams.

"He'll be here soon," Lula said, shifting her books to her other arm. "Cassius is always late."

Darius nodded but didn't move from his post. When Cassius finally appeared, racing through the entrance with his satchel bouncing against his hip and one shoelace trailing in the dust, Darius's face transformed. The change was subtle, a slight lifting at the edges of his lips, a brightening in his eyes, but to Lula, who had studied her brother's expressions for years, it might as well have been a shout of joy.

"Darius! Lula!" Cassius skidded to a halt before them. "Sorry I'm late! Rex got into the neighbor's garbage again and Mama made me help clean it up before school, which isn't fair because it wasn't my fault, but then I found this cool bottle cap in the trash and…" He thrust his hand forward, revealing a flattened metal cap with faded red paint. "Look! It's almost the same color as Pyrrhos!"

Darius leaned closer, examining the cap with the same attention to detail he applied to his drawings.

"Pyrrhos took me to this crystal cave last night," Cassius continued as they walked toward the schoolhouse. "The whole place shined red, and there were these tiny creatures that looked like fireflies but they were shaped like tiny dragons, dragon-flies, get it? They followed me everywhere, landing on my shoulders and singing these songs that rang like church bells but underwater."

Lula rolled her eyes. "That's not how dragons work."

"How would you know?" Cassius challenged. "You don't have one."

"Neither do you," she replied. "Not a real one, anyway."

When Darius's hand found Cassius's sleeve, a light touch silenced both of them. His eyes met Lula's, a silent request for peace.

Over the past weeks, Darius had done more than anyone expected. He still didn't speak often, but he'd begun taking part, showing Miss Thompson more and more answers on his slate, solving number patterns faster than the other students, even nodding when she spoke to him directly. Cassius's constant chatter seemed to anchor him rather than overwhelm. So when Miss Thompson paused by his desk earlier that morning and quietly asked if he'd like to try reading aloud today, he surprised them both by giving the faintest nod.

In the classroom, Miss Thompson moved quietly across the front, writing out the day's lessons on the blackboard while humming a slow, familiar tune, something Darius had heard her sing during morning clean-up. The rhythm settled him, low and predictable. But today, he watched Cassius, who couldn't seem to stay still. Every few seconds,

Cassius leaned over to whisper more about his dream, tapped his pencil against the desk, or shifted in his seat with a creak that snapped Darius's attention sideways.

"Darius," Miss Thompson called, her voice cutting through his distraction. "Would you please read the first sentence for us?"

All the children in the classroom looked toward him. In the past, such attention would have sent him retreating into silence, eyes fixed on his desk. Today, he glanced at Cassius, who gave him an encouraging nod.

"The... first... set...set...settlers... came..." Darius began, his voice barely audible. The words blurred on the page, his concentration fracturing under the combined pressure of the stares and Cassius's restless energy beside him.

"If you can speak a little louder, please, so everyone can hear," Miss Thompson prompted.

Darius tried again, but the sentence tangled in his throat. Sweat beaded along his hairline. When Cassius reached under the desk and tapped Darius's knee three times, a pattern, a lifeline, Darius seized it, his breathing steadying.

"The first settlers... came to the river... valley in spring," he managed, the words emerging slowly but surely. He stopped, exhausted by the effort.

"Thank you, Darius," Miss Thompson said. "Thomas, please continue."

As Thomas took over the reading, Miss Thompson observed Darius with growing concern. For weeks, his progress had been slow, with small steps, but forward. Today, something appeared different. His attention splintered every time Cassius moved or whispered, yet he seemed drawn to these distractions rather than disturbed by them.

During arithmetic, a subject where Darius typically excelled, he stared at his slate without making a single mark. Cassius worked beside him, narrating his thought process in a constant stream of whispers.

"... and if you add seven plus four, that's eleven, then carry the one, except I always forget to carry it, which is why I got in trouble last week when Mrs. Peterson asked me to add up how many eggs we collected and I said seventeen when it was twenty-seven, and she thought I was stealing eggs!"

Darius listened, pencil forgotten in his hand. When Miss Thompson collected their work, his slate remained blank. She paused at his desk, studying him.

"Are you feeling well, Darius?"

He nodded, but his eyes strayed back to Cassius, who was now attempting to balance his pencil on his nose.

At lunch, they sat beneath the oak tree, Lula joining a group of girls nearby but keeping her brother within sight. When Cassius unwrapped his food with animated motions, he launched immediately into a story about how his cousin once found a frog in his lunch pail.

"...and he screamed so loud the teacher thought he was dying, but it was this tiny frog no bigger than my thumb, and then the frog jumped right onto Sally Jefferson's head and she screamed even louder and knocked over her milk, and it went all over Principal Wright's shoes!"

Darius stared at Cassius, the image building in his mind. His lips twitched. Then, without warning, something bubbled up from his chest, a laugh, rusty and unpracticed, but genuine. It spilled into the air between them, startling both boys into momentary silence.

"You laughed!" Cassius exclaimed, his face splitting into a wide grin. "You laughed!"

Darius pressed his fingers to his mouth, as surprised by the utterance as Cassius was.

"Do it again!" Cassius urged. "It sounds like music!"

From across the yard, Miss Thompson paused in her conversation with another teacher. The note of Darius's laughter carried to her, unfamiliar enough that it took her a moment to identify its source. Her expression softened, torn between joy at this breakthrough and concern for his academic regression.

When afternoon lessons began, Darius's distraction deepened. During a pattern recognition exercise, normally his strongest subject, he matched triangles with circles and squares with stars, basic errors that drew furrowed brows from Miss Thompson. Beside him, Cassius worked with unusual concentration, his tongue caught between his teeth.

"I'm doing it like you showed me," Cassius whispered. "See it all at once, not piece by piece."

Darius nodded, but the sequences that had always come so naturally to him now fractured beneath Cassius's constant movement and chatter. Yet he didn't mind. The numbers would return tomorrow, but this, this warm feeling of having someone who didn't need him to be anything other than himself, this was new. This was worth protecting.

As the afternoon of school work came to an end, Darius packed his satchel with careful movements. For once, his mind didn't drift to home and the quiet sanctuary of his window. Instead, he felt a pull toward tomorrow, toward the next story Cassius would tell, the next adventure they would share. School had transformed from a necessary ordeal into the place where his friend waited.

"See you tomorrow?" Cassius asked, already knowing the answer.

Darius nodded, his expression clear and certain.

For the first time, the noise and disorder of school were tied to something he wanted. Cass would be there tomorrow. That made the rest of it easier to bear.

***

The cavern opened like a cut through stone. Its walls drank up every trace of light, leaving scraps of reflection twisting across the black glass. When Pyrrhos approached the entrance, his red scales dulled, his ruby jewels quivering with a hesitant, uneven flow. He paused at the threshold, gathering courage that threatened to abandon him with each shuddering breath.

"Enter," commanded a voice from within, deep as forgotten wells and cold as starless nights.

Pyrrhos obeyed, wings pressed tight against his body as he navigated the narrowing passage. The temperature dropped with each step, frost forming along his scales despite the fire that burned within all dragons of his lineage. When the cavern finally opened before him, the space seemed to expand endlessly, defying the physical boundaries of Somnoria itself.

In the center, coiled in darkness, waited the Obsidian Dragon. Unlike Pyrrhos, whose form remained solid and defined even in the dream realm, the dark dragon shifted constantly, edges blurred into shadow, then sharpened, then faded again. Yet his eyes stayed fixed, darker than the scales around them, pulling at Pyrrhos's gaze like gravity.

"You're late," the darkness said, his voice causing tiny cracks to spiderweb across the floor. "I trust you bring something of value."

Pyrrhos lowered his head in deference. "The children's friendship grows stronger each day. They speak constantly of dreams and dragons."

"And does the quiet one, Darius, suspect anything about your... authenticity?"

"He questions," Pyrrhos said, then hesitated. "Cassius believes wholeheartedly. But Azure may have doubts. He's shown Darius the Hall of Threads."

When the Obsidian Dragon uncoiled, stretching to his full height, shadows writhed around his massive form. His movement released a scent like burning metal. "The Hall of Threads?" Interest flickered across his features. "Azure moves faster than expected with this one."

"Darius differs from other dreamers," Pyrrhos ventured. "His mind works differently than most humans. He sees things others miss."

"Different," the shadow repeated, the word curling through his teeth like smoke. "So that's why Azure clings to a child who can barely form a sentence? The High Priest and Priestess always did favor the broken."

When Pyrrhos flinched, his tail tightened beneath him. "Darius isn't broken. He's kind. Stronger than he seems."

The Obsidian Dragon tilted his head, eyes narrowing, not with fear, but fascination.

"Strange, what draws their favor," he murmured, stepping forward. Frost bloomed in the air with each breath. "A quiet boy, unnoticed... yet the threads bend around him. Curious."

The surrounding darkness twisted like a living thing, pressing in close.

"He's an unusual dreamer. A kind that deserves watching."

A tremor ran through Pyrrhos's wings. "What would you have me do? Cassius trusts me completely."

"Continue as you have been. Encourage friendship. Let Cassius speak endlessly of his dreams with you." The Obsidian Dragon's claws scraped against the obsidian floor, leaving gouges that sealed themselves moments later. "But I want more. I want you to arrange a shared dreamscape."

"A shared dreamscape?" Pyrrhos's jewels flickered with alarm. "That's risky. Shared dreamscapes are rare."

"They are rare because shared dreams require connection between the dreamers. Their friendship creates a bond to make it possible. I want to know what Azure is teaching the boy. What patterns he's showing him. What secrets of Somnoria he's revealing."

"But the Luminaries…"

"Are not here," the Obsidian Dragon cut him off. "They abandoned Somnoria to its fate long ago, leaving us to guard the dream realms without guidance. Or have you forgotten?"

Pyrrhos lowered his gaze. He hadn't forgotten. The High Priest and Priestess had withdrawn from active guidance centuries ago, their direct interventions becoming increasingly rare. In that absence, the Obsidian Dragon's influence had grown, his whispers reaching even the most loyal Dreamers' Dragons in moments of doubt.

The Obsidian Dragon's claws scraped the floor, sealing and reopening the gouges in endless repetition. "The Luminaries call it choice. Beautiful word, isn't it? They gave us choice, then vanished to watch us stumble."

Pyrrhos shifted. "They trust us to —"

"Trust?" The word cracked like splitting stone. "I offer what the Luminaries never could — certainty."

"The boy has been promised greatness by Azure," the Obsidian Dragon continued, his tone shifting to something almost contemplative. "A dreamer of consequence, he called him. Yet all I see is a human child who flinches at loud noises and can't form simple sentences."

"The blue in his eyes…"

"Means nothing without the mind to wield it," the Obsidian Dragon dismissed. "Azure has always seen potential where none exists. It's his greatest weakness."

The cavern temperature dropped further. Frost formed along Pyrrhos's jaw, cracking when he spoke. "And if I refuse?"

The Obsidian Dragon didn't answer immediately. He circled Pyrrhos once, shadows trailing from his form like ink in water. When he spoke again, his voice carried neither threat nor anger, just certainty.

"Then Cassius loses his dragon forever. The connection severs. The dreams end. Is that what you want for your dreamer? To leave him alone in the darkness of ordinary sleep while Darius soars through worlds beyond imagination?"

The question struck Pyrrhos where he was most vulnerable. In the brief time since bonding with Cassius, he'd grown genuinely fond of the boy's boundless enthusiasm, his endless questions, his capacity for wonder. To abandon him now would be cruel, perhaps crueler than the deception itself.

"I'll do as you ask," Pyrrhos conceded, his jewels dimming to dull embers.

"Good." The Obsidian Dragon retreated to the center of the cavern. "Watch. Learn. Report. Do not let Azure see your observations."

"And Cassius? What should I tell him?"

"The truth, of course." A sound like breaking glass escaped the Obsidian Dragon, a laugh, though no humor reached his eyes. "Tell him you want to meet his friend's dragon. Children love nothing more than introducing their special things to each other."

Pyrrhos nodded, already constructing the suggestion he would plant in Cassius's next dream. The guilt weighed on him, a physical presence pressing against his wings.

"You may go," the Obsidian Dragon dismissed him. "And Pyrrhos, your hesitation dishonors you. You are a Dreamers' Dragon. Act like one."

The words followed Pyrrhos as he retreated through the twisting passages, his form growing dimmer with each step. Outside the cavern,

Somnoria waited, crystal spires catching dream-light, fields stretching toward distant mountains, rivers flowing with memories instead of water. Its beauty deepened his shame.

He had been a true Dreamers' Dragon once, chosen by the Luminaries, dedicated to guiding dreamers through the realm of possibility. Now he served two masters, the light he was born to and the darkness that had found his weakness.

As Pyrrhos took flight, shadows curled at the edges of his wings, tendrils of the Obsidian Dragon's influence stretching toward the dreams of a boy with sapphire eyes who slept, unaware that his friendship had become a battleground between forces older than human understanding.

Chapter Twenty-Eight

Candy

Darius slipped into sleep with the same careful precision that marked his waking hours. His breath slowed, deepened, rising and falling beneath the blue blanket pulled to his chin. But tonight, the usual path to Azure's realm, the beautiful crystal spires and eternal twilight sky, did not unfold. Instead, unfamiliar colors bled through the normal order of Darius's dreams, and the scent of sugar pulled him forward like a hand reaching from another dream. Something was different. Someone else was here. A connection, a link, unseen but unmistakable, and it led to Cassius.

He blinked and stood before a door made of peppermint sticks tied with licorice ribbons. It swung open without touch, releasing a wave of sweet-scented air that tickled his nose and made his mouth water. Inside, a candy shop stretched impossibly deep, filled with shelves stacked with jars of sweets, counters piled with perfect fudge squares, and the ceiling dripping chocolate stalactites that somehow never fell.

Rivers of caramel wound through the floor, steaming as they bubbled around rock candy formations. Jellybeans filled barrels bigger than bathtubs, their colors swirled in shapes no factory would attempt. Display cases held elaborate sugar sculptures, castles, dragons, and ships with spun-sugar sails that caught light from nowhere and everywhere.

"Darius! You made it!"

Cass popped up from behind a counter, grinning wide, fingers sticky with some bright blue confection. "I was waiting for you!"

Darius stepped forward, brushing his fingers against a lollipop taller than himself. It felt solid, real, despite the impossibility of the place.

"It's all free," Cass declared, arms spread. "I checked. No grown-ups, candy everywhere!"

He plucked a red lollipop and lifted it out. "Try one. They taste exactly how you want them to taste."

Darius hesitated, then accepted. The candy touched his tongue and became the perfect blend of cherry and his mama's blueberry pie.

"Good, right?" Cass bounced on his toes. "I had one that tasted like Christmas morning, then another like my mama's Sunday fried chicken. Candy shouldn't taste like chicken, but it was amazing!"

The shop's absurdity should have unsettled Darius, triggered his need for order, but dream-logic wrapped around him like his blue blanket and brought order to the chaos surrounding him. When Cass grabbed his wrist and tugged him toward the back, he called, "Look what I found!"

He pointed at barrels of jellybeans, each big enough to swim in. "I've been jumping in them like swimming holes!"

Without waiting, Cass climbed a barrel filled with pink, red, and purple beans. He balanced dramatically, then jumped in like a stone dropped in a well, vanishing beneath the candy. Seconds later, his head popped up, jellybeans clinging to his hair and pajama collar.

"Come on, D! It doesn't hurt at all!"

Darius stepped closer, peering over the rim. He traced the wood grain, counting the rings while calculating if the barrel could hold them both.

"They're not gonna run out," Cass said. "I tried eating to the bottom. They keep appearing. Dream candy, remember?"

Something about that word, dream, clicked. This wasn't his usual dream. It was shared. Linked to Cass. Instead of confusion, curiosity bloomed. He climbed the rungs in a slow, deliberate motion until he stood at the edge.

"Jump!" Cass called, swimming backward in a lazy circle.

Darius closed his eyes. Counted. One. Two. Three. He stepped into empty air. The jellybeans cushioned his fall, surrounding him with clicking, candy-colored spheres. He sank, then bobbed to the surface. Cass waited, grinning.

"Isn't it the best?"

Cass flung a handful of beans into the air. They froze mid-fall, then reshaped into a floating dragon. "You can make them do whatever you want. It's your dream too."

When Darius raised a hand, he looked at a cluster of blue jellybeans. They trembled, lifted, and swirled into Azure's eye, icy iris, vertical pupil, perfect in every detail. The floating eye blinked, then collapsed back into candy.

"That's so cool!" Cass clapped, scattering jellybeans everywhere. "Let's try the chocolate fountain next!"

They explored for what felt like hours, or minutes. Dream-time shifted, stretched, then compressed. They dipped fingers in liquid butterscotch. Built marshmallow towers to the ceiling, then knocked them down giggling.

Behind the counter, Cass pulled out aprons and oversized bow ties.

"Let's play store," he said, tying a big apron over Darius's shoulders. "I'll be the candy maker, and you be the shopkeeper."

Darius nodded and stepped behind the register. The keys clicked beneath his fingers, numbers appearing in a sequence that made no sense, but it made him happy.

"Welcome to Sweet Dreams Candy Shoppe," Cass announced in a deep, grown-up voice. "Where all your sugar wishes come true! I'm making fresh fudge for our most distinguished customers!"

He pantomimed stirring a huge pot, wiping imaginary sweat from his brow.

"It's hot work, making the world's best fudge! Shopkeeper, please help the lady with the purple hat!"

Darius looked up. The shop had filled with shadowy, transparent customers, dream-figures, not quite solid, moving purposefully among displays. A woman-shaped blur with the hint of a purple hat approached the counter.

Without planning, words rose to his lips.

"What would you like today?" he asked, his voice clear and confident in a way it never was awake.

"Two pounds of chocolate bonbons and a stick of rock candy for my son," said the shadow-woman, her voice like rustling paper.

Darius's hands moved automatically, filling a bag, pressing buttons on the register.

"That's fifty-three cents," he declared.

She handed over coins that clinked against the counter but left no marks on the sugar-dusted surface. Darius placed the bag in her transparent hands, and she drifted away, pleased.

"You're a natural!" Cass grinned, dropping his adult voice. "These customers are spending a fortune!"

More shadows approached. Darius served them all, speaking full sentences without effort or fear. A lightness built in his chest, pressure rising until it burst out as laughter, sudden, loud, unrestrained. Startled, he laughed again, harder. Joy broke through the careful restraint he wore like armor.

Cass froze, eyes wide, then joined in. Their laughter echoed through the candy shop, sending ripples through rivers of caramel.

"That's the best sound ever," Cass gasped. "Better than candy."

Darius couldn't stop. Years of quiet joy poured out in waves, his body shaking, tears welling in his eyes and rolling down his cheeks. In the waking realm, the place without dragons, this kind of release would have frightened him. But here, surrounded by impossible sweets and a friend who asked nothing, laughter was freedom.

"We should do this every night," Cass said, climbing onto the counter and swinging his legs. "Our own candy store! We'll invent flavors... fried egg jellybeans! Pickle drops! Mud pie made of mud but tastes like chocolate!"

Darius nodded, breath slowing, his smile wide and unguarded. The dream-stone shone brighter, colors intensifying as if reflecting their happiness.

"Tomorrow," he said, the word smooth, natural. "More tomorrow."

Azure perched on a gumdrop-shaped rooftop, royal blue scales catching the strange light of this unfamiliar dreamscape. His wings folded tight, jewels flickering with vigilance. Beside him sprawled Pyrrhos, ruby-studded tail flicking through cotton candy clouds.

They were opposites. Azure remained precise, each crest-feather aligned, eyes scanning every motion below, sapphires ablaze, pulsing in sync with Darius's heartbeat. Pyrrhos radiated fire, his crimson scales shifting like licking flames. The red jewels on his spine gleamed unevenly, scattered like stars.

"This is... unusual," Azure said, voice low. "I have not given Darius enough dreams of play. And sharing a dream with another dreamer, such moments are rare, even for those guided by dragons."

Below, Darius and Cass raced through spun sugar fields, footprints filling with liquid chocolate before vanishing. Darius ran freely, arms swinging instead of clenched close.

"Unusual doesn't mean bad. Their friendship draws them together within their dreaming," Pyrrhos replied, stretching his wings before tucking them again. "Cass brings joy. His dreams are always wild and bright."

Azure's tail twitched, a sign of unease. "Darius needs structure. His mind seeks order, even here."

"Which is why this may help him," Pyrrhos said, nodding at the scene where Darius traced a perfect spiral in hardened caramel. "He still finds patterns, but he doesn't resist the chaos."

They watched Cass crown Darius with a licorice necklace, naming him "King of Candyland." Darius didn't recoil from the touch; he bowed, laughter returning.

"He's happy," Azure admitted, surprise softening his tone.

"Not every dream is a lesson to be learned," Pyrrhos said. "Sometimes the lesson is remembering how to play."

The words lingered, silencing Azure's rebuttal. Below, Darius built a candy castle with peppermint bricks and frosting mortar. Cass added the flair — jellybean flags, chocolate gargoyles, licorice drawbridges — that somehow made it better, not worse.

"I've shown him wonders," Azure murmured. "The crystal caves, the memory pools, the dream-libraries of time. But never something like this."

"Each dreamer needs different guidance," Pyrrhos replied. "Cass would struggle in your structured realms. Darius might've found this overwhelming, if not for Cass."

Azure nodded. "They balance each other."

"As real friendships do."

They fell silent, watching as Darius took the lead. He assigned candy guards, made Cass the royal taste-tester, and gestured with growing confidence.

On a whim, Darius lifted both hands and studied the licorice drawbridge. Threads emerged, not obvious ones, but wisps of silky color, like melted taffy stretched thin. He twisted his wrists, coaxing them into a swirl.

The licorice thickened, reshaped, becoming more stable, its ends sealed with a spiral pattern. Then, with barely a pause, Darius shaped a gumdrop into a perfect candy sphere and, grinning, wove the threads again to form a shimmering vision of Azure.

When Azure leaned forward, his eyes narrowed in awe. "I have never seen him weave this easily. No strain, no hesitation, he creates as if he were born to it."

"And happily," Pyrrhos added. "He's not thinking about how. He's thinking about what."

Azure's jewels brightened. "Perhaps this is the truest weaving, when the dreamer forgets the lesson and lives it."

But Azure, from his perch, tilted his head. "I feared this connection might weaken him," Azure said. "Distract him from the path ahead."

"And now?" Pyrrhos asked.

"Now I see it strengthens him. Opens doors he's kept shut," Azure said. "There's no illusion here. Children playing as they should."

When Pyrrhos looked away, something unreadable flickered across his face. "Yes. Children."

The candy castle climbed to dizzying heights, its towers piercing cotton clouds. The boys climbed a winding staircase to a balcony overlooking their sweet domain. Darius pointed to candy-starred formations, naming patterns he saw.

"The three jewels," he said.

"Like on Azure's face!" Cass beamed. "Can we fly up there?"

Darius nodded. Instantly, wings sprouted, his, precise and blue; Cass's, red and chaotic. They leapt from the balcony and soared, flight instinctive and unburdened.

"He creates with precision," Azure said. "Even his improvised dreams have logic."

"And Cass brings the spark," Pyrrhos added. "Without him, the logic could trap him."

Then Azure spread his wings, catching warm candy updrafts. "I should guide them."

"No," Pyrrhos interrupted, too quickly. Then, gentler: "Let them have this. Dreamers' Dragons needn't steer every dream."

Azure folded his wings again, thoughtful. "You're right. There's time enough for lessons."

The boys spiraled through banks of marshmallow clouds, laughter trailing behind like comet tails. Darius flew with surprising confidence, executing turns and dives with a precision that defied his age.

"He will be remarkable," Azure murmured, pride in his voice.

"They both will," Pyrrhos corrected.

When Azure studied him with new appreciation, he said, "Your devotion to Cass does you credit. I had... concerns."

"Concerns?" Pyrrhos's tone stayed neutral.

"Your sudden appearance. The timing." Azure's jewels brightened twice. "But I see now, your bond is genuine."

Pyrrhos dipped his head. Below them, the candy dreamscape began to shift. Structures melted and reformed as the boys' imaginations reshaped the world.

"The dream ends soon," Azure said. "The world above calls."

"Until tomorrow," Pyrrhos replied. "Cass will insist on continuing."

When Azure rose, he said, "Then we shall meet again."

"Yes," Pyrrhos said, carefully.

As the dream faded, Azure took flight, vanishing into the dissolving sky. Pyrrhos stayed on the rooftop a moment longer, watching Darius and Cass wave goodbye. They had shared something rare. A dream shaped by two minds, working as one.

When the last sugar spire melted away, Pyrrhos departed. The brightness of his jewels faded from his red scales, leaving them dark and flat. He slipped into the deeper dream streams, paths between dreams, narrow and forbidden. The Luminaries had marked these corridors as off-limits. He went anyway.

Here, the veil thinned. As he passed, Pyrrhos glimpsed stray dream fragments: an old woman flying above her childhood home, a man crushed by endless paperwork, and a child running from faceless monsters. He turned away from their minds and flew harder into the dark.

At last, he reached a tear in the dreamscape: a jagged wound pulsing with inverted light. Its edges curled like burned paper. Cold air seeped out, thick with the scent of stone and something older.

He paused. Then a voice, low and grinding, came from within.

"Enter."

Pyrrhos pushed through.

The obsidian chamber formed around him. The walls swallowed light. The cold hit deep, turning each breath into fog that vanished too fast.

From the shadows emerged the Obsidian Dragon, or perhaps the shadows were him. His enormous body drank in what little light existed. His eyes burned deep copper, fixed and cruel against the dark.

"You're late."

"The dream lingered longer than expected," Pyrrhos said, bowing his head. "I couldn't leave without raising suspicion."

"Did you succeed?"

"Yes." Pyrrhos lifted a claw. A thread of darkness uncoiled from it like smoke. "A direct link to their shared dream."

The thread rose and touched the Obsidian Dragon's chest. He inhaled sharply. His eyes flared, then dimmed.

"Report."

"He's methodical," Pyrrhos began, his voice tightening as the thread pulsed between them. "He sees patterns. He reshaped the drawbridge using thread manipulation, basic weaving, but precise. When Cass added chaos, he adapted. He didn't reject it."

The Obsidian Dragon's tail scraped the floor, gouging the stone.

"His speech?"

"Limited, but intentional. Every word is chosen. And…" Pyrrhos paused. "He laughed. Without restraint."

"Laughed?" The Obsidian Dragon's gaze sharpened. "The silent one?"

"Yes. The more joy he feels, the stronger his connection becomes. To Cass. To the dream. When he laughed, the entire realm changed. Colors deepened. Structures stabilized. His emotions amplify his power."

The Obsidian Dragon watched him, unreadable.

"He is not what I expected," he said at last. "Azure chose his vessel well."

"Not a vessel," Pyrrhos said before thinking. "A child." His voice trailed off as he remembered who he was speaking to.

The dragon's eyes fixed on him. "A child whose eyes match the ancient texts, one of the children foretold to fulfill the prophecy."

Pyrrhos lowered his head. "Yes."

When the Obsidian Dragon circled the vision, his gaze fixed on the boy who counted everything.

"Seven steps to the door. Three breaths before speaking. Such careful control."

Recognition flickered in his tone.

"I was like him once — before the Luminaries taught me that order is another word for prison. Look at him. Every pattern he builds is a plea for certainty, for someone to tell him the rules. The Luminaries would let him struggle forever and call it growth." His voice lowered, almost tender. "I would give him peace. No more choosing. No more failing."

"Watch him. Closely." The Obsidian Dragon stepped forward, his bulk closing the space. "I want to know how he thinks. How he builds. How Azure trains him. And how he touches the deeper dream currents."

"I will."

"And the other one, Cass. His chaos is useful. Together, they build formations I didn't anticipate."

Pyrrhos's gems flickered. "Cass trusts me. Fully."

"As he should." A slow, bitter smile touched the dragon's voice. "You are his dragon."

The words hit hard. Pyrrhos's tail curled in tight.

"Does that trouble you?" the dragon asked, circling him. "Your jewels betray you."

The Obsidian Dragon's eyes narrowed. "Do you not see, Pyrrhos? The boy is not a child. He is an obstacle. The prophecy would mend what I have torn, closing the paths between worlds. You call it salvation. I call it a cage. Would you chain mortals again, leave them stumbling blind in their dreams?"

Pyrrhos's gems flickered uneasily.

"We are freeing them," the dragon pressed, voice smooth as polished stone. "By keeping the veil open, we grant them more than the Luminaries ever allowed. No riddles. No waiting. Power within reach. I offer mercy. Do not confuse it with weakness."

Pyrrhos dipped his head, but the words lodged like thorns. A cage, the dragon had said. Yet when Darius laughed, Pyrrhos had seen no cage, only color and strength.

"I understand," Pyrrhos said. "I worry Azure may grow suspicious."

"Azure sees what he wants, children laughing, forming bonds. His sentiment blinds him." The Obsidian Dragon stopped directly before him. "Unless you've hidden something?"

"Nothing." Pyrrhos forced his light to hold firm. "Azure believes the connection is natural. He trusts it."

"Good. Then our path remains clear." The dragon inhaled. The thread vanished into him like smoke.

"Continue the dreams. Push them. See how far Darius can go, when driven by joy..." He paused. "Or fear."

"Fear?" Pyrrhos's head snapped up. "You want me to frighten them?"

"Not yet." The dragon's voice sank. "But in time..."

The thread snapped. Pyrrhos staggered as it released.

"You may go," the dragon said, already turning away. "Return when there is more."

Pyrrhos backed toward the tear in reality, wings tucked tight. Only after he passed through the seam did he exhale, the warmer air of the regular dreamscape filling his lungs.

As he flew the path back toward Somnoria, his thoughts tangled like knotted thread. Cass's face hovered in his mind, open, trusting, lit with wonder at discovering his dragon. The boy's joy had been real; his excitement infectious. Service to the Obsidian Dragon was never given without price. Pyrrhos had accepted that long ago. But this was the first time he could not ignore who might be made to pay it.

The rubies along his spine flared with conflict, their red flickering between vivid crimson and dull garnet. He had once been a devoted Dreamers' Dragon, protector, guide. Now he walked in the shadows, pretending to serve the light while answering to darkness.

But his affection for Cass, that wasn't a lie. That had become real.

Elsewhere in the dream, Azure perched beside Darius's sleeping form as the boy stirred toward waking. The dragon watched with muted satisfaction as a smile touched Darius's lips, joy from the shared dream still lingering.

"Sweet dreams, indeed," Azure murmured, sapphires blazing with pride and protection.

He didn't sense the shadow-thread that had watched them. Didn't feel the Obsidian Dragon's interest growing. In this moment, Azure saw what comforted him, Darius finding joy and a growing strength through connection and friendship with Cassius Williams.

As morning light spilled into the boy's room, Azure faded from view. Darius's eyes opened, blue as Azure's scales, still full of sugar dreams. Clutched to his chest, a single red scale shimmered… then vanished into skin before he noticed.

The boundary thinned. The deception held.

And Pyrrhos, caught between loyalties, braced for another night of dreams, some shared, some stolen.

CHAPTER TWENTY-NINE

HOME

Augustus Turner pressed the hammer against the bent hinge. The porch steps had needed fixing for months, but time slipped away with work, kids, and life. His muscles ached from the railroad yard, heavy hours spent lifting freight and steel, but this labor was different, necessary, connected to something that mattered. Behind him, the house sighed with dinner preparations: pots clanging, children's voices rising and falling.

The smell of honeysuckle from the edge of their yard mixed with fried onions drifting from the Jenkins house. Grass barely clung in patches along the walkway, worn down by kids' shoes and chickens.

He adjusted the hinge against the wood, testing its fit. Years of Georgia summers had warped the metal, expanding and contracting until it no longer sat right. Like his family, bending but not breaking under pressures he couldn't always explain.

Light footsteps crossed the porch. Augustus didn't look up at first, expecting Theo or Ezra to call him in. But the steps stopped. No voice followed. He turned his head.

Darius stood three feet away, a sheet of paper in one hand. His eyes, those startling eyes, watched the work with fastened attention.

"Hey there, son," Augustus said, setting down the hammer. "You come to help your old man fix this step?"

Darius didn't answer right away. He shifted his weight, gaze dropping to the paper. Crayon smudges, blue and gray, marked his fingers. More drawings. The boy drew constantly now, filling page after page with images he alone understood.

"You want to show me what you got there?" Augustus patted the space beside him.

When Darius approached carefully, each step was deliberate. He sat, leaving six inches between them, not touching, but closer than before.

"I drew Azure," Darius said.

Augustus nodded, careful not to show his surprise at the full sentence. For years, Darius had spoken in fragments. Lately, more words were coming, especially when he talked about his dreams.

When Darius turned the paper toward him, Augustus caught his breath. A dragon filled the page, drawn in striking detail. Blue scales gleamed even through crayon strokes. Gems dotted its long neck and wings. The eyes, thoughtful, kind, seemed impossibly alive.

"That's some fine drawing," Augustus said, genuinely impressed. "You put a lot of work into this."

"Silver in wings." Darius tapped the gray streaks. "Not just blue. Silver … like … stars. Eyes change too. When… he teach."

Augustus set the tools aside, giving his son his full attention. More words in one moment than he'd heard in maybe, ever.

"What kind of things does he teach you?"

Darius traced the outline. "Quiet inside." He paused, struggling to find the words. "Not afraid."

Augustus nodded. He didn't fully understand, but he understood it mattered.

"Different not broken," Darius said, voice steadier.

A lump rose in Augustus's throat. How many nights had he sat with Sadie, wondering what was broken in their boy? Wishing for a child who would play catch, who wouldn't scream at touch, who might one day call him Daddy?

"He big. Not scary," Darius added.

Augustus studied his son's face, once so blank, now eager with wonder. For years, it had been unreadable, locked behind silence. Now he saw peace.

"And he's big?" Augustus asked, gesturing to the dragon towering over a small figure.

"Bigger… our house," Darius said.

Augustus picked up his hammer, turning it over in his hands, needing something to anchor him. Part of him wanted to say dragons weren't real. That this was imagination. But Darius's voice held certainty. His eyes held peace.

Augustus looked at his son, not as the broken child he'd grieved for, but as a boy with secrets and wisdom he might never grasp. Did it matter if Azure was real? If Darius's dreams of a dragon gave Darius peace, if he taught him how to live in a world that often hurt his son, then he would believe in Azure.

"Then you tell him your daddy's grateful."

Surprise flickered across Darius's face. Then came a rare, genuine smile, enough to take Augustus's breath.

"I will," Darius said, folding the drawing and tucking it into his pocket. "He knows. He sees… everything."

They sat in silence as the sun slipped below the horizon. He glanced at the sky, then at the boy beside him. "I see your mama in you. But something else too. I don't know what, but something different," Augustus said, as he gathered his tools. "We should go in."

Darius nodded and stood. Before turning to the door, he placed his small hand on Augustus's shoulder.

Augustus sat still, tools heavy in his lap, his son's touch still warm on his shoulder. He looked up at the first stars, wondering about dragons with voices. About teachers who came in dreams.

His eyes filled. A lump swelled in his throat. He never believed a moment like this would come.

His son spoke and touched his shoulder.

And silently, to whatever or whoever might be listening, Augustus Turner gave thanks.

Sadie finished washing off the kitchen table after preparing dinner. The blackberry pie cooled by the open window, its deep purple filling still bubbling through slits in the golden crust. She'd saved the berries Theo and Ezra brought home last week, transforming their offered buckets into something sweet for after Sunday dinner. Through the window came the rising and falling of children's laughter, Darius's voice among them. Still quieter than the others, but present. Part of the chorus.

Three firm knocks announced Mrs. Jenkins before the back door swung open. She bustled in without waiting, as she always had.

"Lord have mercy, Sadie Turner, that smell would raise the dead," she declared, holding a jar of preserved peaches like an offering. "Thought you might want these for the children. My tree's giving more than I can handle."

Sadie accepted it with a smile. "You're too kind, Evelyn. Come sit. Tea's still good and hot."

Mrs. Jenkins settled into her usual chair, which creaked in protest. Her sharp eyes took everything in, the scrubbed floor, the mended curtains, the schoolwork on the wall. Nothing eluded her notice, which made her both a comfort and a challenge.

"You've got that kitchen looking nice as Sunday," she said, accepting the cup Sadie poured. "Augustus still working long hours?"

"Six days a week now," Sadie replied, sitting across from her. "Down at the railroad yard. With men out of work all over Atlanta, I thank the Lord every day he's still got hours. We're trying to put something aside. Theo outgrows shoes faster than I can patch them. Thank God the school's close enough they don't wear 'em out too quick."

Mrs. Jenkins added sugar, the small clinking of the spoon tapped the cup. A peal of laughter rang from outside, bright, full-throated.

"Was that…" she paused, teacup halfway to her lips. "Darius laughing?"

Sadie nodded, her pride unconcealed. "Playing with his brothers and sisters. Happens more often now."

Mrs. Jenkins lowered her cup. "Well, I declare. I remember when that child couldn't say a word and would scream bloody murder if you brushed against his arm." She leaned in, voice dropping. "I remember when he nearly broke every dish in your cabinet during one of his fits."

The memory still stung, though its edges had dulled. "He's different now. Still has hard days, but fewer. He's finding his way."

"And he's finding his voice, too," Mrs. Jenkins said, glancing toward the window. "I saw him at church last Sunday. Sat still as a mouse. Even shook Pastor John's hand. Didn't say anything, but that's a big step for him. He seems to have made a friend. The little Williams boy, Cassius. I visited his mother, he's quite the little talker isn't he? What an unusual pair, but God puts people in our path for a reason."

Sadie smiled, remembering how long Darius had practiced that handshake with Augustus. How his hand had trembled but stayed extended long enough.

"He's speaking more every day. Full sentences sometimes. Last night he told me he likes it when I sing in the kitchen. It helps him with his words," Sadie continued. "Cassius has helped Darius take a step toward the world. It's wonderful to see him have a friend. Honestly, it's not something I ever thought would happen."

Mrs. Jenkins clasped her hands. "If that ain't a miracle straight from heaven. I told Arthur, 'The Lord is working on that Turner boy,' I said. Our prayer circle's lifted him up every Wednesday for five years now."

Sadie stood to refill their cups, letting the motion ground her. Mrs. Jenkins meant well, and she wasn't wrong. Who was to say where Azure came from, or why he chose Darius?

"It's like he was locked in a room, and someone finally found the key," Mrs. Jenkins said. "Pastor says the Almighty acts in ways we can't understand, especially with children like…” She hesitated. “Well. With special children.”

Sadie’s smile grew. The word special held a new meaning for her now. One that brought warmth to her chest. “Yes, Darius is special.”

“Course he is,” she said. “Special from the day he was born, with those eyes blue as heaven. I meant the Lord’s got plans for children who see the world differently. Bible’s full of ’em.”

Sadie thought of the drawings in Darius’s room, page after page of Azure, done in crayon, charcoal, pencil, whatever was on hand. One morning she caught him teaching Gunny how to breathe “dragon-style,” deep in for four, out for eight, like Azure taught him.

She could have told Evelyn about the dreams. About the dragon who reached her son when no one else could. About the nights she crept to the living room, hoping to catch a glimpse of him. Like a child hoping to spot Santa.

But some wonders weren’t meant to be shared. Whether born of angels or dragon wings, they were no less holy.

“I think you’re right,” Sadie said. “God finds ways to reach all His children.”

A crash from outside interrupted them, followed by Ezra’s indignant yell. Sadie half-rose, but no crying followed, only more laughter.

“Listen to that,” Mrs. Jenkins said. “Playing like any normal child now.” She reached across the table and patted Sadie’s hand. “You keep praying, Sadie Turner. The Lord’s not finished with your boy yet.”

Sadie thought of the drawings of Darius’s dragon and of the calm that had quietly replaced chaos in their home. Of Darius, who now smiled more than he screamed.

“I believe you’re right about that,” she said.

When Mrs. Jenkins finished her tea and rose, she paused as she turned back at the door, her expression unusually soft.

“The Lord don’t always come in the ways we expect, but I see His work in that child of yours.”

Sadie stood in the doorway, watching her cross the street. Sunlight caught the older woman’s gray hair, turning it silver.

"Always," Sadie said, though Evelyn couldn't hear.

Sadie didn't know and tonight she didn't care whether the Lord wore robes of glory or scales of blue, whether He spoke through scripture or in dreams of flight, whether His messengers had halos or horns. All she knew was that her son and her family were healing.

Faith spoke in many tongues, and so did love.

And Sadie Turner was learning to be fluent in both.

Twilight softened the edges of the Turner backyard, turning the familiar into something almost magical. Lightning bugs rose from the tall grass at the property's edge, blinking like stars fallen to earth. The heat of the day lingered but was easing; the air, sweet with honeysuckle and cut grass. In that in-between hour when day surrendered to night, the children's voices rang clearer, laughter echoing off the darkening trees. Five children formed a loose circle beneath the old oak, their faces serious with the business of choosing a game.

"Not hide and seek again," Lula groaned, crossing her arms. "Gunny always gives away where everyone's hiding."

The six-year-old in question stuck out her lip. "Do not!"

"Do too," Ezra said, poking her side. "You giggle every time someone walks past you."

When Darius proposed a game about catching lightning bugs, Ezra ran to the kitchen for jars.

On the porch, Sadie and Augustus sat on the worn steps, watching their children through the gathering dark. Augustus's arm rested across Sadie's shoulders, his fingers tracing slow circles.

"Listen to him," Sadie said, eyes on Darius as he darted through the firefly glow. "All those words, coming now. I used to pray he'd say my name. Just once — 'Mama.' So I'd know he knew who I was to him."

"Now he's teaching the others games," Augustus said.

They watched as Darius knelt beside Lula, helping her count the fluttering specks in her jar. His voice floated across the yard, patient and sure, explaining how one especially bright firefly counted as two.

"It's a miracle," Sadie said, not caring if the word was overused. Sometimes, the old words were the right ones.

"Whatever it is," Augustus said, "I'm grateful."

The game peaked when Theo declared it was time to count their treasure. Beneath the tree, they compared twinkling jars. Arguments broke out, negotiations followed, and through it all, Darius was calm, no longer apart from the moment, but at the center.

Lula won, her jar bright with seventeen lightning bugs to Ezra's fifteen. She accepted her victory with theatrics — her arms stretching high above her head, and then a deep bow, and already planning tomorrow's game.

When Sadie finally called them inside, the children opened their jars. Lightning bugs floated upward, some pausing at their fingertips as if reluctant to leave.

Inside, the house hummed with evening — school reports, light teasing, shoes dropped in corners. The scent of cornbread and blueberry pie lingered in the air.

Augustus leaned back in his chair, one leg crossed. "That boy Darius has been sittin' with, Cassius, right? Loud talker. Saw 'em again today."

Sadie smoothed a wrinkle on her skirt. "Cassius. Loud, yes. But not rough. Doesn't expect much from Darius."

"Talks enough for the both of 'em," Gunny chimed in, legs swinging from the armchair. "Darius listens. Smiles sometimes too."

Ezra glanced up from his book. "Lula said Cassius talks about dragons. Serious about it. Told her he's got his own Dreamers' Dragon."

Theo snorted. "That's a stretch. Boy's got imagination, I'll give him that."

Sadie looked where Darius sat drawing in the dirt with a stick. "Well... whatever it is, it's exactly what Darius needs."

"Or someone who don't mind doin' all the talkin'," Augustus added.

Gunny rested her chin in her palms. "It's nice. Darius never had a friend before, like me, I have Lila."

Theo leaned against the doorframe, arms crossed. "He's happier since Cassius showed up. Stands taller."

"Long time comin'," Augustus said.

"He needed someone his kind of different," Theo added.

Lula grinned. "Peculiar kids always find each other."

Augustus nodded. "Then maybe Darius finally found where he belongs."

Darius was the last to release his lightning bugs. He whispered something no one could hear, then opened his jar. The insects illuminated above his head, dancing around him before drifting into the sky.

Then, with one final burst, Darius ran across the yard, arms stretched like wings. Lightning bugs followed him like sparks from a shooting star. His feet barely touched the ground. His laughter trailed behind like a ribbon of joy.

From the window, his parents watched, not the boy they once mourned, but a child who had found his voice, his place, his belonging. Not despite his differences, but because of them.

Like the lightning bugs, Darius now carried his light into the dark, unafraid.

***

The dream unfolded gently, in waves of color and a gentle hum like a song Mama might sing. Unlike earlier dreams with Cassius that burst into being, this one arrived softly. Stars dotted the dark sky, not constellations he knew, but new ones. Directly overhead, six stars formed a perfect circle, effulgent and brighter than the rest.

Below the hill where Darius sat, a valley incandescent with lights, some drifting like glowworms, others still like distant windows lit from within.

Azure's massive body curled around the hilltop, his tail arcing protectively behind Darius. His scales caught the light, each one reflecting a tiny piece of the sky. Heat radiated from him, a constant warmth holding back the night's chill.

Darius leaned against Azure's side, legs stretched out in the downy grass. His slight frame looked even smaller beside the dragon's bulk. Azure felt like part of him now, like breath or heartbeat.

They sat quiet for a while. Not the kind of quiet that turned empty. The good kind. The kind that radiated stillness and peace.

After a while, Darius spoke.

"It's quieter now," he said. "Not only at home. Inside me, too."

Azure didn't move much, but Darius knew he was listening. He always did.

"I used to hear everything. All at once. People talking. Clocks ticking. Mama's heart when she held me close." He ran his fingers through the grass. "It was like everybody else had a knob to turn things down and mine was broken."

Below them, dream lights shifted and swirled like lightning bugs chasing each other. Darius watched without flinching. That used to be hard.

"And now I got a friend."

Azure's side rose and fell. Slow. Solid. Safe.

"Not just Gunny or Theo or Ezra. Not someone who has to be nice 'cause we live in the same house." He gave a little grin. "Cassius is loud. Real loud." He chuckled. "Talks so much, don't care if I answer or not. Keeps goin'. Like a radio stuck on."

He picked at a thread on his pajama pants. "But I like listenin'. And he listens too. Folks don't think he does, but he remembers what I say."

Up above, a shooting star cut across the sky like a chalk mark.

"We're kinda the same. But backwards. He's noise and movin'. I'm quiet and still." He paused. "He never makes fun when my hands go wild. Or when I take a while to talk. He stays."

A grin crept onto his face.

"He's got a Dreamers' Dragon too. Pyrrhos. All red and shiny. Looks like rubies. Fits Cass. Bright. Loud. He says his wings cut through clouds like fire burning paper."

When Darius turned, resting his palm on Azure's side, he said, "I didn't know anybody else could have one. I thought I was alone."

They sat with that for a while.

"School's still hard," he said. "Kids stare. Most of 'em don't say nothin' 'cause Lula won't let 'em. But some laugh when I move my hands too fast." He moved his fingers in the air. "But I like school. I like knowin' things."

"Miss Thompson lets me step outside when it gets loud." He smiled. "I'm good at math. The numbers make sense."

He pulled his knees in tight. "Readin's harder. Sometimes the letters jump around and it's hard to follow. But I'm workin' on it."

"Some kids like my drawings now," he said. "They say the dragons look grand. Miss Thompson put one on the wall last week."

The grin returned, brighter this time.

"But that first one I drew for Mama and Daddy?" He laughed. "You looked like a goat with chicken legs."

Azure's tail twitched faintly.

Darius laughed. "I been practicin'. I can draw your wings better now, the shape, how they catch the light. Cass says my pictures make dreams feel real. He said that when I showed him the one of y'all flyin' over clouds lookin' like sweet rolls." Darius glanced at his hands, then back at Azure. "You said it'd happen. That my soul would see first… and my hands would catch up. I think they are now. Like you said."

His voice dropped. "I never thought I'd have a friend like him. Someone who picks me, even when I'm quiet. Even when I'm odd."

He rested his cheek against Azure's scales, fingers curling into the familiar ridges. "I'm happy, Azure. I didn't know I could be this happy."

Azure's tail curled in a little closer, wrapping behind.

Another shooting star crossed the sky, its trail lingering longer than it would in the night sky of his everyday world. Darius watched it, head tilted.

"I still get mad sometimes," he said after a moment. "I knocked over Ezra's model airplane yesterday. He kept making engine noises and wouldn't stop when I asked." He hugged his knees tighter. "I said sorry. He helped me fix it."

Azure didn't speak. He didn't need to.

"But I don't scare Gunny anymore," Darius added. "She used to hide behind Mama when I walked into a room. Now she follows me around, asking questions." He smiled, small and real. "She says I tell the best stories."

Below, the lights in the valley blinked out one by one, like houses settling down for the night. The remaining lights shone brighter because of it.

"And Mama doesn't cry in the kitchen anymore," he said, almost whispering. "Not like before. I used to hear her when she thought I was asleep. Crying while she did dishes or folded laundry." He swallowed. "I knew it was because of me. But I couldn't stop being... me."

When Azure lowered his head, his eye met Darius's. The dragon didn't speak, but in that deep sapphire gaze, Darius saw himself, not small, not broken. But seen.

He pressed his hand to Azure's warm side. "You helped me. Not with just words, with... me. You stayed. Even when I couldn't talk. Even when I threw things. You never left. Kind of like my family. You are my family too."

The truth sat between them, too heavy and too simple for a child his age. But Darius had never been a simple child. Azure had known that from the start.

"I still don't understand everything," Darius said. "Why I see patterns other people don't. Why loud sounds hurt me. Why my hands need to move or my body rocks when I need to feel safe." His hand stilled on the dragon's scale. "But I don't need to understand everything now. I like who I am," he said, the words falling into place like puzzle pieces. "Even the way my hands move. Even the quiet." He lifted his chin. "I don't want to be someone else."

Azure's voice came at last. "You are becoming who you already are."

The simple truth of those words settled over Darius like the warmth of his blanket. He closed his eyes, resting his head against Azure's side. Beneath muscle and scale, the dragon's heartbeat thudded strong as a drum.

"Thank you," Darius whispered.

Above them, the six stars twinkled once in unison, bright and sharp against the dark.

When Azure tilted his glorious head back, he asked, not to Darius, not expecting an answer, but as if the sky itself might speak, "What do you think it means? The six stars?"

But Darius answered anyway.

"It means children. Six children." His voice was calm. Certain. "It always has."

When Azure turned to look at Darius, surprised, he saw that Darius wasn't looking at the stars, but at the space between them, as if reading something hidden.

"I see six stars everywhere," he said. "In the sounds, the colors, the dreamscapes. I don't know why."

Azure stilled. For centuries he'd guided dreamers, followed symbols, and recited old prophecies. But he'd never once considered that the number six was literal. That the stars didn't point to some vague destiny, but to six specific children.

"I've said nothing," Darius continued, "because I don't understand it. I just know that's what it means."

Azure exhaled, a slow gust of warm breath. "You're seeing what even dragons have missed."

Darius drew a deep breath, lungs filled with the sweet, clean air of this place between dreaming and waking. His body melted into Azure's warmth. His mind, quiet.

When Azure extended one wing over him, not to shield, but to embrace, it was not protection. Belonging.

Azure's heartbeat rumbled beneath Darius's head, deep as the earth itself. The dragon had taught him not merely to navigate dreams but to carry their calm into the waking world. To find stillness within chaos, beauty in patterns others don't see, and strength through storms. He now knew he belonged in both worlds, within his family and, most importantly, in his own skin. His mind, with its unique perceptions, was rare, not broken. A constellation unlike any other.

As the dream blurred, stars fading into the first muted light of morning, Darius carried his peace across the threshold between worlds.

On the couch, with his blanket tangled around him as birds began their morning songs, Darius Turner opened his eyes. His hand reached beneath the pillow, tracing the dragon drawing.

He was Darius, a dreamer, a dragon-friend, a son and a brother.

Finally, he was home.

Chapter Thirty

Fish

The afternoon silence ended with Miss Thompson releasing the students for the day. Chairs rasped against the worn plank floor as children scrambled to gather books and belongings.

Darius slid his reader and arithmetic notebook into his bag, fingers pressing softly along each edge to ensure corners sat flush and safe. Beside him, Cassius shoveled his things into his satchel with one sweep of his arm, his attention already turned somewhere else. A pencil slipped free and rolled off the desk.

"That was the best dream ever!" Cassius said, loud enough to earn curious glances from nearby students. "All that candy with no stomach aches! Can you still taste it?"

Darius nodded, a smile tugging at the corners of his lips. He tapped a gentle rhythm against the side of his satchel, one, two, three, anchoring himself while Cassius practically vibrated.

"We should dream again tonight," Cassius whispered, leaning so close their shoulders nearly touched. "Something even better, maybe fishing!"

From her desk, Miss Thompson lifted a brow. "Boys, don't dilly-dally. Start walking home."

"Yes, ma'am," Cassius said, then immediately turned back to Darius. "You ever been fishing for real?"

Darius shook his head.

"You're kidding!" Cassius's eyes widened. "Last summer Uncle Walter took me out to the lake. We sat all day on a little wooden boat, and the water was so still you could see the sky reflected in it. We caught fish this big!"

Cassius stretched his arms wide, then drew them in with a sheepish grin. "Maybe about half that big. But still big."

Cassius walked backwards in front of Darius, hands flying. "When that fish pulled my line, it felt like a train grabbed me. My uncle had to grab me to keep me from falling overboard. My heart was pounding, boom, boom, boom."

Cassius thumped his chest for emphasis.

Darius watched in amusement as Cassius barreled on with enthusiasm. "Tonight's dream could be fishing, but magical! Fish changing colors, singing songs, and maybe even granting wishes!"

When Lula appeared at Darius's side, books hugged tight, she said, "Time to go, Darius. Mama's waiting."

"We're planning another dream," Cassius informed her eagerly. "We're going fishing!"

Lula raised a skeptical eyebrow. "You are dreaming the same dreams together?"

Cassius opened his mouth.

"No," Darius said. He cut Cassius a look that meant stop. "Stories."

Lula's eyes moved between them. "Stories," she repeated, testing the word. "Well, don't start believing your stories."

Darius nodded once, serious as a promise.

When Cassius waved energetically, spotting his mother across the yard, he called, "Remember, big fish tonight! Think real hard about it!" He dashed off, stumbling over his untied shoelaces.

Darius watched him go with his hand half-raised.

"You like him, don't you?" Lula asked quietly.

Darius nodded, still watching Cassius until he vanished out of sight.

"Be careful," Lula said. "Real life isn't the same as dreams."

Darius met his sister's gaze firmly. "Better," he said, certain in his simple truth.

At home, he ate dinner fast, not messy or frantic, but with intent. He helped clear the table of the dishes, completed his arithmetic homework, and prepared for bed without needing reminders. When Sadie bent to kiss his forehead, she noticed the change in him: an energy, a presence that hadn't been there before.

"Sweet dreams, baby," she said, smoothing his blanket.

Darius curled his fingers into the blue cloth. Behind his closed eyes, a lake began to take shape. Water called to him. Somewhere across town, another boy did the same, building a dream with both hands and no patience.

Darius awoke to a world of blue. He stood on a sandy shore, facing a clear lake that mirrored a sky filled with clouds shaped like fish. Across the water, Cassius waved enthusiastically, already knee-deep in the water.

"Darius! You're here!" Cassius shouted, splashing closer. "I thought about lakes all evening, this one's perfect!"

The lake was vast, its far edges blurred by mist. Three suns hung overhead, throwing bright streaks across the surface. Fish broke the water in bright arcs, flashing and vanishing again.

"We need something to fish from," Darius said, his voice calm and clear. He lifted his hand, fingers hesitant at first, then more deliberate.

A few wooden planks shimmered into place, edges rough and uneven. They dropped with subtle thuds. More followed, creaking as they stacked into place. The dock formed one board at a time until a narrow crooked platform stretched over the water.

Darius exhaled, surprised it had held. With Azure, he'd made small things, buttons, a pouch, little shapes that vanished as quickly as they formed. In the shared dream with Cassius, candy had appeared in his hands without him even thinking about it. But this… this was the first time he'd shaped something this big on his own.

When Cassius bounded onto the dock, grinning as it swayed, he said, "Whoa. You built that?"

"It's like standing on water!" Cassius shouted, arms stretched out wide for balance.

Darius stepped on next, guiding the dock's gentle shifts. The boards dipped.

Cassius plunged into the lake with a splash.

He came up sputtering and laughing. "You did that on purpose!"

Darius laughed openly, nodding.

When Cassius hauled himself back onto the dock, dripping, he said, "We need something to fish with."

He scanned the shoreline, then darted toward a crooked branch half-hidden beneath a patch of tall grass. With a satisfied grunt, he yanked it free and inspected it like a seasoned angler.

"This'll work."

He pulled a bit of string from his pocket. It was there, as if dreams stocked him the way his mother stocked their pantry. He tied it to the end.

"It's a super fishing stick!" Cassius announced, casting his line with a dramatic flick.

The water stirred.

Pyrrhos rose from below, no longer built for the sky. His body transformed into the sleek sea form of a ruby-scaled sea dragon.

"Today," Pyrrhos said, "we explore underwater."

Cassius jumped with excitement. "You're a fish-dragon. Can we ride? Can we breathe underwater?"

"Yes," Pyrrhos said, lowering himself. "That's why I'm here. And for the record I am not a fish-dragon."

His eyes narrowed in mock offense.

"I'm a sea-dragon," Pyrrhos added. "Big difference."

They climbed on, and Pyrrhos dove smoothly beneath the surface.

Water closed over them in a rush of bubbles. Cassius's cheeks puffed with instinct, then he laughed when his lungs kept working as if he stood in open air. The lake shifted around them, filled with drifting color. Fish glinted past. Coral rose like frozen fireworks.

"Follow me," Pyrrhos said, and angled toward a forest of red coral.

Azure glided in behind.

Pyrrhos led them into the mouth of a sea cave. Pale green crystals studded the stone and cast a lustrous shine through the water. Schools of tiny silver fish darted in and out of the shadows.

Near the back of the cave, a cluster of translucent fish hovered in place. Each had a dark oval mark where an ear might be.

Cassius swam closer. "What are those?"

"Echo fish," Pyrrhos said, a small grin tugging at his mouth. "They repeat whatever sound they hear."

Cass immediately cupped his hands and shouted, "Blub blub!"

The echo fish answered in perfect unison, "Blub blub!" in a high, watery chorus.

Darius smirked. He tapped on a nearby rock, producing three sharp clicks. The fish answered back with the same triple-click, then added an extra, unexpected fourth one.

"Hey, they improved it!" Cass laughed. He spun in place, calling out random noises: "Boing!" "Honk!" Each echoed back, sometimes with odd little embellishments. Ridiculous tones soon reverberated throughout the cave of crystal and stone.

Pyrrhos's tail flicked lazily, amusement in his eyes. "I'll leave you to it. I'm going to see if I can find some bigger fish."

"Bring back a whale!" Cass called after him.

"Or a shark," Darius added with a small grin.

Pyrrhos rumbled a laugh and slipped out of the cave, his crimson form vanishing into the deeper blue.

The water grew colder, pressure building, not from depth, but from something watching him.

Pyrrhos swam toward the depths where light failed to penetrate. The water pressure increased around him, not with physical weight but with something more insidious. He stopped in a ravine between two structures that had been vibrant and singing minutes before but now stood silent and gray, their colors leached away.

Shadows gathered. Not the natural dark of deep water, but something that moved with intention. They wrapped around his legs, crawled across his wings, and then pressed against his scales like searching hands.

"You've grown attached to them."

The voice came from everywhere, filling the water without disturbing it.

"How... touching."

Pyrrhos's tail snapped once. "I followed your instructions," he said. His words came out smaller than he meant. "The boys trust me completely."

"Yes." The word stretched into a hiss. "The quiet one especially. His mind opens in ways I hadn't anticipated."

A black thread materialized in the water, thin as spider silk but unnaturally dark, absorbing light rather than merely blocking it. It slithered through the water toward Pyrrhos, wrapping around one of his front claws before he could retreat.

"They belong to me now," the Obsidian Dragon said. "If you wish them whole, you'll do as you've done before."

Pyrrhos winced. His scales rippled with involuntary shudders. "What do you want from me?"

"Push deeper. Test the quiet one's limits." The thread tightened, biting into his claw. "Find what lies beneath his careful control. The prophecy speaks of blue eyes that see beyond seeing, I am eager to discover what he sees when that control breaks."

"They're children," Pyrrhos protested, his voice barely audible. "Breaking him serves no purpose."

"Purpose."

The single word struck like cold iron.

The air collapsed inward, crushing his chest, as if invisible coils wound tighter with every

syllable. A searing pressure raked his scales, forcing a tremor down his spine.

"You question my purpose?"

Pyrrhos's claws dug into the lake bed, gouging deep furrows in the dream-stone beneath the sand. His wings tight to his body, making himself smaller before the unseen presence.

"No," he said. "I'll do as you ask."

"Good." The thread eased, but didn't release. "The next dream must push boundaries. Fear reveals truth that joy hides."

"Fear?" Lifting his head, Pyrrhos dared the question.

The searing pressure slammed back into his chest, sharper this time, like claws closing around his heart. Breath caught. The thought remained unfinished.

"Children," The Obsidian Dragon said, as if tasting the word. "Yes. You mentioned that. Children grow. These two, faster than most. The quiet one especially."

The thread slid off Pyrrhos's claw but hung suspended in the water, pointing toward the surface where distant figures, the boys and Azure, explored a coral cave.

"Don't forget what's at stake," the Obsidian Dragon said. "Your freedom. Their safety. The balance of Somnoria."

The thread dropped into the lake bed like a spear.

The dream-stone cracked where it struck, black lines spreading outward in a web.

"Tomorrow," the Obsidian Dragon commanded as the presence withdrew. "Test him tomorrow."

The shadows dispersed and slid away into the ravine.

Pyrrhos remained still, staring at the spreading fracture in the lake bed. The cracks crept outward, slow, yet consistent, eating into the foundation of this shared dream.

He turned back toward the cave.

Pyrrhos forced his scales to brighten. He forced his movement into grace. His luster still faltered as he swam, a tell he could not fully conceal.

"Sorry, boys," Pyrrhos called when he reached them. "No big fish in the deep waters."

When Cassius spotted him, he waved. "Pyrrhos! Listen to the echo fish! They repeat what you say but in different voices!"

He showed by calling out, "Hello there!"

A school of tiny silver fish darted around his head, their mouths opening and closing as they echoed, "Hello there!" in voices ranging from deep bass to high soprano.

Darius didn't join in right away.

He studied Pyrrhos with an intensity that sharpened his whole face. His blue eyes tracked the uneven flicker of Pyrrhos's rubies. He noted the faint tremor in the dragon's wings.

"Something wrong?" Darius asked. His question came clean and direct.

When Pyrrhos turned his face away, as if examining an interesting rock formation, he said, "Nothing at all. The dream-dusk brings changes, that's all."

Cassius followed Darius's gaze and hesitated for the first time. "He's fine," he said, as though he was trying to convince himself.

Azure drifted closer, his movements casual but his attention fixed.

"What kind of changes did you observe in the depths?" Azure asked.

"Currents shifting. Colors are fading," Pyrrhos said. "Nothing unusual."

Azure's jewels flashed once, twice in a deliberate rhythm.

Pyrrhos flinched.

Something passed between them without words: a question pressed, an answer withheld.

"We should return to the surface," Azure said. "Dream-night brings different wonders than day."

"But I like it down here," Cassius protested. "The echo fish still have lots to say!"

"The surface has stars," Darius said, still watching Pyrrhos. "Stars that tell stories."

Azure inclined his head. "Indeed."

They rose through the water. Pyrrhos swam a little apart, his body angled away from the others. He glanced down once.

Far below, the web of cracks kept spreading across the lake bed.

When Azure shifted position as they passed over the fracture, he placed himself between it and the boys, as if the movement meant nothing.

His placement meant everything.

The dream continued. Under its surface, something had changed. Something that would not unmake itself because a child laughed.

CHAPTER THIRTY

CHAPTER THIRTY-ONE

CHOICE

They climbed out of the lake onto a shoreline remade by night.

The sky was crowded with stars, not scattered the way they were at home, but arranged. Constellations held shape like deliberate sketches: dragons, strange animals, doorways outlined by moving points that refused to sit still. The sand beneath their feet looked like crushed crystal and retained a gentle warmth, like a stone that had been sitting near a stove all day.

Water ran off their hair and sleeves in thin streams.

Then it changed its mind.

Droplets reversed and lifted, drifting upward to join low clouds that hovered close enough to touch. The clouds carried their own faint burn, like paper lanterns left lit after a church supper.

"I'm starving," Cassius announced. "Can you get hungry in dreams? Because I feel like I could eat an entire dream cow."

Darius scanned the beach. The starlight caught in his eyes, turning them sharper, darker. He knelt and placed both palms flat against the sand.

A blue trace spread outward from his fingertips in clean loops and linked circles, the lines forming symbols that looked older than handwriting. Not decoration. Instruction.

"Fire," he said.

Flames rose from the center, not orange but deep blue at the base, shifting through green, and violet at the tips. Heat radiated outward, but the sand beneath didn't burn or blacken.

"Dream fire!" When Cassius dropped to his knees beside the flames, he said, "Does it burn? Or is it..."

He thrust his hand toward the flames, then pulled back with a yelp.

"Nope. Definitely burns."

"Careful," Darius cautioned, his voice soft but firm. "Still fire."

Pyrrhos settled into the sand nearby, his sea-dragon form unwinding into a loose coil. The dampness from the lake still clung to his scales, steam rising from them in thin spirals that caught the colored light.

"Even here," Pyrrhos said, "things keep their nature. Dreams make them seem different."

When Azure landed opposite the fire, he folded his wings with the same precision he brought to everything, as if order itself followed him. "Form changes," he said. "Essence does not."

Cassius snapped his fingers. "We should cook those dream fish! I bet they taste as good as my brother Sam's when he brings back a load from fishin'."

He closed his eyelids and moved his hands in randomly, pretending to weave fishing sticks.

Darius watched, amused, and then produced two sticks with sharp ends and placed them in front of Cass's feet.

When Cass opened his eyes and stared, for one bright second, he believed he'd done it.

"Look," he said, grinning. "Roasting sticks."

Then he caught Darius's expression, and the grin shifted, smaller but still there. A little disappointment. A little understanding.

"Cooking sticks," Darius corrected, almost smiling.

"Whatever they're called." Cassius shoved one into Darius's hand. "Let's catch dinner."

They waded into the shallows where schools of dream fish drifted in lazy circles. Cassius speared one with translucent rainbow scales. It didn't bleed or thrash. It changed, becoming a clean, ready fish, its scales turning into edible jewels that snapped faintly between his fingers.

Darius caught a smaller one with clockwork insides. When his stick pierced it, the gears stilled, and the fish became ordinary, as if the dream had decided it had played enough.

They brought their catch back to the fire.

Cassius showed how to hold the sticks over the flames, turning them over and over to cook evenly. "My granddaddy taught me this. We went camping by the creek once, and he showed me how to cook fish right from the water. Mama wasn't happy when I came home smelling like smoke and fish guts."

The fish cooked quickly, their scales sizzling and releasing aromas that changed every few seconds, from butter to cinnamon to something wild and unfamiliar. When they bit into the flesh, the flavor shifted with each chew, sweet to savory to tangy and back again.

"This is better than actual food!" Cassius declared through a mouthful. "We should bring some home for breakfast."

"Doesn't work that way," Darius said, picking a tiny gear from his teeth.

They ate in comfortable silence, the fire crackling with tones instead of the pops and hisses, sounding as though someone were plucking a few careful notes on a distant instrument. Above them, the constellations continued their slow dance, forming and reforming into stories written by their light.

When Cassius finished first and tossed the stick into the fire, where it burned with bright yellow flames before disappearing, he scooted closer to Pyrrhos, leaning his back against the dragon's warm scales.

"You know what?" Cassius tipped his head up. "You're the best dragon ever. Not that Azure isn't great too," he added hastily with a glance toward the blue dragon, "but you're mine. That makes you special."

Pyrrhos's wings shifted, feathering out then smoothing back against his body. "I'm honored you think so."

"It's not thinking," Cassius said. "It's knowing." He patted the red scales beside him. "You showed up right when I needed someone to understand me. Nobody else ever did that before Darius."

Across the fire, Darius watched. He set aside his empty cooking stick and reached into his pocket, withdrawing a thin strand of blue thread-light, thicker than ones he'd used to create the dock. Gold and silver wove through it, braided tight.

He stood and walked around the fire to Pyrrhos. Without speaking, he held out the thread, offering it with both hands.

When Pyrrhos lifted his head, ruby eyes fixed on the offering, he asked, "What is this?"

"Friendship," Darius said. "From me."

Cassius sat up straighter. "Did you make that? It's beautiful! Like a tiny rope of stars!"

Darius nodded, still holding the thread toward Pyrrhos. "For connections. To find each other."

When Pyrrhos extended one claw with visible hesitation, the thread floated from Darius's hands to land across his talons, settling there with the weight of trust. For a moment, Pyrrhos's jewels stuttered, bright then dull, like a heart missing a beat.

"I…" His voice caught. He tried again. "Thank you."

He lowered his gaze, curling his claw around the pulsing strand as though to keep it safe. For the first time in a long time, he let himself believe it might last.

Darius returned to his place by the fire. The gift given, he seemed content to watch the flames cycle from blue to green to violet and back again.

Cassius yawned, stretching his arms above his head. "I'm getting sleepy in my dream. Is that usual? Can you sleep inside a dream?"

Azure spoke without looking up. "Dreams can nest."

"Nest? Like a bird?" Cassius asked, already curling up against Pyrrhos's warmth. "Think I'll try it anyway."

Within minutes, his breathing slowed.

Darius's eyelids grew heavy too. A blue blanket formed beneath him as he lay down, as natural as a habit. His eyes met Azure's for a beat before they closed. A wordless exchange. Permission. Warning. Both.

When the boys slipped into deeper sleep, Azure rose.

He crossed the sand to Pyrrhos and extended one wing over Cassius's small, sleeping body. Protective, yes. Also claiming space.

"You cannot serve two masters," Azure said without preamble, his voice low but carrying clearly in the night air. "One will cost you everything."

Pyrrhos didn't lift his head or meet Azure's gaze. "I don't know what you mean."

"The crack in the lake bed." Azure's voice stayed level. "The shadow that follows you. The voice that commands you when you think no one sees."

Pyrrhos remained silent, his claw closing around Darius's thread.

"He trusts you," Azure said, glancing at Darius curled by the fire. "They both do. Trust is not easy to rebuild once it breaks."

"I would never harm them," Pyrrhos said. The words came out fierce, almost desperate.

"Not willingly, perhaps." Azure's tail swept a perfect arc through the sand. "That is not the same as never."

The fire between them sputtered, flames momentarily turning black before resuming their rainbow hues. When Pyrrhos flinched at the change, his wings drew tighter around his body.

"I have no choice," he said at last.

"There is always choice." Azure turned away, the conversation finished. "Even in the deepest darkness."

Pyrrhos watched him go.

Then looked down at the thread still clutched in his claw. It continued to glow with unwavering light, a physical manifestation of Darius's trust.

With a quick, furtive movement, Pyrrhos pressed the thread against his chest.

His scales parted like water, revealing a hollow near his heart. He placed the thread inside and closed the opening, hiding Darius's gift in the one place that still felt like his.

The dream thinned around the edges.

Stars dimmed. The three moons sank toward an impossible horizon. The fire lowered to embers. Morning pressed at the edge of everything, drawing the boys back toward waking.

Through it all, Pyrrhos stayed awake, one wing around Cassius, eyes fixed on the shoreline as if he could hold the world together by staring hard enough.

Far behind them, deep under the lake, the fracture widened. Black lines continued creeping toward land, slow as roots, patient as hunger.

Azure saw them coming.

He said nothing.

Some warnings landed better without words.

The night passed.

Morning waited.

And in the narrow space between dreaming and waking, choices hung suspended — quiet, weighty, and close enough to touch.

PART III

CHAPTER THIRTY-TWO

VIOLATION

Darius opened his eyes to find himself standing on his own front porch, bare feet cold against familiar boards. The moon hung overhead, too large and pale, casting shadows that fell wrong across the yard. This wasn't how his dreams with Azure began. Never, since that first dream with Azure, did his dreams begin at home. Usually, a mist, a field, or the crystal paths of Somnoria would emerge.

"Azure?"

His voice came out small, swallowed by thick air.

He stepped forward. The porch creaked beneath him with a wet thud, like cloth dropping. His counting began automatically. One, two, three. Even the numbers turned slippery in this light, unable to hold.

The rail beneath his hand shifted texture with each breath. Rough bark. Smooth glass. Then something soft and sticky that made his stomach turn. He pulled away, fingers tingling with an eerie sensation of wrongness.

Where was Azure?

His dragon had never failed to answer. Not once in all their nights together. Darius rotated his head, scanning the bloated moon-bright sky for any trace of blue wings.

Silence pressed against his ears. Deliberate. Crafted. Not the absence of sound but the presence of quiet, as if something held its breath beyond sight.

A shadow passed overhead. No shape. No source. Darkness spilling across the porch like ink. Cold struck him like a physical blow, the kind that started in bones and worked outward. The shadow didn't speak. It didn't need to.

You are alone here.

Black-ink purple light bled through the air. Not the warm purple of sunset. This was nightshade purple, bruised, spoiled — dark. The porch dissolved beneath his feet. Planks softened, sagged, and lost their shape. Wood became smoke, thick, oily smoke that rolled against his shins and left a bitter film behind. Smoke unraveled into threads, and the threads turned tacky the moment they touched him. They wrapped around his ankles and stuck. They climbed in strings that stretched, snapped, and rejoined, racing up his legs, his stomach, his chest, and then to his throat. The binding didn't clamp down. It clung. It moved when he swallowed, learning him, taking permission he never gave.

"Azure!"

He tried to scream. The tendon-like dream-matter webbed across his mouth, and over his jaw. It tasted of ash and copper.

Corruption.

The tarry binding oozed down his throat, banded his arms and burrowed into his ears. Each thread pulled at something deeper, at the part of him that knew how to dream, stealing his connection strand by strand.

His counting scattered. His anchor slipped away like water through spread fingers.

Then the world collapsed.

It reformed at the edge of a chasm.

And across the impossible gulf —

Azure.

Relief surged so fast his knees nearly folded. His dragon stood tall, wings spread, jewels catching what little light remained. Then Darius's gaze snapped into focus, and the relief didn't fade.

It failed.

Azure's scales were dull, and colorless, drained to dead gray. His jewels were dark as river stones.

Black tentacles rose from the void at Azure's feet. They didn't lash. They *lifted*, slow and certain, and coiled around his legs. They moved with a tacky drag, as if the air itself stuck to them. A sour, damp stench rode the gap and hit Darius's nose, thick as mold in a closed cellar.

The coils climbed.

They spiraled up with practiced strength, and where they touched, Azure's blue didn't just fade—it erased. Color gave way to bare gray, then to a stripped nothing that made Darius's stomach roll.

Azure jerked once, like a chain had snapped inside him.

Azure made a sound Darius had never heard. It carried across the chasm in pieces—part roar, part plea, all pain.

More tentacles erupted. They braided over wings, pressed into his chest, and climbed his throat. They pinned him without hurry, like they had all the time in the world.

When Azure's eyes found Darius, the command hit harder than fear. *Run. Get away.*

"Not... your... fault..." Azure forced out as coils crushed his throat.

The tentacles turned.

They reached for Darius next.

They crossed the chasm like distance meant nothing. They didn't stretch; they *arrived*. They moved with calm inevitability, like ink spilling downhill.

The threads already on Darius's ankles tugged in answer.

The binding around his throat tightened, timed to the beat of his swallow. It matched the pull it had on Azure, strand for strand—one web, one count, one trap.

Azure bucked once. His wings shuddered against the coils and gained nothing.

Azure groaned again, broken and raw. The sound caught, then tore free.

It might have been Darius's name.

It might have been goodbye.

Chapter Thirty-Three

Aftermath

The scream tore out of him before consciousness fully returned. It ripped up his throat, raw and animal, dragging him back into his body with violence that left his chest burning. Darius lurched upright on the couch; his blanket twisted around his legs like bindings. Sweat slicked his skin. He felt like he was burning up, yet cold all at once. The room was dark, but familiar.

The memory of the porch, the shadow. Of Azure.

His stomach rolled. Bile surged, bitter and hot, coating the back of his throat. He swallowed hard, hands grabbing for his blanket, fists closing so tight the fabric bit into his palms. One breath. Then two. Still too fast. His heart hammered against his ribs like something trying to escape.

The taste clung to his mouth — ash and copper, thick as the dream-matter that had webbed across his jaw. He worked his tongue against his teeth, desperate to scrub it away, but the flavor persisted. Rotted. Corrupted. Real enough to make him gag.

His fingers trembled against the blanket. When he tried to release his grip, they wouldn't obey. The muscles locked, frozen in the same position they'd been when the tentacles climbed Azure's throat. His throat burned where the bindings had pressed. He touched it with shaking fingers. Nothing. No marks. No tacky residue. But the sensation remained, tight and suffocating, like phantom hands still learning the shape of his swallow.

Footsteps pounded down the hall.

When Sadie burst through the doorway, breath sharp, hair loose around her face, she crossed the room in three strides and dropped to her knees in front of him. Her arms reached for his shoulders.

He flinched at first.

It was instinctive, and violent. His body jerked away from her touch, shoulders slamming against the couch cushions. Not her. Not Mama. But his skin screamed that anything touching him would bind, would climb, would steal.

Sadie froze. Hands suspended in the air between them. Pain flickered in her mind. It had been years since he recoiled at her touch. "Darius. Baby, it's Mama. I'm here."

His chest heaved. He stared at her hands — warm brown skin, familiar calluses, nothing like the black coils that had wrapped Azure. But his body wouldn't believe it. Every nerve fired warning signals. Every muscle tensed for invasion.

"You're safe," she said. Her voice dropped lower, softer. "You're home. You're on the couch. It's just me and you."

He shook. Hard, bone-deep tremors that rattled his teeth and turned his breath into ragged gasps. His hands flew to his ears, pressing hard, trying to shut out the phantom sound of Azure's broken roar. But it echoed inside his skull where hands couldn't reach.

Sadie lowered her hands to her lap. She didn't push. "That's all right. I'll stay right here. You don't have to do anything."

262

Minutes crawled past. Darius's breathing stayed jagged, his body locked in rigid terror. Sweat cooled on his skin, turning clammy. His nightshirt stuck to his back. When he shifted, the fabric pulled, and the sensation shot through him like the sticky threads climbing his legs. He gasped, hands scrambling at the cloth, yanking it away from his body.

"Easy," Sadie murmured. "You're all right."

But he wasn't. His fingers found his throat again, pressing against the phantom binding. The tightness persisted, synchronized with his pulse. Each swallow reminded him of the coils mapping his body, claiming what was never theirs. His stomach lurched again. He bent forward, certain he would be sick, but nothing came except dry heaves that left his ribs aching.

Sadie shifted closer, not touching, just present. "Was it a bad dream?"

He managed a nod, still hunched over his knees. The movement sent his vision swimming.

"The worst kind," she said. Her voice wrapped around him like her arms couldn't. "The kind that follows you out."

Yes. That was it exactly. The nightmare hadn't stayed in his sleep. It clung to his skin, coated his mouth, squeezed his throat. Even now, fully awake in his own living room with Mama kneeling beside him, the shadow's presence pressed against his awareness. Watching. Waiting.

His hands wouldn't stop shaking.

"I'm going to hum now," Sadie said. "You don't have to do anything. Just listen if you want."

The sound started low, barely louder than breath. An old hymn she carried in her bones. Rivers. Crossing. Staying afloat. The melody wound through the air between them, patient and sure. Darius lifted his head slightly, just enough to see her face. Tears tracked down her cheeks, but her expression stayed calm.

The trembling in his chest eased by degrees. Not gone. Not even close. But fractionally less violent. He counted his breaths the way Azure taught him. One. Two. Three. The numbers slipped and scattered, but he caught them again. Four. Five. Six.

"That's it," Sadie whispered, her humming never breaking. "That's my boy."

Before the dreams, her touch would have been too much. Too close. Too loud against his skin. He would have twisted away, fought it, screamed harder. But now his body knew what comfort felt like. How sensation could soothe instead of assault. Slowly, fraction by fraction, he let himself lean toward her.

When his shoulder finally made contact with her arm, she didn't grab him. She stayed still, letting him control the pressure, the placement, the pace. He pressed closer. Then closer still. When his forehead touched her collarbone, he collapsed against her like strings cut.

Sadie's arms came around him then, gentle but firm. One hand settled between his shoulder blades. The other cradled the back of his head. She rocked him without asking, her chest rising and falling beneath his cheek.

The smell of her hit him all at once. Lavender soap. Baked bread. Home. It cut through the copper taste, through the phantom stench of corruption that had ridden across the chasm. He breathed it in, desperate, using it to scrub the nightmare from his lungs.

She rocked him. He shook against her, body purging the terror in waves. Sharp, hitching breaths gave way to deeper sobs he couldn't voice. His fingers fisted in her nightgown, holding on like she might dissolve into shadow.

"You don't have to tell me," she said against his hair. "You don't have to say a word."

Minutes passed. Maybe longer. The house clicked and sighed around them. The night outside remained unremarkable. Whatever had followed him out of the dream did not show itself here. Or maybe it couldn't. Maybe Mama's arms created a barrier the darkness couldn't cross.

But inside, the violation persisted. His safe place had been entered. His protector touched. Azure bound, voice taken, eyes dimming to dead gray. The fear wasn't of death. It was of silence. Of isolation. Of being alone in a world that had taught him he was less.

The thing in the dark had shown him exactly what it wanted him to see. And even clutched in his mother's arms, another terror pressed up beneath the first.

What if Azure was gone?

What if he fell asleep and found only darkness?

His grip on Sadie's nightgown tightened. She felt it and anchored him closer. "I got you. I'm not letting go."

The trembling lessened but never fully stopped. His throat still burned. His stomach still churned. But surrounded by lavender and safety, exhaustion crept in around the edges. His body, wrung out and spent, began the slow descent toward sleep he feared.

"I scared," he managed. The words scraped out, barely sound.

"I know, baby." Sadie's hand moved in slow circles on his back. "But you're not alone. Not ever."

When dawn finally thinned the dark, Darius's grip had loosened. His breathing evened. His body slept, heavy and spent, cheek still pressed against Sadie's shoulder. She did not move until the light was full, and even then, she held him longer, whispering prayers over his head that he wouldn't remember but his spirit might keep.

***

Grass cooled his feet.

Darius did not move at first. He stayed frozen, listening for the echo of wrongness. His throat constricted. His pulse spiked. The air around him felt too similar to the nightmare — quiet, vast, watching.

The breeze blew gently, carrying no stench of corruption. Nothing reached for him with sticky intent.

"Azure," he said. His voice cracked on the name.

Wings swept low. Blue filled his vision — solid, precise, real. Jewels caught the twin moons and threw them back cleanly, each facet bright and whole. When Azure landed and folded his wings, he lowered his head until they were level.

Relief hit Darius so hard his knees buckled. He pitched forward, hands slamming into grass to keep from falling. A sob tore loose, raw with fear and gratitude tangled into one sound.

Azure moved closer, his presence a wall between Darius and every shadow. "It wasn't one of our dreams."

Darius nodded, unable to lift his head. His shoulders shook.

"It followed me," he managed.

"Yes."

"Was it real?" The question came out broken, desperate.

"It was a nightmare." Azure's voice carried weight, certainty. "Nightmares feel real because they use what already lives inside you. Fear. Memory. The shape of things you love twisted into weapons."

Darius lifted his head, eyes searching Azure's scales. His jewels were bright. Not gray. No tentacles. No dead eyes dimming to nothing. He reached out, fingers shaking, and touched Azure's foreleg.

Solid. Warm. Real.

"You were hurt," Darius said.

"No." The answer came without hesitation. "I am here. Whole. Unharmed."

But Darius remembered the coils climbing. The sound Azure made when his throat crushed. The command in his eyes: Run. Get away.

His hand pressed against his own throat. The phantom binding pulsed there, synchronized with his heartbeat. "It still —" He searched for a word. "Stings."

Azure studied him, gaze penetrating. "Come."

Darius stood on shaking legs. Azure turned, leading him across grass that felt too normal after violation. They walked in silence. Darius counted steps instead of breaths. One. Two. Three. The numbers helped. Always had.

When they stopped, Azure faced him again. "Not everything needs naming yet."

Darius swallowed hard. The binding sensation tightened, then eased. "I don't know what was real."

"Enough of it was." Azure's answer offered no comfort, only truth. "The darkness exists. It knows you now. And it will try again."

The words should have terrified him. They did. But beneath the fear ran something sharper — recognition. Whatever haunted his nightmare hadn't been random. It had a purpose. It had targeted him specifically, used Azure specifically, and violated his sanctuary with deliberate intent.

"Why?" His voice barely carried.

Azure's jewels flashed, catching light that came from everywhere and nowhere. "Because you matter. Because what you can become frightens it."

Darius stood in grass cooled by twin moons, body still shaking from nightmare residue, throat still burning from phantom bindings. And somewhere beyond the dream realm, beyond Somnoria's crystal spires, a darkness waited that knew his name.

CHAPTER THIRTY-FOUR

BECOMING

The dream did not dissolve.

It tightened around him, the way certainty replaces doubt, the way morning light claims the edges of night. The grass beneath Darius's feet cooled, no longer shifting with the emptiness that had followed him from the nightmare.

Azure stood before him, whole and unmistakably real.

Darius did not move closer. He did not retreat. He waited, throat still tender from phantom bindings, body aware in the way it remained after pain had passed but memory had not. The fear from the nightmare lingered in his muscles, a residue he couldn't shake through will alone.

Azure watched him with eyes that saw more than surface. When he finally spoke, his voice carried weight without urgency. "Come with me."

Darius's pulse quickened. Something in Azure's tone suggested this would not be like their other lessons, the gentle explorations of Somnoria's crystal paths. This was deliberate. Chosen.

"It is time for one of the most important lessons I can give you." Azure's wings shifted slightly, jewels catching light that came from everywhere and nowhere. "You are safe within this realm of dreams. There is no better time than the present."

The world responded before Darius could.

Silence spread outward from where they stood, not empty but intentional, as if the dream itself braced for what would come. The clearing reshaped beneath his feet, moss deepening to cushion each step, light thinning into clean, deliberate bands that striped the ground. The air thickened with texture, becoming something he could almost touch.

When Azure moved beside him, vast and grounded, his presence filled the space like a truth too large to question. His wings folded with care, each movement precise.

"This dreamscape is not like the others," Azure said. "Here, you will not merely practice skills. You will learn who you are."

Darius tilted his head, listening not just with his ears but with the part of him that had learned to read sensation the way others read words. The clearing hummed with possibility, with potential waiting to take shape.

"The skills you've gathered, the strength you've grown — these are not separate from you." Azure's voice dropped lower, more intimate. "They are you. This realm will test your senses, stretch your patience, stir the storm inside you. But I am near, always near. You will not face these trials by yourself."

Darius drew breath, feeling it fill his lungs completely, then release. His counting began automatically. One. Two. Three. The rhythm steadied him.

"It is time to learn not who you are alone," Azure said, "but what you can become."

Darius exhaled slowly, letting the words sink into the marrow of him. What he could become. Not what others expected. Not what limitations had been placed upon him by doctors or neighbors or even family who loved him but couldn't always see him. What he, Darius Turner, could become when the world bent to meet him instead of demanding he contort to fit its shape.

"Do not look with your eyes," Azure instructed. "Feel it through your skin. Every hair. Every pore. In your sinew and marrow."

Darius didn't speak, but his head tilted in that particular way that meant he was listening with his whole body. His eyes drifted half-closed, pupils dilating as he drank in every detail. The air grew thick with textures he had no words for in waking life. He sensed the vibration of insects humming conversations too high-pitched for ordinary hearing, the inaudible murmur of roots speaking to one another underground, the tiny flex of petals blooming in motion so slow it seemed like stillness.

He didn't simply see these things. He sensed them as shape and sound, color and rhythm, the way a musician might hear a symphony in the rustling of leaves.

His body moved without conscious command. He dropped to one knee and placed his palm flat against the earth. The moss cooled his skin immediately, but beneath that surface sensation he discerned something warmer, like breath rising from a sleeping giant. He pressed harder, then drew a circle with his fingertip — slow, deliberate, feeling the dream respond to his touch.

The trees responded.

Their branches leaned inward, rustling in tones he knew weren't wind. A spiral of mist lifted from the center of the clearing and unspooled above him, forming an image midair that shimmered with ethereal clarity. A wide field materialized, golden and phosphorescent under a lavender sky that hurt to look at directly. Strange stalks grew tall and straight in perfect lines, their heads shimmering with a brittle-bright quality that made Darius's stomach tighten.

Grain. But unlike any grain he had seen in the waking world or in dreams before this moment.

In the vision, children ran through the field, laughing, scooping up handfuls of the golden grain and eating them with delighted abandon. Their movements flowed smooth and effortless. One girl spun in circles, eyes bright, but the light in her face seemed off. Darius flinched. The laughter rang hollow, looped, like a song played too many times until the joy wore thin and only the mechanics remained.

He felt it then. The absence beneath the beauty. Not dangerous exactly. Not pain. Something worse.

Stasis.

The vision cracked for a moment, as if glass strained under pressure it was never meant to bear, then vanished in a flutter of gold dust that dissolved before touching the ground.

When Azure stepped forward, jewels dimming slightly, he asked, "Did you see it?"

Darius nodded. He touched his chest with one hand, then swept it outward in a single decisive motion. The gesture spoke more clearly than words could have.

Tainted.

Azure's gaze lingered where the field had been, his ancient eyes seeing layers Darius couldn't yet access. "Yes. This field has been planted here. Something is shifting in the dreamscape, changing in ways I have not witnessed before."

Darius rose slowly, muscles cautious. He did not smile. But his eyes were clear, alert in a way they had not been since the nightmare. Whatever that vision meant, whatever darkness waited beyond Somnoria's borders, he would face it when the time came.

He glanced at Azure, then skyward, where the vision had appeared and disappeared.

Somewhere ahead, something was waiting for him.

They arrived without walking.

One moment Darius and Azure were rising through trees wrapped in ribbons of light; the next, they stood in a long, cathedral-like corridor carved from starlight and glass. The transition happened so smoothly Darius couldn't pinpoint when movement became arrival, when intention became manifestation.

The Hall of Echoes.

Sound here did not bounce or fade the way it did in the waking world. It lingered, suspended in the air like memory made audible. The atmosphere was permeated with moments lived and lost, not memories to be seen but feelings to be experienced. Joy and fear and shame and triumph all existing simultaneously in tone, vibration, and the spaces between silence. The walls pulsed, not with color, but with emotion given texture.

Azure said nothing, allowing the hall to speak for itself.

When Darius took a tentative step forward, the floor beneath him rippled — not visually, but internally, like stepping into a memory encased beneath the skin of the world. A soft whimper met his ears, followed by the sharp crack of a plate breaking, then a child's scream. His own voice, younger and more terrified.

The dream didn't show the scene. It offered the feeling. The shame of not understanding what he'd done wrong. The confusion when Mama's face crumpled. The helpless rage that followed, building until it drowned out everything else.

Darius froze.

His breathing grew shallow, fingers curling at his sides until nails bit into palms. He knew this memory intimately, knew every terrible second of what came next. The slap of footsteps running. The rush of panic as hands reached for him. His mother's voice, tender and trembling, trying desperately to reach him while he flailed against everything — her arms, the world, himself.

"It's not hurting you now," Azure said behind him. "It's showing you that you survived it."

The words unlocked something in Darius's chest. He forced his fingers to uncurl, forced air into lungs that had forgotten how to expand. One breath. Then another. He stepped forward.

A new note vibrated nearby. It was laughter, bright and unrestrained. His siblings playing outside, their voices weaving together in harmony he'd wanted so desperately to join. Warmth spread through his chest, bittersweet and sharp.

"I wanted to be part of it." The words emerged quiet but clear. "But I couldn't get the words out. And then I got angry because I couldn't explain. And it got worse."

He took another step, this time with more certainty.

As he moved through the hallway, sounds washed over him in waves. Each one carried a moment from his life, a fragment of the boy he'd been: the fear in Gunny's cries when the storm broke loose, the pleading in his mother's voice as she tried to pull him back from it, and the aftermath — the wreck left behind in the rooms and in the people. He tried to show them he loved them. He just didn't know how to get it out before everything shattered.

He winced, not from pain, but from recognition.

But he didn't stop walking.

Step by step, he moved forward, letting the echoes roll through him. They no longer overwhelmed the way they once would have. Instead they flowed like Mama's humming, constant and sure, marking time without demanding anything in return. He passed anger and fear, shame and frustration, each emotion acknowledged but not dwelt upon.

Then he reached a point where the tone changed completely — a soothing hum, deep and safe, vibrating through the hall with the resonance of home. Azure's voice. Their first meeting. The first time Darius hadn't been afraid of his own mind, the first time someone had looked at him and seen strength instead of brokenness.

Darius exhaled fully, shoulders dropping.

"It's not just memory," he said, running his fingers through the air as if tracing invisible strings. "It's music. My whole life is music." He paused, considering. "Out of tune in some places, but still music. Still worth listening to."

He drew the path of each echo with his hands, following melodies only he could hear. When he looked ahead, more memories waited in the distance, more truths suspended in sound and sensation. But he no longer braced for their arrival.

He was listening. Learning. Letting the past teach him instead of haunt him.

"I used to think the dream was about escaping." His voice carried clearly through the hall, each word deliberate. "But it's not. It's teaching me. Helping me carry the things I couldn't hold before."

A faint golden tone rang out somewhere far ahead, new yet familiar, like a song he'd heard once in childhood and never quite forgotten. The future, whispering.

Darius turned toward it, pulse steady.

"I'm ready," he said to Azure, to the hall, to himself. "What's next?"

The sky changed without warning.

One breath they stood in the Hall of Echoes, surrounded by the music of memory; the next, they emerged beneath a vast dome of floating glass that stretched beyond sight in every direction. The air here buzzed with silent expectation, as if the realm suspended itself perfectly still to see what Darius would do.

Suspended above and around them, a thousand shards of translucent crystal hovered midair, each one impossibly suspended by forces he couldn't name. The fragments caught and refracted light, creating patterns that shifted too quickly to follow. Some reflected complete scenes — a dragon's eye blinking slow, a child's hand reaching toward starlight, a crown broken cleanly in two. Others remained blank, or worse — flickered between possibilities too fast to hold, showing futures that existed and didn't exist simultaneously.

When Darius took a slow step forward, neck craned back to take in the impossible architecture of glass and light, Azure spoke beside him. His voice carried reverence, the kind reserved for sacred things. "They call this the Skyglass. It's a puzzle left by the first dreamers, before my time or any living dragon's. No one has solved it. It doesn't ask for logic or cleverness. It asks for something else entirely."

Darius tilted his head, that familiar gesture of deep listening.

The pieces weren't still. They rotated on invisible axes, shifting and spinning, like they were listening right back to him. He could feel their rhythm. It was not linear, not fixed to any pattern he'd encountered before. It was like trying to follow six melodies at once, each playing a different version of truth, each insisting it alone possessed the answer.

His eyes closed. Better to see with other senses.

A girl's laughter again — was that Sara, the girl from his picture, from the vision? The sound was familiar yet unknown. Then something colder underneath, a current of darkness threading through innocence. Then heat built slowly, like dragon fire gathering deep in a chest before release.

He opened his eyes. The glass flared in return, responding to his attention.

Without hesitation, without fear or doubt, he stepped into the center of the chamber.

"Wait —" Azure started, wings half-spreading in protective instinct, but stopped himself.

Darius raised one hand, palm open to the glass above. Then the other. Slowly, as if moving underwater where resistance shaped every gesture, he spun in a circle. The hum of the glass passed through him, vibrating in his bones. With each rotation, his body remembered more, the tones and notes he'd heard in dreams he hadn't understood until this moment, shapes he'd glimpsed and dismissed, patterns that had seemed random but now revealed their structure.

The shards responded, shifting like they recognized him. Like they'd been waiting.

He hummed a single note, low and clear, rising from somewhere deeper than his throat.

The pieces moved.

Not toward symmetry. Not toward the kind of order that made sense to ordinary eyes. But toward meaning, toward truth arranged in its own language.

They spiraled inward, forming a constellation that blazed against the darkness. Six stars, each illuminating blue fire. Beneath them, a flicker materialized — a crown cracked down the middle, split by force or intention. Around it, a dragon's wing spread wide and dark, cast in shadow that seemed to breathe.

Left behind, blazing in the air like a brand burned into the fabric of the dream itself, hung a symbol Darius had never seen but somehow knew:

Six stars. One crown. A path unfolding into futures not yet written.

For the first time since entering Somnoria, Darius looked beyond the immediate dream, not with fear or confusion, but with clarity that cut through every doubt. The pieces fell together in his mind, assembling themselves into understanding.

"We're not alone," he said, voice steady. "I saw them. The others with eyes like mine." He paused, letting the weight of it settle. "And I think they're already dreaming. Somewhere. Somewhen."

The wind changed.

Azure lifted his head sharply, ancient instincts flaring. "Hold still. Something has changed in the outer realms."

He turned toward a horizon only dragons could see, jewels dimming with concern.

"Let's return to safer ground."

Darius obeyed, stepping back from the constellation that still burned overhead. But before they could move, the sky split open, not with rain, but with color made violent. Cascading rivers of red and violet streaked across the clouds, colliding with bursts of gold and teal in explosions that hurt to witness. Sounds poured down like thunder made of bells and whispers, the pitch rising into a chaotic, shimmering scream that threatened to tear thought apart.

The dream trembled. The ground beneath Darius rippled like water disturbed.

"This is not meant to hurt you," Azure said quickly, positioning himself between Darius and the worst of the storm. "But it is meant to test you. To see if you can hold yourself together when everything pulls you apart."

Darius clenched his fists, breath catching in his throat.

The overwhelming cascade of sensation he'd spent his whole life trying to escape crashed over him. It was like being small again, younger and helpless, when he needed to cover his ears and close his eyes but the pressure still built and built until he had to bang his head against something solid just to make it stop, to replace the chaos with pain he could control.

His knees buckled. He fell hard, palms slamming into the ground that wouldn't hold still.

The colors struck the earth around him, pulsing in jagged waves of sound made visible. He could hear every single shade. Each one carried a different texture, a different urgency, screaming for attention simultaneously. It was chaos, but underneath the randomness he sensed a pattern, a structure he couldn't yet name but recognized instinctively.

When his palms pressed flat against the trembling ground, he forced his eyes closed.

He breathed the way Azure had taught him.

In. Four counts.

Out. Eight counts.

The breath anchored him when nothing else could. His fingers started tracing a pattern in the air. He didn't understand it, had never learned it in any lesson, but it felt safe. Like truth, somehow.

The storm paused.

When Darius opened his eyes and looked straight into the heart of the chaos, he raised one hand and drew a spiral, slow and deliberate.

A gust of gold wind folded inward, responding to his command.

Then red. Then violet. Each hue bent toward the pattern he drew, following the invisible architecture his fingers traced. Not calmed, not silenced, but seen. Acknowledged. Given shape instead of allowed to rampage.

Darius stood on shaking legs, surrounded by a dimming cyclone of light that spun around him like a wall between safety and storm. His smile emerged calm, not triumphant. This wasn't victory over the chaos. It was conversation, the kind he'd always wanted to have with a world that shouted too loud and moved too fast.

"I'm not afraid of you," he said to the colors, to the storm, to every overwhelming sensation that had ever made him feel broken.

The storm stilled.

The last of the wind curled like a ribbon around his wrist, gentle now, almost tender, before vanishing into the sky.

Azure studied him for a long moment, jewels pulsing with something that might have been pride or perhaps recognition that his student had surpassed expectation.

"You're ready for the mirror," Azure said finally.

Darius nodded, heart beating steady, eyes shining with purpose.

"I want to see who I truly am."

The mirror waited in a clearing of absolute stillness — no wind, no rustle of leaves, no sound beyond the heartbeat of the dream itself, keeping time.

It wasn't a mirror of glass or polished metal.

It floated before them, a pane of light suspended between two elder trees whose roots dug deeper than earth could measure. Its surface was neither smooth nor flat but curved like water bound in impossible tension. Around it, the world faded into diffused shadow. The dream itself seemed to hold its breath, waiting.

Darius approached with steps that grew smaller as he drew closer, some part of him both desperate and terrified to see what the mirror would reveal.

He saw nothing at first. Just light reflecting light, empty as unmarked paper.

Then, little by little, images formed.

A boy stood in the mirror's surface. It was him, but fundamentally not. This version spoke quickly, words tumbling out with easy confidence. He laughed without restraint. His hands stayed still at his sides instead of flicking through counts and patterns. Words flowed from him like rivers, and everyone around him nodded, smiling, understanding perfectly. He was normal. Ordinary. Expected.

Darius tilted his head, studying this stranger wearing his face.

Another version flickered into place, replacing the first. This one stood taller, older, a sword slung across his back with casual authority. His eyes sparkled with confidence bordering on arrogance. He led armies, shook hands with kings, commanded respect through presence alone. He looked like heroes from the stories Lula read aloud, like someone whose life made sense to everyone who witnessed it.

Expected. Predictable. A story someone else had written.

Then another image emerged.

A scholar bent over books, surrounded by admiration. A musician whose fingers coaxed beauty from instruments Darius didn't recognize. Versions of himself shaped by what others might call success, by definitions of worth that had nothing to do with who he actually was.

He took a step back.

Azure's voice came soft, almost tender. "These are echoes of who you might have been — if you were born in another body, another life, another path. They are not lies. They are simply not you."

Darius stood perfectly still, watching the parade of possibilities that would never come to pass.

"I don't want to be anyone else," he said.

The words emerged quiet but absolute. He had spent his life being told, in ways both gentle and cruel, that he needed to change. To speak more. To move less. To be easier, quieter, more like everyone else. And here the mirror offered him exactly that — a thousand versions of himself smoothed into shapes that fit comfortably in the world.

He didn't want them.

He stepped closer to the mirror and reached into his dream-cloak. From a small pouch at his side, he pulled free a shard of Skyglass, one piece from the puzzle he had solved earlier, still glowing with the light of understanding.

With slow, certain movements that betrayed no doubt, he raised it and pressed it to the mirror's surface.

The glass rippled like water struck by stone, and the false selves vanished.

Now the mirror showed him as he truly was. An eight-year-old boy with fierce, brilliant eyes that saw the world in ways others couldn't imagine. He stood barefoot in moss, hands covered in dream-ink from drawing patterns only he could see, mind alert and burning with thoughts too complex for simple words. The six stars formed a constellation behind him, points of light that marked him as different and would mark the others yet to come.

This version of him didn't try to fit into spaces too small for what he contained. He didn't explain or apologize for taking up room in the world. He simply was. And the dream loved him for it, and celebrated him exactly as he stood.

Azure lowered his grand head beside him, jewels catching Darius's reflection and multiplying it a thousand times. "After this," he said, "nothing will fit the way it did before. Once you accept who you are — truly accept it — the world will ask more of you than it asks of most. Some of it will hurt. Some of it will cost you. I will walk with you, but I will not lie to you. It will not be easy."

"I accepted it a long time ago," Darius said, eyes still fixed on the glowing image of himself shining in the mirror. "This is just the first time I knew it."

The mirror pulsed once, silver, then deep blue, and dissolved into the night air like mist burned away by morning.

No applause followed. No flare of triumphant light. Just peace settling over the clearing like snow.

Darius turned to Azure, shoulders straight, eyes clear.

"I'm ready."

CHAPTER THIRTY-FIVE

LESSONS

The morning after seeing his true self in the mirror, Darius moved through the world differently.

Not visibly. His hands still flicked through their familiar counts. His feet still found the same worn path between home and school. But inside, something fundamental had changed. The boy who had looked back at him from that floating pane of light, the fierce-eyed, unashamed, marked by constellation, walked beside him now in waking hours. When other children stared at his silence or his strange movements, he no longer felt the old pull to shrink, to apologize for taking up space. He was different. The dream had shown him that different was not the same as broken.

Azure's words echoed through his thoughts as he settled into his desk that morning: *Once you accept who you are — truly accept it — the world will ask more of you than it asks of most. Some of it will hurt. Some of it will cost you.*

The six stars still burned behind his eyes when he blinked. The cracked crown. The dark wing spreading. Somewhere, others like him were already dreaming. Already gathering. The knowing sat in his chest like a weight and a gift simultaneously. A responsibility he hadn't asked for but somehow recognized as his.

By recess, the dream realm's intensity had faded enough for ordinary concerns to resurface. Like Cass's relentless curiosity. Like the simple pleasure of drawing what he'd seen while his best friend chattered beside him.

Shadows from the pecan tree blotched the grass where Darius and Cass sat during recess. The schoolyard buzzed with shouts and laughter, but this corner stayed quiet, far enough from the swings for Cass to concentrate and Darius to think. Darius hunched over his notebook, pencil gliding across the page. Cass plucked leaves from low branches, tearing them into neat strips.

"That ain't normal clouds," Cass said, peeking over Darius's shoulder at the swirling shapes. "Clouds got bumps. These look like somebody pulled cotton candy apart real slow."

Darius remained silent, while his pencil wavered, then continued, lines looping from last night's dream.

"Your dreams are all floaty and serious," Cass went on, stuffing a pecan into his mouth. He grimaced and spat it out. "You dream like an old man."

Darius's shoulders shook with silent laughter. He flipped to a new corner of the page, sketching Azure's wingtip arched across a field of stars.

"Last night I rode a pickle through the sky, and the stars were lightning bugs," Cass said. "What'd you dream about? More of those string things?"

Darius nodded, shading in the curve of Azure's wing.

"How come your dragon teaches you serious stuff and Pyrrhos plays games?" Cass folded a leaf into quarters. "Not that I'm complainin'. Games are better than lessons. But still."

Darius flipped the page again, sketching delicate threads intersecting at sharp angles. His hand moved with certainty rarely seen in his waking movements, dream-memory guiding the pencil.

When Cass leaned closer, curiosity overtook his usual restlessness. "That what they look like? The threads?"

Darius nodded.

"And you can... touch 'em?"

Another nod.

"Why you gotta learn it?" Cass asked, quieter now. "Is that what you weave and make things appear in a dream?"

Darius looked back to his notebook. His fingers drummed, one, two, three. Azure had never said not to share dream weaving, but it had always felt personal.

"Do you think you can show me how?" Cass asked, then scratched the back of his neck. "I mean... could you? Sometime?"

Darius didn't answer right away. He looked back down at his notebook. He'd never thought about teaching someone else. Dream weaving wasn't like drawing or talking. It didn't come from his head, it came from somewhere quieter. Deeper.

"I don't know if I can teach you," he said. "Azure's been showin' me for a long time now. Almost three years." He paused, watching the faint lines he'd sketched fade. "It's more somethin' I feel than somethin' I know."

Cass opened his mouth, closed it, then gave a sharp nod like he understood, even if he didn't.

Around them, the schoolyard spun on, children playing with jump ropes, bouncing balls, and lots of laughter from the group of girls Lula was sitting next to. None of it touched the space they shared beneath the tree. None of those kids had dragons.

Cass leaned in a little. "Can I watch then? I won't mess anything up, I swear." His usual bounce was gone, replaced by something quieter. "I'll be quiet. Well... not so much quiet, but careful.

But I won't touch nothin' unless I'm s'posed to."

A smile tugged at Darius's lips. Cass not touching anything was hard to imagine. Still, in his chaos, there was some kind of magic.

"I could look," Cass added. "Like when you showed me how to draw. I'll sit still this time. Promise."

Darius studied him, weighing the risks. Azure might not approve. The threads might not respond to another presence. But something inside him nudged forward, an instinct deeper than logic.

"Tonight?" Darius asked. One word, layered with meaning.

Cass's eyes widened. "No foolin'? You'll let me come?"

Darius nodded, returning to his drawing, adding pressure to a strand that now shined brighter than the rest.

He wondered what Azure would say, how he'd explain Cass's presence. But the worry sat far off compared to the excitement rising in his chest.

"What's it feel like?" Cass asked. "The threads. When you touch them."

Darius tilted his head, thinking. He reached for Cass's hand and pressed two fingers to the inside of his wrist, where his pulse beat.

"Like a heartbeat? Are they slimy?" Cass guessed.

Darius grinned. Then lifted his hand to the sunlight streaking through the pecan branches.

"So, not slimy, but like sunlight?" Cass murmured. His brow furrowed as he tried to picture it. "So... alive. They feel alive?"

A rare full smile spread across Darius's face.

The bell rang. The boys were so engrossed in their discussion that it took them by surprise. Cass jumped up as usual. Darius closed his notebook with care, slipping it into his satchel.

"Tonight," Cass said, not asking.

Darius nodded. A flicker of anticipation ripped through him. He would share them, Azure's lessons, his truth. Not in solitude, but with someone who might understand.

The island hovered in empty space, a disc of marble suspended in lavender mist. Stars hung close overhead, watchful.

Darius stood barefoot at the center, his dream-self steadier than his waking body. Azure perched at the island's edge, his wings half-unfurled, and his sapphire jewels lit from within as he watched his charge.

Around them, the air shimmered with unseen currents, waiting to be noticed.

When Azure extended one wing, sweeping it in a slow arc, where the tip passed, faint strands of light appeared, quivering like plucked strings.

"Dreams are connections," Azure said. His wing completed its arc, leaving a trail of shimmering filaments. "A weaver does not create these threads. They already exist. The weaver reveals them and guides them."

Darius stepped closer, his eyes reflecting the threads' glow. He raised a hand, hesitating.

"Reach, not just with your hands, but with the intent of creation," Azure said. "Listen first."

Darius reached toward a pale blue thread, his hand hovering above it. His eyes narrowed, watching.

His breathing slowed, syncing with something beyond himself. When he opened his eyes again, he understood.

He touched the thread.

Light rippled from the contact, racing along the strand like fire on a fuse. The thread brightened, lifted to his fingertip as if recognizing him.

"Excellent," Azure said, pride clear in his voice. "Now draw it toward you. Deliberately, like Mama pulling a stitch through cloth."

When Darius curled his finger, the thread followed. It bent, stretched, held shape. He guided it into an arc, watching it respond to his will.

"Set your eyes to the threads. They will answer," Azure said. "Emotion shapes it. Intention guides it. But its nature remains its own. Remember this: we do not force the dream. We invite —"

"I FOUND YOU!"

The shout shattered the calm, and the thread vanished.

Darius and Azure both turned.

Cass stood at the island's edge, barefoot in bright red pajamas, his grin impossibly wide. "Whoa, this place is fancy," he said, trotting across the marble. His steps sent ripples through the smooth surface. He spun in place, arms outstretched. "Everything's so... clean."

When Azure stiffened, wings drawing in, the sapphires along his jaw dimmed.

"What is the meaning of this?" he asked Darius.

Before Darius could speak, Cass jogged to his side. "He invited me," he said with a shrug. "Said I could watch." He poked the air where the thread had been. "Sorry 'bout that."

Darius glanced at Cass, then shaped his hands with clarity: Be quiet. Be still.

"I can do that," Cass promised, though he swayed in place. "Quiet as a mouse." He zipped his lips, then immediately added, "Where's Pyrrhos?"

A rush of wind answered as Pyrrhos descended, ruby-studded scales catching starlight. He landed gracefully, tail curling behind him in a perfect spiral.

"We meant no disruption," Pyrrhos said, voice deeper and warmer than Azure's. "Cass was... persistent."

Azure's jewels pulsed, twice. Darius recognized the signal: displeasure.

"Dream weaving is not performance," Azure said. "It demands concentration, discipline and most importantly — silence."

"We'll stay back," Pyrrhos replied, placing a claw gently on Cass's shoulder. "Curiosity is the beginning of all learning."

Azure's tail swept the marble. "Curiosity without discipline tangles threads. Destroys dreams."

"I can be disciplined," Cass insisted, fingers already reaching toward a shimmer in the air. Pyrrhos caught his wrist.

"Perhaps," Pyrrhos offered, "a demonstration would help. Show him what happens when threads are mishandled."

Azure glanced from Pyrrhos to Cass, then to Darius, who stood still, patient.

"Very well," Azure said at last. "But at the first disruption, you both withdraw." His gaze hardened. "Dreams are not toys. They carry power you cannot understand."

"Yes, Mr. Azure, Sir," Cass said, unusually solemn. He folded his legs and sat, hands on his knees. "Ready."

Azure turned back to Darius. "Begin again. Show him what listening truly means."

Darius closed his eyes. The interruption had scattered his attention, but the threads remained. He extended a hand, fingers spread, sensing more than seeing. Soon, he found it, a thread that vibrated with quiet strength, its frequency aligned with something inside him.

He drew it into view. It gleamed silver-blue, pulsing between his fingers. Carefully, he began to shape it, guiding, not pushing.

A second thread appeared, drawn to the harmony. Darius wove them together, forming a simple shape, two loops intersecting into a circle.

"That's it?" Cass said, awe softening his voice. "That's dream weaving?"

Darius nodded, holding the shape with confidence.

The woven circle hovered in the air, threads of light pulsing. When Cass leaned in, eyes wide with curiosity, his usual restlessness stilled. His fingers twitched at his sides, eager to touch, to try.

"Can I try?" Cass blurted, eyes fixed on a scarlet thread.

Azure glanced at Pyrrhos, then back at Cass. "Cassius, dream weaving requires years of practice. Darius has trained for years."

Cass's shoulders dropped. "But it looks easy when Darius does it."

Pyrrhos moved closer. "It isn't. You're seeing the part after the struggle."

Cass clenched his fists. His jaw worked once, like he was swallowing something bitter. "I hate only watching Darius weave."

For a moment, no one corrected him. The lavender mist persisted. The woven circle pulsed, steady in Darius's hands.

Then Azure said, quieter, "Your lessons differ from Darius's."

Cass kicked lightly at the marble, eyes down. "Still feels unfair. He gets cool powers, and I stand around."

Pyrrhos's claw settled on his shoulder. "Your gift is creation, Cassius. You make new dreams."

Azure nodded once. "That is strength."

Cass's expression softened, accepting but still wistful. "I guess it's like how Darius draws better, but I run faster."

Darius smiled, relieved by his friend's understanding.

From behind them, Pyrrhos observed with care, especially how Darius paused before touching threads, fingers fluttering like he was listening. When Darius added a third thread with ease, Pyrrhos's eyes narrowed.

"You hear them, don't you?" he asked. "Not merely sense them, hear them."

Darius nodded, surprised by the accuracy.

"A rare ability," Pyrrhos said. "Even among practiced weavers."

"Darius sees things right," Cass said, pride overtaking his jealousy.

Darius ducked his head, a shy smile forming. His circle grew, incorporating the scarlet thread that Cass had wanted to try. Now it radiated in harmony with the others.

"Look!" Cass shouted. "You used the one that was supposed to be mine!"

"He did so on your behalf," Azure said. "A gift between friends."

Cass beamed. "So part of that circle is mine too?"

Darius nodded, hands shaping the growing creation. The scarlet thread brightened in response.

"Interesting," Pyrrhos murmured, too quiet for the boys to hear. "The threads respond not to the weaver alone, but to those close to them." He watched Darius's every motion, the precision, the pauses, the listening.

Above, the stars shifted into celestial shapes mirroring Darius's pattern below. The lesson continued in shared awe, two boys, two dragons, suspended in lavender mist, joined by threads both seen and unseen.

Azure guided Darius through another sequence. Threads multiplied under his hands, forming a lattice above the floor. Cass stood quietly nearby, watching closely. Darius now wove on his own, Azure only stepping in to correct misalignments.

"You're building a dream bridge," Azure said as Darius linked two vibrant threads. "A path between separate dream states."

Cass edged closer. "You mean he can make a road from my dreams to his? So I could go back to the candy place even without Darius inviting me?"

"With enough skill," Azure confirmed, "that's possible."

While the trio set their eyes on the lattice, Pyrrhos stepped back, movements silent. The crimson jewels along his spine dimmed to dull embers. At the island's edge, he spread his wings and vanished into the mist without a ripple.

Pyrrhos slipped into the mist where the dream thinned.

He extended a claw into the thin place, and the dream recoiled.

A tear opened in the fabric of the world, its edges curling like burned paper. Pyrrhos reached through, claws scraping against something resistant, until his grip closed around a thread unlike any Azure had revealed. This one drank light. The air bent around it, everything flattening as if swallowed.

"I've found something," Pyrrhos said.

His voice did not echo. It vanished.

The response came as weight. Cold pressure settled over his thoughts, vast and patient. The Obsidian Dragon did not speak so much as take up space, as if it had always been there.

"Report."

Pyrrhos tightened his grip despite the burn along his claw. "The quiet one advances faster than expected."

The thread pulsed.

"He weaves with precision. Threads respond to him instinctively. What takes others years —"

"Explain."

Pyrrhos swallowed. "He listens. Before shaping, before command. He hears the threads' intent and suggests instead of forcing."

Silence pressed down. Not absence — assessment.

"Azure permits this."

"Yes. He adapts his teaching around it." Pyrrhos glanced toward the distant island, barely visible through the mist. "There is more. When the boy incorporated a thread tied to Cass's emotions, the sequence strengthened."

The dark thread twisted, alive now. Hungry.

Connection, the Obsidian Dragon thought, and the word carried satisfaction. *Always the weakness.*

"Should I sever it?" Pyrrhos asked.

The pressure deepened, deliberate.

"No. Let it deepen. Let him trust."

The presence expanded, sinking into Pyrrhos's bones.

"Roots do not break stone by force. They wait," the Obsidian Dragon continued.

Pyrrhos didn't move.

"Watch."

A pause — measured, cruel.

"Do not interfere. Yet."

The thread went slack, unraveling into black mist that evaporated. The weight withdrew, leaving cold behind.

Pyrrhos flexed his claw, frost melting from his scales.

He turned back toward the island.

The lesson continued.

And the stone, unseen, continued to crack.

As he approached, the dream clarified, Darius weaving, Azure guiding, Cass brimming with energy. None had noticed he'd gone.

When Pyrrhos landed lightly and returned his rubies to full brilliance, he said, "Remarkable progress. Your student has natural talent."

Azure nodded. "More than talent. Understanding."

Darius connected the final threads, his bridge between dreams now whole. His eyes fixed, no strain, his movements fluid.

"I want to try it!" Cass said, bouncing beside the structure.

"Not tonight," Azure replied. "It must stabilize."

Darius nodded, lowering his hands. The work was done, rough, but real. He glanced toward Pyrrhos, a silent question in his eyes.

Pyrrhos inclined his head. "Well done, young weaver."

The praise was sincere, despite the lies it sat atop. As the dream began to fade and dawn brushed against sleep's edge, Pyrrhos felt the weight of his role.

The boy deserved better than to be a pawn.

But the Obsidian Dragon's words echoed like prophecy:

Trust is how the root slips beneath the stone.

And Pyrrhos knew:

The stone was already cracking.

Chapter Thirty-Six

Picnic

The sun dipped behind the giant oak trees on the grounds of the church, cooling off the congregation from the evening's heat after Sunday's evening sermon. Picnic blankets dotted the grass, laden with dishes still warm from ovens and skillets: fried chicken, potato salad, greens seasoned to perfection. Lanterns flickered, casting cozy light across smiling faces.

When Mrs. Williams settled into her lawn chair next to Mrs. Jenkins, fanning herself lightly with a folded church program, she said, "Well, Evelyn, it's a blessing to see Cass playing with someone who doesn't mind all his talking, someone with the patience to take it in stride."

"He's been talkin' non-stop about fishin' with Darius," Evelyn Jenkins said, shaking her head with affectionate bewilderment. Her husband, Arthur, chuckled beside her, eyes crinkling warmly.

"Never had a friend quite like that before," Mrs. Williams admitted. Her gaze drifted to the cluster of children near the edge of the yard. Cassius's voice rose brightly above the rest, animated and insistent. "He usually talks nonstop around others. I worry, you know."

When Pastor John approached quietly, smiling warmly as he overheard the exchange, he said, "God has a way of bringing friends together, Mrs. Williams. Perhaps Darius is exactly who Cassius needed and vice versa."

Sam, Cass's older brother, lanky and thoughtful, lounged nearby, monitoring Cass with a protective gaze. He nodded, his voice quiet but clear. "Cass keeps saying they're fishin' in dreams. Catching impossible things."

"Dream fishin'?" Pastor John's eyebrows lifted, amused.

"Cass tells the wildest stories," Sam continued. "He says their catches are big as cars and got stars inside 'em."

Mrs. Williams laughed, shaking her head. "Cass and his imagination. He's always had stories bigger than himself."

Augustus Turner, within earshot, exchanged a quick glance with his wife, Sadie. He cleared his throat. "That's the sort of adventure boys love."

Ezra and Theo exchanged quiet smirks, knowing more than they would say. When Lula tugged on her mother's sleeve, she said, "Mama, Cass said they caught a fish that sang songs."

Sadie offered a careful smile. "Did he now? Well, every fisherman's entitled to stretch the truth a little."

Laughter rippled through the adults, masking quiet suspicions. Darius stood near Cass, quietly sketching in the dust with a stick, listening intently as his friend continued weaving their dream adventures for anyone who would listen. Gunny flopped down beside them, hands on her hips. "Every time y'all sit this quiet, something weird happens. I'm saying."

Cass rolled his eyes. "We're eatin'."

"That's what you said last time," she shot back, already stealing a cookie.

Pastor John chuckled warmly, placing a comforting hand on Mrs. Williams's shoulder. "Well, imagination's a mighty gift. Who knows? I reckon they're catchin' stars."

Across the yard, Miss Thompson stood alone near the dessert table, arranging leftover pies with practiced efficiency. She'd attended the evening service as she did most Sundays, finding comfort in the familiar hymns and Pastor John's steady voice. But tonight, her attention kept drifting to a particular student who sat cross-legged in the grass, drawing patterns with a stick while his friend talked enough for both of them.

When Sadie approached with an empty serving dish, Miss Thompson smiled. "Mrs. Turner. Lovely sermon this evening."

"It was," Sadie agreed, setting down the dish. She followed Miss Thompson's gaze to where Darius sat. "He's doing well, isn't he? At school?"

Miss Thompson's smile deepened, becoming something warmer, more personal. "He's special, Mrs. Turner. Truly." She glanced around, then lowered her voice. "Might we speak a moment? About Darius?"

Sadie's posture shifted slightly, the automatic tension of a mother preparing for difficult news. "Of course."

They moved away from the dessert table, finding a quieter spot beneath a magnolia tree where the lantern light barely reached. Miss Thompson folded her hands, choosing her words with care.

"I want you to know," she began, "I'm learning things about how your son thinks."

The tension in Sadie's shoulders eased slightly. "Go on."

"He notices patterns — in numbers, shapes, the way things line up." Miss Thompson chose her words carefully. "Last week, I wrote a sequence on the board. He completed it, but couldn't tell me how. When I asked him to explain, he drew it instead. That helped me understand his thinking."

Sadie's hand pressed against her chest. "He's always seen patterns. Since he was small. Wallpaper, tree branches, the way rain falls."

"His drawings..." Miss Thompson paused, shaking her head. "Mrs. Turner, they're exceptional. The detail, the precision. I've taught for many years and I've never seen a child draw like that." She leaned forward. "But here's what confuses me. He can barely write his name legibly. His letters are shaky, uneven. He struggles with reading. Yet he can draw a dragon with scales so detailed I can count each one."

She spread her hands. "I don't understand it. How can his hand do one thing so beautifully and not the other? It's like there are two different children in one body."

"He draws constantly at home," Sadie said softly. "Fills page after page. Dragons, mostly. Always dragons."

"I've noticed." Miss Thompson smiled. "The other children ask him to draw for them now. He's become... respected, in his way. They don't always understand him, but they recognize something special."

"And Cassius?" Sadie asked. "How are they together? In class?"

Miss Thompson's expression shifted, becoming thoughtful. "That friendship is good for both of them. Cassius needs someone who listens without judgment. Someone who doesn't mind his constant chatter or his restlessness." She paused. "And Darius needs someone who doesn't require him to be anything other than what he is."

"Cassius talks enough for both of them," Sadie said with a small laugh.

"He does." Miss Thompson's smile returned. "But I've noticed something interesting. When Cassius gets overwhelmed, and he does, though he hides it with noise, Darius notices. He'll tap Cassius's hand, three times, always three. A pattern. And Cassius settles."

Sadie's eyes widened. "He does that at home. When his siblings get too loud or too close. Three taps. His way of saying 'enough' without words."

"Cassius has learned to read it." Miss Thompson glanced toward the boys again. "They've developed their own language. Not words, but understanding."

For a moment, both women watched the children. Darius had set down his stick and was now listening to Cassius with complete attention, his blue eyes focused and present in a way that still sometimes surprised his mother.

"There's something else," Miss Thompson said quietly. "Something I probably shouldn't mention, but I feel you should know."

Sadie turned to her, waiting.

"The other teachers ... parents too." Miss Thompson hesitated. "Some of them don't understand what I see in Darius. They think I'm being too lenient. Some believe that he shouldn't be in our school or that he should behave like the other children." Her voice firmed. "But I don't listen to them. What they see as deficits, I see as differences that need different approaches."

Sadie's throat tightened. "Thank you. You don't know what it means, to have someone see him truly."

"I do see him," Miss Thompson said. "I see a child who thinks differently, who experiences the world in ways most of us can't imagine." She paused, her expression honest. "But Mrs. Turner, I won't lie to you. It won't be easy for him. The world isn't built for children like Darius. He'll face people who don't understand, who won't try to understand. School will be hard. Life will be hard."

Sadie's eyes burned. She'd known this, but hearing it said aloud made it real.

"But he has something many children don't have," Miss Thompson continued, her voice steady. "He has a mother who fights for him. And now he has a teacher who will too, for as long as I'm able." She touched Sadie's arm gently. "I can't promise he'll be fine. But I can promise I'll do everything in my power to help him learn, to keep him safe in my classroom, and to make sure others see the Darius we see."

Sadie nodded, unable to speak past the tightness in her throat. After years of judgment and pity, here was someone offering something different. Not false hope, but partnership.

"One day at a time," Miss Thompson said, her voice carrying quiet steel. "One person at a time. That's all we can do."

"One day at a time. That's what my husband Augustus has always said. One day at a time," Sadie said, and for the first time in years, she didn't feel quite so alone.

The two women stood together in companionable silence, watching Darius trace another pattern in the dirt while Cassius's animated voice carried across the yard. Around them, the picnic continued its gentle wind-down, families gathering children and dishes, lanterns beginning to dim.

"He talks about his dreams," Sadie said after a moment. "More than he talks about anything else. Stories about a dragon named Azure who teaches him things. Beautiful, impossible things."

Miss Thompson tilted her head. "Cassius mentions dreams too. Dragons and adventures. They seem to share them, somehow. The same stories, the same details."

"Imagination," Sadie said, though her voice held a question.

"Perhaps." Miss Thompson smiled. "Or perhaps something we don't have words for yet. Either way, it brings him joy. And after everything..." She didn't finish, but Sadie understood.

After everything — the years of screaming, of fear, of wondering if her son would ever find peace — joy was no small thing.

"Thank you, Miss Thompson," Sadie said again. "For seeing him. For believing in him."

"It's easy to believe in something true," Miss Thompson replied. She glanced toward the dessert table where other parishioners were beginning to gather. "I should help with the cleanup. But Mrs. Turner? If you ever need someone to talk to, about Darius or anything else... my door is always open."

Sadie nodded, not trusting her voice. Miss Thompson squeezed her arm once more, then moved away, returning to the practical work of gathering dishes and folding tables.

Sadie remained beneath the magnolia tree for another moment, watching her son. Darius had stood now, offering his hand to help Cassius up. The gesture was small, natural, the kind of thing any child might do. But for Darius, who had once recoiled from all touch, who had screamed when hands came too close — it was everything.

Augustus appeared at her side, his presence warm and steady. "What was that about?"

"Miss Thompson wanted to tell me about Darius's progress," Sadie said. "His mathematics, his drawings. How his friendship with Cassius is good for both of them."

"She's not wrong." Augustus slipped his arm around her waist.

Sadie leaned into him, watching as Darius and Cassius made their way back toward the adults, Gunny trailing behind them still protesting something. "I know. But it's different, hearing it from someone outside the family. Someone who sees him every day, in a place where he has to work harder to be understood."

"She's good for him," Augustus observed. "That teacher."

"She is," Sadie agreed. "She sees what we see."

The evening continued its gentle progression toward night. Families called to children, gathered belongings, exchanged final pleasantries. The Turner family moved as one unit, collecting their dishes and blankets, making sure everyone was accounted for before beginning the walk home.

As the picnic wound down and families began gathering their belongings, the familiar anxious desire to head home tugged at Darius. Later that night, safely tucked in bed beneath his quilt, his dreams carried him far from the familiar church grounds, guiding him once again into a world suspended between sky and earth.

CHAPTER THIRTY-SIX

301

Chapter Thirty-Seven

Flight

Darius stood at the edge of a towering, sheer cliff overlooking booming waves and screaming seabirds. His bare feet gripped cool grass while wind whipped his cheeks. His arms extended, fingers tracing invisible designs. Where his hands moved, threads of light appeared, weaving themselves into a bridge that stretched toward a nearby floating mass of rock.

Azure was near, perched on a stone ledge above the cliff — but he did not intervene. The dragon's jewels glowed faintly as his gaze followed every movement, measuring, waiting. He had shown Darius how to weave, had guided his hands through practice, but now he wanted to see what the boy would attempt alone. This was the moment to step back, to discover not what could be taught, but what Darius could build when left to himself.

"Hurry up!" Cassius bounced on his toes behind Darius, his impatience visible in every muscle. "Make it a scary one this time!"

When Darius glanced back, a rare smile tugged at his lips. His fingers twisted in a complicated gesture, and the bridge responded, its solid center splitting into three narrow paths that braided around each other.

"That's more like it!" Cassius clapped his hands, then charged forward without hesitation.

The bridge shifted beneath Cassius's feet, paths splitting and reconnecting with each step. He stumbled, arms pinwheeling, one foot slipping into empty air. For a heartbeat, he hung suspended over the endless drop.

When Darius's hand tightened, the bridge solidified enough for Cassius to regain his balance.

"Whoa!" Cassius laughed, bright and fearless. "Almost got me that time!"

He continued his mad dash across the braided light, each footfall sending ripples through the structure. When he reached the far island, he spun around and waved triumphantly.

"Your turn!"

Darius stayed put, content to remain where he stood. His fingers continued their dance, sending new bridges sprouting in all directions, some narrow and thin, others wide as boulevards, but each one unique in color and texture.

"Fine, I'll have to make my own fun." When Cassius crouched down, pressing his palms against the grassy earth of his island, his face scrunched in concentration, pretending to weave his own creation. Darius grinned and leaned down with both hands and touched the gentle landing below his feet. The ground beneath his hands bulged, then split. Small shapes leapt forth, creatures with stubby legs and spiral horns, their hooves leaving rainbow trails where they stepped.

"Sky goats!" Cassius announced, straightening up with pride. "Did I do that? Come on, little guys, show Darius what you can do!"

The goats, no larger than puppies, bleated and bounded toward the bridge. They leapt onto the braided light, their rainbow hooves never slipping despite the narrowness of the path. There was chaos to their movement, yet they jumped from strand to strand with impossible agility, sometimes passing through each other like mist.

From high above, Azure descended in a spiral, his massive wings catching air currents that existed in dreams. He circled the playful goats, his deep laugh rumbling through the air.

"Well done, young dreamers," Azure called. "You've surpassed yesterday's creations already."

Darius nodded, acknowledging the praise without breaking his concentration. Some connected to islands, others looped back on themselves or ended in platforms that hung unsupported in the blue.

A streak of red fire cut through the network of bridges as Pyrrhos arrived, his ruby-studded form blazing against the sky. He executed a tight barrel roll around one of Darius's constructions before landing beside Cassius, sending the sky goats scattering with excited bleats.

"Impressive architecture," Pyrrhos observed, his tail sweeping in an appreciative arc. "But how fast can you navigate it?" He nudged Cassius with one massive claw. "Care for a race, dreamer?"

Cassius's eyes lit up. "You're on! But no flying, that's cheating. You have to run the bridges like me."

When Pyrrhos lowered himself, his wings clenched against his frame. "Agreed. From here to the blue island and back." He pointed with his snout toward a distant mass topped with blue-leafed trees. "Ready?"

"Set!" Cassius crouched, muscles tensing.

"GO!" they shouted together.

They launched forward, Cassius's small form darting across the nearest bridge while Pyrrhos thundered behind, his bulk somehow supported by Darius's light constructions. The dragon's claws gripped each strand with precision, his movements surprisingly agile despite his size.

When Cassius reached the first junction and hesitated, choosing between three possible paths, Pyrrhos seized the opportunity, veering onto a narrow bridge that curved sharply left. Flames licked from his nostrils, leaving a trail of fire that hung in the air behind him.

"No fair!" Cassius shouted, choosing the middle path. "You didn't say anything about fire trails!"

"You said no flying!" Pyrrhos called back, his voice carrying a note of playfulness rarely heard. "Fire is fair game!"

Azure circled above the race, his wings creating currents that rippled through the dream. Then he noticed something wrong, the bridges farther ahead wavered, their light flickering where it should have remained solid. His gaze tracked to a point beyond the blue island where the sky itself seemed to fold inward, colors draining into a pinprick of darkness.

"Darius," Azure called. "Pull back the bridges."

Below, Darius lifted his head, fingers still tracing configurations in the air. The web of light constructions stretched too far now, reaching into regions of the dreamscape he hadn't explored before. He sensed the instability, threads vibrating at dissonant frequencies, structures bending under pressures that shouldn't exist here.

Something had noticed the strain — not the bridges themselves, but the way they were pulled between them.

Cassius raced ahead, oblivious to the danger. His feet barely touched each strand as he moved across the narrowing paths, laughter trailing behind him like a banner. Pyrrhos followed, his massive form somehow nimble on the light bridges, ruby jewels flashing with each step.

"I'm winning!" Cassius shouted back. "Told you I'm faster than…"

The bridge beneath him lurched. Light strands unraveled at their far ends, the dissolution racing toward him like fire along a fuse. Cassius stumbled, his confident stride breaking into an awkward shuffle.

"What's happening?" He grabbed at a handrail that dissipated between his fingers.

Twenty yards ahead, the pinprick of darkness expanded, unfurling into a swirling vortex that pulled at the dream fabric. Bridges stretched toward it, their straight lines bending into curves that spiraled inward. The blue island itself tilted, trees uprooting as its edges crumbled toward the hungry void.

"Cassius, stop!" Pyrrhos halted, claws digging into the bridge for purchase. "Turn back now!"

When Cassius tried to pivot, the bridge beneath him snapped. He plunged downward, fingers snatching at broken light strands that disintegrated in his grasp. His scream tore through the dreamscape, high and terrified.

"No!" Darius's hands flashed through emergency patterns, weaving a new structure beneath the falling boy. Threads materialized, knitting themselves into a net, but they formed reluctantly. The net sagged under forces it wasn't designed to resist, then unraveled at the edges, dissolving faster than Darius could repair it.

When Pyrrhos launched from his position, wings unfurling in a burst of crimson, he dove toward Cassius with single-minded focus. Fire streamed from his nostrils, not the playful flames from before but desperate, scorching heat that left the air shimmering in his wake.

Cassius tumbled through space, the vortex's pull accelerating his fall. Wind rushed past his ears, drowning his screams. The darkness below opened wider, revealing glimpses of something ancient and cold at its center, obsidian scales shifting in impossible geometries, eyes that absorbed light rather than reflected it, unblinking.

Azure flew after them, but Pyrrhos had the head start. The red dragon tucked his wings and dove, closing the distance to Cassius with terrifying speed. Flames enveloped his form, not consuming him but extending his reach, wrapping around the boy seconds before he would have been swallowed by the void.

When Pyrrhos snapped his wings open, the sudden resistance nearly tore them from their sockets. He curled his body around Cassius, shielding the small form with wings and tail, creating a cocoon of scales and fire. The vortex pulled at them both, hungry for the double prize.

"Hold on to me," Pyrrhos growled, his voice strained. "Don't let go, no matter what you see."

Cassius clung to the dragon's neck, face buried against hot scales. Through tears, he glimpsed something reaching from the vortex, a tendril of pure darkness, formed not of matter but of absence, stretching toward them with terrible purpose.

Pyrrhos beat his wings with desperate strength, fighting both gravity and the vortex's unnatural pull. Each downstroke pushed them a few feet higher, away from the grasping tendrils of darkness. Fire coursed along his scales, intensifying until he blazed like a second sun in the dream sky.

"It knows you now," he panted, muscles straining. "It's tasted your fear."

The tendril retreated as Pyrrhos gained altitude, but the vortex remained, a wound in reality that seemed to watch them with malevolent awareness. Pyrrhos glanced toward the nearest stable island, judging distance against his failing strength.

"We won't make it back to the others," he decided. "Hold tight."

He angled toward a small outcropping, barely more than a floating rock with a few stunted trees. His flight path wobbled, wings struggling to maintain lift. When they reached the island, he couldn't manage a proper landing. They crashed through branches, tumbling across hard ground until coming to rest against a boulder.

Cassius lay curled in the protective cage of Pyrrhos's forearms, shaking violently. The dragon's wings remained wrapped around him, though they drooped with exhaustion, several membrane tears visible where light shone through.

"Are you hurt?" Pyrrhos asked, his voice dropping to a gentleness that contrasted sharply with the fire still smoldering along his scales.

Cassius shook his head, though tears streamed down his face. "What was that thing? It felt..." He shuddered. "It knew me. Like it was waiting for me."

When Pyrrhos shifted, allowing Cassius to sit up while maintaining the protective circle of his body, his ruby jewels dimmed to a subdued luster, conserving energy while they recovered.

"Some dreams turn dark," he said carefully. "Not all forces in the dreamscape wish dreamers well."

"It almost got me." Cassius wiped at his face with dirty hands, leaving smudged trails across his cheeks. "If you hadn't."

"I will always come for you." Pyrrhos touched his snout tenderly to Cassius's forehead. "Always."

The simplicity of the promise hung in the air between them. Cassius looked up, meeting the dragon's gaze directly. Something passed between them, an understanding deeper than their brief acquaintance should allow, trust beyond explanation.

"You're hurt." Cassius reached toward a tear in Pyrrhos's wing, fingers hovering over the damage.

"It will heal." Pyrrhos folded his wings, hiding the injury. "Dragons recover quickly."

In the distance, Azure and Darius approached, crossing what remained of the bridge network with cautious steps. The vortex had shrunk back to a pinprick, though its presence lingered like a smudge against the perfect blue. Not gone. Waiting.

Pyrrhos watched their approach, his expression guarded once more. The fierce protective instinct that had driven him to dive after Cassius settled into something deeper, more troubling. It wasn't duty that had compelled him to act, not the obligation of a Dreamers' Dragon to his assigned charge.

It was something dangerously close to love.

If the Obsidian Dragon touched him, this boy with his endless questions and boundless heart, Pyrrhos would burn the realm down himself.

The realization shocked him. His loyalty should remain with the ancient powers, with the bargain he'd struck. Yet here, curled protectively around Cassius's small form, he knew with terrible certainty that his priorities had shifted.

The ledge floated beneath a canopy of dream stars, their light casting long shadows across the weathered stone. When Azure landed, wings folding against his sides as he surveyed the damage, Darius slipped from his back, immediately moving toward Cassius who remained tucked against Pyrrhos's side, the dragon's wing draped over him like a blanket. The protective posture seemed natural enough, but Azure's jewels pulsed with subtle intensity as he noted the tremble in Pyrrhos's tail, the way his ruby eyes darted toward the distant pinprick of darkness before settling on Cassius again.

"Are you harmed?" Azure asked, addressing both of them while his gaze lingered on the tears in Pyrrhos's wing membrane.

"Just scared," Cassius replied, his usual boundless energy subdued. "Pyrrhos saved me. He flew so fast the air caught fire."

When Pyrrhos shifted, adjusting his wing to better conceal the damage, he said, "The vortex appeared without warning. I've never seen anything like it in this region of the dreamscape."

Azure circled them once, his movements measured and precise. "Strange indeed. Dream structures don't collapse without cause." His tail swept across the stone, leaving a trail of blue light. "Especially bridges woven by a dreamer of Darius's caliber."

When Darius knelt beside Cassius, his hand hovering near his friend's shoulder without quite touching it, his eyes tracked to the gashes in Pyrrhos's wing, then to the dragon's face, studying something there that only he seemed to notice.

"It was reaching for me," Cassius said, hugging his knees to his chest. "From inside the black hole thing. Something with cold hands. I felt it before I saw it."

Pyrrhos's scales rippled, a tremor running beneath the surface. "Dreams can manifest our deepest fears. The void may have been nothing more than…"

"It wasn't fear," Cassius interrupted. "It knew me. Called my name without speaking."

Silence settled over the group. Darius's fingers traced a design in the air, not weaving bridges this time, but drawing. Lines of light formed beneath his fingertips, creating an image that hung suspended above the stone: Pyrrhos in flight, wrapped in protective flames, wings extended around a small human figure. The image captured the rescue perfectly, but as it completed, shadows leaked into the edges, tendrils of darkness that crept inward, reaching toward both dragon and boy.

Pyrrhos stared at the drawing, ruby jewels dimming. "Your dreamer sees too deep," he murmured, too low for Cassius to hear.

Azure studied the drawing, then Pyrrhos. "Darius perceives things others may look past."

Darius continued adding details, the shadows taking more definite shape, curling like smoke around Pyrrhos's tail, reaching toward his heart. In the drawing, Pyrrhos's eyes held something complex: determination, but also guilt.

When Cassius pushed himself up, fascination temporarily overriding his fear, he said, "That's amazing! You made me look way braver than I was." He touched the light image, fingers passing through his own representation. "Can you make it move? Show Pyrrhos doing that barrel roll when he caught me?"

Azure stepped forward, breaking the moment with deliberate motion. "Cassius, there's something I believe Darius wanted to show you on the far side of this island. A stream that flows upward, carrying dream fish that sing when touched."

"You mean for true?" Cassius perked up, natural curiosity returning. "Like singing-singing or weird dream noises?"

"See for yourself." Azure nodded toward Darius. "Take him there."

Darius hesitated, glancing between Azure and Pyrrhos. Understanding flickered across his face, Azure wanted them alone. He nodded once and extended his hand to Cassius, who took it without question.

"Don't go near the edges," Pyrrhos called after them. "Stay where we can see you."

The boys moved away, Cassius already peppering Darius with questions about singing fish. When they disappeared behind a cluster of twisted dream trees, Azure turned to Pyrrhos, all pretense of casualness gone.

"You burn too hot tonight," Azure said, his voice low but carrying weight. "Your jewels pulse with more than protective instinct."

Pyrrhos straightened, wings folding tight against his body. "He almost died. My reaction was appropriate to the threat."

"The threat." Azure moved closer, towering over the smaller dragon. His sapphires flared with cold light. "Which appeared precisely when Darius extended his bridges into uncharted territory. Territory you suggested they race toward."

"You think I orchestrated this?" Pyrrhos bristled, the ridges along his spine lifting. "I dove after him. Tore my wings saving him."

"Yes." Azure circled Pyrrhos. "With genuine fear. With genuine care." He paused directly before the red dragon. "Which makes me wonder what game you play, Pyrrhos. Your attachment to the boy is real. Yet you guide him toward danger."

"I guide him toward nothing." Pyrrhos shifted, moving back a step. "Dreams have their own currents. Not everything follows our design."

"Indeed." Azure's tail swept across the ground between them, leaving a line that pulsed like a question mark. "Tell me, then. What would you trade to keep him alive?"

The query lingered, heavy with implications. Pyrrhos turned away, wings twitching with suppressed tension.

"My duty is to protect my dreamer," he said finally. "As yours is to protect Darius."

"You didn't answer my question." Azure remained perfectly still, watching every twitch of Pyrrhos's scales. "What would you sacrifice? Your position among the Dreamers' Dragons? Your connection to the ancient powers? Your loyalty to…"

"Enough." Pyrrhos spun back, flames flickering around his mouth. "You ask questions you have no right to pose."

Azure didn't flinch from the fire. "I ask because Darius senses what I see. The shadow in your flames. The hesitation in your guidance." His voice softened. "And because the boy trusts you completely."

Pyrrhos's fire died, replaced by something close to shame. "I would never harm Cassius."

"Intentionally, no." When Azure turned as Darius and Cassius reappeared, the latter soaking wet and laughing, he added, "But harm comes in many forms."

Cassius bounded toward them, trailing droplets that evaporated into steam before hitting the stone. "Darius pushed me in! The fish don't sing; they scream! Like when Gunny tries to sing like Sister Alma!" He collapsed against Pyrrhos's side, instinctively seeking the dragon's warmth. "This place is amazing."

When Pyrrhos curled his wing around the boy, the gesture automatic and protective, his eyes met Azure's over Cassius's head, and something passed between the dragons, an acknowledgment of an impasse, of questions that remained dangerously unanswered.

The stars overhead lost their radiance, touched by a light that didn't belong here. Morning was coming. Darius glanced skyward, the dream around him already fading.

"Time to go," Azure said. "The day calls you back."

Cassius yawned, suddenly heavy-lidded. "Can we come back tomorrow? I want to try the bridges again. Without the scary parts."

"Of course," Pyrrhos promised, though his jewels dimmed as he spoke. "I'll be waiting."

As the dream dissolved around them, Azure maintained eye contact with Pyrrhos until the very last moment. The question remained between them, suspended in the fading dreamscape:

What would you trade to keep him alive?

And the more troubling question beneath it — at what cost to the dreamer himself?

Morning sunlight filtered through the worn curtains of the Turner home, casting a warm light across the wooden floor. Darius stowed his drawings into his pouch, smoothing the leather flap with deliberate strokes. The dream clung to him like cobwebs, the terror in Cassius's eyes as he fell, the darkness reaching from the vortex, the strange tension between Azure and Pyrrhos. His fingers paused on the satchel's buckle, feeling the weight of knowledge, he couldn't properly express.

"Darius! Breakfast!" Lula called from the kitchen, her voice cutting through his thoughts.

He traced the outline of his notebook through the worn leather once more, then secured the buckle with a sharp click.

Breakfast passed in its familiar motion, oatmeal portioned into the exact center of his bowl, milk poured to the precise line he preferred, the family's voices washing over him in an order he could predict. Ezra told a long story about a frog he'd caught and lost again. Lula reviewed spelling words under her breath. Their mother reminded everyone about church clothes needing mending.

Darius ate methodically, his mind elsewhere. When he finished, he carried his bowl to the basin, rinsed it exactly three times, and placed it on the drying rack.

"You're mighty quiet this morning," his mother observed, pressing a kiss to the top of his head. "More than usual."

Darius nodded but offered no explanation. How could he explain what he'd seen? The shadow in Pyrrhos's flames, the way Azure's jewels dimmed with suspicion, the drawing that had formed beneath his fingertips without conscious thought?

Outside, the spring morning greeted them with birds singing and the scent of magnolias. Lula walked beside Darius, her hand occasionally brushing his arm in the habitual, protective way she'd perfected. Ezra raced ahead, then circled back, unable to maintain the slower pace of his siblings.

"There's Cassius," Ezra announced, pointing down the dirt road where a familiar round-faced figure bounded toward them.

Cassius approached at a run, his satchel slapping against his hip, one shoelace untied and flapping with each step. Dark circles hung beneath his eyes, but his face gleamed with excitement that sleep deprivation couldn't dim.

"Darius! Do you remember? I was so scared!" he called. "The floating islands and bridges made of light and…" He broke off, suddenly remembering their agreement about dream-talk. "I mean, I made it all up. For a story. That I'm writing."

"You don't write stories," Ezra said, squinting skeptically. "You can barely write your spelling words."

"Shows what you know." Cassius tossed his head. "I'm excellent at stories." He fell into step beside Darius, leaning close to whisper, "I remember everything this time. Every single part."

Lula watched them with narrowed eyes. "What kind of story?" she asked, positioning herself on Darius's other side like a shield.

"Adventure stuff." Cassius waved his hand vaguely. "Dragons and magic and falling through the sky."

"Falling?" Darius spoke for the first time that morning, the word emerging faint but clear.

"Yeah! In my... story... the main character falls off this bridge and almost gets eaten by this swirling black hole thing," Cassius continued, gaining momentum. "But then this amazing red dragon swoops down and catches him, and they're both on fire but the fire doesn't burn them, it protects them!"

He showed with elaborate hand gestures, nearly hitting Ezra who dodged with practiced ease.

"Sounds like something you ate didn't agree with you," Ezra said with a snort. "Mama says spicy food before bed gives you crazy dreams."

"It wasn't a dream," Cassius insisted, then caught himself. "I mean, it wasn't from spicy food. It was my imagination. For my story."

They walked in silence for several moments. Only the cadence of their footsteps on the packed dirt and distant roosters announced the morning. Darius stared straight ahead, his fingers tapping — three-beat against his thigh.

"You fine?" Cassius nudged Darius's arm. "You're even quieter than normal. Didn't you like the dream? I mean, the story I made up?"

Lula shot Cassius a warning look. "Maybe he's tired. Not everyone wants to talk all the time, you know."

"I know that," Cassius said, rolling his eyes. "I'm not stupid."

When Darius stopped walking suddenly, the others continued a few steps before realizing he'd fallen behind. He stood in the middle of the road, hands pressed flat against his sides, eyes fixed on Cassius with unusual intensity.

"Pyrrhos..." Darius began, struggling to form the words he needed. "He looked scared."

Cassius turned back, head tilting in confusion. "When he saved me? Of course he was scared! I was falling into that black hole thing! You should've seen it, Darius. He flew so fast his whole body caught fire, and then he wrapped me up in his wings and…"

"Not that kind." Darius's jaw tightened, frustration creasing his brow. "Different scared."

"What's he talking about?" Ezra asked, looking between them. "Who's Pie-rose?"

"Nobody," Cassius said quickly. "A character in my story."

When Lula took Ezra's arm, she said, "Let's walk ahead a bit. They're talking about their game." She pulled her brother forward, giving Darius space while keeping them in sight.

When they were out of earshot, Darius tried again. "He hides things." His hand moved in a subtle motion, tracing the shadow he'd drawn in the dream. "You don't see?"

Cassius's expression shifted, enthusiasm dimming into something guarded. "See what? Pyrrhos saved my life."

"Azure watched him." Darius struggled, the concepts clear in his mind but resistant to language. "Something … wrong."

"There's nothing wrong with Pyrrhos." Cassius's voice sharpened. "He's perfect. He's brave and strong and he caught me when I was falling and he gave his word he'd always come for me. Just because Azure is all fancy and teaches you special dream magic doesn't mean Pyrrhos isn't as good. You're just seeing things you want to see."

The accusation hung between them, sharp-edged and unexpected. Darius stood motionless, hands returning to his sides. His face settled into the careful blank expression he used when overwhelmed, but his eyes remained fixed on Cassius's face, absorbing the rejection.

He nodded once, not agreement, but acknowledgment. Without a word, he stepped around Cassius and continued walking toward school, pace fast and measured.

"Darius, wait…" Cassius called, regret already coloring his tone. "I didn't mean…"

But Darius didn't turn back. He joined Lula and Ezra, fitting himself into the space beside his sister who immediately adjusted her stride to match his. The familiar gesture of understanding settled around him like a blanket.

Behind them, Cassius stood alone for a moment, caught between pride and shame. Then he ran to catch up, his usual boundless energy subdued. The four children continued toward the schoolhouse visible in the

distance, morning sunlight washing over them, the dream adventure fading into the sharpness of waking reality and the first crack in a friendship
too new to withstand such strain.

CHAPTER THIRTY-SEVEN

Chapter Thirty-Eight

Tension

That crack widened in the hours that followed.

Cassius stayed quiet through most of the morning lessons, but his foot never stopped bouncing. He tapped his pencil on his desk, though never in time, never in sync.

Darius noticed. He always noticed.

By the time math came, the tension had grown teeth.

The pencil scratched against paper with quiet precision. Darius traced each number in his workbook, the math problems unfolding like a map he alone could navigate. Around him, twenty-three students bent over identical sheets. The classroom was hushed, pencils whispering, and the occasional sigh.

Miss Thompson moved between desks, her sensible shoes tapping gently as she offered guidance here, encouragement there.

Sunlight slanted through tall windows. The wall clock ticked steadily, marking time in clean, predictable intervals. Darius worked through his pattern recognition exercise, pencil gliding in smooth strokes as he connected the sequence. His eyes narrowed. The rest of the room faded.

When Cass's pencil clattered to the desk beside him, he stretched his arms overhead, fingers splayed wide, then slouched back in his chair.

"Done," he said loudly, earning a few glances. He flipped his paper with a flourish, surveying the room like a king finished with court.

When Miss Thompson approached, scanning his work, she said, "Check number seven again, Cass."

"But I'm finished."

"Not quite." She tapped the problem and moved on.

Cass sighed. He scribbled something quickly, then flipped the page back over. His leg bounced, foot tapping a sharp, repeating beat that vibrated through the desks and scattered Darius's concentration.

Darius paused. His pencil hovered above problem twelve. The numbers wavered, distorted by the subtle shaking. He shifted in his seat, creating space.

When Cass picked up his pencil and tapped the eraser, the rhythm began. Tap-tap-tap. Pause. Tap-tap-tap-tap. The tapping grew uneven, sharp enough to grate. A tuneless hum followed.

Thomas, ahead of them, turned around. "Shh."

"What? I'm just sitting here," Cass said. He stopped tapping, but began spinning his pencil instead, a yellow blur flickering in Darius's peripheral vision.

Darius pressed harder, the lead carving darker lines. His shoulders hunched, creating a barrier around his work. Problem twelve needed attention: 3, 7, 15, 31…

When Cass leaned closer, breath warm, he said, "Hey, you almost done? I drew somethin' funny on the back of my paper."

No response.

"Hey," he said again, nudging Darius's elbow. "Guess what Azure'd look like in a Sunday dress?"

The pencil paused.

Cass snorted. "All stiff and fancy, like one o' them church ladies with a hat and shiny shoes. Bet he'd trip over his tail tryin' to curtsey."

He chuckled to himself. "Maybe pink. With ruffles and a little crown made of his jewels."

The tapping resumed, louder. Tap-tap-TAP. His knee bounced faster. The humming grew louder.

"Cass," Miss Thompson called. "Please settle down and find something quiet to do."

"Yes, ma'am." He stopped tapping, fingers drumming silently now. "What number are you on?" he said. "I bet I can help."

Darius's breathing shortened. Eyes fixed on the page, but the numbers blurred. His pencil trembled.

Cass's voice, the tapping, the bounce, they swirled and began to collide while stacking louder and louder. Pencil scratches. Clock ticking. Lula's worried glance.

"I think red would look better," Cass said. "Red dress for a red dragon, get it? But yours is blue so…"

The system tipped.

When Darius slammed both hands over his ears, his pencil clattered to the floor. A raw screech ripped from his throat, guttural and unfiltered. He swept his arm across the desk. Workbooks and papers flew, scattering like startled birds.

Silence fell.

Miss Thompson crossed the room swiftly. "Everyone, continue working please."

Lula rose halfway, face tight. "Darius…"

He dropped to the floor, crawling beneath his desk. Back to the wood, knees to his chest, hands covering his ears, fingers digging into his scalp. Rocking. Forward and back, again and again.

"I was just talking!" Cass blurted, confused and embarrassed. "I didn't do anything!"

Miss Thompson knelt nearby but didn't touch him. "Darius, it's all right. Take some deep breaths for me."

The rocking intensified. Eyes squeezed shut. Ragged gasps.

Lula approached slowly, ignoring Miss Thompson's gesture to stay back. She knelt beside him, silent, close, but didn't touch. After a moment, she began to hum, low and steady, the opening of Wade in the Water, the song their mother sang while cleaning.

The tune slipped past the noise. Darius's rocking slowed, hands still over his ears.

"That's right," Lula murmured. "Like at home."

When Miss Thompson touched Lula's shoulder, she said, "You're doing wonderfully. Can you stay with him while I talk to the class?"

Lula nodded, humming without pause.

Miss Thompson stood and addressed the room. "Let's take a short break. Everyone line-up for early recess."

Students filed out, stealing glances at the desk where Darius huddled. Cass lingered, shoulders hunched.

"I didn't mean to upset him," he said.

"I know you didn't," Miss Thompson said. "But sometimes what we mean and what we do don't match. It still matters."

Cass joined the line.

Once the room emptied, she returned to Darius. "It's quiet now. Would you like some fresh air?"

After a moment, his hands lowered. Eyes opened, red-rimmed, distracted.

"Come on, baby," Lula coaxed, using their mother's tone. "It's just you and me and Miss Thompson."

Darius gradually uncurled. Movements cautious. Miss Thompson stepped back, giving him space. He didn't take Lula's hand but allowed her to walk beside him to the door.

As they left, Miss Thompson gathered the scattered pages. One drawing had torn nearly in half, not a math page, but a careful picture of Darius and Azure flying through starry skies. The rip split them cleanly apart.

***

Wind swept across the barren mountaintop, scouring the stone clean of everything but memory. No trees reached for the sky; no birds circled the crags. The runes remained silent, etched deep and glowing, their light rising and fading in quiet accord with the sapphires along Azure's spine. This was no idle dreamscape, but a sanctum of reckoning.

Azure perched at the cliff's edge, wings half-spread, twilight winds threading through the vast silence. Below, the clouds churned, layers of indigo and bruised violet hiding the realms beneath.

A fracture shimmered into being behind him.

When Pyrrhos emerged through it, his ruby scales dimmed, wings folding tight, he landed with less force than usual, more controlled. Warier.

"You summoned?" he asked, claws scraping lightly against stone. "I don't usually receive personal invitations."

Azure didn't turn. "You've avoided mine long enough."

Pyrrhos circled, not approaching. "Difficult morning. The boys fought. Cassius was unsettled."

"He was primed," Azure said. "Before the schoolyard, before the classroom. You know this."

"I didn't cause it."

"No," Azure agreed. "But you fanned the flame."

Pyrrhos's eyes narrowed. "They're children. Jealousy passes. Friends forgive."

"You speak of it as if it's outside you."

When Azure rose, turning, his eyes caught the glow of the runes and amplified it. "You are the fault line beneath them, Pyrrhos. I've watched it deepen."

Pyrrhos bristled, tail twitching once. "I've tried to protect him."

A pause.

Azure took one step closer. "Yes. I believe you."

Pyrrhos blinked.

"I believe you love him. That's the danger."

His wings shifted. "He nearly died. You saw it. If I'd been seconds slower…"

"I saw it," Azure interrupted. "I also saw the fire change when you caught him. Shadows threaded through it. A dragon's flame reflects his heart."

Pyrrhos looked away. "He trusts me."

"And what of your trust?" Azure asked. "Where have you placed it?"

Silence. The gems along Pyrrhos's neck flickered once, then dimmed.

Azure's voice lowered. "You disappear after shared dreams. You watch more than guide. You flinch when he says your name."

"I flinch because I fear losing him," Pyrrhos snapped, then regretted it. His claws scraped small furrows into the stone. "He saved me too, Azure. He brought me back to life."

"Then honor him with truth."

"I can't."

The admission dropped like a blade. Pyrrhos's shoulders sagged. For a moment, the wind stilled.

A black thread shimmered faintly along his flank, thin as a crack, pulsing low. Azure's gaze fell on it.

"You are not false," he said. "But you are not whole."

Pyrrhos looked down. "I don't know how to stop."

"Then let someone help you."

At that, Pyrrhos backed away. The thread along his spine twitched, and his rubies flared too brightly. "My duty is to Cass."

"And what will you become to fulfill it?"

Pyrrhos said nothing. The air between them thinned.

At last, he turned. "He'll dream soon. He'll need me."

Azure didn't stop him. "Go," he said. "But know this, protection built on silence becomes a cage."

When Pyrrhos spread his wings and lifted off, the black thread pulsed once, then vanished into the clouds with him.

Azure stood alone, the wind scraping over stone, whispering a language older than dragons. His sapphires dulled. He turned toward a rune: a circle, cracked down the center.

"So it begins," he murmured.

And the sky swallowed the light.

The school day ended with the same bell that had begun it, the brass tone echoing across the emptying playground. Most students rushed toward the freedom of the streets, but Lula and Darius remained beneath the oak tree at the yard's far edge. They knelt in the dirt, using sticks to trace designs. Lula drew flowers and houses; Darius crafted precise geometric designs, each line clean despite the crude tool.

Miss Thompson observed from the door, her leather-bound notebook clutched to her chest. After the morning's incident, she'd kept Darius close, letting him sit apart, excusing him from recitations. Now he seemed calmer. Drawing steadied him.

When Cass emerged last, his usual energy subdued, he paused at the stairs, eyes scanning until they found Darius and Lula. His fingers tightened on his satchel straps before he squared his shoulders and crossed the yard.

Lula noticed him first. She straightened, moving a bit closer to her brother. "School's over, Cass."

"I know." He stopped a few feet away, arms crossed. Dirt smudged his cheek. A folded drawing stuck from his pocket, the one he'd hidden all afternoon. He kicked a pebble. "You mad at me or something?"

The question hung unanswered. Darius kept drawing, stick moving in slow, continuous strokes.

"He's busy," Lula said, firm but calm.

"I can see that." Cass stepped closer. "I wanted to say sorry about this morning. I wasn't trying to bother you during math."

Darius's stick paused, then resumed.

"Maybe tomorrow," Lula said. "He needs quiet after today."

Cass shifted his weight. "I said I was sorry. What else am I supposed to do?"

"Nothing," Lula replied. "Please give him space."

"That's all anybody says!" Cass's voice rose. "Give Darius space. Be quiet around Darius. Wait for Darius to be ready. What about what I need?"

Lula stood, brushing her skirt. "Keep your voice down. You're making it worse."

"Making what worse? He won't even look at me!" Cass stepped closer. "I wanted to talk about my dog. That's all. I didn't mean to mess up his stupid math problems."

Darius pressed harder into the dirt. His shoulders tensed.

"That's enough," Lula said, stepping between them. "Leave him alone."

"Why? Because he's special?" Cass flushed. "Miss Thompson lets him sit all by himself. You speak for him. He never talks, but everyone listens like he's magic!"

The stick snapped in Darius's hands. He stayed still, eyes on the broken piece.

"That's not fair," Lula said. "You don't understand…"

"I understand plenty!" Cass shouted. Then his voice cracked. "Even his dragon's better! Azure teaches him threads and real dream stuff. Pyrrhos…"

He stopped.

"Pyrrhos what?" Lula's tone sharpened.

Cass's mouth opened, then closed. He looked down, kicking dirt over Darius's pattern.

"He saved my life." The words slipped out, quieter now. "Pyrrhos did. He caught me when I fell. He promised he'd always come for me."

His voice dropped further, barely above a whisper. "But Darius thinks something's wrong."

When Darius looked up, their eyes met, not with forgiveness. Not even understanding. But recognition.

A thread stretched taut between them. Not visible, not spoken. But it held.

Then, Darius did something unexpected. He placed the broken stick down, rose, and walked away.

Not toward Lula. Not to hide. Simply walked away. Across the sunlit yard toward the iron gate. Each step precise. No anger. No fear. Just distance.

"Darius?" Lula called after him, voice uncertain. No response came. She scrambled to gather their things. "Now you've done it," she muttered, chasing his retreating form.

Cass stood alone beside the trampled pattern, breath catching in his throat. The anger had bled out, leaving silence. He watched Darius grow smaller, Lula's curls bobbing as she caught up to him.

"I didn't mean it like that," he whispered. No one heard.

The playground was deserted. Even Miss Thompson had returned inside. The classroom door was shut.

When Cass pulled a crumpled paper from his pocket, a blue and red dragon soared across a charcoal sky. The blue one was bold and graceful, wings stretched wide. The red one looked small and off-balanced. Its eyes too big. Its rubies smudged.

He stared at it, lips pressed tight. Then crumpled it again, harder this time.

"Stupid," he muttered. "Stupid, stupid, stupid."

He kicked at the dirt, scattering the last remnants of Darius's drawing. The dust clung to his shoes. Satisfaction didn't come. The air was thick and heavy with something unspoken.

When Cass walked to the oak and sank beneath it, drawing his knees to his chest, the posture mirrored Darius that morning, curled in, closed off. A single leaf drifted past, brushed his shoulder, and landed beside the crumpled dragon.

"I didn't mean it," he said again. "I wanted him to talk to me."

No one answered. Even the wind had gone still.

Warmth lingered like fire cooling under ash.

Moonlight filtered through the thin curtains of Cass's bedroom, painting silver stripes across warped floorboards. The room lay in disarray, marbles scattered, books stacked into leaning towers, and clothes slumped over the chair. Even in sleep, Cass remained tense beneath his patchwork quilt, curled on his side, spine rigid, clutching something tightly beneath his pillow.

At the edge of Cass's bed, Pyrrhos watched.

His form shimmered faintly on the edge of reality, real enough to cast shadows, unreal enough to pass through air. The rubies along his spine flickered low, as if unwilling to draw attention. His gaze never wavered from the boy.

Cass mumbled, shifting. The quilt twisted. The paper slipped free.

A dragon, hand-drawn, blue and red streaking over a starry background. The blue one soared with elegance. The red... crooked, its wings uneven, lines too thick, eyes too big. Flawed. Loved.

"He loves that boy," Pyrrhos whispered. "But fear always follows love."

The air shifted.

A shadow slithered into the room, not cast by moonlight, but cut from it. It moved where light should be. A tendril coiled out from the corner, silent and slow.

"Good," the Obsidian Dragon's voice, cold and final, hissed.

Pyrrhos stood taller, rubies brightening. "Obsidian."

The shadow coiled tighter, rising to meet him. "You hesitate."

Pyrrhos flared his wings. "He nearly died. I caught him. I saved him."

"As you should," the thread hissed, its surface rippling with dark runes. "He must survive, to become useful."

"He's more than useful." Pyrrhos's voice burned low. "He's not some vessel to shape."

"No," the shadow said, curling closer. "He is yours to break or protect. But protect him too much, and he'll remain weak."

Pyrrhos moved between Cass and the shadow. "You think pain makes them stronger?"

"It separates them. And separation is the beginning of power."

The thread struck, looping around Pyrrhos's foreleg. His ruby scales dulled where it touched, dimming to a sickly gray. Pyrrhos gritted his teeth.

"Refuse," the shadow said, "and he pays the price."

The threat settled like ice in the room. Cass shivered in his sleep, fingers curling tighter around the edge of the paper.

"I will continue," Pyrrhos said. "But not for you."

The shadow paused. "You cannot win both ways."

"I know."

The thread slithered back toward the corner. "Then prepare. The next dream seals it."

"What happens then?" Pyrrhos asked.

But the shadow had vanished.

Silence returned, deeper now. Cass turned in his sleep, his face softening, breath even.

Pyrrhos stepped closer. He gazed down at the boy who trusted him completely.

"I'll protect you," he murmured. "Even if it ends me."

He crouched low and spread his wings over the quilt, a ruby canopy that touched no fabric but cast warmth all the same. His tail curled near Cass's feet. For a moment, the boy stilled, peaceful at last.

Outside, clouds swept across the moon, plunging the room into deeper dark. But the rubies along Pyrrhos's spine flared, resolute, and defiant.

Not for obedience.

Not for the Obsidian Dragon.

For the child who now slept beneath his wings.

Chapter Thirty-Nine

Reconciliation

Morning light streamed through the windows, catching dust dancing in silent currents. The usual chatter of twenty-four children settling in had dulled to a hush. When Darius slid into his seat beside Lula, blue eyes fixed on the desktop, his fingers traced the familiar grooves worn by years of pencils and elbows. Three desks away, Cass sat motionless, his stillness sharper than Darius's calm.

Lula stacked her books, her gaze shifting between her brother and Cass. The space between them stretched like a barrier. She reached into her satchel, pulled out Darius's notebook, and placed it neatly before him.

"Do you want your pencils?" she asked, voice low to match the room's mood.

Darius nodded once, fingers still sweeping the desk's geography.

Miss Thompson moved among rows, checking homework, offering her usual quiet warmth. When she paused at Cass's desk, noting the arithmetic sheet perfectly aligned, she said, "Thank you, Cass. Are you feeling well today?"

Cass nodded, eyes lowered. "Yes, ma'am."

The flat response hung in the air. No bouncing words. No commentary. Just the soft rip of paper under his desk as his fingers tore a corner of his worksheet into thin strips. His leg bounced against the chair rung, jittering faster with every unanswered question.

The morning passed through reading and history. Maps unfurled, battle sites pinned in color. Hands raised, books opened, questions answered. Cass stayed quiet, shredding paper into confetti piles on his lap. His pencil rolled unused across the desk.

When Thomas stumbled over the Gettysburg Address, forgetting "four score and seven," the pause stretched. Any other day, Cass would've whispered the answer loud enough for half the room. Today, he stared at the curls of paper under his hand.

When Darius's turn came, he pushed out each word, halting, stuttering, mumbling, but he made it through. Lula's approving nod carried pride. Cass's turn followed. His voice was flat, barely audible. His shoulders sagged lower with each phrase.

Miss Thompson stopped behind him during writing. "Your penmanship has improved today," she offered.

Cass froze, then muttered, "Thank you, ma'am," without looking up.

She lingered, waiting for the usual rush of explanation, a story, an opinion. None came.

When Miss Thompson crouched beside him, lowering her voice, she said, "Cassius, would you step outside with me for a moment?"

He shoved the paper bits into his desk and followed, dragging his feet. In the hallway, he wouldn't meet her eyes. His hands picked at a loose thread on his sleeve until it unraveled.

"What's going on today?" Miss Thompson asked.

Cass's words tumbled out in a rush, barely connected. "Darius, he, he don't get it, Azure talks to him, he don't listen, there's dragons, real dragons, you don't see them, they pick us, they —"

Miss Thompson blinked, trying to follow. "Cassius," she said. "Dragons?"

"They're real!" Cass said, louder now. "In dreams! He thinks he's better 'cause Azure picked him…" His words caught, his voice cracking. "He's supposed to be my friend."

Miss Thompson waited until his breathing slowed. "Maybe I don't understand about dragons," she admitted. "But I do understand about friends. It appears as though a misunderstanding came between you two."

Cass scuffed his shoe against the floor. "He don't want me no more."

"Maybe he doesn't know how to show it today," Miss Thompson said. "Friendship isn't about who's better or worse. It's about forgiving and trying again. Do you think you could try again?"

Cass hesitated, chewing at his thumbnail. At last, he gave a tiny shrug.

"That's a start," she said. "You don't have to say it perfectly. But you do need to be honest. When you're ready, tell Darius what matters to you. Not the dragons. The part about being his friend."

Cass nodded, his foot tapping again, but slower this time.

The lunch bell rang. Tin pails lifted, paper bags rustled. The room exhaled. Darius rose, notebook in one hand, lunch pail in the other. Lula stood beside him, a protective shadow, while Miss Thompson guided Cass back inside.

"We'll sit by the fence today," she said, not asking.

Cass stayed seated, watching them from his chair. His hand reached toward his notebook, then stopped. When most of the class had filed out, he stood and walked to the playground, settling beneath a different tree, far from his usual oak.

That afternoon, free drawing time was their reward. Darius opened his notebook, pencil moving with familiar ease. Around him, children sketched stick figures and horses. Miss Thompson wandered among the students' desk, offering praise and quiet suggestions.

Across the room, Cass bent over his own notebook. Gone were his sprawling doodles. Now he fixed his eyes on a single page. Occasionally, he glanced at Darius, then returned to pressing hard lines into paper. Once, he tore a scrap from the corner, scribbled something quick, and half-rose as if to cross the aisle. But he froze, crumpled the scrap into his fist, and sat back down.

Lula noticed but said nothing. Her own drawing, a neat row of identical flowers, grew steadily beneath her pencil.

Darius's page filled with lines forming Azure's shape, this version curled inward, wings wrapped tight, jewels barely visible. The eyes remained blank. His pencil hovered above the space, then moved on, adding detail to the coiled tail.

"What a peaceful afternoon," Miss Thompson murmured as she passed. "Sometimes too much quiet lets thoughts grow loud." Her gaze drifted between the boys, her words floating above the children's heads.

The day wound down. Chairs tucked under desks. Erasers clapped outside. Assignments copied from the board into rows. Through it all, silence lingered between Darius and Cass, solid as a wall.

When the final bell rang, Darius closed his notebook on the unfinished drawing. The blank eyes disappeared between pages, but his thoughts lingered on the boy across the room. Would Cass finish that story he was writing?

From the other side of the room, Cass folded a paper with careful creases, slipped it into his pocket, and glanced at Darius's desk. He almost walked over, biscuit from lunch still wrapped in wax paper in his other hand, but turned away at the last second. What was Darius drawing? Would he ever show him again?

Both wanted to say sorry.

Neither knew how.

They left through different doors, paths splitting at the gate with no words exchanged.

But the questions followed.

And where questions remained, so did the thread between them.

Sleep took Darius with precision, no stutter, no stumble. Each muscle let go in order: shoulders, arms, then the tight spot near his spine. His breath settled. The world faded, not with a jolt, but like someone dimming the lights, one layer at a time.

But the dream didn't unfold into sapphire skies or spiral towers. No Azure. No Cassius. No heat of Pyrrhos's flame.

It was thick fog, heavy, and suffocating.

It pressed close, stealing depth and color. Even the surface under his feet felt vague, as if the dream had been stripped of detail on purpose.

He raised his hand, watching his fingers vanish into the mist. Three cautious steps followed, each counted aloud. The terrain under him wasn't solid or liquid, but something between, somewhat yielding, yet firm enough to hold his weight.

"Some lessons need absence before presence can be understood," Azure's voice came first, then the dragon emerged. His massive form built itself from transparency to gleaming blue.

Darius greeted him with a raised hand, then gestured to the empty space.

"This place exists between realms," Azure said, settling onto his haunches. "Where dreams haven't yet taken shape. Perfect for today's lesson."

His tail swept a semicircle, clearing space between them. "You've learned to weave space, to create dream-bridges. Now we try something harder: weaving memory. Not facts, but emotion."

Darius tilted his head.

"Emotional memory holds stronger than the physical," Azure said. "The touch of your mother's hand when you were sick. The low hum of your father's laughter." His voice softened. "Or the warmth of friendship."

Darius looked away, fingers twitching.

"To begin," Azure said. "Recall a moment tied to emotion. Hold it strong in your mind. Then reach for the threads."

When Darius closed his eyes, his breathing slowed. When he opened them again, his hands lifted, fingers splayed. But this time, they trembled.

"Emotional threads resist," Azure said. "They hide beneath protection."

Hands moved through the fog, searching. Sweat dotted his brow. His arms shook.

Nothing.

"You're trying too hard," Azure said. "Emotion isn't captured. It's invited."

Exhaling, Darius let his hands fall. The fog stirred.

"Even threads between friends fray," Azure said. "But they're not gone."

The silence that followed was still and thoughtful.

"Your friendship with Cass changed you both," Azure continued. "His chaos brought movement to your calm. Your quiet gave his noise shape." He touched his snout to Darius's head. "Different isn't broken. Strong bridges often span the widest gaps."

Darius's fists clenched, then loosened. He raised his hands again, this time slower, gentler. His eyes half-lidded, his breath centered and slow.

"Listen for the emotion first," Azure said. "The thread will follow."

Darius turned his palms up, not reaching, but offering. Fog condensed into droplets along his skin. He stayed still.

Then, something shifted between his hands, not color — but a change in the air. A suggestion of form. His fingers curved around it without touching.

"You've found it," Azure said. "Now coax it to form."

The thread responded, vibrating faintly. His left hand rotated, creating a breeze in the fog that helped it grow. A faint blue light emerged, flickering like a shy flame.

"Emotional threads carry your mark," Azure said. "This one shines with your color, but it wavers."

Darius studied it. His thumb brushed the thread, steadying the uneven pulse.

"The connection was always there," Azure said. "Weaving doesn't create, it reveals."

The color deepened. Darius continued, careful and measured. Around them, the fog thinned, shapes emerging at the edges, familiar contours beneath the mist.

"Trust what you feel," Azure said. "Memory speaks clearly when we stop judging."

Darius nodded. The thread shined brighter, casting soft blue shadows across his face. It wasn't as strong as his previous weavings, but it was enough. A fragile bridge, beginning to be built.

The fog continued to part, exposing the dream world beyond. The lesson stretched on, one thread at a time, stitched by quiet hands that remembered how to create when words could not.

Cass tumbled into sleep like he did everything else, all at once, without caution. His dreams usually burst with color and impossible joy, candy mountains and talking animals. But tonight, his dream formed unhurried, and reluctant, as if echoing the weight he'd carried all day. Murky water crept around his ankles, cold and thick. Mist hung in tattered curtains between skeletal trees, their branches reaching like desperate fingers. Each step echoed twice, three times, warped and disorienting.

"Hello?" Cass called. His voice bounced back, hello, hello, hello, mocking and strange.

He pushed forward, mud clinging to his feet. The swamp shifted, distances stretching and collapsing. A moss-covered log appeared ahead, faintly luminescent. Cass sank onto it and hugged himself.

"Not much fun, is it?" The voice came from behind, familiar, subdued.

When Pyrrhos emerged from the mist, his red scales dulled like old brick, the rubies on his spine barely flickered. He crept with hesitancy, wings tucked in close.

"This isn't your usual dream," he said, settling beside the log. His bulk displaced the water, sending ripples across the swamp.

Cass didn't look at him. "Didn't know you were coming."

"I always come." Pyrrhos lowered his head to meet the boy's downcast eyes. "Every night since we met."

"Doesn't matter." Cass kicked at the water, sending droplets that froze midair before falling. "Nothing does."

Pyrrhos's tail curled around the log, creating a loose barrier. "Your friendship with Darius matters."

"He hates me now." Cass picked at the moss, watching it dissolve. "I said mean things. I ruined his drawing."

"Friends fight."

"He was my first friend," Cass said quietly. "Nobody else ever sat with me before. They all want me to shut up, sit still, not be me."

His fingers curled into the moss. "But Darius didn't care."

"And you were mine," Pyrrhos said, voice low. "But I haven't told you everything. And now I must."

Cass tensed. "What are you talking about?"

The swamp hushed. Even the frogs fell silent.

"I didn't find you by accident," Pyrrhos said. "I wasn't drawn to you because of your spark or questions or chaos, though I came to love those things."

Cass stood. "Then why? Why me?"

"I was sent. Because of your link to Darius." Pyrrhos's wings folded tighter. "To see what Azure protects."

"Sent?" Cass's voice cracked. "By who?"

A distant rumble stirred the mist.

"By the Obsidian Dragon."

Cass didn't know the name, but the air changed. The swamp darkened. Trees creaked as if recoiling.

"You're not my dragon?" he whispered.

"I am," Pyrrhos said fiercely. "But I wasn't meant to be. I was meant to observe. To report. To manipulate, if needed."

"So, all of it was fake?" Cass said, eyes filling with tears.

"The flying, the fishing, the stories…"

"No. That was mine." Pyrrhos moved closer but didn't touch him. "I was supposed to play a part. I stopped. You changed me."

"How?" Cass whispered.

"You trusted me. You talked to me without shame. You made me laugh."

Pyrrhos paused.

"And when you fell, I didn't hesitate. I caught you because I needed you to live, not for the plan. For me."

The swamp reacted, water brightening, mist thinning.

Cass sat back down, jaw tight. "Darius warned me. He knew something was wrong."

"I know." Pyrrhos's rubies dimmed. "And I hated myself for confirming it."

"The fight?" Cass asked. "Was that part of it?"

"No. That was pain and fear. But I was supposed to use it."

He paused. "Instead... I'm telling you now. I'm breaking the rules."

Cass stared at him, trying to see the lie, and failing.

"Why now?"

"Because I'd rather be destroyed than betray you."

The mist shifted, folding back like breath drawn in. A strip of dry land unfurled beneath their feet.

"I still want to fix it with Darius," Cass whispered. "That's the one thing I know is real."

Pyrrhos sank beside him. "I am real too. Not the way you thought. But real in the ways that matter."

Cass leaned forward, elbows on his knees, mind racing. He didn't move when Pyrrhos lay beside him, one wing curled around, not to shield, not to trap, but to be near.

They sat that way for a long while, raw, quiet, changed.

Cass finally spoke, voice hollow. "So, what now? You tell me all this and... then what?"

"I wait," Pyrrhos said. "For your choice."

"And if you'll have me... I fight beside you."

Cass didn't answer. His hands pressed into his lap, knuckles white.

Then the mist shifted. A pulse of blue, faint but familiar, threaded through the air, not cold like the Obsidian's shadow, but calm and even, like breath. Cass looked up.

A path of crystal light unraveled from the dark, flowing forward through the swamp, inviting, not demanding.

Cass turned to Pyrrhos. "That's him, isn't it? Darius."

Pyrrhos nodded once. "He's asking you to dream again."

Cass crept closer. "Even after everything."

"Because he knows what it is to forgive."

Cass wavered, then stepped onto the thread. Pyrrhos followed in silence, ruby light warming with each step.

High above the crystal paths, perched on a frozen cascade, Azure and Pyrrhos watched the boys walk beneath them. The dragons remained half-shadowed by refracted dream light.

"He wove that thread from emotion," Azure said. "Not technique. Not logic. But from a tether of trust."

Pyrrhos exhaled through his nose. "And Cass followed, even knowing the truth." His voice carried awe, and shame. "He's stronger than I ever gave him credit for."

"Perhaps friendship," Azure murmured, "is the truest dream weaving of all."

Below, Darius and Cass stepped side by side. The thread linking them shimmered red and blue. Where they walked, fractures sealed. Shadows receded. The dream stabilized, not around them, but just within them.

"The Obsidian Dragon will not be pleased," Pyrrhos said. "This defies him."

Azure turned. "And what of you, Red? Where do you stand now?"

Pyrrhos didn't hesitate. "With the boy. Even if it ends me."

They watched in silence as the boys spoke, Cass animated, Darius composed. The dreamscape softened. Pools cleared. Towers mended.

Neither noticed the first shift above them. Stars blinked out — not into darkness, but absence.

"... and tomorrow I'll show you my new marbles," Cass was saying. "One looks like it has a galaxy in it."

He stopped. "Did it get cold?"

Darius turned slowly. Frost curled from their words. The colors around them faded.

Cass stepped closer. "Something isn't right."

The thread between them flickered — then buckled. Darius gripped his end tight, his attention sharpening.

340

Ahead, the dream cracked open. From beneath, darkness bled upward.

Before Azure could answer, the hum deepened into a growl, raw, and angry. Crystals vibrated, then shattered. Shards fell across the trembling ground.

"Move," Darius said, tugging Cass toward a spiraling crystal staircase.

They ran. The thread stretched, dimming with each quake. Halfway up, a step vanished beneath Cass's foot. He slipped with a yelp.

Darius grabbed the back of his shirt, yanking him to safety.

"Thanks," Cass panted.

The ground roared. Vast. Old. Hungry.

Azure's wings unfurled, feathers flaring. Sapphires lit up against the darkness. His tail swept across the perch, clearing space.

"He comes," Azure said.

Pyrrhos extended his neck toward the boys. "Hurry. The boundary weakens."

They climbed faster. The staircase collapsed behind them. The thread between them thinned to a faint flicker, but neither let go.

At the top, Pyrrhos coiled around Cass, shielding him. After a moment, he extended one wing to shelter Darius too.

"Who's coming?" Cass asked, voice tight.

"The Obsidian Dragon," Azure answered, staring at the now-starless sky. "The reconciliation drew his attention."

Below, the central reflection pool darkened, surface thickening. Something vast stirred beneath. Wherever it touched, crystal turned to obsidian, slick, sickening.

"Can't you stop him?" Cass asked, pressing against Pyrrhos's side.

"Not alone," Azure said. "And not tonight."

The realm buckled. Lights vanished. Crystals crumbled into shadow. The growl rose from every direction, as if the dream itself spoke.

"Hold to each other," Azure ordered, stepping between the boys and the approaching void. "Your thread may be your greatest defense."

They tightened their grip. The thread flickered, then steadied, faint but holding.

When Pyrrhos glanced at Azure, then lowered his head to Cass, he said, "Whatever happens, know this: I chose you."

The dreamscape convulsed. Something rose from the corrupted pool, blacker than night, shifting, formless. Two eyes opened — unblinking.

"Leave. Wake up," Azure commanded.

"Now."

As the boys slipped from the dream, the last thing they saw was Azure, unmoving, defiant, a mountain of blue fire standing against a storm of shadow.

CHAPTER FORTY

SACRIFICE

The candy melted in thick, bubbling streams that hissed as they hit the ground. The jellybean hills they once dove into like swimming holes now oozed black sludge, reeking of burnt sugar.

"We didn't wake up," Cass said, voice thin beneath the squelching decay. "Azure told us to, and I tried, but... we're still dreaming."

Darius nodded, fingers tapping his thigh, one, two, three, a rhythm to anchor him against the unraveling world. The sky above hung low and metallic, like tarnished copper. Chocolate rain fell in thick, sticky drops that clung like tar.

"This isn't right." Cass wiped at his face, smearing the black streaks. "Our candy place was happy. This is…"

A crack split the ground between them. They leapt apart as the once-gentle caramel river boiled over, its surface blistering. Rock candy fish breached — now mutated, gasping with twisted mouths — before vanishing again.

When Darius grabbed Cass's wrist and yanked him back from the river's edge, peppermint trees contorted in windless air, their trunks writhing into grotesque humanoid shapes. A low moan echoed from them, eerie and discordant.

"What's wrong? It's like the dream is sick," Cass said, inching closer. "It's like our dream is dying. What did we do?"

Sapphire sparks flashed in the sky. Azure emerged, wings spread wide, his form coalescing from light to substance. He landed amidst the boys and the corrupted terrain. Jewels along his jaw flared in uneven pulses.

"This isn't your doing," Azure said tightly. "Someone intercepted your waking. Pulled you sideways into... this."

A second burst, ruby red, announced Pyrrhos. His scales, usually brilliant, had dulled. His tail lashed, wings tight to his body.

"It's gone," Cass said, reaching for him. "It's all ruined."

"Not ruined," Pyrrhos murmured, eyes scanning the shadows. "Corrupted. Turned against you."

The rain thickened, each drop a glob of black sludge. Where it struck, the landscape melted into scorched, bone-like structures. When Darius tugged Azure's wing, pointing to the castle they'd built together, now it sagged like wax, its spires crooked, its windows stretched into gaping mouths.

"Yes," Azure said, following the gesture. "It holds meaning for you both. That's why he chose it."

"Who?" Cass asked, voice cracking.

Pyrrhos curled around them. "He's found us."

The earth shuddered. The caramel river hardened to a crust that cracked like glass. Hills flattened, leaving behind a plain littered with jagged shards.

"Behind me," Azure commanded, spreading his wings to shield them.

The shadow swelled, aligning into the rough shape of a dragon, massive, reptilian, ever-shifting.

"What is that?" Cass said.

"The Obsidian Dragon," Pyrrhos said, voice hollow. "Corrupter of dreams."

The entity loomed, blotting out the last hints of light. Its body seethed with movement, constantly reforming.

When it spoke, no mouth moved; the words vibrated through the air. "The famous Azure. Still guarding lost causes."

Azure's jewels flared. "This dream is protected. You need to leave."

A low, rumbling laugh rolled through the ground, opening fresh cracks. "Protected? By you and the traitor?" The volcanic eyes turned to Pyrrhos. "Your jewels dim, Red. Guilt suits you."

Pyrrhos flinched but stood his ground. His rubies flickered, faint but firm.

The shadow slithered lower, peering at the boys. When Darius stepped forward, shielding Cass, he raised his hands, fingers searching for threads.

"So, this is the Threadbearer," the Obsidian Dragon mused. "A broken child with sapphire eyes. This is Azure's hope?"

Tendrils of shadow extended toward Darius. "Show me what power this child has."

"And the Luminaries call it free choice," the dark dragon continued. "All while congratulating themselves on an ending they claim not to see."

He paused.

"I provide true freedom."

Azure's wings flared. "You speak of freedom while building cages."

The Obsidian Dragon's form solidified, revealing deep ragged scars. "I speak of purpose. Every dragon who follows me chose to. Every dreamer I guide knows exactly where they stand. No riddles. No tests. Just truth."

"Your truth," Azure countered.

"The one truth that matters," the Obsidian Dragon said. "Power belongs to those strong enough to wield it. I provide what the Luminaries refuse — direction."

When Darius stepped forward, hands weaving, he said, "Not... want... that."

The dark dragon fixed on him. "You don't know what you want, child. That's why you need me."

Darius didn't back away. His hands stayed raised, blue eyes unflinching.

"Leave him alone!" Cass shouted, voice cracking.

His eyes shifted. "And the chatterbox. The one who speaks without saying anything worth hearing."

Cass froze.

Smoke slithered toward him. "Tell me, boy, how does it feel to know your dragon was never truly yours?"

Before Cass could answer, Azure stepped between them, wings flaring wide, sapphires ablaze.

"Enough," Azure commanded. "This dream ends now."

The Obsidian Dragon swelled, obsidian shards clattering like teeth. "No, Azure. This dream is only beginning."

When Azure launched upward, wings cleaving the thick air, the sapphires across his body erupted in blue flame as he circled once and dove, jaws parted in a roar that echoed through the marrow of the dream.

The collision cracked the sky. Light slammed into shadow. Candy cliffs crumbled like brittle sugar, and the ground trembled beneath them.

"Stay together!" Pyrrhos shouted from below, wings clenched tight. He watched the battle above. Torn between orders and the boy he swore to protect.

Azure spun, carving arcs of radiant flame through the Obsidian Dragon's swirling form. Wherever blue light struck, darkness unraveled but only to reassemble, shards clicking into place, like bones.

"Fascinating," the Obsidian Dragon purred. "Such loyalty. Such misplaced faith."

It didn't strike back. Instead, tendrils reached downward, brushing the fractured landscape. Where they touched, corruption spread in concentric rings, seeping like ink into a page.

"Why won't you fight?" Azure demanded, wheeling for another pass.

"Why fight," the voice coiled. "When the dream itself fights for me?"

346

When tendrils stabbed into the ground, the realm convulsed. From the corrupted soil rose twisted threads, warped imitations of dream weaving. They pulsed like veins, sharp as wire.

"Pyrrhos!" Azure roared. "Protect them!"

Pyrrhos hesitated. His rubies flickered, caught in a war between master and bond. His eyes locked on Cass. Then on the shadow. Then back.

With a growl ripped from his core, he broke free. "The threads," he gasped. "They'll listen to you." Pyrrhos launched into the air, his wings beating with a force that tore leaves from the peppermint trees.

Below, Darius yanked Cass aside as a corrupted thread speared the ground behind him. More followed, hunting lines, slicing the air.

"What do we do?" Cass cried, dodging again. "They're everywhere!"

Darius stopped, anchoring Cass beside him. His gaze sharpened. He extended both hands, palms wide, reaching inward and outward at once.

"You can't stop them!" Cass gasped. "There's too many!"

Darius said nothing. He searched the space between his hands.

A thread shimmered, thin and fragile with blue light flickering from his fingertips.

Above them, Pyrrhos met Azure. Ruby and sapphire surged side by side, flame colliding with smoke. Each strike tore shadow apart, but it reformed fast, adapting, and multiplying.

"It's working," Cass whispered. "You're doing it."

The thread brightened and stretched. Darius took a deep slow breath and shaped it with careful precision. Blue light unfurled outward, sealing into a dome around them.

A corrupted thread slammed into it.

The impact shrieked like splitting glass.

The dome shuddered — but held.

Darius trembled. Sweat dotted his brow. Still, he shaped the weave.

Above, the dragons battled through the dark. For every shape Azure shattered, two more rose, half-formed and relentless.

Inside the dome the air rang like a struck bell. The shield flexed and strained.

"You're holding them back," Cass breathed. "You're stopping them."

High above, the Obsidian Dragon watched. Its charcoal-red eyes narrowed. "Interesting. Raw talent. Undisciplined. But… significant."

The corrupted threads withdrew.

Then vanished into the ground.

The dome didn't reach below.

The earth erupted. Twisted threads speared upward from beneath their feet.

"Move!" Cass shouted.

They dove apart.

The dome collapsed as Darius fell backwards, concentration breaking. Blue light unraveled in mid-air.

He tried again — hands flying — but the threads slipped through his grasp like water.

"Behind you!" Cass yelled.

Darius turned.

A barbed thread hovered inches from his face, coiling with hunger, its barbs flexing toward his eyes.

He stumbled back.

It followed.

Above, Azure broke away from the fight and dove hard.

"Hold on!"

Then, a deep voice cut through the sky — cold, commanding.

"Enough, Pyrrhos."

The Obsidian Dragon loomed behind the veil, his presence splitting the dream fabric.

"The Luminaries may have shaped you," he said, "but it was I who revealed your true flame. You are mine. Do as I command."

A pause.

"Now"

Pyrrhos faltered. His wings locked mid-beat.

"That's better," the Obsidian Dragon murmured. "You've burned in my shadow for years. You cannot unmake what you are."

Cassius stopped breathing.

The ruby dragon turned, slow, and uncertain. The flames around him dulled. His gaze dropped.

"Pyrrhos?" Cass whispered.

For one terrible moment, he hovered — half-turned, eyes dim — and began to descend.

The Obsidian Dragon extended a clawed hand, threads coiling like smoke.

"I was forged by fire," Pyrrhos said. His voice weak and shaking. "But I choose what I burn for."

Pyrrhos exploded upward.

Flame erupted from his chest, wild and bright. Pyrrhos surged like a comet, wings flared wide as he slammed into darkness. He didn't flinch. He roared as they collided.

The sky split.

Cliffs cracked. The caramel river froze mid-flow. The Obsidian Dragon staggered, reeling from the impact.

Cass gasped. "He's fighting it. For me."

Pyrrhos continued his charge, claws raking through shadow and scale. Black venom hissed from open wounds. Obsidian shards rained like hail.

"You will not have him!" Pyrrhos roared.

The beast's tail lashed around his middle and methodically then began constricting with cruel and deliberate intent, savoring it. His ribs flexed inward, past where they should bend, until the first one snapped. Then another. Each break forced more air from his lungs, more fire from his throat, until nothing was left but a thin, broken keen. And still, Pyrrhos refused to give into him.

His rubies ignited, fed not by rage, but by memory. By laughter. By stubborn joy. By every moment Cass made him laugh and feel like a Dreamers' Dragon again.

That light burned against the dark.

"You think sentiment saves you?" the Obsidian Dragon hissed. "You were never a protector. Merely a failed Dreamers' Dragon — useful and broken."

Pyrrhos bared his teeth, smoke curling from his jaws.

"I may be broken, but I choose him."

They rose, locked together, spiraling through the fractured sky.

Below, Darius knelt beside Cass, hands pressed to the trembling ground, holding the dream in place.

"Azure!" he cried.

Azure flew toward them, then stopped.

He saw it.

The flare building inside Pyrrhos's core.

"Don't," Azure said. "Not alone."

When Pyrrhos turned his head and met Azure's eyes, he said, *"Take care of him."*

And let go.

He twisted midair, wings clamping tight around the Obsidian Dragon.

Then he detonated.

The blast wasn't fire.

It was a memory.

Every shared moment of joy, anger, wonder, and loyalty, erupted in ruby flame.

The shockwave tore through the obsidian armor, fracturing it, exposing molten wounds beneath.

The creature screamed.

It staggered back. Not destroyed — but injured.

For the first time, fear took hold.

Then Pyrrhos fell. His wings, torn, burnt and thin, hung in ribbons. Ruby scales dulled to gray, smeared with ash and blood. When Cassius reached him as Azure caught Pyrrhos's broken body, lowering him with care to the ground, the earth trembled beneath Cass's knees.

The child screamed.

"I'm sorry," Pyrrhos rasped, each breath shuddering like glass about to break.

"For what?" Azure's voice was soft, but Cass barely heard it, drowned by the rip tearing out of his own chest.

"For the time I wasted trying not to care." Pyrrhos coughed. Smoke curling from his nose.

When Cass pressed his face into Pyrrhos's snout, feeling the dragon's once warm scales, now cooling rapidly under his shaking hands, he said, "Don't go. You can't go. You can't leave me. I just got you. Please don't die. I love you… I love you… I —"

Cass pleaded with Pyrrhos to stay with him, knowing his words would not be granted. "Please… don't… please." Pyrrhos's eyes, rimmed with gold, blinked with effort. "And I love you, Cassius Williams. I was yours," he whispered, "from the first riddle you told that didn't make sense."

Cass's tears spilled hot onto Pyrrhos's face. "Stay. I need you. I'll do better. I promise. I'll fix it. I'll —"

"I was sent to spy," Pyrrhos said, voice ragged. "But I chose love. You did that for me. I thank you for making me a true Dreamers' Dragon again." Blood bubbled at the edge of his mouth.

When Darius stepped forward, his face streaked with silent tears, his hand hovered near the writhing black barb in Pyrrhos's chest, the wound seething with sick, oily light.

"No," Azure said. "Remove it, and he passes now."

Cass's hands shook as he stroked his dragon's muzzle, trying to memorize every line, every scar. "You said it before. In the swamp. But not all of it."

Pyrrhos's eyes flicked to Darius.

"I was sent to watch you," he admitted. "To unravel your gift." He coughed again, a spasm wracking his body. "Forgive me."

Darius nodded. He placed a trembling hand on Cass's shoulder. The touch was real, anchoring, not distant, but of a true friend bringing comfort to a hurt soul.

"I didn't deserve you," Cass whispered. The words tasted like ash.

"No," Pyrrhos said, a faint smile tugging at his mouth. "It was I who didn't deserve you."

Black venom spread beneath his scales. "He promised certainty," Pyrrhos gasped, "but gave nothing but chains." His eyes found Cass. "You taught me the difference. Real love is letting someone choose badly — and loving them anyway."

High above, the shadow curled tighter, its shards scraping together like snapping bones.

"First sacrifice," the Obsidian Dragon said. "Meaningless. One fallen spy changes nothing." He withdrew into shadow, but paused.

"The boy with sapphire eyes will sleep soon enough. They all do." His voice sharpened. "Some until their hair turns white. Some until they forget dreaming."

Azure's tail lashed. "You know nothing of their strength."

"I know everything." The dragon's laugh was winter through bones. "I've watched them all. The girl whose ashes still whisper. The twins who dance in tomorrow's shadows. And this one..."

His gaze locked on Darius. "I'm not your enemy. I'm the one who ends the lie."

His jaw tightened. "You'll grow old in silence while the world forgets dragons ever existed."

"You're wrong," Cass shouted.

"Am I?" The Obsidian Dragon's form wavered. "Ask your friend about the color of silence. Ask him what happens when words become too heavy to carry."

When Azure stepped in front of them, wings flared, he said, "No more."

"Dreamers' Dragons don't die," the Obsidian Dragon said. "They return to the Source."

Pyrrhos's form faded, edges dissolving into the night.

"Will it hurt?" Cass asked, voice small and broken.

"No," Azure whispered. "It'll feel like falling into a silent dream."

Pyrrhos's tail curled weakly around Cass's leg — one last anchor.

"Remember our dreams," Pyrrhos breathed.

"I will," Cass swore, voice raw. "Every dream. I promise."

Cass bent over him as the dragon's warmth faded. His own breath slowed, his lungs shallow, struggling. The world spun, broken and lost, as Darius knelt beside him, a silent witness to the end of everything Cassius had known.

"Your threads show promise," the Obsidian Dragon hissed.

"That's why I'm here." He paused.
"To make sure you never finish."

Chapter Forty-One

The Color of Silence

The Obsidian Dragon shrank into the darkness hissing and laughing at the destruction he left behind as if folding in on itself like a dying star. The black barb in Pyrrhos's chest splintered, fissures racing through it. It shattered with a crack — like bones breaking.

The ruby at Pyrrhos's chest lifted from his body. As it separated, something gleamed within; a thread of starlight woven through its heart.

Darius gasped. "My thread."

"Hidden ... protected ..." Pyrrhos breathed, his voice fading. "For when ... time ... calls."

When Pyrrhos pulled Cass closer with his tail, he said, "Listen ... important ..."

"I'm here." Cass pressed against him.

"The dreaming ... isn't done. Others will come." His eyes clouded. "Some ... already turned to dust. Some ... still waiting to breathe. But you..." He set his eyes on Cass with effort. "You'll be there."

"What do you mean?" Cass asked.

Three of Pyrrhos's scales circled Cass before pressing into his skin — wrist, heart, throat. They burned for a moment, then vanished, leaving the faintest trace of warmth.

"The scales will remember," Pyrrhos whispered. "They will answer when the circle closes."

"Protection," Pyrrhos continued. "A warding for the long winter ahead."

"What winter?" Cass's voice cracked.

"Not yours," Pyrrhos's eyes found Darius. "His."

"When he sleeps awake... when years stack like fallen leaves ... you will still be there," Pyrrhos said. "Not as you are — but as your thread continues."

Azure watched with growing understanding. "You're binding them across the wheel of time."

"Small magic," Pyrrhos managed. "But enough. When the last eyes open ... when the youngest call to their elders ... these marks will answer."

Cass looked to Darius then at Azure. "What's he talking about?"

Azure said nothing.

When Darius stepped forward, Pyrrhos was already fading.

Azure's wings locked. The ruby's inner thread caught the light, and his sapphire eyes burned brighter. He did not speak. Some truths belonged to time itself.

Cass crushed Pyrrhos closer, burying his face in the dragon's neck, desperate to hold in the warmth, the scent of smoke and cinnamon. "Don't leave me. Please. I can't ... I can't ... do this without you."

Pyrrhos's voice was smoke, fading and knowing this was goodbye and knowing what was tucked inside the red gem. "I'll be there ... in the ruby ... in the dreams we built."

Darius's voice trembled, barely a whisper. "Thank you."

Pyrrhos managed a smile, teeth stained with blood. "The quiet one … speaks."

"You're worth it," Cass gasped, voice splintering, snot and tears pouring down his face. "I'm sorry I talked too much."

"I love all of you … even … the … talking," Pyrrhos said, eyes growing glassy, breath ending.

Silence crashed down. The world seemed to hold its breath as what was left of Pyrrhos faded into the dream realm.

The Obsidian Dragon's form wavered. For one heartbeat, scales became visible. Scarred and ancient.

"Another dragon lost to choice," he said. "This is what freedom costs. This is what the Luminaries allow."

A pause, cut thin as a blade.

"His blood is on their hands, not mine."

Cass stayed on his knees, hands trembling as he cupped the ruby, the sole remnant of Pyrrhos still warm against his skin. He rocked back and forth, silent sobs wracking his body.

When Darius lowered himself beside him and leaned in, shoulder to shoulder, he offered no words. Just presence.

"He's gone," Azure murmured. Grief roughened his voice. "He was brave. Truer than his beginnings."

Cass turned, eyes red and swollen. "He wasn't supposed to die. He was meant to be mine."

"He was yours," Azure said. "In the way that truly counted."

The ruby grew cold in Cass's palm.

"Your bond was real," Azure continued. "Even if born in shadow. And no dreamer walks alone."

When Darius reached for the ruby, looked deep inside to see a faint blue rope of stars inside, then paused, meeting Cass's gaze with a silent question, Cass nodded, unable to speak.

Darius pressed the ruby back into Cass's shaking hands. "Keep. Always keep."

Cass clutched it to his chest, feeling his heart pound against the stone. "What now?" he whispered. "I can't dream like Darius. I don't have a dragon."

"Not yet," Azure said.

Azure lifted his head, eyes narrowing, as if seeing something far away and full of promise.

Cass swallowed. "What's he doing?"

"Watch," Darius said.

Above, threads appeared, silver, gold, braiding into a colorful sphere.

"A message," Darius said. "To Somnoria."

Inside the sphere, an egg formed.

When Azure opened his eyes, he said, "When the time is right, Cass will receive a true Dreamers' Dragon. One born of choice."

The sphere spun. Then vanished skyward.

"Where'd it go?" Cass asked.

"To the Luminaries," Azure said. "A request has been made."

Cass looked down at the ruby. "Will my new dragon be like Pyrrhos?"

"No," Azure said. "But the love you gave him will shape what comes."

When Darius placed his hand over Cass's, together, they cradled the last of Pyrrhos's light. The ruby dimmed to a subtle pulse, the thread inside settling like a heartbeat returning to rest.

When Azure lowered his head, watching the marks on Cass's skin where the scales had burned in, he said, "It is done."

"It hurts," Cass said.

"It will fade," Azure said. "Not vanish. The marks are not for now."

When Darius stepped closer, gaze flicking between the ruby, Cass, and the space where Pyrrhos had been, he said, "He said… I'll sleep."

Azure's tone softened. "He saw what might be, not what must be. Time folds differently for dragons. Do not fear what you don't yet understand."

Cass frowned. "Then what did he mean about the youngest and oldest?"

Azure didn't answer for a moment. He looked at the two children — shaken, but still standing.

"Some truths are seeds," he said at last. "They don't open until their season."

Cass shook his head, breath hitching.

"Dragons," he muttered. "Y'all ever talk normal?"

The caramel river cracked again. Somewhere in the peppermint grove, something moaned — like a place trying to recall what it used to be.

Azure's gaze swept the ruined candy hills, the warped trees, the blackened rain that had thinned to a drizzle.

"This dream will heal," he said quietly. "But not today. Your hearts have to heal first."

The air shifted. Echoes dulled. Edges softened.

Cass reached toward the fading light, but his hand passed through it.

"Azure —" he started.

"Rest," Azure said. "The waking world is calling."

The dream began to slip away. When Darius reached for Cass's hand and gripped it hard as the world dissolved, the last image was of Azure, wings spread against a pale gold sky — watching the boundary like a gatekeeper, holding the dark back as long as he could.

* * *

Morning sunlight spilled across the school steps, warming the worn brick to a gentle pink-orange. Darius and Cass sat side by side, neither touching nor speaking, their shoulders hunched against memories too large for their small bodies. They had arrived early, claiming this quiet corner of the schoolyard before the day's chaos began. Occasional glances passed between them, carrying questions and answers that required no voice.

The school bell wouldn't ring for another twenty minutes. Around them, the world continued its ordinary cycles, birds called from the oak tree's branches, a delivery truck rattled past the playground fence, early arrivals trickled into the schoolyard in twos and threes. None approached the two boys on the steps. Something in their posture, in the invisible

barrier of shared experience surrounding them, kept others at a respectful distance.

Cass's hand slipped into his pocket for the fifth time that morning,
fingers curling around something small and hard. Not everything crossed
the veil. Only what grief forged, or love gave freely. Pyrrhos's last gift
had made it through, not as magic, but as meaning. Its surface remained
cool against his skin, no trace of the pulsing light that had marked it as
part of Pyrrhos.

Darius watched this repeated gesture without comment. His own
hands rested on his knees, perfectly still except for his right index finger
tapping on his leg in his usual pattern. His blue eyes looked particularly
vivid today, almost too bright against his dark skin.

Miss Thompson walked up the path from the parking lot, her sensible
shoes crunching against the gravel. When she spotted the boys immediately, her steps slowed as she approached. The greeting that normally
would have bubbled forth remained unspoken as she noted their expressions, Cass's raw and open grief, Darius's focused intensity. With a small
nod that acknowledged their presence without demanding a response,
she continued up the steps and into the school building.

More students arrived. The schoolyard filled with voices and movement, jump ropes slapping against dirt, treasures being traded, yesterday's
arguments reignited or forgotten. The ordinary chaos of childhood
flowed around Darius and Cass like water around stones in a stream.

"He died for me," Cass finally said, the words barely audible above the
schoolyard noise. His fingers tightened around the ruby in his pocket.
"Actually died. For me."

Darius turned slightly, studying his friend's profile. The morning light
caught in Cass's unshed tears, turning them to brief diamonds at the corners of his eyes.

"He was supposed to be bad," Cass went on, voice strengthening. "A
spy. Not real. But he jumped in and fought the Obsidian Dragon anyway." His shoulders rounded. "Nobody's ever done anything like that
for me before."

He hesitated, frowning as if something hovered out of just reach. "I keep thinking there was more … something he said. But every time I try to remember, it slips away."

Darius's eyes narrowed, distant, like he was listening for a murmur too soft for anyone else to hear. He tapped once against his knee: one, two, three … pause.

Cass shook his head. "Doesn't matter, I guess. He saved us. That's what I'll remember."

Darius nodded. Somewhere behind his calm gaze, fragments of dream flickered — scales, light, words that burned and faded. He could still see Pyrrhos's tail around Cass's leg, still see the ruby lifting free, then the words came in broken flashes. Sleeping awake. Marks. The circle closes. He tried to line them up into sense. They wouldn't stay.

Darius nodded once, acknowledgment rather than agreement. His gaze drifted to Cass's pocket where the ruby lay hidden, then back to his friend's face.

"I keep thinking," Cass said, "what if the new dragon doesn't like me? What if it's all proper and serious and doesn't want to play stupid games or listen to my stories or …" His voice caught. "What if nothing's ever that good again?"

Darius's hand moved from his knee, hesitated in the air between them, then settled lightly on Cass's shoulder. The touch was brief. Still, it offered comfort, and it held understanding.

When Lula approached from across the schoolyard, textbooks clutched against her chest, she paused several yards away, noting her brother's position beside Cass. Her eyebrows rose in surprise, then lowered in understanding. With a small nod to herself, she altered her course, joining a group of girls beneath the oak tree instead of interrupting the boys' conversation.

Darius reached into his own pocket and extracted a folded piece of paper, creases sharp and precise from meticulous handling. With the same attention he gave to all his creations, he unfolded it once, twice, smoothing it flat against his knee.

When Cass glanced down, then froze, his breath caught loud in his throat.

On the page, drawn in Darius's unmistakable style, Pyrrhos curled around a sleeping Cass. The dragon's wings formed a shelter, his jeweled scales catching dream-light that seemed to burn from the paper itself. The detail was exceptional, each ruby precisely placed, each scale perfectly defined, even the subtle texture of Pyrrhos's skin where scales gave way to softer flesh. But most striking was the expression Darius had captured, fierce protectiveness mingled with gentle affection, a dragon who had found his purpose in guarding this one small, remarkable human.

"When did you …" Cass began, then stopped. Fresh tears spilled onto his cheeks, tracking silent paths to his chin. "How did you know to draw this before it happened?"

Darius tapped his temple, then his chest. The gesture contained no words but needed none. Some things were known through minds that saw patterns invisible to others, and some through hearts that recognized truth before it manifested.

He held out the drawing.

"I can't take this," Cass protested. "It's too good. I'll wreck it."

Darius pushed the drawing closer, eyes intent on his friend's face. His expression contained all the stubborn certainty that marked his rare but unshakeable decisions.

When Cass accepted the paper with reverent hands, touching the lines as if they might rearrange themselves beneath his fingers, he said, "Thank you." Then, looking up with tears still tracking down his face: "You're my best friend, D. Even if your dreams are way too serious."

The first bell rang, its brass voice calling students toward the schoolhouse doors. Children gathered books and abandoned games, the schoolyard emptying. Lula glanced toward her brother, questioning whether to wait.

Darius bobbed his head in her direction, then turned back to Cass. A smile touched his lips, small but genuine, reaching his eyes and transforming his usually solemn face. He stood, offering his hand to help Cass up.

When Cass tucked the drawing carefully into his notebook before accepting the offered hand, together they climbed the remaining steps, pausing at the schoolhouse door.

"You think we'll dream tonight?" Cass asked, his voice steadier now.

Darius nodded.

"Good dreams or bad dreams?" Cass pressed, one hand unconsciously moving to the pocket that concealed Pyrrhos's ruby.

Darius considered the question with his characteristic thoroughness. His eyes lifted to the morning sky, tracking formations in clouds that others might find random. When he looked back at Cass, his expression bore neither false comfort nor unnecessary fear, merely truth, offered to a friend strong enough to bear it.

"Both," he said. "Always both."

Cass nodded, accepting this wisdom that seemed beyond his friend's years. He squared his shoulders, drawing strength from Darius's continuous presence and from the weight of the ruby in his pocket, a talisman between worlds, a promise that sacrifice created new beginnings.

As the last of the children disappeared through the door, Darius lingered a moment longer, his gaze drifting back toward his home, to a world out of view. He thought of Mama's quiet humming in the kitchen that morning, the way she'd paused, for a moment, when he met her eyes and said "Good morning" without prompting. How her hand had fluttered to her mouth, hiding either a smile or a prayer.

He remembered Lula's nod from under the oak tree, small but sure, the way she no longer hovered but still noticed. Theo and Ezra on the porch, tossing jabs back and forth over who left the tools out, but this time, when he passed by, Ezra tossed him a crooked grin and Theo added, "Don't let Cass eat all your lunch again." No teasing. Simply included because he belonged.

He thought of Gunny's laughter echoing across the yard that weekend, sticky with peaches, tugging his hand toward the garden hose. And Daddy, quiet, calloused Daddy, resting a hand on his shoulder with a weight that said everything words could not.

They didn't know everything about Azure. They knew nothing about threads or how dreams bent time. But they were why he kept walking between those worlds.

This was his world. And he would protect it.

Side by side, Darius and Cass walked into the schoolhouse, carrying their shared experiences like invisible strings that bound them together, one boy who spoke through silence, one who filled silence with words, both forever changed by dreams that bridged their differences.

The door closed behind them, separating the ordinary world of arithmetic and history from the wondrous realms they visited in sleep. But the boundary between those worlds had thinned, allowing magic to flow in both directions.

Somewhere in the distance, beyond sight but not beyond hope, a dragon egg stirred, suspended in golden thread, for the day when Cass would need a new guide through dreams worth having.

Deep within the threads of dream, a story waited to begin again.

Not yet.

Not until silence finds its color.

END OF BOOK

CLOSING CREDITS

ACKNOWLEDGMENTS

This story began with a dream — a literal one. When my oldest son was in second grade, he would come home spinning tales about a little boy named Darius and the adventures he went on. The name stayed with me. Then, one night, I dreamed of that same boy, drifting into sleep and soaring through his dreams beside a dragon. I woke the next morning and wrote a poem, and that small poem was the first spark of everything that followed. The story changed shape many times over the years. First a picture book, then a chapter book, then something far larger. Until it finally became the novel you hold now. That it became a real book at all is something I will never take lightly.

To my husband: you heard this story in every form it ever wore. Every draft, every chapter, every scene I revised more times than either of us could count and you stayed my most patient and honest reader through all of it. When I lost the thread, you helped me find it again. This book is steadier for having been built beside you.

To Christian, Mason, and Mikky: thank you for your patience through the countless hours this book asked of me, and for believing it would one day exist even when it lived only in pieces. And to my granddaughters, who remind me exactly why the stories still ahead are worth writing.

To the autism community. The individuals and families whose lives, struggles, and fierce love taught me far more than any research ever could — thank you. To the parents and caregivers who give so much of themselves, so often without rest or recognition: what I learned from watching that devotion lives in every page.

To my students and their families: working beside you has changed me. You have taught me patience, humility, resilience, and the countless forms that communication can take. Darius is his own character, and this is his own story, but it was shaped by the courage I have witnessed in all of you, and written with deep respect for everyone who lives daily with silence, misunderstanding, and hope.

To the early readers and the writing community who walked through rough chapters alongside me: thank you for your honesty and your faith in this story. And to my brother-in-law Andy at Window Light Studio, one of the very first to read these pages — thank you for letting them move you the way they did. The lyrics you were inspired to write, set to such beautiful music, gave *The Color of Silence* a new level of experience, a voice that carries far beyond the page. I am endlessly grateful for that gift.

And finally, to every reader who opens this book: thank you. I hope Darius stays with you.

ABOUT THE AUTHOR

C.J. Gryffin is a writer and special education teacher whose storytelling is deeply shaped by her work with children with autism and other significant support needs. Through both her teaching and her writing, she is drawn to stories about courage, family, resilience, and the quiet strength often overlooked by the world.

Her debut novel, *The Color of Silence*, is the first book in *A Dreamers' Dragon Novel* series. The story began with a literal dream and stayed with her for eighteen years before finally making its way to the page.

C.J. lives in Utah with a full heart, a busy imagination, and a deep love for her family, who inspire her work in more ways than they know.

Continue the Journey

Dreamers' Dragons: The Awakening
Book Two of A Dreamers' Dragon Novel series

The veil between the dream realm and the waking world is thinning.

What began in silence with Darius Turner now widens into something far greater—and far more dangerous. Across centuries, children marked by sapphire-blue eyes are bound to a prophecy none of them fully understand. As the boundary between worlds weakens, dreams no longer remain safely asleep. Old powers stir. Hidden paths reopen. And somewhere in the vast reaches of Somnoria, darkness begins to gather with purpose.

In 2025, Tim and Sara begin their journey with their Dreamers' Dragon, Azar. What starts as wonder soon opens the door to a realm far larger, stranger, and more perilous than either of them imagined. As they take their first steps into Somnoria, they discover that dreams carry weight, choices matter, and not every presence in the dream world comes with good intent.

Elsewhere, Jackie and Jareth are drawn deeper into forces already in motion—forces tied to prophecy, forgotten truths, and dangers that have been waiting far longer than they know. The dream realm is changing, and the children moving through it are beginning to sense that they are part of something much older than themselves.

At the same time, Saoirse follows the pull of prophecy through shifting dream paths, chasing answers that never come easily. Guided by instinct and sharpened by trial, she moves toward the same converging threads as the others, unaware of how deeply their fates are already entwined.

Above them all, the stakes continue to rise. Somnoria is no longer a place of mystery alone. It is becoming a battleground of memory, destiny, and deception. As shadows lengthen and the dreamers draw closer to the truth, each of them must decide what to trust—and what they are willing to risk.

In **Dreamers' Dragons: The Awakening**, the world grows wider, the danger grows sharper, and the prophecy begins to stir in earnest.

The children are no longer only dreaming.

They are awakening.

Thank You for Reading

Stories grow through the voices of readers like you.

If this story meant something to you, the best way you can help it reach other readers is by leaving a short review.

QR Codes

Leave an Amazon Review

Leave a Goodreads Review

Join the Dream

Scan the QR code to receive:
Updates on Dreamers' Dragons Book Two
Exclusive bonus scenes
Artwork from Somnoria

www.cjgryffin.com